P9-ASN-400

THE *PLAYBOY* BOOK OF SCIENCE FICTION

THE *PLAYBOY* BOOK OF SCIENCE FICTION

Edited by Alice K. Turner

HarperPrism

HarperPrism
A Division of HarperCollins*Publishers*
10 East 53rd Street, New York, NY 10022-5299

These are works of fiction. The characters, incidents, and dialogues are products of the authors' imagination and are not to be construed as real. Any resemblance to actual events or persons, living or dead, is entirely coincidental.

Copyright © 1998 by Playboy Enterprises, Inc. All rights reserved. No part of this book may be used or reproduced in any manner whatsoever without written permission of the publisher, except in the case of brief quotations embodied in critical articles and reviews. For information address HarperCollins Publishers, 10 East 53rd Street, New York, NY 10022-5299.

"The Word Processor." is reprinted by permission of the author. Copyright © Stephen King. All rights reserved.

HarperCollins®, 📖®, and HarperPrism® are trademarks of HarperCollins Publishers, Inc.

HarperPrism books may be purchased for educational, business, or sales promotional use. For information, please write: Special Markets Department, HarperCollins Publishers, 10 East 53rd Street, New York, NY 10022-5299.

Printed in the United States of America

First printing: May 1998

Designed by Elliott Beard

Library of Congress Cataloging-in-Publication Data is available from the publisher.

Visit HarperPrism on the World Wide Web at
http://www.harperprism.com

98 99 00 01 02 ❖/RRD 10 9 8 7 6 5 4 3 2 1

Contents

INTRODUCTION

FROM THE OUTSET, in 1953, *Playboy* has welcomed science fiction to its pages. Imagination, innovation, and daring have always been the magazine's stock in trade; no wonder it has drawn so many stellar authors from the field. And they have been loyal. Ray Bradbury was the very first young, contemporary author chosen for reprint in the early years when *Playboy* could not yet afford to publish original fiction, he was one of the first to be paid for original material—and he is still a favorite decades later.

The new magazine offered science fiction writers some things they couldn't get elsewhere in those days: first, the opportunity to break out from the genre magazines to a far larger public. Then too, genre magazines, which counted teenagers as a substantial part of their readership, were restrictive regarding content and *Playboy* offered the creative freedom to write for an adult audience. And eventually, as a market, *Playboy* simply looked better than the genre competition, especially after the attention given to "The Fly," by George Langelaan (July, 1957), which almost immediately inspired the first of many movies.

In July and August of 1963, in place of the Interview, the magazine ran an innovative and influential panel entitled *1984 and Beyond*. A dozen top science fiction writers, including four collected here (Bradbury, Arthur C. Clarke, Frederik Pohl, William Tenn), gathered to predict the future. The speculations are amusing to read today, some of them pretty accurate (the Russian socialist empire would collapse), some not (telepathic sex). The most creative result of the panel may have been to inspire Clarke, over the next fifteen years, to continue a series of highly regarded articles on science and futuristics for *Playboy*. He, too, still appears in our pages as he enters his ninth decade.

Because of the difficulties of choosing from the wealth of excellent material accumulated over forty-five years, a few rules are in play here. You will find no more than one story from each author, though some (Bradbury and Robert Silverberg come to mind) contributed far more frequently than others. There's been an effort to mix it up, tossing the lighthearted pieces that readers enjoy together with more serious work, and short stories with longer ones. No stories from *The Playboy Book of Science Fiction and Fantasy*, published in 1966, are included, even though that book is a hard-to-find collector's item today. And, speaking of fantasy, you won't find it here, or at least not much of it, given the inevitable genre overlap.

Most of these authors are well known, a few of them famous. Over the years, we have published science fiction by lesser lights too, even a few first-timers (we've included one of those), but in a collection like this one, in a field where even the top talents still write short stories (this is rare in the mainstream), it's inevitable. They're a wildly diverse group. We think you'll enjoy their stories.

RAY
BRADBURY

THE LOST CITY OF MARS

January 1967

Ray Bradbury and *Playboy* are longtime partners. His novel *Farenheit 451,* with its scathing indictment of book-burning and censorship, appeared in three installments from March through May of 1954—a bold move for the fledgling magazine at the height of the McCarthy period. These were reprints; *Playboy* could not yet afford to pay for original fiction. Soon it could, however, and since then, dozens of Bradbury stories have appeared in the magazine, and the end is nowhere in sight. He sat for the Playboy Interview in May 1996. Nebula Grandmaster Bradbury is one of the best-known, best-loved, and most frequently anthologized authors in the world, with hundreds of stories to his credit. In the field of science fiction (as opposed to fantasy, or horror), his masterpieces are *The Martian Chronicles* and *Farenheit 451.* Much of his short work was collected into a huge volume, *The Stories of Ray Bradbury*, in 1980, but many stories have appeared since then, and these are periodically collected in book form, most recently in *Driving Blind*.

Born in Illinois in 1920, Bradbury has lived in Los Angeles since his teens, and, not surprisingly, has frequently connected with the movie business. He wrote the screenplay of *Moby Dick* for John Huston, an encounter he has returned to several times in stories and memoirs. *Farenheit 451* was filmed by François Truffaut and *The Illustrated Man* also became a movie. Bradbury created the screen treatments for *It Came From Outer Space* and *The Beast from 20,000 Fathoms*, popular B-thrillers of the 1950s. Stories were adapted for television in *The Twilight Zone* (and, quite similarly, for the old ET series of horror comics) and he wrote most of the episodes for *Ray Bradbury Theater*, a weekly series still in reruns. *The Martian Chronicles* ran as a miniseries in 1980. He has also written plays and a good deal of poetry. It's a pleasure to present a vintage story that really is science fiction, with rocket ships and astronauts and a return to Mars.

THE GREAT EYE floated in space. And behind the great eye somewhere hidden away within metal and machinery was a small eye that belonged to a man who looked and could not stop looking at all the multitudes of stars and the diminishings and growings of light a billion billion miles away.

The small eye closed with tiredness. Captain John Wilder stood holding to the telescopic devices that probed the Universe and at last murmured, "Which one?"

The astronomer with him said, "Take your pick."

"I wish it were that easy." Wilder opened his eyes. "What's the data on that last star?"

"Same size and reading as our sun. Planetary system, possible."

"Possible. Not certain. If we pick the wrong star, God help the people we send on a two-hundred-year journey to find a planet that may not be there. No, God help me, for the final selection is mine, and I may well send myself on that journey. So, how can we be sure?"

"We can't. We just make the best guess, send our starship out and pray."

"You are not very encouraging. That's it. I'm tired."

Wilder touched a switch that shut up tight the greater eye, this rocket-powered space lens that stared cold upon the abyss, saw far too much and knew little, and now knew nothing. The rocket laboratory drifted sightless on an endless night.

"Home," said the captain. "Let's go home."

And the blind beggar-after-stars wheeled on a spread of fire and ran away.

The frontier cities on Mars looked very fine from above. Coming down for a landing, Wilder saw the neons among the blue hills and thought, we'll light some worlds a billion miles off, and the children of the people living under these lights this instant, we'll make them immortal. Very simply, if we succeed, they will live forever.

Live forever. The rocket landed. Live forever.

The wind that blew from the frontier town smelled of grease. An aluminum-toothed jukebox banged somewhere. A junk yard rusted beside the rocketport. Old newspapers danced alone on the windy tarmac.

Wilder, motionless at the top of the gantry elevator, suddenly wished not to move down. The lights suddenly had become people and not words that, huge in the mind, could be handled with elaborate ease.

He sighed. The freight of people was too heavy. The stars were too far away.

"Captain?" said someone behind him.

He stepped forward. The elevator gave way. They sank with a silent screaming toward a very real land with real people in it, who were waiting for him to choose.

At midnight the telegram bin hissed and exploded out a message projectile. Wilder, at his desk, surrounded by tapes and computation cards, did not touch it for a long while. When at last he pulled the message out, he scanned it, rolled it in a tight ball, then uncrumpled the message and read again:

FINAL CANAL BEING FILLED TOMORROW WEEK. YOU ARE INVITED CANAL YACHT PARTY. DISTINGUISHED GUESTS. FOUR-DAY JOURNEY TO SEARCH FOR LOST CITY. KINDLY ACKNOWLEDGE.

I. V. AARONSON.

Wilder blinked, and laughed quietly. He crumpled the paper again, but stopped, lifted the telephone and said:

"Telegram to I. V. Aaronson, Mars City I. Answer affirmative. No sane reason why, but still—affirmative."

And hung up the phone. To sit for a long while watching this night that shadowed all the whispering, ticking and motioning machines.

The dry canal waited.

It had been waiting 20,000 years for nothing but dust to filter through in ghost tides.

Now, quite suddenly, it whispered.

And the whisper became a rush and wall-caroming glide of waters.

As if a vast machined fist had struck the rocks somewhere, clapped the air and cried "Miracle!," a wall of water came proud and high along the channels, and lay down in all the dry places of the canal and moved on toward ancient deserts of dry bone surprising old wharves and lifting up the skeletons of boats abandoned countless centuries before when the water burnt away to nothing.

The tide turned a corner and lifted up—a boat as fresh as the morning itself, with new-minted silver screws and brass pipings, and bright new Earth-sewn flags. The boat, suspended from the side of the canal, bore the name Aaronson I.

Inside the boat, a man with the same name smiled. Mr. Aaronson sat listening to the waters live under the boat.

And the sound of the water was cut across by the sound of a hovercraft, arriving, and a motor bike, arriving, and in the air, as if summoned with magical timing, drawn by the glimmer of tides in the old canal, a number of gadfly people flew over the hills on jetpack machines and hung suspended as if doubting this collision of lives caused by one rich man.

Scowling up with a smile, the rich man called to his children, cried them in from the heat with offers of food and drink.

"Captain Wilder! Mr. Parkhill! Mr. Beaumont!"

Wilder set his hovercraft down.

Sam Parkhill discarded his motor bike, for he had seen the yacht and it was a new love.

"My God," cried Beaumont, the actor, part of the frieze of people in the sky dancing like bright bees on the wind. "I've timed my entrance wrong. I'm early. There's no audience!"

"I'll applaud you down!" shouted the old man, and did so, then added, "Mr. Aikens!"

"Aikens?" said Parkhill. "The big-game hunter?"

"None other!"

And Aikens dived down as if to seize them in his harrying claws. He fancied his resemblance to the hawk. He was finished and stropped like a razor by the swift life he had lived. Not an edge of him but cut the air as he fell, a strange plummeting vengeance upon people who had done nothing to him. In the moment before destruction, he pulled up on his jets and, gently screaming, simmered himself to touch the marble jetty. About his lean middle hung a rifle belt. His pockets bulged like those of a boy from the candy store. One guessed he was stashed with sweet bullets and rare bombs. In his hands, like an evil child, he held a weapon that looked like a bolt of lightning fallen straight from the clutch of Zeus, stamped, nevertheless: MADE IN U. S. A. His face was sun-blasted dark. His eyes were cool surprises in the sun-wrinkled flesh, all mint-blue-green crystal. He wore a white porcelain smile set in African sinews. The earth did not quite tremble as he landed.

"The lion prowls the land of Judah!" cried a voice from the heavens. "Now do behold the lambs driven forth to slaughter!"

"Oh, for God's sake, Harry, shut up!" said a woman's voice.

And two more kites fluttered their souls, their dread humanity, on the wind.

The rich man jubilated.

"Harry Harpwell!"

"Behold the angel of the Lord who comes with Annunciations!" the man in the sky said, hovering. "And the Annunciation is—"

"He's drunk again," his wife supplied, flying ahead of him, not looking back.

"Megan Harpwell," said the rich man, like an entrepreneur introducing his troupe.

"The poet," said Wilder.

"And the poet's barracuda wife," muttered Parkhill.

"I am not drunk," the poet shouted down the wind. "I am simply *high*." And here he let loose such a deluge of laughter that those below almost raised their hands to ward off the avalanche.

Lowering himself, like a fat dragon kite, the poet, whose wife's mouth was now clamped shut, bumbled over the yacht. He made the motions of blessing same, and winked at Wilder and Parkhill.

"Harpwell," he called. "Isn't that a name to go with being a great modern poet who suffers in the present, lives in the past, steals bones from old dramatists' tombs, and flies on this new egg-beater wind-suck device, to call down sonnets on your head? I pity the old euphoric saints and angels who had no invisible wings like these so as to dart in oriole convolutions and ecstatic convulsions on the air as they sang their lines or damned souls to hell. Poor earthbound sparrows, wings clipped. Only their genius flew. Only their muse knew airsickness—"

"Harry," said his wife, her feet on the ground, eyes shut.

"Hunter!" called the poet. "Aikens! Here's the greatest game in all the world, a poet on the wing. I bare my breast. Let fly your honeyed bee sting! Bring me, Icarus, down, if your gun be sun-beams kindled in one tube, let free in single forest fires that escalate the sky to turn tallow, mush, candlewick and lyre to mere tarbabe. Ready, aim, fire!"

The hunter, in good humor, raised his gun.

The poet, at this, laughed a mightier laugh and, literally, exposed his chest by tearing aside his shirt.

At which moment a quietness came along the canal rim.

A woman appeared, walking. Her maid walked behind her. There was no vehicle in sight, and it seemed almost as if they had wandered a long way out of the Martian hills and now stopped.

The very quietness of her entrance gave dignity and attention to Cara Corelli.

The poet shut up his lyric in the sky and landed.

The company all looked together at this actress who gazed back without seeing them. She was dressed in a black jump suit that was the same color as her dark hair. She walked like a woman who has spoken little in her life and now stood facing them with the same quietness, as if waiting for someone to move without being ordered. The wind blew her hair out and down over her shoulders. The paleness of her face was shocking. Her paleness, rather than her eyes, stared at them.

Then, without a word, she stepped down into the yacht and sat in the front of the craft, like a figurehead that knows its place and goes there.

The moment of silence was over.

Aaronson ran his finger down the printed guest list.

"An actor, a beautiful woman who happens to be an actress, a hunter, a poet, a poet's wife, a rocket captain, a former technician. All aboard!"

On the afterdeck of the huge craft, Aaronson spread forth his maps.

"Ladies, gentlemen," he said. "This is more than a four-day drinking bout, party, excursion. This is a search!"

He waited for their faces to light properly, and for them to glance from his eyes to the charts, and then said:

"We are seeking the fabled Lost City of Mars, once called Dia-Sao, the City of Doom. Something terrible about it. The inhabitants fled as from a plague. The City left empty. Still empty now, centuries later."

"We," said Captain Wilder, "have charted, mapped and cross-indexed every acre of land on Mars in the last fifteen years. You can't mislay a city the size of the one you speak of."

"True," said Aaronson, "you've mapped it from the sky, from the land. But you have *not* charted it via water, for the canals have been empty until now! So we shall take the new waters that fill this last canal and go where the boats once went in the olden days, and see the very last new things that need to be seen on Mars." The rich man continued: "And somewhere on our traveling, as sure as the breath in our mouths, we shall find the most beautiful, the most fantastic, the most awful city in the history of this old world. And walk in that city and—who knows?—find the reason why the Martians ran screaming away from it, as the legend says, thousands of years ago."

Silence. Then:

"Bravo! Well done." The poet shook the old man's hand.

"And in that city," said Aikens, the hunter, "mightn't there be weapons the like of which we've never seen?"

"Most likely, sir."

"Well." The hunter cradled his bolt of lightning. "I was bored of Earth, shot every animal, ran fresh out of beasts, and came here looking for newer, better, more dangerous man-eaters of any size or shape. Plus, now, new weapons! What more can one ask? Fine!"

And he dropped his blue-silver lightning bolt over the side. It sank in the clear water, bubbling.

"Let's get the hell out of here."

"Let us, indeed," said Aaronson, "get the good hell out."

And he pressed the button that launched the yacht.

And the water flowed the yacht away.

And the yacht went in the direction toward which Cara Corelli's quiet paleness was pointed: beyond.

The poet opened the first champagne bottle. The cork banged. Only the hunter did not jump.

The yacht sailed steadily through the day into night. They found an ancient ruin and had dinner there and a good wine imported 100,000,000 miles from Earth. It was noted that it had traveled well.

With the wine came the poet, and after quite a bit of the poet came sleep on board the yacht that moved away in search of a city that would not as yet be found.

At three in the morning, restless, unaccustomed to the gravity of a planet pulling at all of his body and not freeing him to dream, Wilder came out on the afterdeck of the yacht and found the actress there.

She was watching the waters slip by in dark revelations and discardments of stars.

He sat beside her and thought a question.

Just as silently, Cara Corelli asked herself the same question, and answered it.

"I am here on Mars because not long ago for the first time in my life, a man told me the truth."

Perhaps she expected surprise. Wilder said nothing. The boat moved as on a stream of soundless oil.

"I am a beautiful woman. I have been beautiful all of my life. Which means that from the start people lied because they simply wished to be with me. I grew up surrounded by the untruths of men, women and children who could not risk my displeasure. When beauty pouts, the world trembles.

"Have you ever seen a beautiful woman surrounded by men, seen them nodding, nodding? Heard their laughter? Men will laugh at anything a beautiful woman says. Hate themselves, yes, but they will laugh, say no for yes and yes for no.

"Well, that's how it was every day of every year for me. A crowd of liars stood between me and anything unpleasant. Their words dressed me in silks.

11

"But quite suddenly, oh, no more than six weeks ago, this man told me a truth. It was a small thing. I don't remember now what it was he said. But he didn't laugh. He didn't even smile.

"And no sooner was it out and over, the words spoken, than I knew a terrible thing had happened.

"I was growing old."

The yacht rocked gently on the tide.

"Oh, there would be more men who would, lying, smile again at what I said. But I saw the years ahead, when beauty could no longer stomp its small foot, and shake down earthquakes, make cowardice a custom among otherwise good men.

"The man? He took back his truth immediately, when he saw that he had shocked me. But it was too late. I bought a one-way fare to Mars. Aaronson's invitation, when I arrived, put me on this new journey that will end . . . who knows where."

Wilder found that during this last he had reached out and taken her hand.

"No," she said, withdrawing. "No word. No touch. No pity. No self-pity." She smiled for the first time. "Isn't it strange? I always thought, wouldn't it be nice, someday, to hear the truth, to give up the masquerade? How wrong I was. It's no fun at all."

She sat and watched the black waters pour by the boat. When she thought to look again, some hours later, the seat beside her was empty. Wilder was gone.

On the second day, letting the new waters take them where it wished to go, they sailed toward a high range of mountains and lunched, on the way, in an old shrine, and had dinner that night in a further ruin. The Lost City was not much talked about. They were sure it would never be found.

But on the third day, without anyone's saying, they felt the approach of a great presence.

It was the poet who finally put it in words.

"Is God humming under His breath somewhere?"

"What a fierce scum you are," said his wife. "Can't you speak plain English even when you gossip?"

"Damnit, listen!" cried the poet.

So they listened.

"Don't you feel as if you stood on the threshold of a giant

blast-furnace kitchen and inside somewhere, all comfortably warm, vast hands, flour-gloved, smelling of wondrous tripes and miraculous viscera, bloodied and proud of the blood, somewhere God cooks out the dinnertime of life? In that caldron sun, a brew to make the flowering forth of life on Venus, in that vat, a stew broth of bones and nervous heart to run in animals on planets ten billion light-years gone. And isn't God content at His fabulous workings in the great kitchen Universe, where He has menu'd out a history of feasts, famines, deaths and reburgeonings for a billion billion years? And if God be content, would He not hum under His breath? Feel your bones. Aren't the marrows teeming with that hum? For that matter, God not only hums. He sings in the elements. He dances in molecules. Eternal celebration swarms us. Something is near. Sh."

He pressed his fat finger to his pouting lips.

And now all were silent, and Cara Corelli's paleness searchlighted the darkening waters ahead.

They all felt it. Wilder did. Parkhill did. They smoked to cover it. They put the smokes out. They waited in the dusk.

And the humming grew nearer. And the hunter, smelling it, went to join the silent actress at the bow of the yacht. And the poet sat to write down the words he had spoken.

"Yes," he said, as the stars came out. "It's almost upon us. It has . . ." he took a breath, ". . . arrived."

The yacht passed into a tunnel.

The tunnel went under a mountain.

And the City was there.

It was a city within a hollow mountain with its own meadows surrounding it and its own strangely colored and illumined stone sky above it. And it had been lost and remained lost for the simple reason that people had tried flying to discover it or had unraveled roads to find it, when all the while the canals that led to it stood waiting for simple walkers to tread where once waters had trod.

And now the yacht filled with strange people from another planet touched an ancient wharf.

And the City stirred.

In the old days, cities were alive or dead if there were or were not people in them. It was that simple. But in the later days of life on Earth or Mars, cities did not die. They slept. And in their dreamful coggeries and enwheeled slumbers they remembered how once it was or how it might be again.

So as, one by one, the party filed out on the dock, they felt a great personage, the hidden, oiled, the metaled and shining soul of the metropolis slide in a landfall of muted and hidden fireworks toward becoming fully awake.

The weight of the new people on the dock caused a machined exhalation. They felt themselves on a delicate scales. The dock sank a millionth of an inch.

And the City, the cumbrous Sleeping Beauty of a nightmare device, sensed this touch, this kiss, and slept no more.

Thunder.

In a wall 100 feet high stood a gate 70 feet wide. This gate, in two parts, now rumbled back, to hide within the wall.

Aaronson stepped forward.

Wilder moved to intercept him. Aaronson sighed.

"Captain, no advice, please. No warnings. No patrols going on ahead to flush out villains. The City wants us in. It welcomes us. Surely you don't imagine anything's *alive* in there? It's a robot place. And don't look as if you think it's a time bomb. It hasn't seen fun and games in—what? Do you read Martian hieroglyphs? That cornerstone. The City was built at least twenty thousand years ago."

"And abandoned," said Wilder.

"You make it sound like a plague drove them—"

"Not a plague." Wilder stirred uneasily, feeling himself weighed on the great scales beneath his feet. "Something. Something . . ."

"Let's find out! In, all of you!"

Singly, and in pairs, the people from Earth stepped over the threshold.

Wilder, last of all, stepped across.

And the City came more alive.

The metal roofs of the City sprang wide like the petals of a flower.

Windows flicked wide like the lids of vast eyes to stare down upon them.

A river of sidewalks gently purled and washed at their feet, machined creek-ways that gleamed off through the City.

Aaronson gazed at the metal tides with pleasure. "Well, by God, the burden's off me! I was going to picnic you all. But that's the City's business now. Meet you back here in two hours to compare notes! Here goes!"

And saying this, he leaped out onto the scurrying silver carpet that treaded him swiftly away.

Wilder, alarmed, moved to follow. But Aaronson cried jovially back:

"Come on in, the water's fine!"

And the metal river whisked him, waving, off.

And one by one they stepped forward and the moving sidewalk drifted them away. Parkhill, the hunter, the poet and his wife, the actor, and then the beautiful woman and her maid. They floated like statues mysteriously borne on volcanic fluids that swept them anywhere, or nowhere, they could only guess.

Wilder jumped. The river seized his boots gently. Following, he went away into the avenues and around the bends of parks and through fiords of buildings.

And behind them, the dock and the gate stood empty. There was no trace to show they had arrived. It was almost as if they had never been.

Beaumont, the actor, was the first to leave the traveling pathway. A certain building caught his eye. And the next thing he knew, he had leaped off and edged near, sniffing.

He smiled.

For now he knew what kind of building he stood before, because of the odor that drifted from it.

"Brass polish. And, by God. that means only one thing!"

Theater.

Brass doors, brass rails, brass rings on velvet curtains.

He opened the door of the building and stepped in. He sniffed and laughed aloud. Yes. Without a sign or a light, the smell alone, the special chemistry of metals and dust torn free of a million tickets.

And above all . . . he listened. The silence.

"The silence that waits. No other silence in the world waits. Only in a theater will you find that. The very particles of air chafe themselves in readiness. The shadows sit back and hold their breath. Well . . . ready or not . . . here I come . . ."

The lobby was green velvet undersea.

The theater itself: red velvet undersea, only dimly perceived as he opened the double doors. Somewhere beyond was a stage.

Something shuddered like a great beast. His breath had dreamed it alive. The air from his half-opened mouth caused the curtains 100 feet away to softly furl and unfurl in darkness like all-covering wings.

Hesitantly, he took a step.

A light began to appear everywhere in a high ceiling where a school of miraculous prism fish swam upon themselves.

The oceanarium light played everywhere. He gasped.

The theater was full of people.

A thousand people sat motionless in the false dusk. True, they were small, fragile, rather dark, they wore silver masks, yet—people!

He knew, without asking, they had sat here for endless centuries.

Yet they were not dead.

They were—he reached out a hand. He tapped the wrist of a man seated on the aisle.

The hand tinkled quietly.

He touched the shoulder of a woman. She chimed. Like a bell.

Yes, they had waited some few thousand years. But then, machines have a property of waiting.

He took a further step and froze.

For a sigh had passed over the crowd.

It was like the sound, the first small sound a newborn babe must make in the moment before it really sucks, bleats and shocks out its wailing surprise at being alive.

A thousand such sighs faded in the velvet portieres.

Beneath the masks, hadn't a thousand mouths drifted ajar?

He moved. He stopped.

Two thousand eyes blinked wide in the velvet dusk.

He moved again.

A thousand silent heads wheeled on their ancient but well-oiled cogs.

They looked at him.

An unquenchable cold ran wild in him.

He turned to run.

But their eyes would not let him go.

And, from the orchestra pit: music.

He looked and saw, slowly rising, an insect agglomeration of instruments, all strange, all grotesquely acrobatic in their configurations. These were being softly thrummed, piped, touched and massaged in tune.

The audience, with a motion, turned their gaze to the stage.

A light flashed on. The orchestra struck a grand fanfare chord.

The red curtains parted. A spotlight fixed itself to front center, blazing upon an empty dais where sat an empty chair.

Beaumont waited.

No actor appeared.

A stir. Several hands were lifted to left and right. The hands came together. They beat softly in applause.

Now the spotlight wandered off the stage and up the aisle.

The heads of the audience turned to follow the empty ghost of light. The masks glinted softly. The eyes behind the masks beckoned with warm color.

Beaumont stepped back.

But the light came steadily. It painted the floor with a blunt cone of pure whiteness.

And stopped, nibbling, at his feet.

The audience, turned, applauded even louder now. The theater banged, roared, ricocheted with their ceaseless tide of approbation.

Everything dissolved within him, from cold to warm. He felt as if he had been thrust raw into a downpour of summer rain. The storm rinsed him with gratitude. His heart jumped in great compulsive beats. His fists let go of themselves. His skeleton relaxed. He waited a moment longer, with the rain drenching over his upthrust and thankful cheeks and hammering his hungry eyelids so they fluttered to lock against themselves, and then he felt himself, like a ghost on battlements, led by a ghost light, lean, step, drift, move down and along the incline, sliding to beautiful ruin, now no longer walking but striding, not striding but in full-tilted run, and the masks glittering, the eyes hot with delight and fantastic welcoming, the flights of hands on the disturbed air in upflung dovewinged rifle-shot flight. He felt the steps collide with his shoes. The applause slammed to a shutdown.

He swallowed. Then slowly he ascended the steps and stood in the full light with a thousand masks fixed to him and two thousand eyes watchful, and he sat in the empty chair, and the theater grew darker, and the immense hearth-bellow breathing softer out of the lyre-metal throats, and there was only the sound of a mechanical beehive thrived with machinery musk in the dark.

He held onto his knees. He let go. And at last he spoke:

"To be or not to be—"

The silence was complete.

Not a cough. Not a stir. Not a rustle. Not a blink. All waited. Perfection. The perfect audience. Perfect, forever and forever. Perfect. Perfect.

He tossed his words slowly into that perfect pond and felt the soundless ripples disperse and gentle away.

"—that is the question."

He talked. They listened. He knew that they would never let him go now. They would beat him insensible with applause. He would sleep a child's sleep and arise to speak again. All of Shakespeare, all of Shaw, all of Molière, every bit, crumb, lump, joint and piece. *Himself* in repertory!

He arose to finish.

Finished, he thought: Bury me! Cover me! Smother me deep!

Obediently, the avalanche came down the mountain.

Cara Corelli found a palace of mirrors.

The maid remained outside.

And Cara Corelli went in.

As she walked through a maze, the mirrors took away a day, and then a week, and then a month and then a year and then two years of time from her face.

It was a palace of splendid and soothing lies. It was like being young once more. It was being surrounded by all those tall bright glass mirror men who would never again in your life tell you the truth.

Cara walked to the center of the palace. By the time she

stopped, she saw herself 25 years old, in every tall bright mirror face.

She sat down in the middle of the bright maze. She beamed around in happiness.

The maid waited outside for perhaps an hour. And then she went away.

This was a dark place with shapes and sizes as yet unseen. It smelled of lubricating oil, the blood of tyrant lizards with cogs and wheels for teeth, which lay strewn and silent in the dark, waiting.

A titan's door slowly gave a slithering roar, like a backswept armored tail, and Parkhill stood in the rich oily wind blowing out around him. He felt as if someone had pasted a white flower on his face. But it was only a sudden surprise of a smile.

His empty hands hung at his sides and they made impulsive and completely unconscious gestures forward. They beggared the air. So, paddling silently, he let himself be moved into the garage, machine shop, repair shed, whatever it was.

And filled with holy delight and a child's holy and unholy glee at what he beheld, he walked and slowly turned.

For as far as his eye could see stood vehicles.

Vehicles that ran on the earth. Vehicles that flew in the air. Vehicles that stood ready with wheels to go in any direction. Vehicles with two wheels. Vehicles with three or four or six or eight. Vehicles that looked like butterflies. Vehicles that resembled ancient motor bikes. Three thousand stood ranked here, four thousand glinted ready there. Another thousand were tilted over, wheels off, copper guts exposed, waiting to be repaired. Still another thousand were lifted high on spidery repair hoists, their lovely undersides revealed to view, their disks and tubes and coggeries all intricate and fine and needful of touching, unbolting, revalving, rewiring, oiling, delicately lubricating . . .

Parkhill's palms itched.

He walked forward through the primeval smell of swamp oils among the dead and waiting to be revived ancient but new armored mechanical reptiles, and the more he looked the more he ached his grin.

The City was a city all right, and, to a point, self-sustaining. But, eventually, the rarest butterflies of metal gossamer, gaseous

19

oil and fiery dream sank to earth, the machines that repaired the machines that repaired the machines grew old, ill and damaging of themselves. Here then was the bestial garage, the slumberous elephant's bone yard where the aluminum dragons crawled rusting out their souls, hopeful of one live person left among so much active but dead metal, that person to put things right. One God of the machines to say, you Lazarus-elevator, rise up! You hovercraft, be reborn! And anoint them with leviathan oils, tap them with magical wrench and send them forth to almost eternal lives in and on the air and above the quicksilver paths.

Parkhill moved among 900 robot men and women slaughtered by simple corrosion. He would cure their rust.

Now.If he started now, thought Parkhill, rolling up his sleeves and staring off down a corridor of machines that ran waiting for a solid mile of garage, shed, hoist, lift, storage bin, oil tank and strewn shrapnel of tools glittering and ready for his grip; if he started now, he might work his way to the end of the giant's ever-constant garage, accident, collision and repair-works shed in 30 years!

A billion bolts to be tightened. A billion motors to be tinkered! A billion gross anatomical mysteries to lie under, a grand oil-dripped-upon orphan, alone, alone, alone with the always beautiful and never talking back hummingbird-commotion devices, accouterments and miraculous contraptions.

His hands weighed him toward the tools. He clutched a wrench. He found a 40-wheeled low running sled. He lay down on it. He sculled the garage in a long whistling ride. The sled scuttled.

Parkhill vanished beneath a great car of some ancient design.

Out of sight, you could hear him working on the gut of the machine. On his back, he talked up at it. And when he slapped it to life, at last, the machine talked back.

Always the silver pathways ran somewhere.

Thousands of years now they had run empty, carrying only dust to destinations away and away among the high and dreaming buildings.

Now, on one traveling path, Aaronson came borne like an aging statue.

And the more the road propelled him, the faster the City exposed itself to his view, the more buildings that passed, the more parks that sprang into sight, the more his smile faded. His color changed.

"Toy," he heard himself whisper. The whisper was ancient. "Just another," and here his voice grew so small it faded away, ". . . another toy."

A supertoy, yes. But his life was full of such and had always been so. If it was not some slot machine, it was the next-size dispenser or a jumbo-size razzmatazz hi-fi stereo speaker. From a lifetime of handling metallic sandpaper, he felt his arms rubbed away to a nub. Mere pips, his fingers. No, handless, and lacking wrists. Aaronson, the Seal Boy!!! His mindless flippers clapped applause to a city that was, in reality, no more and no less than an economy-size jukebox ravening under its idiot breath. And— he knew the tune! God help him. He *knew* the tune.

He blinked just once.

An inner eyelid came down like cold glass.

He turned and trod the silver waters of the path.

He found a moving river of steel to take him back toward the great gate itself.

On the way, he met Cara Corelli's maid, wandering lost on her own silver stream.

As for the poet and his wife, their running battle tore echoes everywhere. They cried down 30 avenues, cracked panes in 200 shops, battered leaves from 70 varieties of park bush and tree, and only ceased when drowned by a thundering fountain display they passed, like a rise of clear fireworks upon the metropolitan air.

"The whole thing is," said his wife, punctuating one of his dirtier responses, "you only came along so you could lay hands on the nearest woman and spray her ears with bad breath and worse poetry."

The poet muttered a foul word.

"You're worse than the actor," said his wife. "Always at it. Don't you ever shut up?"

"Don't you?" he cried. "Ah God, I've curdled inside. Shut up, woman, or I'll throw myself in the founts!"

21

"No. You haven't bathed in years. You're the pig of the century! Your picture will grace the *Swine Herder's Annual* next month!"

"That *did* it!"

Doors slammed on a building.

By the time she got off and ran back and fisted the doors, they were locked.

"Coward!" she shrieked. "Open up!"

A foul word came echoing out, dimly.

"Ah, listen to that sweet silence," he whispered, to himself, in the great shelled dark.

Harpwell found himself in a soothing hugeness, a vast womb-like building, over which hung a canopy of pure serenity, a starless void.

In the middle of this room, which was roughly a 200-foot circle, stood a device, a machine. In this machine were dials and rheostats and switches, a seat and a steering wheel.

"What kind of junk is this?" whispered the poet, but edged near, and bent to touch. "Christ-off-the-cross and bearing mercy, it smells of what? Blood and mere guts? No, for it's clean as a virgin's frock. Still it does fill the nose. Violence. Simple destruction. I can feel the damn carcass tremble like a nervous highbred hound. It's full of *stuffs*. Let's try a swig."

He sat in the machine.

"What do I twig first? This?"

He snapped a switch.

The Baskerville-hound machine whimpered in its dog slumberings.

"Good beast." He flicked another switch. "How do you go, brute? When the damn device is in full tilt, where to? You lack wheels. Well, surprise me. I dare."

The machine shivered.

The machine bolted.

It ran. It dashed.

He held tight to the steering wheel.

"Holy God!"

For he was on a highway, racing fast.

Air sluiced by. The sky flashed over in running colors.

The speedometer read 70, 80.

And the highway ribboned away ahead, flashing toward him. Invisible wheels slapped and banged on an increasingly rough road.

Far away, ahead, a car appeared.

It was running fast. And—

"It's on the wrong side of the road! Do you see that, wife? The wrong side."

Then he realized his wife was not here.

He was alone in a car racing—90 miles an hour now—toward another car racing at a similar speed.

He veered the wheel.

His vehicle moved to the left.

Almost instantly, the other car did a compensating move and ran back over to the left.

"The damn fool, what does he think—where's the blasted brake?"

He stomped the floor. There was no brake. Here was a strange machine indeed. One that ran as fast as you wished, but never stopped until what? it ran itself down? There was no brake. Nothing but—further accelerators. A whole series of round buttons on the floor, which, as he tromped them, surged power into the motor.

Ninety, 100, 120 miles an hour.

"God in heaven!" he screamed. "We're going to hit! How do you like that, girl?"

And in the last instant before collision, he imagined she rather liked it fine.

The cars hit. They erupted in gaseous flame. They burst apart in flinders. They tumbled. He felt himself jerked now this way, now that. He was a torch hurtled skyward. His arms and legs danced a crazy rigadoon in mid-air as he felt his peppermint-stick bones snap in brittle and agonizing ecstasies. Then, clutching death as a dark mate, gesticulating, he fell away in a black surprise, drifting toward further nothings.

He lay dead.

He lay dead a long while.

Then he opened one eye.

23

He felt the slow burner under his soul. He felt the bubbled water rising to the top of his mind like tea brewing.

"I'm dead," he said, "but alive. Did you see all that, wife? Dead but alive."

He found himself sitting in the vehicle, upright.

He sat there for ten minutes thinking about all that had happened.

"Well now," he mused. "Was that not interesting? Not to say fascinating? Not to say almost exhilarating? I mean, sure, it knocked the stuff out of me, scared the soul out one ear and back the other, hit my wind and tore my seams, broke the bones and shook the wits, but, but, but, wife, but, but, but, dear sweet Meg, Meggy, Megeen. I wish you were here, it might tamp the tobacco tars out of your half-ass lungs and bray the mossy graveyard back-breaking meanness from your marrow. Let me see here now, wife, let's have a look, Harpwell-my-husband-the-poet."

He tinkered with the dials.

He thrummed the great hound motor.

"Shall we chance another diversion? Try another embattled picnic excursion? Let's."

And he set the car on its way.

Almost immediately, the vehicle was traveling 100 and then 150 miles per hour.

Almost immediately, an opposing car appeared ahead on the wrong side of the road.

"Death," said the poet. "Are you always here, then? Do you hang about? Is this your questing place? Let's test your mettle!"

The car raced. The opposing car hurtled.

He wheeled over into the far left lane.

The opposing car shifted, homing toward Destroy.

"Yes, I see, well, then, this," said the poet.

And switched a switch and jumped another throttle.

In the instant before impact, the two cars transformed themselves. Shuttering through illusory veils, they became jetcraft at take-off. Shrieking, the two jets banged flame, tore air, yammered back sound-barrier explosions before the mightiest one of all—as the two bullets impacted, fused, interwove, interlaced blood, mind and eternal blackness, and fell away into a net of strange and peaceful midnight.

I'm dead, he thought again.

And it feels fine, thanks.

He awoke at the touch of his own smile.

He was seated in the vehicle.

Twice dead, he thought, and feeling better each time. Why? isn't that odd? Curiouser and curiouser. Queer beyond queerness.

He thrummed the motor again.

What this time?

Does it locomote? he wondered. How about a big black choo-choo train out of half-primordial times?

And he was on his way, an engineer. The sky flicked over, and the motion-picture screens or whatever they were pressed in with swift illusions of pouring smoke and steaming whistle and huge wheel within wheel on grinding track, and the track ahead wound through hills, and far on up around a mountain came another train, black as a buffalo herd, pouring belches of smoke, on the same two rails, the same track, heading toward wondrous accident.

"I see," said the poet. "I do begin to see. I begin to know what this is used for; for such as me, the poor wandering idiots of a world, confused, and sore put upon by mothers as soon as dropped from wombs, insulted with Christian guilt, and gone mad from the need of destruction, and collecting a pittance of hurt here and scar tissue there, and a larger portable wife griev-ance beyond, but one thing sure, we do want to die, we do want to be killed, and here's the very thing for it, in convenient quick pay! So pay it out, machine, dole it out, sweet raving device! Rape away, death! I'm your very man."

And the two locomotives met and climbed each other. Up a black ladder of explosion they wheeled and locked their drive shafts and plastered their slick negro bellies together and rubbed boilers and beautifully banged the night in a single outflung whirl and flurry of meteor and flame. Then the locomotives, in a cum-brous rapine dance, seized and melted together with their violence and passion, gave a monstrous curtsy and fell off the mountain and took a thousand years to go all the way down to the rocky pits.

The poet awoke and immediately grabbed the controls. He was humming under his breath, stunned. He was singing wild tunes. His eyes flashed. His heart beat swiftly.

"More, more, I see it now, I know what to do, more, more, please, O God, more, for the truth shall set me free, more!"

He hoofed three, four, five pedals.

He snapped six switches.

The vehicle was auto-jet-locomotive-glider-missile-rocket.

He ran, he steamed, he roared, he soared, he flew. Cars veered toward him. Locomotives loomed. Jets rammed. Rockets screamed.

And in one wild three-hour spree he hit 200 cars, rammed 20 trains, blew up 10 gliders, exploded 40 missiles, and, far out in space, gave up his glorious soul in a final Fourth of July death celebration as an interplanetary rocket going 200,000 miles an hour struck an iron planetoid and went beautifully to hell.

In all, in a few short hours he figured he must have been torn apart and put back together a few times less than 500.

When it was all over, he sat not touching the wheel, his feet free of the pedals.

After a half hour of sitting there, he began to laugh. He threw his head back and let out great war whoops. Then he got up. shaking his head, drunker than ever in his life, really drunk now, and he knew he would stay that way forever, and never need drink again.

I'm punished, he thought, really punished at last. Really hurt at last, and hurt enough, over and over, so I will never need hurt again, never need to be destroyed again, never have to collect another insult or take another wound, or ask for a simple grievance. God bless the genius of man and the inventors of such machines, that enable the guilty to pay and at last be rid of the dark albatross and the awful burden. Thank you, City, thank you, old blueprinter of needful souls. Thank you. And which way out?

A door slid open.

His wife stood waiting for him.

"Well, there you are," she said. "And still drunk."

"No," he said. "Dead."

"Drunk."

"Dead," he said, "beautifully dead at last. Which means, free. I won't need you anymore, dead Meg-Meggy-Megeen. You're set free, also, like an awful conscience. Go haunt someone else, girl.

Go destroy. I forgive you your sins on me, for I have at last forgiven myself. I am off the Christian hook. I am the dear wandering dead who, dead, can at last live. Go and do likewise, lady. Inside with you. Be punished and set free. So long, Meg. Farewell. Toodle-oo."

He wandered away.

"Where do you think you're going?" she cried.

"Why, out into life and the blood of life, and happy at last."

"Come back here!" she screamed.

"You can't stop the dead, for they wander the Universe, happy as children in the dark field."

"Harpwell!" she brayed. "Harpwell!"

But he stepped on a river of silver metal.

And let the dear river bear him laughing until the tears glittered on his cheeks, away and away from the shriek and the bray and the scream of that woman, what was her name? no matter, back there, and gone.

And when he reached the gate he walked out and along the canal in the fine day, heading toward the far towns.

By that time, he was singing every old tune he had known as a child of six . . .

Behind him, by the strange building that had set him free, his wife stood a long while staring at the metal path that had floated him away. Then slowly she turned to glare at the enemy building. She fisted the door once. It slid open, waiting. She sniffed. She scowled at the interior.

Then, steadily, hands ready to seize and grapple, she advanced. With each step she grew bolder. Her face thrust like an ax at the strange air.

Behind her, unnoticed, the door closed.

It did not open again.

It was a church.

It was not a church.

Wilder let the door swing shut.

He stood in cathedral darkness, waiting.

The roof, if roof there was, breathed up in a great suspense, flowed up beyond reach or sight.

The floor, if floor there was, was a mere firmness beneath. It, too, was black.

27

And then the stars came out. It was like that first night of childhood when his father had taken him out beyond the city to a hill where the streetlights could not diminish the Universe. And there were a thousand, no ten thousand, no ten million billion stars filling the darkness. The stars were manifold and bright, and they did not care. Even then he had known: They do not care. If I breathe or do not breathe, live or die, the eyes that look from all around don't care. And he had seized his father's hand and gripped tight, as if he might fall up into that abyss.

Now, in this building, he was full of the old terror and the old sense of beauty and the old silent crying out after mankind. The stars filled him with pity for small men lost in so much size.

Then yet another thing happened.

Beneath his feet, space opened wide and let through yet another billion sparks of light.

He was suspended as a fly is held upon a vast telescopic lens. He walked on a water of space. He stood upon a transparent flex of great eye, and all about him, as on a night in winter, beneath foot and above head, in all directions, were nothing but stars.

So, in the end, it was a church, it was a cathedral, a multitude of far-flung universal shrines, here a worshiping of Horsehead Nebula, there Orion's galaxy, and there Andromeda, like the head of God, fiercely gazed and thrust through the raw dark stuffs of night to stab his soul and pin it writhing against the backside of his flesh.

God, everywhere, fixed him with shutterless and unblinking eyes.

And he, a bacterial shard of that same Flesh, stared back and winced but the slightest.

He waited. And a planet drifted upon the void. It spun by once with a great mellow autumn face. It circled and came under him.

And he stood upon a far world of green grass and great lush trees, where the air was fresh, and a river ran by like the rivers of childhood, flashing the sun and leaping with fish.

He knew that he had traveled very far to reach this world. Behind him lay the rocket. Behind lay a century of travel, of sleeping, of waiting, and now, here was the reward.

"Mine?" he asked the simple air, the simple grass, the long simplicity of water that spilled by in the shallow sands.

And the world answered wordless: Yours.

Yours without the long travel and the boredom, yours without 99 years of flight from Earth, of sleeping in kept tubes, of intravenous feedings, of nightmares dreamed of Earth lost and gone, yours without torture, without pain, yours without trial and error, failure and destruction. Yours without sweat and terror. Yours without a falling down of tears. Yours. Yours.

But Wilder did not put out his hands to accept.

And the sun dimmed in the alien sky.

And the world drifted from under his feet.

And yet another world swam up and passed in a large parade of even brighter glories.

And this world, too, spun up to take his weight. And here, if anything, the fields were richer green, the mountains capped with melting snows, far fields ripening with strange harvests, and scythes waiting on the edge of fields for him to lift and sweep and cut the grain and live out his life any way that he might.

Yours. The merest touch of weather upon the hairs within his ear said this. Yours.

And Wilder, without shaking his head, moved back. He did not say no. He thought his rejection.

And the grass died in the fields.

The mountains crumbled.

The river shallows ran to dust.

And the world sprang away.

And Wilder stood again in space where God had stood before creating a world out of chaos.

And at last he spoke and said to himself:

"It would be easy. Oh Lord, yes, I'd like that. No work, nothing, just accept. But . . . You can't *give* me what I want."

He looked at the stars.

"Nothing can be given, ever."

The stars were growing dim.

"It's really very simple. I must borrow, I must earn. I must take."

The stars quivered and died.

"Much obliged and thank you, no."

The stars were all gone.

He turned and, without looking back, walked upon darkness. He hit the door with his palm. He strode out into the City.

29

He refused to hear if the machine Universe behind him cried out in a great chorus, all cries and wounds, like a woman scorned. The crockery in a vast robot kitchen fell. By the time it hit the floor, he was gone.

It was a museum of weapons.

The hunter walked among the cases.

He opened a case and hefted a weapon constructed like a spider's antennae.

It hummed, and a flight of metal bees sizzled out the rifle bore, flew away and stung a target-mannequin some 50 yards away, then fell lifeless, clattering to the floor.

The hunter nodded with admiration, and put the rifle back in the case.

He prowled on, curious as a child, testing yet other weapons here and there that dissolved glass or caused metal to run in bright yellow pools of molten lava.

"Excellent! Fine! Absolutely great!"

His cry rang out again and again as he slammed cases open and shut, and finally chose the gun.

It was a gun that, without fuss or fury, did away with matter. You pressed the button, there was a brief discharge of blue light and the target simply vanished. No blood. No bright lava. No trace.

"All right," he announced, leaving the place of guns, "we have the weapon. How about the game, the grandest beast ever in the long hunt?"

He leaped onto the moving sidewalk.

An hour later he had passed a thousand buildings and scanned a thousand open parks without itching his finger.

He moved uneasily from treadway to treadway, shifting speeds now in this direction, now in that.

Until at last he saw a river of metal that sped underground.

Instinctively, he jumped toward that.

The metal stream carried him down into the secret gut of the City.

Here all was warm blood darkness. Here strange pumps moved the pulse of the City. Here were distilled the sweats that lubricated the roadways and lifted the elevators and swarmed the offices and stores with motion.

The hunter half crouched on the roadway. His eyes squinted. Perspiration gathered in his palms. His trigger finger greased the metal gun, sliding.

"Yes," he whispered. "By God, now. This is it. The City itself . . . the great beast. Why didn't I think of that? The animal City, the dread carnivore that has men for breakfast, lunch and dinner, it kills them with machines, it munches their bones like bread sticks, it spits them out like toothpicks, and it lives long after they die. The City, by God, the City. Well now . . ."

He glided through dark grottoes of television eyes that showed him remote parkways and high towers.

Deeper within the belly of the underground world he sank as the river lowered itself. He passed a school of computers that chattered in maniac chorus. He shuddered as a cloud of paper confetti from one titan machine, holes punched out to perhaps record his passing, fell upon him in a whispered snow.

He raised his gun. He fired.

The machine disappeared.

He fired again. A skeleton strutwork under yet another machine vanished.

The City screamed.

At first very low and then very high, then, rising, falling, like a siren. Lights flashed. Bells began to ricochet alarms. The metal river shuddered under his feet. He fired at television screens that glared all white upon him. They blinked out and did not exist.

The City screamed higher until he raved against it, himself.

He did not see, until it was too late, that the road on which he sped fell into the gnashing maw of a machine that was used for some purpose long forgotten centuries before.

He thought that by pressing the trigger he would make the terrible mouth disappear. It did indeed vanish. But as the roadway sped on and he whirled and fell as it picked up speed, he realized at last that his weapon did not truly destroy, it merely made invisible what was there and what still remained, though unseen.

He gave a terrible cry to match the cry of the City. He flung out the gun in a last blow. The gun went into cogs and wheels and teeth and was twisted down.

The last thing he saw was a deep elevator shaft that fell away for perhaps a mile into the earth.

He knew that it might take him two minutes to hit the bottom. He shrieked.

The worst thing was, he would be conscious . . . all the way down . . .

The rivers shook. The silver rivers trembled. The pathways, shocked, convulsed the metal shores through which they sped.

Wilder, traveling, was almost knocked flat by the concussion.

What had caused the concussion he could not see. Perhaps, far off, there was a cry, a murmur of dreadful sound, which swiftly faded.

Wilder moved. The silver track threaded on. But the City seemed poised, agape. The City seemed tensed. Its huge and various muscles were cramped, alert.

Feeling this, Wilder began to walk as well as be moved by the swift path.

"Thank God. There's the gate. The sooner I'm out of this place the happier I'll—"

The gate was indeed there, not a hundred yards away. But, on the instant, as if hearing his declaration, the river stopped. It shivered. Then it started to move back, taking him where he did not wish to go.

Incredulous, Wilder spun about and, in spinning, fell. He clutched at the stuffs of the rushing sidewalk.

His face, pressed to the vibrant grill-work of the river-rushing pavement, heard the machineries mesh and mill beneath, humming and agroan, forever sluicing, forever feverish for journeys and mindless excursions. Beneath the calm metal, embattlements of hornets stung and buzzed, lost bees bumbled and subsided. Collapsed, he saw the gate lost away behind. Burdened, he remembered at last the extra weight upon his back, the jet-power equipment that might give him wings.

He jammed his hand to the switch on his belt. And in the instant before the sidewalk might have pulsed him off among sheds and museum walls, he was airborne.

Flying, he hovered, then swam the air back to hang above a casual Parkhill gazing up, all covered with grease and smiling from a dirty face. Beyond Parkhill, at the gate, stood the frightened maid. Beyond even further, near the yacht at the landing, stood

Aaronson, his back turned to the City, nervous to be moving on.

"Where are the others?" cried Wilder.

"Oh, they won't be back," said Parkhill, easily. "It figures, doesn't it? I mean, it's quite a place."

"Place!" said Wilder, hovered now up, now down, turning slowly, apprehensive. "We've got to get them out! It's not safe."

"It's safe if you like it. I like it," said Parkhill.

And all the while there was a gathering of earthquake in the ground and in the air, which Parkhill chose to ignore.

"You're leaving, of course," he said, as if nothing were wrong. "I knew you would. Why?"

"Why?" Wilder wheeled like a dragonfly before a trembling of storm wind. Buffeted up, buffeted down, he flung his words at Parkhill, who didn't bother to duck but smiled up and accepted. "Good God, Sam, the place is hell. The Martians had enough sense to get out. They saw they had overbuilt themselves. The damn City does everything, which is too much! Sam!"

And at that instant, they both looked round and up. For the sky was shelling over. Great lids were vising in the ceiling. Like an immense flower, the tops of buildings were petaling out to cover themselves. Windows were shutting down. Doors were slamming. A sound of fired cannons echoed through the streets.

The gate was thundering shut.

The twin jaws of the gate, shuddering, were in motion.

Wilder cried out, spun round and dived.

He heard the maid below him. He saw her reach up. Then, swooping, he gathered her in. He kicked the air. The jet lifted them both.

Like a bullet to a target he rammed for the gate. But an instant before he reached it, burdened, the gates banged together. He was barely able to veer course and soar upward along the raw metal as the entire City shook with the roar of the steel.

Parkhill shouted below. And Wilder was flying up, up along the wall, looking this way and that.

Everywhere, the sky was closing in. The petals were coming down, coming down. There was only a last small patch of stone sky to his right. He blasted for that. And kicking, made it through, flying, as the final flange of steel clipped into place and the City was closed to itself.

33

He hung for a moment, suspended, and then flew with the woman down along the outer wall to the dock, where Aaronson stood by the yacht staring at the huge shut gates.

"Parkhill," whispered Wilder, looking at the City, the walls, the gates. "You fool. You damned fool."

"Fools, all of them," said Aaronson, and turned away. "Fools. Fools."

They waited a moment longer and listened to the City, humming, alive, kept to itself, its great mouth filled with a few bits of warmth, a few lost people somewhere hid away in there. The gates would stay shut now, forever. The City had what it needed to go on a long while.

Wilder looked back at the place, as the yacht took them back out of the mountain and away up the canal.

They passed the poet a mile farther on, walking along the rim of the canal. He waved them off. "No. No. thanks. I feel like walking. It's a fine day. Goodbye. Go on."

The towns lay ahead. Small towns. Small enough to be run by men instead of the towns running them. He heard the brass music. He saw the neon lights at dusk. He made out the junk yards in the fresh night under the stars.

Beyond the towns stood the silver rockets, tall, waiting to be fired off and away toward the wilderness of stars.

"Real," whispered the rockets, "real stuff. Real travel. Real time. Real space. No gifts. Nothing free. Just a lot of good brute work."

The yacht touched into its home dock.

"Rockets, by God," he murmured. "Wait till I get my hands on you."

He ran off in the night, to do just that.

URSULA K. LE GUIN

NINE LIVES

November 1969

Ursula K. Le Guin is the jewel in the crown of late twentieth-century science fiction, a bright symbol of the field's increasing confidence in itself as an important branch of contemporary writing. Winner of four Nebulas and five Hugos, testament to her popularity and respect among writers and fans, she has also won the National Book Award for children's literature, and she is certainly the only self-proclaimed genre writer to publish regularly in *The New Yorker* and—like the proverbial 500-pound gorilla—anywhere else she wishes. Success has made her fearless: her 1985 novel, *Always Coming Home* takes the form of a collage of sociological reports, poetry, recipes, drawings (by Margaret Chodos) and a musical cassette (by Todd Barton)—and it sold rather well! She is also one of the few science fiction writers to have invented a device so indispensable that it has been taken up by many others subsequently: this is the "ansible," a faster-than-light transmissions contrivance that makes planet-to-planet communication possible. In the far future, if and when post-Einsteinian physics manufactures such a thing, it will probably be named just that.

Le Guin was born in 1929 to Alfred and Theodora Kroeber, both distinguished in the field of anthropology, a study that has clearly influenced her own work. Her extraordinary fourth novel, *The Left Hand of Darkness,* made her famous. Published as a paperback original in 1969, it won both the Nebula and the Hugo, and it has never been out of print. An intense and subtle exploration of the nature of sexuality, sexism, and racial or cultural prejudice, it may have had more influence on later science fiction than any other single book since H. G. Wells's *War of the Worlds.* All her early books, a later novel, *The Disposessed,* an overtly political work and another double award-winner, and a number of novellas and short stories are set in a universe populated by people from the planet Hain—hence they are known as the Hainish series. "Nine Lives" is not part of the Hainish sequence, but it is a very well-known story, one that explores the now hotly debated topic of cloning in a typically thoughtful, and moving way.

SHE WAS ALIVE inside but dead outside, her face a black and dun net of wrinkles, tumors, cracks. She was bald and blind. The tremors that crossed Libra's face were only quiverings of corruption; underneath, in the black corridors, the halls beneath the skin, there were crepitations in darkness, ferments, chemical nightmares that had gone on for centuries. "Oh, the damned flatulent planet." Pugh murmured, as the dome shook and a boil burst a kilometer to the southwest, spraying silver pus across the sunset. The sun had been setting for the past two days.

"I shall be glad to see a human face."

"Thanks," said Martin.

"Oh, yours is human, to be sure," said Pugh, but I've seen it so long I can't see it."

A clutter of rad-vid signals crowded the communicator that Martin was operating, faded, returned as face and voice. The face filled the screen; young, powerful, the nose of an Assyrian king and the eyes of a samurai, the skin bronze, eyes the color of iron: magnificent. "Is that what humans look like?" said Pugh with awe. "I'd forgotten."

"Shut up, Owen, we're on."

"Libra Exploratory Mission Base, come in, please, this is Passerine launch."

"Libra here. Beam fixed. Come on down, launch."

"Expulsion in seven E seconds. Hold on." The screen blanked and sparkled.

"Do you think the whole lot of them look like that?" said Pugh, still bemused. "Martin, you and I are uglier men than I thought."

"Shut up, Owen. . . ."

For 22 minutes, Martin followed the landing craft down by signal and then, through the cleared dome, they saw it, small star high in the blood-colored east, sinking. It came down neat and quiet, Libra's thin atmosphere carrying little sound. Pugh and Martin closed the headpieces of their imsuits, zipped out of the dome air locks and ran with soaring strides, Nijinsky and Nureyev, toward the boat. Three equipment modules came floating down at four-minute intervals and 100-meter intervals east of the boat. "Come on out," Martin said on his suit radio, "we're waiting at the door."

"Come on in, the methane's fine," said Pugh.

The hatch opened and the young man they had seen on the screen flung himself out with one athletic twist and leaped down onto the shaky dust and clinkers of Libra. Martin shook his hand, greeted him, but Pugh stared at the hatch, from which another young man emerged with the same neat twist and jump, followed by a young woman, who emerged with the same twist, ornamented by a wriggle, and the jump. Like the first one, they were tall, with bronze skin, black hair, high-bridged nose, epicanthic fold, the same face. They all had the same face. The fourth was emerging from the hatch with the identical neat jump movement of the three others. "Martin, *bach*," said Pugh, "we've got a clone."

"Right," said one of the newcomers, "we're a tenclone, John Chow's the name. You're Lieutenant Martin?"

"No, I'm Owen Pugh."

"Alvaro Guillen Martin," said Martin formally. Another girl was emerging, the same beautiful face: Martin stared at her and his eyes rolled like a nervous pony's. Evidently, he had never given any thought to cloning and was suffering technological shock.

"Steady," Pugh said in the Argentine dialect, "it's only excess twins." He stood close by Martin's elbow. He was glad of the contact.

It is hard to meet a stranger. Even the greatest extrovert meeting even the meekest stranger knows a certain dread, though he may not know he knows it. Will he make a fool of me, wreck my image of myself, invade me, destroy me, change me? Will he be different from me? Yes, that he will. There's the terrible thing: the strangeness of the stranger.

After two years on a dead planet, and the last half year spent as a team of two with only radio contact with the rest of their crew, two men working hard and seeing nobody else at all for six mortal months; after that, it's even harder to meet a stranger, however welcome he may be. For you're out of the habit, you've lost the touch; and so the fear revives, the primitive anxiety, the old dread.

The clone, five males and five females, had done in a couple of minutes what a man might have done in 20: It had greeted Pugh and Martin, had a look at Libra, unloaded the boat and now was ready to go. As they set off, Martin asked, "Which of you did I speak to during flight?" His voice was rather sharp.

"Me, John Aleph. Also Yod got a word in," one said, nodding at a second one, who appeared all at once to be younger and smaller.

"Big Aleph generally talks first," this one said. But the next moment, as they all float-bounced along, Pugh couldn't tell which one was Aleph and which one Yod.

The dome filled with them, a hive of golden bees. They hummed and buzzed quietly, filled up all silences, all spaces with a honey-brown flood of human presence. Martin looked bewilderedly at the long-limbed girls, whose smile was a little gentler than that of the boys, though no less radiantly self-possessed.

"Self-possessed," Owen Pugh murmured to his friend, "that's it. Think of it, to be oneself ten times over. Nine seconds for every motion, nine ayes on every vote. It would be glorious!" But Martin was asleep. And the John Chows had all gone to sleep at once. The dome was filled with their quiet breathing. They were young, they didn't snore. Martin sighed and snored, his Hershey bar–colored face relaxed in the dim afterglow of Libra's primary, set at last. Pugh had cleared the dome and stars looked in, Sol among them, a great company of lights, a clone of splendors. Pugh slept and dreamed of a one-eyed giant who chased him through the shaking halls of hell.

Pugh watched the clone's awakening from his sleeping bag. They all got up within a minute, except for one pair, a boy and a girl, who lay snugly tangled and still sleeping in one bag. Seeing this, there was a shock like one of Libra's earthquakes within Pugh, a very deep tremor. Yet consciously, he was pleased at the sight; there was no other such comfort on this dead hollow world. More power to them who made love. One of the others stepped gently on them; they woke; the girl sat up, flushed and sleepy, with bare golden breasts. One of her sisters murmured something to her, she shot a glance at Pugh and disappeared into the sleeping bag, followed by a faint giggle, from another direction a brief fierce stare, from yet another direction a voice: "Christ, we're used to having a room to ourselves. Hope you don't mind, Captain Pugh."

"It's a pleasure," Pugh said half truthfully. He had to stand up then, wearing only the shorts he slept in, and he felt like a plucked rooster, all white scrawn and pimples. The United Kingdom had come through the Great Famines rather well, losing less than half its population: a record achieved by rigorous food control. Black-marketeers and hoarders had been executed. Crumbs had been shared. Where in richer lands many had died and a few had thrived, in Britain fewer died and none throve. They all got lean. Their sons were lean, their grandsons lean, small, brittle-boned, easily infected. They had replaced the survival of the fittest with the survival of the fairest. Owen Pugh was a scrawny little man. But he was there.

Just at the minute, he could have wished he wasn't.

At breakfast, a John said, "Now, if you'll brief us, Captain Pugh—"

"Owen, then."

"Owen, we can work out our schedule. Has anything new concerning the mine turned up since your last report to your mission? We saw all your reports when Passerine was in orbit around Planet V."

Martin did not answer, though the mine was his discovery and project: Pugh did his best. It was hard to talk to them, the same expression of intelligent interest on the same faces, all leaning forward at almost the same angle. Over the Exploitation Corps insignia on their tunics, each had a name band, first name John and last name Chow, of course, but the middle names different. The men were Aleph, Kaph, Yod, Gimel and Samekh; the women Sadhe, Daleth, Zayin, Beth and Resh. Martin buttered and chewed his toast, and suddenly interrupted: "You're a team, aren't you?"

"Right," said two Johns.

"God, what a team! I hadn't seen the point. How much do you each know what the others are thinking?"

"Not at all, properly speaking," replied one of the girls, Zayin.

The others watched her with the proprietary, approving look they had. "True ESP is still unachieved. But we do think alike, having the same equipment. So, given the same problem or stimulus, we are likely to be thinking the same thing at the same time. Explanations are easy, a word or two. We seldom misunderstand one another. It does facilitate our working as a team."

"Christ, yes," said Martin. "Pugh and I have spent seven hours out of ten for six months misunderstanding each other. What about emergencies—are you good at meeting the unexpected problem as a nor—an unrelated team?"

"Statistics so far indicate that we are," Zayin answered readily. "We can't brainstorm as singletons can, we can't profit from the interplay of varied minds; but we have a compensatory advantage. Clones are drawn from the best human material, individuals of I. I. Q. ninety-ninth percentile, genetic constitution alpha double A, and so on. So we have more to draw on than most individuals do."

"And it's multiplied by a factor of ten. Who is—who was John Chow?"

"A genius, surely," Pugh said politely. His interest in cloning was not so newly roused and hungry as Martin's.

"Leonardo Complex type," said Yod. "Biomath; also a cellist and an undersea hunter and interested in structural engineering problems, and so on. Died before he'd worked out his major theories."

"Then you each represent a different facet of his mind, his talents?"

"No," said Zayin, shaking her head in time with several others. "We share the basic equipment and tendencies, of course, but we're all engineers in the Planetary Exploitation line. A later clone might be trained to develop other aspects of the basic equipment. It's merely a matter of education. The genetic substance is identical. We are John Chow. But we were trained differently."

Martin looked shell-shocked. "How old are you?"

"Twenty-three."

"You say he—died young. Had they taken some germ cells from him beforehand or something?"

Gimel took over: "He died at twenty-four in an air-car crash. They couldn't save the brain but took some intestinal cells and cultured them. Reproductive cells aren't used for cloning, since they have only half the chromosomes. Intestinal cells happen to be easy to despecialize and reprogram for total growth."

"All chips off the old block," Martin said valiantly. "But how can . . . some of you be female . . . ?"

Beth took over: "It's easy to program half the clonal mass back to the female. Just delete the male gene from half the cells and they revert to the basic: that is, the female. It's trickier to go the other way, have to hook in artificial Y chromosomes. So they mostly clone from males, since clones function best when bisexual."

"It's an elaborate process," Aleph said. "Each new generation has to be cloned from cells, the fetuses incubated in Ngama Placentae, then given to trained foster-parent groups. Did you know that we cost the Government about $3,000,000 apiece?"

"But how about you, don't you—" Martin asked, still struggling.

"Breed?" Beth finished for him. "Yes and no. The men are permitted to crossbreed with approved singletons. But as for the women—we're sterile. Deleting the Y chromosome from our original cell makes us so. John Chow in his pure form dies with us—unless, of course, there is a decision to clone him again or a biological breakthrough that would create fertile clone females." They spoke in even, objective tones, as if none of this had any personal relevance whatsoever.

Question time was over. "Well," said one of the Johns, and all changed mood, like a flock of starlings that changes course in one wing flick, following a leader so fast that no eye can see which leads. They were ready to go. "How about a look at the mine? Then we'll unload the equipment. Some nice new models in the roboats, you'll want to see them. Right?" Had Pugh or Martin not agreed, they might have found it hard to say so. Polite as the Johns were, their decisions were unanimous, tenfold: They carried. Pugh, commander of Libra Base Two, felt a qualm. How could he boss this supermanwoman-entity-of-ten around? And a genius, at that. He stuck with Martin as they suited for outside. Neither said anything.

Four apiece in the three large air sleds, they slipped off north from the dome, over Libra's dun rugose skin, in starlight.

"Desolate," one said.

A boy and a girl were with Pugh and Martin. Pugh wondered if they were the two that had shared a sleeping bag last night. No doubt they wouldn't mind if he asked them. Sex must be as handy as breathing, to them. Did you two breathe last night?

"Yes," he said, "it is desolate."

"This is our first time Off, except training on Luna, of course," said the softer voice, the girl.

"How'd you take the big hop?"

"They doped us. I wanted to experience it." That was the boy, a bit wistful. They seemed to have more personality, only two at a time. Did repetition of the individual negate individuality?

The Mountains of Merioneth showed leprotic in starlight to the east, a plume of freezing gas trailed silver from a venthole to the west, the sled tilted groundward. The twins braced for the stop at the same moment, each with a slight protective gesture to the other. Your skin is my skin, Pugh thought with admiring envy. What would it be like, then, to have somebody as close to you as that? Always to be answered when you spoke; never to be in pain alone. Love your neighbor as you love yourself. . . . That problem was solved. The neighbor was the self: the love was perfect.

And here was Hellmouth, the mine.

Pugh was the Libra Exploratory Mission's extraterrestrial geologist, Martin his technician and cartographer; but when, in the course of a local survey, Martin had discovered the uranium mine, Pugh had given him full credit, as well as the onus of prospecting the lode and planning the Exploit Crew's job. These kids had been sent out from Earth years before Martin's reports got there and had not known what their job would be until they got here: the Exploitation Corps had sent them only in the well-founded hope that there might be a job for them on Libra or the next planet out. The Government wanted uranium too urgently to wait while reports drifted home across the light-years. The stuff was like gold, old-fashioned but essential. Worth mining extraterrestrially and shipping interstellarly. Worth its weight in people, Pugh thought sourly, watching the tall young men and women go, one by one, glimmering in starlight, into the black hole Martin had named Hellmouth.

It was silent on Libra; it was silenter inside Libra. Dead black.

Their homeostatic forehead lamps brightened. Twelve nodding gleams ran along the moist, wrinkled walls. Pugh heard Martin's radiation counter peeping 20 to the dozen up ahead. "Here's the drop-off," said Martin's voice in the suit intercom, drowning out the peeping and the dead silence around. "We're in a side fissure, this is the main vertical vent in front of us." The black void gaped, its far side not visible in the head-lamp beams. "Last traces of vulcanism from two thousand to twenty-five hundred E years ago. Nearest fault twenty-eight miles east, in the Trench. It's seismically as safe as anything you can find on Libra. The big basalt flow overhead stabilizes all these substructures, as long as it remains stable itself. Your central lode is thirty-six meters down, running in a series of five bubble caverns for two hundred and ten meters northeast. It is a lode, a pipe of very high-grade ore. You saw the percentage figures in the report Passerine picked up when it contacted our System Survey Team, right? Extraction's going to be no problem. All you've got to do is get the bubbles topside."

"Take off the lid and let 'em float up." He heard an identical-sounding voice from ten mouths. "Open the thing right up."—"Safer that way."—"Solid basalt roof: How thick, ten meters here?"—"Three to fifteen, the report said."—"Blow good ore all over the lot."—"Use this access we're in, straighten a bit and run slider rails."—"Import burros."—"Have we got enough propping material?"—"What's your estimate of total pay-load mass, Martin?"

"Well, say over five million kilos and under eight."

"The Transport Crew will be by here in ten E months; we'll have enough for them to start packaging."

The first one—Aleph? (Hebrew, the ox, the leader)—swung onto the ladder and down; the rest followed. Pugh and Martin stood alone at the cavern's edge. Pugh set his intercom to exchange only with Martin's suit and noticed Martin doing the same. It was a little wearing, hearing one person think aloud in ten voices.

"A great gut," Pugh said, looking down into the black pit, its veined and warted walls catching stray gleams of head lamps far below. "A cow's bowel. A bloody great constipated intestine."

They were silent. Martin's counter peeped like a lost chicken. They stood inside the dead but epileptic planet breathing oxygen from tanks, wearing suits impermeable to corrosives and harmful radiations, resistant to a 200-degree range of temperatures, tearproof and as shock-resistant as possible, given the soft vulnerable stuff inside.

"I hate this place," Martin said. "I like mines, caves, you know. But this one's a bitch. Mean. You can't ever let down in here. I guess this lot can handle it, though. They know their stuff."

"Wave of the future, Martin, *bach*."

The wave of the future came swarming up the ladder, swept Martin to the shaft entrance, gabbled until one called order: "Martin can't understand us all at once."

"But we can," said another. "Let's get this thought out now. Do we have enough material for supports?"

"If we convert one of the extractor-servos to anneal, yes."

"Sufficient if we miniblast?"

"Kaph can calculate stress."

"How broad's that basalt lid?"

Pugh looked at them, so many thoughts jabbering in a busy brain, and at Martin standing silent among them, and at Hellmouth and the wrinkled plain.

"Settled. How does that strike you as a preliminary schedule, Martin?"

"It's your baby," Martin said.

By day five of their stay on Libra, the Johns had all their material and equipment unloaded and operating and were ready to start opening up the mine. They worked with total efficiency. Pugh was fascinated and frightened by their effectiveness, their confidence, their independence. A clone, he thought, might be, in fact, the first truly stable, self-reliant human being. It would be sufficient to itself sexually, emotionally, intellectually and ethically. Any member of it would always receive the complete support and approval of his peers. Nobody else was needed.

Two of the clone stayed in the dome, doing calculations and paperwork, with frequent sled trips to the mine for samples, measurements and tests. A girl and a boy, Zayin and Kaph, they were the mathematicians of the clone. That is, as Zayin explained, all ten had had thorough mathematical training from the ages of three to 21; but from 21 to 23, she and Kaph had gone on with math, while the others intensified other specialties—geology, mining engineering, electronic engineering, equipment robotics, applied atomics, and so on. "Kaph and I feel," she said, "that we're closer to what John Chow was in his lifetime. But, of course, he was principally in biomath, and they didn't take us very far in that."

"They needed us most in this field," Kaph said, with the patriotic priggishness they sometimes evinced.

Pugh and Martin continued to be able to distinguish this pair from the others, Zayin by gestalt, Kaph only by a discolored left fourth fingernail, acquired from an ill-aimed hammer at the age of six. No doubt, there were many such differences, physical and psychological, among them: Nature might be identical, nurture could not be. But the differences were hard to find.

Social training partly disguised their basic indifference to others: They had the standardized American friendliness. "Do you come from Ireland, Owen?"

"Nobody comes from Ireland, Zayin."

"There are lots of Irish-Americans."

"To be sure, but almost no Irish. A couple of thousand in all the island, last I knew. By the third Famine, there were no Irish left at all but the priesthood, and they are all celibate: or nearly all."

Zayin and Kaph smiled stiffly. They didn't quite get Owen. "What are you, then, topologically?" Kaph asked.

Pugh replied, "A Welshman."

"Is that Welsh that you and Martin speak together?"

None of your business, Pugh thought, but said, "No, it's his dialect, not mine: Argentinean. Descendant of Spanish. We've had a world to ourselves for half a year. . . . Sometimes a man likes to speak his native language, that's all."

"Is Wells quaint?" asked Zayin.

"Wells? Oh, Wales, it's called. Yes. Wales is quaint." Pugh switched on his rock cutter, which prevented further conversation by a synapse-destroying whine; and while it whined, he turned his back and said a profane word in Welsh.

That night, he used the Argentine dialect for private communication. "Do they pair off in the same couples, or change every night?"

Martin looked surprised. A prudish expression, unsuited to his features, appeared for a moment. It faded. He, too, was curious. "I think it's random."

"Don't whisper, man, it sounds dirty-minded. I think they rotate on a schedule. So that nobody gets omitted."

Martin gave a vulgar laugh and smothered it. "What about us? Aren't we omitted?"

"That doesn't occur to them. It never will."

"What if I propositioned one of the girls?"

"She'd tell the others and they'd decide as a group."

"I am not a bull," Martin said, his dark, heavy face heating up. "I will not be judged—"

"Down, down, *machismo*," said Pugh. "Do you mean to proposition one?"

Martin shrugged, looking sullen. "Let 'em have their incest," he said.

"Incest or masturbation, is it?"

"I don't care, if they'd do it out of earshot!"

The clone's early attempts at modesty had soon worn off, unmotivated by any deep defensiveness of self or awareness of others. Pugh and Martin were daily deeper swamped under the intimacies of its constant emotional-sexual-mental interchange: swamped yet excluded.

"Two months to go," said Martin one evening.

In 60 days, the full crew of their Exploratory Mission was due back from a survey of the four other planets of the system. Pugh was aware of this.

"Are you crossing off the days on the calendar?" he jeered. He was irritable lately, while Martin was sullen.

"Pull yourself together, Owen."

"What do you mean?"

"What I say."

They parted in contempt and resentment.

Pugh came in after a day alone on the Pampas, a vast plain the nearest edge of which was two hours south by jet. He was tired, but refreshed by solitude. They were not supposed to take long trips alone but lately had often done so. Martin stooped under bright light, drawing one of his elegant, masterly charts: The whole face of Libra this one was, the cancerous profile. The dome was otherwise empty, seeming dim and large, as it had before the clone came. "Where's the golden horde?"

Martin grunted ignorance, crosshatching. He straightened his back to glance round at the sun, squatting feebly like a great red toad on the eastern plain, and at the clock, which said 18:45. "Some big jumps today," he said, returning to his map. "Lot of crates fell over. Take a look at the seismo."

The needle jiggled and wavered on the roll. It never stopped jiggling here. Back in midafternoon, the roll had recorded five quakes of major intensity; twice the needle had hopped off the roll. The attached computer had been activated to emit a slip reading, EPICENTER 61' N BY 42'4" E.

"Not in the Trench this time."

"Wasn't it? It felt a bit different from usual. Sharper."

"In Dome One, I used to lie awake all night, feeling the ground jump. Queer how you get used to things."

"Go spla if you didn't. What's for dinner?"

"I thought you'd have cooked it."

"Waiting for the clone."

Feeling put-upon, Pugh got out a dozen dinner boxes, stuck two in the Instobake, pulled them out. "All right, here's dinner."

"Been thinking," Martin said, coming to table. "What if some clone cloned itself? Illegally, I mean. Made a thousand duplicates—ten thousand. Whole army. They could make a tidy power grab, couldn't they?"

"But how many millions would each of this lot cost to rear? Artificial placentae and all that. It would be impossible to keep secret, unless they got a planet to themselves. . . . Back before the Famines, when there were national governments, they talked about that: Clone your best soldiers, have whole regiments of them. But the food ran out before they could play that game." They were speaking amicably, as they used to.

"Funny," Martin said, chewing. "They left early this morning, didn't they?"

"Before I did, all but Kaph and Zayin. They thought they'd get the first payload above ground today. What's up?"

"They weren't back for lunch," said Martin, immobile.

"They won't starve, to be sure."

"They left at seven."

"So they did." Then Pugh saw it. The air tanks held eight hours' supply.

"Kaph and Zayin carried out spare cans when they left. Or they've got a heap out there."

"They did, but they brought the whole lot in to recharge. There they are." He pointed to one of the stacks of stuff that cut the dome into rooms and alleys.

"There's an alarm signal on every imsuit."

"It's not automatic."

Pugh was tired and still hungry. "Sit down and eat, man. That lot can look after itself."

Martin sat down, but after a minute, he said, "There was a big quake, Owen. The first one. Big enough it scared me for a minute."

After a little pause, Pugh sighed and said, "All right."

Unenthusiastically, they got onto the two-man sled that was always left for them and headed it north. The long sunrise covered everything in poisonous red Jell-O. The horizontal light and shadow made it hard to see, raised walls of fake iron ahead of them, which they slid through, turned the convex plain beyond Hellmouth into a great dimple full of bloody water. They slowed, bumped down, jumped off. Around the tunnel entrance, a wilderness of machinery stood, cranes and cables and servos and wheels and diggers and robocarts and sliders and control huts, all slanting and bulking incoherently in the red light. Martin ran into the mine. He came out again and went straight to Pugh. "Oh, God, Owen, it's down," he said. Pugh went in and saw, five meters from the entrance, the shiny, moist, black wall that ended the tunnel. Newly exposed to air, it looked organic, like visceral tissue. The tunnel entrance, enlarged by blasting and double-tracked for robocarts, seemed unchanged till he noticed thousands of tiny spider-web cracks in the walls. The floor was wet with some sluggish fluid.

"They were inside," Martin said.

"They may be still. They surely had extra air cans—"

"Look, man, look, look at the basalt flow, at the roof: Don't you see what the quake did? Look at it."

The low hump of land that roofed the caves still looked queer, like an optical illusion. It seemed to have sunk down, leaving a vast dimple, or pit. It, too, was cracked with many tiny fissures, Pugh saw when he walked upon it. From some, a whitish gas was seeping, and the sunlight on the surface of the gas pool was shafted as if in the waters of a dim red lake.

"It isn't on the fault. There's no fault here!"

"They wouldn't all have been inside, Martin. Look at the mess here, the equipment; they may be up here, some of them."

Martin followed him and searched dully, then actively. He spotted the air sled. It had come down unguided and stuck at an angle in a pothole of colloidal dust. It had carried two riders. One was half sunk in the dust, but all his suit meters registered normal functioning; the other hung strapped onto the tilted sled. Her imsuit was cut open in several places on the broken legs and the body was frozen hard as any rock. That was all they found. As both regulation and custom demanded, they cremated the dead body at once with the laser guns they carried and had never used before. Pugh, knowing he was going to be sick, wrestled the survivor onto the two-man sled and sent Martin off to the dome with him. Then he vomited and flushed the waste out of his suit and, finding one four-man sled undamaged, followed after Martin, shaking as if the cold of Libra had got through to him.

The survivor was Kaph. He was in deep shock. They found a swelling on the occiput that might mean concussion, but no fracture showed on their tiny diagnoser.

Pugh brought two glasses of food concentrate and two chasers of aquavit. "Come on," he said. Martin obeyed, drinking off the tonic. They sat down near the cot and sipped the aquavit.

Kaph lay immobile, face like beeswax, hair bright black to the shoulders, lips stiffly parted for faintly gasping breaths.

"It must have been the first shock, the big one," Martin said. "It must have slid the whole structure sideways. Till it fell in on itself. Like on ball bearings. There must be gas layers in the lateral rocks, like those formations in the 31st Quadrant. But there wasn't any sign—" As he spoke, the world slid under them. Things leaped and clattered, hopped and jigged, shouted, Ha! Ha! Ha! "It was like this, only worse, at fourteen hundred hours," reason said shakily in Martin's voice, amid the unfastening and ruin of the world. But unreason sat up, as the tumult lessened and things ceased dancing, and screamed aloud.

Pugh leaped across his spilled aquavit and held Kaph down. The muscular body flailed him off. Martin pinned the shoulders down. Kaph screamed, struggled, choked; his face blackened. "Oxy," Pugh said, and his hand found the right needle in the medical kit as if by homing instinct; while Martin held the mask, he struck the needle home to the vagus nerve, restoring Kaph to life.

"Didn't know you knew that stunt," Martin said, breathing hard.

"The Lazarus Jab, my father was a doctor, it doesn't always work," Pugh said. "I want that drink I spilled. Is the quake over? I can't tell."

"Aftershocks. It's not just you shivering."

"Why did he suffocate like that?"

"I don't know, Owen. Look in the book."

Kaph was breathing normally and his color was restored; only the lips were still darkened. They poured a new shot of courage and sat down by him again, with the medical guide. "Nothing about cyanosis or asphyxiation under 'shock' or 'concussion.' He can't have breathed in anything with his imsuit on. I don't understand. *Mother Mog's Home Herbalist* would be more use than this. . . . 'Anal hemorrhoids,' fie!" Pugh said, riffling through the index, and pitched the guide to a crate table. It fell short, because either Pugh or the table was still unsteady.

"Why didn't he signal?"

"Sorry?"

"The eight inside the mine never had time. But he and the girl were outside, or in the vent. Maybe she was near the entrance and got hit by the first slides. He was outside, in the control hut, maybe. He ran in, pulled her out, got her onto the sled, started for the dome. And all that time, never pushed the panic button in his imsuit. Why not?"

"Well, he had that whack on the head. I doubt he realized the girl was dead, even. But I don't know if he'd have thought to signal us. They looked to one another for help. For everything."

Martin's face was like an Indian mask, grooves at the mouth corners, eyes of dull coal. "What must he have felt, then, when the quake came and he was outside, alone—"

As if in answer, Kaph screamed.

He came up off the cot in the heaving convulsions of one suffocating, knocked Pugh down with his flailing arm, staggered blindly into a stack of crates and fell to the floor, lips blue, eyes white. Martin dragged him back onto the cot and gave him a whiff of oxygen, then knelt by Pugh, who was just sitting up, and wiped at his cut cheekbone. "Owen, are you all right, are you going to be all right, Owen?"

"I think I am," Pugh said. "Why are you rubbing my face with that?"

It was a small length of computer tape, now spotted with Pugh's blood. Martin threw it away. "I thought it was a towel. You clipped your cheek on that box there."

"It didn't hurt till you rubbed it with the tape. Is he out of it?"

They stared down at Kaph lying stiff, his teeth a white line inside dark parted lips.

"Like epilepsy. Brain damage, maybe?"

"What about shooting him full of meprobamate?"

Pugh shook his head. "I don't know what's in that shot we gave him that the kit recommends for shock."

"Maybe he'll sleep it off now."

"I'd like to, myself. Between him and the earthquake, I'm getting a bit run down."

"Go on. I'm not sleepy."

Pugh cleaned his cut cheek and pulled off his shirt, then paused.

"No chance at all, you think?"

Martin shook his head.

Pugh lay down on top of his sleeping bag. After what seemed to be half a minute or so, he was wakened by a hideous, sucking, struggling sound. He staggered up, found the needle, tried three times to jab it in correctly and failed, began to massage over Kaph's heart. "Mouth-to-mouth," he said, and Martin obeyed. Presently. Kaph drew a deep harsh breath, his heartbeat steadied, his rigid muscles began to relax.

"How long did I sleep?"

"Half an hour."

They stood up, sweating. The ground shuddered, the fabric of the dome sagged and swayed. Libra was dancing her awful polka again, her *Totentanz*. The sun, though rising, seemed to have grown larger and redder. A lot of gas and particles must have been stirred up in the feeble dead atmosphere.

"What's wrong with him, Owen?"

"I think he's dying with them."

"Them—but they're dead—"

"Nine of them. They all died, they were crushed or suffocated. They were all him, he is all of them. They died and now he's dying their deaths, one by one."

"Oh, pity of God," Martin said.

The next time was much the same. The fifth time was worse, for Kaph fought and raved, trying to speak but getting no words out, as if his mouth were stopped with rocks or clay. After that, the attacks grew weaker, but so did he. The eighth seizure came at about 4:30, and Pugh and Martin worked till 5:30, doing everything they could to keep life in the body that seemed to slide without protest into death. Martin said, "The next will finish him." And it did; but Pugh breathed his own breath into the inert lungs, until he himself passed out.

He woke. The dome was opaqued: and no light on. He lay on his cot. He listened and heard the breathing of two sleeping men. He slept, and nothing woke him till hunger did.

The sun was well up over the dark plains and the planet had stopped dancing. Kaph lay asleep; Pugh and Martin drank tea and looked at him with proprietary triumph.

When he woke, Martin went to him? "How are you, old man?" There was no answer. Martin turned away.

Pugh took his place and looked into the brown, dull eyes that gazed toward but not into his own. Like Martin, he quickly turned away. He heated food concentrate and brought it to Kaph but did not meet his gaze. "Come on, drink."

Kaph drank a sip, choked. "Let me die," he said.

"You are not dying."

Kaph spoke with clarity and precision: "I am nine tenths dead," he said. "There is not enough of me left alive."

That precision convinced Pugh and, because he believed, he fought it. "No," he said, peremptorily. "They are dead. The others, your brothers and sisters. But you're alive. You're not even much hurt. You're them, you're him, John Chow. Your life's in your own hands now."

The boy lay still, looking into a darkness that was not there.

The second day after the quake, Martin took the Exploit Crew's hauler and a set of robos over to Hellmouth to salvage equipment and protect it from Libra's sinister atmosphere. Pugh stayed in the dome, doing paperwork, unwilling to leave Kaph by himself. Kaph sat or lay and stared into his darkness and never spoke. The days went by, silent.

The radio spat and spoke: the Mission calling from the ship. "We'll be down on Libra in five weeks, Owen. Thirty-four E days, nine hours, I make it, as of now. How's tricks in the old dome?"

"Not good, Chief. The Exploit Crew was killed, all but one of them, six days ago. In the mine, an earthquake."

The radio crackled and sang starsong. Sixteen seconds' lag each way; the ship was out around Planet III now. "Killed, the whole lot but one? Listen, you and Martin are all right?"

"We're all right here."

Thirty-two seconds.

"The Exploit Crew that Passerine left out here with us may take over the Hellmouth project, then, instead of the Quadrant Seven project. We'll settle that when we come down. One way or another, you and Martin will be relieved at Dome Two."

Later on, Pugh said to Kaph, "You may be asked to stay here with the other Exploit Crew, if they go to work at Hellmouth. The chief won't command it. But you know the ropes here." Knowing the exigencies of Far Out life, he wanted to warn the young man.

Kaph said nothing. Since he said, "There is not enough of me left alive," he had not spoken a word.

"Owen," Martin said on suit intercom, "he's spla. Insane. Psychotic."

"He's doing very well for a man who's died nine times."

"Well? Like a turned-off android is well? The only emotion he has left is hate."

"That's not hate, Martin. Listen, it is true that he has, in a sense, been dead. I cannot imagine what he feels. But it is not hatred. He can't even see us. It's too dark."

"Throats have been cut in the dark. He hates us because we're not Aleph and Yod. Because we outlived them."

"Maybe. But I think he's alone. He doesn't see us or hear us, that's the truth: He never had to see anyone else before. He never was alone before. He had himself to see, talk with, live with, nine other selves all his life. He doesn't know how you go it alone, he must learn. Give him time."

Martin shook his heavy head. "Spla," he said. "Just remember, when you're alone with him, that he could break your neck one-handed. What I can't stand is his eyes."

"He can't stand ours, I expect," said Pugh, a short, soft-voiced man with a bruised cheekbone. They were just outside the dome air lock, programming one of the Exploit servos to repair a damaged hauler. They could see Kaph sitting inside the great half egg of the dome like a fly in amber. "He'll get better, I think."

"Hand me the insert pack there. What makes you think so?"

"He has a strong personality, to be sure."

"Strong? Wrecked. Nine tenths dead, as he put it."

"But he is not dead. He is a live man: John Kaph Chow. He had a jolly queer upbringing, but after all, every boy has got to break free of his family. He will do it."

"I can't see it."

"Think about it a bit, Martin; what's this cloning for? To repair the human race, isn't it? We're in a bad way. Look at me. My I. I. Q. and G. C. are about half this John Chow's. Yet they wanted me so badly for the Far Out Service that when I volunteered, they took me and fitted me out with an artificial lung and corrected my myopia. Now, if there were enough good, sound men around, would they be taking one-lunged, shortsighted Welshmen?"

"Didn't know you had an artificial lung."

"I do, though. Not tin, you know. Human, grown in a tank from a bit of somebody else's lung: cloned, if you like. That's how they make replacement organs, you know, the same general idea as cloning, but bits and pieces, instead of whole people. It's my own lung now. But my point is, there are too many like me these days and not enough like John Chow. They're trying to raise the level of the human genetic pool, which must be a pretty mucky little puddle since the population crash. So if a man is cloned, he's a tough, sound man. It's only logic, to be sure."

Martin grunted; the servo began to hum.

Kaph had been eating little; he had trouble swallowing his

food, choking on it, so that he would give up trying after a few bites. He had lost eight or ten kilos. Along about three weeks after the earthquake, his appetite began to pick up; and one day, he began to look through the clone's possessions, its sleeping bags, kits and papers, which Pugh and Martin had stacked neatly in a far angle of a packing-crate "room." He sorted, destroyed a heap of papers and oddments, made a small packet of what remained, then relapsed into his walking coma.

Two days later, he spoke. Pugh was trying to correct a flutter in the tape player, a job for Martin, but Martin had the jet out, checking their maps of the West Pampas. "Do you want me to do that?" Kaph said tonelessly.

Pugh jumped, controlled himself, gave the machine to Kaph. The young man took the player apart, put it back together and left it on the table.

"Put on a tape," Pugh, busy at another table, said with careful casualness.

Kaph put on the topmost tape, a chorale. He lay down on his cot and seemed to pay no attention to the music.

After that, he took over several routine jobs one by one. He undertook nothing that wanted initiative; and if asked to do anything, he made no response at all, impassive as the deaf.

"He's doing well," Pugh said in Argentinean.

"He's not. He's settling into a machine role. Does what he's programmed to do, no reaction to anything else, including other humans. He's worse off than he was when he didn't function at all. He's not human anymore."

"What is he, then?"

"Dead."

Owen winced. "Well, good night," he said in English. "Good night, Kaph."

Martin responded; Kaph did not.

Next morning at breakfast, Kaph reached across Martin's plate for the butter. "Why don't you ask for it?" Martin said with the geniality of repressed exasperation. "I can pass it."

"I can reach it," Kaph said in his flat voice.

Martin shrugged and laughed. Pugh, tense, jumped up and turned on the rock cutter.

Later on, "Lay off that, please, Martin," he said.

"Manners are important in small isolated crews, some kind of manners, whatever you work out together. He's been taught that, everybody in Far Out knows it; why does he deliberately flout it?"

"Don't you see, Kaph's never known anybody but himself?"

Martin brooded and then broke out, "Then, by God, this cloning business is dead wrong. It won't do. What are a lot of duplicate geniuses going to do for us when they don't even know we exist?"

Pugh nodded. "They might be wiser to separate the clones and bring them up with others. But they make such a grand team, too useful to waste."

"Do they? I wonder. If this bunch had been ten average inefficient ET engineers, would they all have been in the same place at the same time? Would they all have got killed but one? What if, when the cave-in started, what if all those kids ran the same way—farther into the mine, maybe, to save the one that was farthest in? Even Kaph was outside and went in. . . . It's hypothetical. But I keep thinking, out of ten ordinary confused guys, more might have got out."

"I don't know. It's true that identical twins tend to die at about the same age, even when they have never seen each other. Identity and death, it is very strange."

The days went on. Kaph went on the same way. Pugh and Martin snapped at each other a good deal. Pugh complained of Martin's snoring; offended, Martin moved his cot clear across the dome and did not speak to Pugh for 30 hours. Kaph spoke to neither, except when compelled.

The day before the Mission ship was to come in, Martin announced he was going over to Merioneth.

"We haven't done some of the paperwork we had six months to do; I thought at least you'd be giving me a hand with the computer to finish the rock analyses." Pugh's tone was aggrieved.

"Kaph can do that. I want one more look at the Trench. Have fun," Martin added in dialect, and laughed, and left.

"What is the language you and he speak?"

"Argentinean. I told you that once, didn't I?"

"I don't know." After a while, the young man added, "I have forgotten a lot of things, I think."

"It wasn't important, to be sure," Pugh said gently. "Will you give me a hand running the computer, Kaph?"

He nodded.

Pugh had left a lot of loose ends and the job took them all day. Though Kaph's flat voice got on Pugh's nerves, he was a good co-worker, quick and systematic, much more so than Pugh himself. And then, there was only this one day left before the ship came, the old crew, comrades and friends.

During tea break, Kaph said, "What would happen if the Mission ship crashed?"

"They'd be killed."

"What would happen to you?"

"We'd radio SOS all signals and live on half rations till the rescue cruiser from Area Three Base came. Four and a half E years away, it is. We have life support here for three men for, let's see, maybe between four and five years. A bit tight, it would be."

"Would they come for three men?"

"Of course."

Kaph said no more.

"Enough cheerful speculations," Pugh said cheerfully, rising to get back to work. He slipped sideways and the chair avoided his hand; trying to regain balance, he brought up hard against the dome hide. "My goodness," he said, reverting to his native idiom, "what is it?"

"Quake," said Kaph.

The teacups bounced on the table with a plastic cackle, a litter of papers slid off a box, the skin of the dome swelled and sagged. Underfoot, there was a huge noise, half sound, half shaking, a subsonic boom.

Kaph sat unmoved. An earthquake would not frighten a man who had died in an earthquake.

Pugh, white-faced, his wiry black hair sticking out, a frightened man, said, "Martin's in the Trench."

"What trench?"

"The big fault line. The epicenter for these local quakes. Look at the seismograph." Pugh struggled with the stuck door of a still-jittering locker.

"Where are you going?"

"Take the jet and go locate him."

"Martin took the jet. Sleds aren't safe to use during quakes. They go out of control."

"For God's sake man, shut up."

Kaph stood up, frowning, speaking slowly, as usual. "It's unnecessary to go out after him now. It's taking an unnecessary risk."

"If his alarm goes off, radio me," Pugh said, closed the headpiece of his suit and ran to the lock. As he went out, Libra picked up her ragged skirts and danced a belly dance from under his feet clear to the red horizon. A vent south of the dome belched up a slow-flowing bile of black gas.

Inside the dome, Kaph saw the sled go up, tremble like a meteor in the dull red daylight and vanish to the northeast. The hide of the dome quivered, the earth coughed.

A bell rang loudly, a red light flashed on and off on the central control board. The sign under the light read SUIT 2 and, scribbled under that, A. G. M. Kaph did not turn the signal off. He tried to radio both Pugh and Martin but got no reply.

He went back to work when the aftershocks decreased, and finished up Pugh's job. It took him about two hours. Every half hour, he tried to radio Suit One and got no reply, then Suit Two and got no reply. The red light had stopped flashing after an hour. It was dinnertime, so Kaph cooked dinner for one and ate it.

He lay down on his cot.

The aftershocks had ceased, except for faint rolling tremors at long intervals. The sun hung in the west, oblate, pale-red, immense. It did not sink visibly. There was no sound at all.

Kaph got up and began to walk around the messy, half-packed-up, over-crowded, empty dome. The silence continued. He went to the player and put on the first tape that came to hand. It was music, pure electronically produced notes, no voices. It ended. The silence continued.

The child's dream: There is no one else alive in the world but me. In all the world.

Low, north of the dome, a meteor flickered.

Kaph's mouth opened, as if he were trying to say something, but no sound came. He went hastily to the north wall and peered out into the gelatinous red light.

The sled came in, sank, the light went out. Two figures blurred the air lock. When they came in, Kaph stood close by the lock. Martin's imsuit was covered with some kind of dust, so that he looked raddled and warty, like the surface of Libra. Pugh had him by the arm.

"Is he hurt?"

Pugh shucked his imsuit, helped Martin peel off his. "Shaken up," he said, curt.

"A bit of cliff fell onto the jet," said Martin, sitting down at the table and waving his arms. "Not while I was in it, though. I was parked, see, and poking about that carbon-dust area, when I felt things humping. So I ran out onto a nice bit of early igneous I'd noticed from above. Good footing, and out from under the cliffs. Then I saw this piece of the cliff fall over onto the flier, quite a sight it was; and after a while, I thought the spare air cans were in the flier, so I started leaning on my panic button. But I didn't get any radio reception; that's happened before during quakes, so I didn't know if the signal was getting through. And things went on jumping around and pieces of the cliff coming off. Got so dusty it was hard to see anything. I was really beginning to wonder what I'd do for breathing in the small hours, you know, when I saw old Owen zigging up the Trench in all that dust and junk, like a big ugly bat—"

"Want to eat?" said Pugh.

"Of course, I want to eat. How did you come through the quake here, Kaph? No damage I can see. It wasn't a big one, actually, was it, what's the seismo say? My trouble was I was in the middle of it. Felt like Richter ten there—total destruction of planet—"

"Sit down," Pugh said. "Eat."

After dinner, Martin's spate of talk ran dry and he went off to his cot, still in the remote angle where he had removed it when Pugh complained of his snoring. "Good night, you one-lunged Welshman," he said across the dome.

"Good night, then."

There was no more out of Martin. Pugh opaqued the dome, turned the lamp down to a yellow glow less than a candle's light and sat doing nothing, saying nothing, withdrawn.

"I finished up the computations," Kaph said.

Silence.

"The signal from Martin's suit came through, but I couldn't get through to you or him."

Pugh said with effort, "I should have waited. He had two hours of air left, even with only one can. He might have been heading home when I left."

The silence came back, but punctuated now by Martin's long, soft snores.

"Do you love Martin?"

Pugh looked up with an angry face. "Martin is my friend. We've worked together a long time. He's a good man." After a while, he asked, less belligerently, "Why did you ask that?"

Kaph said nothing, but he looked up at Pugh. His face was changed, as if he were glimpsing something he had not seen before. His voice was also changed. "How can you . . . How do you . . . ."

But Pugh could not tell him. "I don't know," he said. "It's practice, partly. I don't know. We're each of us alone, to be sure. What can you do but hold your hand out in the dark?"

Kaph's strange glance dropped, burned out by its own intensity.

"I'm tired," Pugh said. "That was no picnic, looking for him, in all that black dust and muck, and mouths opening and shutting in the ground. . . . I'm going to bed. The ship will be transmitting to us by six or so." He stood up and stretched.

"It's a clone," Kaph said. "The other Exploit Crew they're bringing with them."

"Is it, then?"

"Yes. They came out with us on the Passerine. A twelveclone."

Kaph sat in the small yellow aura of the lamp, seeming to look past it at what he feared: the new clone, the multiple self of which he was not a part. A lost piece of a broken set, a fragment, inexpert at solitude, not knowing even how you go about giving love to another individual, now he must face the tremendous closed self-sufficiency of a clone of 12; that was a lot to ask of the poor fellow, to be sure. Pugh put a hand on his shoulder in passing. "You won't be asked to stay here, then. You can go home. Or, since you're Far Out, maybe come on farther out with us. We need men. No hurry deciding. You'll make out all right."

Pugh's quiet voice trailed off; he stood unbuttoning his coat, stooped a little with fatigue. Kaph looked at him, as if he were seeing a thing he had never seen before; saw him: Owen Pugh, the other, the stranger who held his hand out in the dark.

"Good night," Pugh mumbled, crawling into his sleeping bag and half asleep already, so that he did not hear Kaph reply after a pause, repeating, across darkness, benediction.

NORMAN SPINRAD

DEATHWATCH

November 1965

Norman Spinrad's best-known early novels, *Bug Jack Baron* and *The Iron Dream,* both caused a stir when they were published. The first involved an interactive-investigative TV host (interactive—call-in—television did not exist in 1969, and the *Sixty Minutes* format was not yet standard) who uncovers an appalling traffic in human lives; the mercenary sex of the depicted TV biz was considered shocking in the science fiction world at the time, though it would cause hardly a blink now. *The Iron Dream* was an alternate biography of Hitler, here a pulp novelist of right-wing bent whose sadistic fantasies are sublimated in his books. (Some real-life writers come to mind.) Spinrad has written many novellas and short stories (collected in, among others, *The Star-*

Spangled Future), and he is considered to be one of the best essayists and reviewers in the genre. His most recent novel is *Russian Spring*. "Deathwatch" is a brief take on one of science fiction's perennial themes, that of immortality.

THE OLD MAN'S breathing was shallow now, dry and brittle, each breath an effort of no little significance. His head rested on the pillow like a dried and shriveled nut on a napkin.

The man standing at the foot of the bed stared impassively into indefinite space. His strong, unlined face showed no emotion—though there was a strange look, indeed, about his eyes, a deep, ageless resignation that seemed grossly out of place on a face that could be no more than 25.

The woman leaning her head on his shoulder had long, thick, honey-colored hair framing a young face wet with tears. Now and then a sob would wrack her body, and the man would stroke her hair with near-mechanical tenderness. He would pass his tongue slowly over his lips as if searching for words of comfort.

But there were no words and there was no comfort. The only sound in the room was the rasping breath of the old man in the bed sighing the dregs of his life away . . .

He smiled happily at his wife as she cuddled the newborn baby in her arms. He was, like all babies to all parents, a beautiful baby: weight, nine pounds; skin, ruddy; voice, excellent.

A son, he thought. *My* son. Secretly, he was relieved. While the doctors had assured them that there was no reason in the world why they could not have children, he had always had that inane, irrational feeling that he would never really be able to *know* that it was true until this moment, when he could actually reach out and touch his son.

He chucked the baby under the chin, and it cooed satisfactorily. All was right with the world . . .

Until a half hour later, when the doctor told him the truth about his child. The invisible but inescapable truth.

It took him a while to fully understand. And when he finally did, his first thought was: How will I tell *her?*

To his great relief and mystification, his wife took it better than he did. At least she seemed to. Or was it merely that built-in anesthetic that women seem to have that lets them blot out any tragedy that is far enough in the past or far enough into the indefinite future?

Whatever it was, he was grateful for it. Bad enough for a man to have to look ahead decades into the future and face the inevitable, to have to live with the thought of it long before the reality itself . . .

For a woman, *let her just have her son.*

He was a boy, just like any other boy, wasn't he? Like every other normal boy. He would learn to walk, to talk, to play with other children. He'd probably have the mumps, and maybe chickenpox, too. There'd be good report cards and bad ones, he'd come home with black eyes and skinned knees . . .

Not a monster. A boy like any other boy. A woman could forget. A woman could lose herself in just being a mother.

But for how long could he make himself feel like a father?

The mutation was called immortality, perhaps inaccurately, since it would take forever to know whether it was really possible to live forever.

Nevertheless, men and women began to be born who did not grow old and die.

Not that they were invulnerable; they simply did not age. A balance was struck in their systems at about the age of 20, and from that age on, the body renewed itself; nervous system, circulatory system, endocrine system, digestive system—all retained their youthful vigor indefinitely.

They were not supermen. They could succumb to the usual diseases. They were just as prone to accidents as other men. They were neither better nor wiser. The mutation, like most other successful mutations, was a narrow one—it produced otherwise ordinary human beings who would not age.

The why of the mutation was, of course, one of those basically unanswerable riddles of evolution. Why do men have no tails? Why do birds have wings? Why intelligence itself?

Immortality was just one more in nature's endless series of experiments. Like all the others, it was, in itself, neither a gift nor a curse. It was whatever men would make of it.

And what it would make of men.

He tried earnestly to be a good father. He was not gruff with his son—if anything, he was too gentle, for he could not look at that boyish face without a pang of regret, without a feeling of sadness.

He did try his best. He tried to be a companion to his son: fishing trips, camping, games—they did the usual father-son things together. And later on, he tried to be his son's confidant, to share his dreams and yearnings and trials. He tried as few fathers try.

But it all fell flat.

Because it was all mechanical, it was all hypocritical. For there was one thing he could not bring himself to try, there was one thing he could not bear.

He could not let himself love his son.

And though he would scarcely admit it, even to himself, he was relieved when his son graduated from college and took a job 3000 miles away across the continent. It was as if half of a great weight were lifted from his shoulders: as if a dagger that had been hanging directly over his head had been moved across the room.

His wife took it like all mothers take it—it hurt to have a continent between her son and herself, but the hurt would grow numb with time . . .

The immortality mutation bred true. It would be passed along from generation to generation like any other dominant gene. Two immortals could produce immortal children, just as two dark-haired people produce dark-haired children.

The immortals would breed as fast as ordinary men, and since youth and potency would be theirs forever, they would be able to produce an unlimited number of offspring in their millennial life spans.

Since the immortals, in the long run, could easily outbreed

mortals, the entire human race would someday be heir to the gift of immortality. In the long run.

In the short run . . .

Their son wrote home, and when he did, the answering letters were invariably written by his mother and countersigned, unread, by his father.

There were trips home every year or so, visits that his mother waited eagerly for and that his father dreaded. There was no hostility between father and son, but there was no warmth either—neither genuine pleasure at meeting nor sorrow at parting . . .

He knew that he had closed his son out of his heart. It was a cold, calculating thing to do. He knew that, too.

But he knew that he *had* to do it, for the sake of his own sanity, to be a rock that his wife could lean on . . .

It was a sacrifice, and it was not without its cost. Something within him seemed to shrivel and die. Pity, compassion, love became academic, ersatz emotions to him. They could not move him—it was as if they were being described to him by somebody else.

And occasionally he found himself lying awake next to his sleeping wife, in the loneliest hours of the night, and wishing that he could cry at least one real tear.

Just one . . .

The laws of genetics are statistical—the coldest form of mathematics. A dominant gene, like the immortality gene, breeds more or less true. Immortality was dominant, death was becoming recessive.

But recessive does not necessarily mean extinct.

Every so often—and the frequency may be calculated by the laws of genetics—two dark-haired people produce a blond, two healthy people a diabetic, two ordinary people a genius or an immortal, two immortals . . .

The old man's breath was stilled now. His heart gave one last futile flutter and gave up the fight.

Now there were only two lives in the room, two lives that would go on and on and on and on . . .

The man searched his heart futilely for some hint of genuine pain, some real and human emotion beyond the bitterness that weighed him down. But it was an old bitterness, the bitterness between father and son that was the fault of neither . . .

The woman left his side and tenderly, with the tears streaming down her creamy cheeks, she stroked the white mane of the dead old man.

With a trembling sob, she pressed her soft smooth skin against the wrinkled leather of his cheek.

And, finally, after long cold decades, a dam within her husband burst, and the torrent of sternly suppressed love and sorrow flooded the lowlands of his soul.

Two lone and perfect tears escaped his still-impassive eyes as he watched his wife touch her warm young lips to that age-wrecked face.

And kiss their son goodbye.

DAMON KNIGHT

MASKS

July 1968

Like many other science fiction writers, Damon Knight started as a teenage fan. Born in 1922 in Oregon, he began to write stories in the 1940s and has never stopped—two collections appeared as recently as 1991: *One Side Laughing: Stories Unlike Other Stories* and *God's Nose*. His latest novel is *Humpty Dumpty: An Oval*. During a long career, he has been a prominent critic, an editor of magazines and many anthologies, and is the founder and first president of the Science Fiction Writers of America. In addition to offering important legal and medical benefits to members, this essential organization votes yearly on the coveted Nebulas, awards presented by writers to writers for the best novel and stories in a given year. SFWA bestowed the title of Grandmaster, given for an entire body of work, on Knight in 1994.

Together with his wife, the well-known science fiction and mystery writer Kate Wilhelm, he founded the famous Clarion Science Fiction Writers Workshops in 1968; these are still flourishing and they have had a significant influence on American science fiction. (George Alec Effinger and Lucius Shepard, both with stories in this book, are Clarion graduates.) Knight's writing is often ironic but this story, "Masks," plays it straight. Compare it with Joe Haldeman's "More Than the Sum of His Parts" published seventeen years later.

THE EIGHT PENS danced against the moving strip of paper, like the nervous claws of some mechanical lobster. Roberts, the technician, frowned over the tracings while the other two watched.

"Here's the wake-up impulse," he said, pointing with a skinny finger. "Then here, look, seventeen seconds more, still dreaming."

"Delayed response," said Babcock, the project director. His heavy face was flushed and he was sweating. "Nothing to worry about."

"OK, delayed response, but look at the difference in the tracings. Still dreaming, after the wake-up impulse, but the peaks are closer together. Not the same dream. More anxiety, more motor pulses."

"Why does he have to sleep at all?" asked Sinescu, the man from Washington. He was dark, narrow-faced. "You flush the fatigue poisons out, don't you? So what is it, something psychological?"

"He needs to dream," said Babcock. "It's true he has no physiological need for sleep, but he's got to dream. If he didn't, he'd start to hallucinate, maybe go psychotic."

"Psychotic," said Sinescu. "Well—that's the question, isn't it? How long has he been doing this?"

"About six months."

"In other words, about the time he got his new body—and started wearing a mask?"

"About that. Look, let me tell you something: He's rational. Every test—"

"Yes, OK, I know about tests. Well—so he's awake now?"

The technician glanced at the monitor board. "He's up. Sam and Irma are with him." He hunched his shoulders, staring at the

73

EEG tracings again. "I don't know why it should bother me. It stands to reason, if he has dream needs of his own that we're not satisfying with the programmed stuff, this is where he gets them in." His face hardened. "I don't know. Something about those peaks I don't like."

Sinescu raised his eyebrows. "You program his dreams?"

"Not program," said Babcock impatiently. "A routine suggestion to dream the sort of thing we tell him to. Somatic stuff, sex, exercise, sport."

"And whose idea was that?"

"Psych section. He was doing fine neurologically, every other way, but he was withdrawing. Psych decided he needed that somatic input in some form, we had to keep him in touch. He's alive, he's functioning, everything works. But don't forget, he spent forty-three years in a normal human body."

In the hush of the elevator, Sinescu said, "Washington."

Swaying, Babcock said, "I'm sorry; what?"

"You look a little rocky. Getting any sleep?"

"Not lately. What did you say before?"

"I said they're not happy with your reports in Washington."

"Goddamn it, I know that." The elevator door silently opened. A tiny foyer, green carpet, gray walls. There were three doors, one metal, two heavy glass. Cool, stale air. "This way."

Sinescu paused at the glass door, glanced through: a gray-carpeted living room, empty. "I don't see him."

"Around the el. Getting his morning checkup."

The door opened against slight pressure; a battery of ceiling lights went on as they entered. "Don't look up," said Babcock. "Ultraviolet." A faint hissing sound stopped when the door closed.

"And positive pressure in here? To keep out germs? Whose idea was that?"

"His." Babcock opened a chrome box on the wall and took out two surgical masks. "Here, put this on."

Voices came muffled from around the bend of the room. Sinescu looked with distaste at the white mask, then slowly put it over his head.

They stared at each other. "Germs," said Sinescu through the mask. "Is that rational?"

"All right, he can't catch a cold, or what have you, but think about it a minute. There are just two things now that could kill him. One is a prosthetic failure, and we guard against that; we've got five hundred people here, we check him out like an airplane. That leaves a cerebrospinal infection. Don't go in there with a closed mind."

The room was large, part living room, part library, part workshop. Here was a cluster of Swedish-modern chairs, a sofa, coffee table; here a workbench with a metal lathe, electric crucible, drill press, parts bins, tools on wallboards; here a drafting table; here a free-standing wall of bookshelves that Sinescu fingered curiously as they passed. Bound volumes of project reports, technical journals, reference books; no fiction, except for *Fire* and *Storm* by George Stewart and *The Wizard of Oz* in a worn blue binding. Behind the bookshelves, set into a little alcove, was a glass door through which they glimpsed another living room, differently furnished: upholstered chairs, a tall philodendron in a ceramic pot. "There's Sam," Babcock said.

A man had appeared in the other room. He saw them, turned to call to someone they could not see, then came forward, smiling. He was bald and stocky, deeply tanned. Behind him, a small pretty woman hurried up. She crowded through after her husband, leaving the door open. Neither of them wore a mask.

"Sam and Irma have the next suite," Babcock said. "Company for him; he's got to have somebody around. Sam is an old Air Force buddy of his and, besides, he's got a tin arm."

The stocky man shook hands, grinning. His grip was firm and warm. "Want to guess which one?" He wore a flowered sport shirt. Both arms were brown, muscular and hairy; but when Sinescu looked more closely, he saw that the right one was a slightly different color, not quite authentic.

Embarrassed, he said, "The left, I guess."

"Nope." Grinning wider, the stocky man pulled back his right sleeve to show the straps.

"One of the spin-offs from the project," said Babcock. "Myoelectric, servo-controlled, weighs the same as the other one. Sam, they about through in there?"

"Maybe so. Let's take a peek. Honey, you think you could rustle up some coffee for the gentlemen?"

"Oh, why, sure." The little woman turned and darted back through the open doorway.

The far wall was glass, covered by a translucent white curtain. They turned the corner. The next bay was full of medical and electronic equipment, some built into the walls, some in tall black cabinets on wheels. Four men in white coats were gathered around what looked like an astronaut's couch. Sinescu could see someone lying on it: feet in Mexican woven-leather shoes, dark socks, gray slacks. A mutter of voices.

"Not through yet," Babcock said. "Must have found something else they didn't like. Let's go out onto the patio a minute."

"Thought they checked him at night—when they exchange his blood, and so on?"

"They do." Babcock said. "And in the morning, too." He turned and pushed open the heavy glass door. Outside, the roof was paved with cut stone, enclosed by a green-plastic canopy and tinted-glass walls. Here and there were concrete basins, empty. "Idea was to have a roof garden out here, something green, but he didn't want it. We had to take all the plants out, glass the whole thing in."

Sam pulled out metal chairs around a white table and they all sat down. "How is he, Sam?" asked Babcock.

He grinned and ducked his head. "Mean in the mornings."

"Talk to you much? Play any chess?"

"Not too much. Works, mostly. Reads some, watches the box a little." His smile was forced; his heavy fingers were clasped together and Sinescu saw now that the finger tips of one hand had turned darker, the others not. He looked away.

"You're from Washington, that right?" Sam asked politely. "First time here? Hold on." He was out of his chair. Vague upright shapes were passing behind the curtained glass door. "Looks like they're through. If you gentlemen would just wait here a minute, till I see." He strode across the roof. The two men sat in silence. Babcock had pulled down his surgical mask; Sinescu noticed and did the same.

"Sam's wife is a problem," Babcock said, leaning nearer. "It seemed like a good idea at the time, but she's lonely here, doesn't like it—no kids—"

The door opened again and Sam appeared. He had a mask on,

but it was hanging under his chin. "If you gentlemen would come in now."

In the living area, the little woman, also with a mask hanging around her neck, was pouring coffee from a flowered ceramic jug. She was smiling brightly but looked unhappy. Opposite her sat someone tall, in gray shirt and slacks, leaning back, legs out, arms on the arms of his chair, motionless. Something was wrong with his face.

"Well, now," said Sam heartily. His wife looked up at him with an agonized smile.

The tall figure turned its head and Sinescu saw with an icy shock that its face was silver, a mask of metal with oblong slits for eyes, no nose or mouth, only curves that were faired into each other. "Project," said an inhuman voice.

Sinescu found himself half bent over a chair. He sat down. They were all looking at him. The voice resumed, "I said, are you here to pull the plug on the project?" It was unaccented, indifferent.

"Have some coffee." The woman pushed a cup toward him.

Sinescu reached for it, but his hand was trembling and he drew it back. "Just a fact-finding expedition," he said.

"Bull. Who sent you—Senator Hinkel?"

"That's right."

"Bull. He's been here himself; why send you? If you are going to pull the plug, might as well tell me." The face behind the mask did not move when he spoke, the voice did not seem to come from it.

"He's just looking around, Jim," said Babcock.

"Two hundred million a year," said the voice, "to keep one man alive. Doesn't make much sense, does it? Go on, drink your coffee."

Sinescu realized that Sam and his wife had already finished theirs and that they had pulled up their masks. He reached for his cup hastily.

"Hundred percent disability in my grade is thirty thousand a year. I could get along on that easy. For almost an hour and a half."

"There's no intention of terminating the project," Sinescu said.

"Phasing it out, though. Would you say phasing it out?"

"Manners, Jim," said Babcock.

"OK. My worst fault. What do you want to know?"

Sinescu sipped his coffee. His hands were still trembling. "That mask you're wearing," he started.

"Not for discussion. No comment, no comment. Sorry about that; don't mean to be rude; a personal matter. Ask me something—" Without warning, he stood up, blaring, "Get that damn thing out of here!" Sam's wife's cup smashed, coffee brown across the table. A fawn-colored puppy was sitting in the middle of the carpet, cocking its head, bright-eyed, tongue out.

The table tipped, Sam's wife struggled up behind it. Her face was pink, dripping with tears. She scooped up the puppy without pausing and ran out. "I better go with her," Sam said, getting up.

"Go on; and, Sam, take a holiday. Drive her into Winnemucca, see a movie."

"Yeah, guess I will." He disappeared behind the bookshelf wall.

The tall figure sat down again, moving like a man; it leaned back in the same posture, arms on the arms of the chair. It was still. The hands gripping the wood were shapely and perfect but unreal; there was something wrong about the fingernails. The brown, well-combed hair above the mask was a wig; the ears were wax. Sinescu nervously fumbled his surgical mask up over his mouth and nose. "Might as well get along," he said, and stood up.

"That's right, I want to take you over to Engineering and R and D," said Babcock. "Jim, I'll be back in a little while. Want to talk to you."

"Sure," said the motionless figure.

Babcock had had a shower, but sweat was soaking through the armpits of his shirt again. The silent elevator, the green carpet, a little blurred. The air cool, stale. Seven years, blood and money, 500 good men. Psych section, Cosmetic, Engineering, R and D, Medical, Immunology, Supply, Serology, Administration. The glass doors. Sam's apartment empty, gone to Winnemucca with Irma. Psych. Good men, but were they the best? Three of the best had turned it down. Buried in the files. *Not like an ordinary amputation, this man has had everything cut off.*

The tall figure had not moved. Babcock sat down. The silver mask looked back at him.

"Jim, let's level with each other."

"Bad, huh?"

"Sure it's bad. I left him in his room with a bottle. I'll see him again before he leaves, but God knows what he'll say in Washington. Listen, do me a favor, take that thing off."

"Sure." The hand rose, plucked at the edge of the silver mask, lifted it away. Under it, the tan-pink face, sculptured nose and lips, eyebrows, eyelashes, not handsome but good-looking, normal-looking. Only the eyes wrong, pupils too big. And the lips that did not open or move when it spoke. "I can take anything off. What does that prove?"

"Jim, Cosmetic spent eight and a half months on that model and the first thing you do is slap a mask over it. We've asked you what's wrong, offered to make any changes you want."

"No comment."

"You talked about phasing out the project. Did you think you were kidding?"

A pause. "Not kidding."

"All right, then open up, Jim, tell me: I have to know. They won't shut the project down; they'll keep you alive, but that's all. There are seven hundred on the volunteer list, including two U.S. Senators. Suppose one of them gets pulled out of an auto wreck tomorrow. We can't wait till then to decide: we've got to know now. Whether to let the next one die or put him into a TP body like yours. So talk to me."

"Suppose I tell you something, but it isn't the truth."

"Why would you lie?"

"Why do you lie to a cancer patient?"

"I don't get it. Come on. Jim."

"OK, try this. Do I look like a man to you?"

"Sure."

"Bull. Look at this face." Calm and perfect. Beyond the fake irises, a wink of metal. "Suppose we had all the other problems solved and I could go into Winnemucca tomorrow; can you see me walking down the street—going into a bar—taking a taxi?"

"Is that all it is?" Babcock drew a deep breath. "Jim, sure there's a difference, but for Christ's sake, it's like any other prosthesis—people get used to it. Like that arm of Sam's. You see it, but after a while you forget it, you don't notice."

"Bull. You pretend not to notice. Because it would embarrass the cripple."

Babcock looked down at his clasped hands. "Sorry for yourself?"

"Don't give me that," the voice blared. The tall figure was standing. The hands slowly came up, the fists clenched. "I'm in this thing. I've been in it for two years. I'm in it when I go to sleep, and when I wake up. I'm still in it."

Babcock looked up at him. "What do you want, facial mobility? Give us twenty years, maybe ten, we'll lick it."

"No. No."

"Then what?"

"I want you to close down Cosmetic."

"But that's—"

"Just listen. The first model looked like a tailor's dummy, so you spent eight months and came up with this one, and it looks like a corpse. The whole idea was to make me look like a man, the first model pretty good, the second model better, until you've got something that can smoke cigars and joke with women and go bowling and nobody will know the difference. You can't do it, and if you could, what for?"

"I don't— Let me think about this. What do you mean, a metal—"

"Metal, sure, but what difference does that make? I'm talking about shape. Function. Wait a minute." The tall figure strode across the room, unlocked a cabinet, came back with rolled sheets of paper. "Look at this."

The drawing showed an oblong metal box on four jointed legs. From one end protruded a tiny mushroom-shaped head on a jointed stem and a cluster of arms ending in probes, drills, grapples. "For moon prospecting."

"Too many limbs," said Babcock after a moment. "How would you—"

"With the facial nerves. Plenty of them left over. Or here." Another drawing. "A module plugged into the control system of a spaceship. That's where I belong, in space. Sterile environment, low grav, I can go where a man can't go and do what a man can't do. I can be an asset, not a goddamn billion-dollar liability."

Babcock rubbed his eyes. "Why didn't you say anything before?"

"You were all hipped on prosthetics. You would have told me to tend my knitting."

Babcock's hands were shaking as he rolled up the drawings. "Well, by God, this just may do it. It just might." He stood up and turned toward the door. "Keep your—" He cleared his throat. "I mean, hang tight, Jim."

"I'll do that."

When he was alone, he put on his mask again and stood motionless a moment, eye shutters closed. Inside, he was running clean and cool: He could feel the faint reassuring hum of pumps, click of valves and relays. They had given him that: cleaned out all the offal, replaced it with machinery that did not bleed, ooze or suppurate. He thought of the lie he had told Babcock. *Why do you lie to a cancer patient?* But they would never get it, never understand.

He sat down at the drafting table, clipped a sheet of paper to it and with a pencil began to sketch a rendering of the moon-prospector design. When he had blocked in the prospector itself, he began to draw the background of craters. His pencil moved more slowly and stopped; he put it down with a click.

No more adrenal glands to pump adrenaline into his blood, so he could not feel fright or rage. They had released him from all that—love, hate, the whole sloppy mess—but they had forgotten there was still one emotion he could feel.

Sinescu, with the black bristles of his beard sprouting through his oily skin. A whitehead ripe in the crease beside his nostril.

Moon landscape, clean and cold. He picked up the pencil again.

Babcock, with his broad pink nose shining with grease, crusts of white matter in the corners of his eyes. Food mortar between his teeth.

Sam's wife, with raspberry-colored paste on her mouth. Face smeared with tears, a bright bubble in one nostril. And the damn dog, shiny nose, wet eyes . . .

He turned. The dog was there, sitting on the carpet, wet red tongue out *left the door open again* dripping, wagged its tail twice, then started to get up. He reached for the metal T square, leaned back, swinging it like an ax, and the dog yelped once as metal sheared bone, one eye spouting red, writhing on its back, dark stain of piss across the carpet and he hit it again, hit it again.

The body lay twisted on the carpet, fouled with blood, ragged black lips drawn back from teeth. He wiped off the T square with a paper towel, then scrubbed it in the sink with soap and steel wool, dried it and hung it up. He got a sheet of drafting paper, laid it on the floor, rolled the body over onto it without spilling any blood on the carpet. He lifted the body in the paper, carried it out onto the patio, then onto the unroofed section, opening the doors with his shoulder. He looked over the wall. Two stories down, concrete roof, vents sticking out of it, nobody watching. He held the dog out, let it slide off the paper, twisting as it fell. It struck one of the vents, bounced, a red smear. He carried the paper back inside, poured the blood down the drain, then put the paper into the incinerator chute.

Splashes of blood were on the carpet. the feet of the drafting table, the cabinet, his trouser legs. He sponged them all up with paper towels and warm water. He took off his clothing, examined it minutely, scrubbed it in the sink, then put it in the washer. He washed the sink, rubbed himself down with disinfectant and dressed again. He walked through into Sam's silent apartment, closing the glass door behind him. Past the potted philodendron, overstuffed furniture, red-and-yellow painting on the wall, out onto the roof, leaving the door ajar. Then back through the patio, closing doors.

Too bad. How about some goldfish.

He sat down at the drafting table. He was running clean and cool. The dream this morning came back to his mind, the last one, as he was struggling up out of sleep: *slithery kidneys burst gray lungs blood and hair ropes of guts covered with yellow fat oozing and sliding and oh god the stink like the breath of an outhouse no sound nowhere he was putting a yellow stream down the slide of the dunghole and*

He began to ink in the drawing first with a fine steel pen, then with a nylon brush, *his heel slid and he was falling could not stop himself falling into slimy bulging softness higher than his chin, higher and he could not move paralyzed and he tried to scream tried to scream tried to scream*

The prospector was climbing a crater slope with its handling members retracted and its head tilted up. Behind it the distant ringwall and the horizon, the black sky, the pin-point stars. And he was there, and it was not far enough, not yet, for the earth hung overhead like a rotten fruit, blue with mold, crawling, wrinkling, purulent and alive.

KURT VONNEGUT, JR.

WELCOME TO THE MONKEY HOUSE

January 1968

Kurt Vonnegut, Jr., claims he doesn't write science fiction. Okay by us, whatever the man says. He does seem to write satires of science fiction, or maybe that's his alter ego, Kilgore Trout, down-at-heels sci-fi writer, writing them under the better-known Vonnegut name. (It's a switch on Stephen King/Richard Bachman.) Certainly, many of his best-known books, from *Player Piano* (1952) to *The Sirens of Titan* (1959) to *Cat's Cradle* (1962) even to *Slaughterhouse-Five* (1965) and beyond, borrow quite a lot from science fiction. Vonnegut, famously born a Hoosier (from Indiana, that is) in 1922, lived for many years on Cape Cod, and now lives in New York City and Long Island. His collection of stories, *Welcome to the Monkey House*, takes its title from this bright satire on sex and science fiction. We hope you won't find the story out of place here.

SO **PETE CROCKER,** the sheriff of Barnstable County, which was the whole of Cape Cod, came into the Federal Ethical Suicide Parlor in Hyannis one May afternoon—and he told the two six-foot Hostesses there that they weren't to be alarmed, but that a notorious nothinghead named Billy the Poet was believed headed for the Cape.

A nothinghead was a person who refused to take his ethical birth-control pills three times a day. The penalty for that was $10,000 and ten years in jail.

This was at a time when the population of Earth was 17 billion human beings. That was far too many mammals that big for a planet that small. The people were virtually packed together like drupelets.

Drupelets are the pulpy little knobs that compose the outside of a raspberry.

So the World Government was making a two-pronged attack on overpopulation. One pronging was the encouragement of ethical suicide, which consisted of going to the nearest Suicide Parlor and asking a Hostess to kill you painlessly while you lay on a Barcalounger. The other pronging was compulsory ethical birth control.

The sheriff told the Hostesses, who were pretty, tough-minded, highly intelligent girls, that roadblocks were being set up and house-to-house searches were being conducted to catch Billy the Poet. The main difficulty was that the police didn't know what he looked like. The few people who had seen him and known him for what he was were women—and they disagreed fantastically as to his height, his hair color, his voice, his weight, the color of his skin.

"I don't need to remind you girls," the sheriff went on, "that a nothinghead is very sensitive from the waist down. If Billy the Poet somehow slips in here and starts making trouble, one good kick in the right place will do wonders."

He was referring to the fact that ethical birth-control pills, the only legal form of birth control, made people numb from the waist down.

Most men said their bottom halves felt like cold iron or balsa wood. Most women said their bottom halves felt like wet cotton or stale ginger ale. The pills were so effective that you could blindfold a man who had taken one, tell him to recite the Gettysburg Address, kick him in the balls while he was doing it, and he wouldn't miss a syllable.

The pills were ethical because they didn't interfere with a person's ability to reproduce, which would have been unnatural and immoral. All the pills did was take every bit of pleasure out of sex.

Thus did science and morals go hand in hand.

The two Hostesses there in Hyannis were Nancy McLuhan and Mary Kraft. Nancy was a strawberry blonde. Mary was a glossy brunette. Their uniforms were white lipstick, heavy eye make-up, purple body stockings with nothing underneath and black-leather boots. They ran a small operation—with only six suicide booths. In a really good week, say the one before Christmas, they might put 60 people to sleep. It was done with a hypodermic syringe.

"My main message to you girls," said Sheriff Crocker, "is that everything's well under control. You can just go about your business here."

"Didn't you leave out part of your main message?" Nancy asked him.

"I don't get you."

"I didn't hear you say he was probably headed straight for us."

He shrugged in clumsy innocence. "We don't know that for sure."

"I thought that was all anybody *did* know about Billy the Poet: that he specializes in deflowering Hostesses in Ethical Suicide Parlors." Nancy was a virgin. All Hostesses were virgins. They also had to hold advanced degrees in psychology and nursing. They also had to be plump and rosy, and at least six feet tall.

America had changed in many ways, but it had yet to adopt the metric system.

Nancy McLuhan was burned up that the sheriff would try to protect her and Mary from the full truth about Billy the Poet—as though they might panic if they heard it. She told the sheriff so.

"How long do you think a girl would last in the E.S.S.," she said, meaning the Ethical Suicide Service, "if she scared *that* easy?"

The sheriff took a step backward, pulled in his chin. "Not very long, I guess."

"That's very true," said Nancy, closing the distance between them and offering him a sniff of the edge of her hand, which was poised for a karate chop. All Hostesses were experts at judo and karate. "If you'd like to find out how helpless we are, just come toward me, pretending you're Billy the Poet."

The sheriff shook his head, gave her a glassy smile. "I'd rather not."

"That's the smartest thing you've said today," said Nancy, turning her back on him while Mary laughed. "We're not scared— we're *angry*. Or we're not even *that*. He isn't *worth* that. We're *bored*. How boring that he should come a great distance, should cause all this fuss, in order to—" She let the sentence die there. "It's just too absurd."

"I'm not as mad at *him* as I am at the women who let him do it to them without a struggle"—said Mary—"who let him do it and then couldn't tell the police what he looked like. Suicide Hostesses at that!"

"Somebody hasn't been keeping up with her karate," said Nancy.

It wasn't just Billy the Poet who was attracted to Hostesses in Ethical Suicide Parlors. All nothingheads were. Bombed out of their skulls with the sex madness that came from taking nothing they thought the white lips and big eyes and body stocking and boots of a Hostess spelled *sex, sex, sex*.

The truth was, of course, that sex was the last thing any Hostess ever had in mind.

"If Billy follows his usual M. O.," said the sheriff, "he'll study your habits and the neighborhood. And then he'll pick one or the other of you and he'll send her a dirty poem in the mail."

"Charming," said Nancy.

"He has also been known to use the telephone."

"How brave," said Nancy. Over the sheriff's shoulder, she could see the mailman coming.

A blue light went on over the door of a booth for which Nancy was responsible. The person in there wanted something. It was the only booth in use at the time.

The sheriff asked her if there was a possibility that the person in there was Billy the Poet, and Nancy said, "Well, if it is, I can break his neck with my thumb and forefinger."

"Foxy Grandpa," said Mary, who'd seen him, too. A Foxy Grandpa was any old man, cute and senile, who quibbled and joked and reminisced for hours before he let a Hostess put him to sleep.

Nancy rolled her eyes. "We've spent the past two hours trying to decide on a last meal."

And then the mailman came in with just one letter. It was addressed to Nancy in smeary pencil. She was splendid with anger and disgust as she opened it, knowing it would be a piece of filth from Billy.

She was right. Inside the envelope was a poem. It wasn't an original poem. It was a song from olden days that had taken on new meanings since the numbness of ethical birth control had become universal. It went like this, in smeary pencil again:

> *We were walking through the park,*
> *A-goosing statues in the dark.*
> *If Sherman's horse can take it,*
> *So can you.*

When Nancy came into the suicide booth to see what he wanted, the Foxy Grandpa was lying on the mint-green Barca-lounger, where hundreds had died so peacefully over the years. He was studying the menu from the Howard Johnson's next door and beating time to the Muzak coming from the loud-speaker on the lemon-yellow wall. The room was painted cinder block. There was one barred window with a Venetian blind.

There was a Howard Johnson's next door to every Ethical

Suicide Parlor, and vice versa. The Howard Johnson's had an orange roof and the Suicide Parlor had a purple roof, but they were both the Government. Practically everything was the Government.

Practically everything was automated too. Nancy and Mary and the sheriff were lucky to have jobs. Most people didn't. The average citizen moped around home and watched television which was the Government. Every 15 minutes his television would urge him to vote intelligently or consume intelligently, or worship in the church of his choice, or love his fellow men, or obey the laws—or pay a call to the nearest Ethical Suicide Parlor and find out how friendly and understanding a Hostess could be.

The Foxy Grandpa was something of a rarity, since he was marked by old age, was bald, was shaky, had spots on his hands. Most people looked 22, thanks to antiaging shots they took twice a year. That the old man looked old was proof that the shots had been discovered after his sweet bird of youth had flown.

"Have we decided on a last supper yet?" Nancy asked him. She heard peevishness in her own voice, heard herself betray her exasperation with Billy the Poet, her boredom with the old man. She was ashamed, for this was unprofessional of her. "The breaded veal cutlet is very good."

The old man cocked his head. With the greedy cunning of second childhood he had caught her being unprofessional, unkind, and he was going to punish her for it. "You don't sound very friendly. I thought you were all supposed to be friendly. I thought this was suppose to be a pleasant place to come."

"I beg your pardon," she said. "If I seem unfriendly, it has nothing to do with you."

"I thought maybe I bored you."

"No, no," she said gamely, "not at all. You certainly know some very interesting history." Among other things, the Foxy Grandpa claimed to have known J. Edgar Nation, the Grand Rapids druggist who was the father of ethical birth control.

"Then *look* like you're interested," he told her. He could get away with that sort of impudence. The thing was, he could leave any time he wanted to, right up to the moment he asked for the needle—and he had to *ask* for the needle. That was the law.

Nancy's art, and the art of every Hostess, was to see that volunteers didn't leave, to coax and wheedle and flatter them patiently, every step of the way.

So Nancy had to sit down there in the booth, to pretend to marvel at the freshness of the yarn the old man told, a story everybody knew, about how J. Edgar Nation happened to experiment with ethical birth control.

"He didn't have the slightest idea his pills would be taken by human beings someday," said the Foxy Grandpa. "His dream was to introduce morality into the monkey house at the Grand Rapids Zoo. Did you realize that?" he inquired severely.

"No. No, I didn't. That's very interesting."

"He and his eleven kids went to church one Easter. And the day was so nice and the Easter service had been so beautiful and pure that they decided to take a walk through the zoo, and they were just walking on clouds."

"Um." The scene described was lifted from a play that was performed on television every Easter.

The Foxy Grandpa shoehorned himself into the scene, had himself chat with the Nations just before they got to the monkey house. "'Good morning, Mr. Nation,' I said to him. 'It certainly is a nice morning.' 'And a good morning to *you*, Mr. Howard,' he said to me. 'There is nothing like an Easter morning to make a man feel clean and reborn and at one with God's intentions.'"

"Um." Nancy could hear the telephone ringing faintly, naggingly, through the nearly soundproof door.

"So we went on to the monkey house together, and what do you think we saw?"

"I can't imagine." Somebody had answered the phone.

"We saw a monkey playing with his private parts!"

"No!"

"Yes! And J. Edgar Nation was so upset he went straight home and he started developing a pill that would make monkeys in the springtime fit things for a Christian family to see."

There was a knock on the door.

"Yes?" said Nancy.

"Nancy," said Mary, "telephone for you."

When Nancy came out of the booth, she found the sheriff choking on little squeals of law-enforcement delight. The telephone was tapped by agents hidden in the Howard Johnson's. Billy the Poet was believed to be on the line. His call had been traced. Police were already on their way to grab him.

"Keep him on, keep him on," the sheriff whispered to Nancy, and he gave her the telephone as though it were solid gold.

"Yes?" said Nancy.

"Nancy McLuhan?" said a man. His voice was disguised. He might have been speaking through a kazoo. "I'm calling for a mutual friend."

"Oh?"

"He asked me to deliver a message."

"I see."

"It's a poem."

"All right."

"Ready?"

"Ready." Nancy could hear sirens screaming in the background of the call.

The caller must have heard the sirens, too, but he recited the poem without any emotion. It went like this:

> *"Soak yourself in Jergen's Lotion.*
> *Here comes the one-man population explosion."*

They got him. Nancy heard it all—the thumping and clumping, the argle-bargle and cries.

The depression she felt as she hung up was glandular. Her brave body had prepared for a fight that was not to be.

The sheriff bounded out of the Suicide Parlor in such a hurry to see the famous criminal he'd helped catch that a sheaf of papers fell from the pocket of his trench coat.

Mary picked them up, called after the sheriff. He halted for a moment, said the papers didn't matter anymore, asked her if maybe she wouldn't like to come along. There was a flurry between the two girls, with Nancy persuading Mary to go, declaring that she had no curiosity about Billy. So Mary left, irrelevantly handing the sheaf to Nancy.

The sheaf proved to be photocopies of poems Billy had sent to Hostesses in other places. Nancy read the top one. It made much of a peculiar side effect of ethical birth-control pills: They not only made people numb—they also made people piss blue. The poem was called *What the Somethinghead Said to the Suicide Hostess*, and it went like this:

> *I did not sow, I did not spin,*
> *And thanks to pills, I did not sin.*
> *I loved the crowds, the stink, the noise.*
> *And when I peed, I peed turquoise.*
>
> *I ate beneath a roof of orange;*
> *Swung with progress like a door hinge.*
> *'Neath purple roof I've come today*
> *To piss my azure life away.*
>
> *Virgin Hostess, death's recruiter,*
> *Life is cute, but you are cuter,*
> *Mourn my pecker, purple daughter—*
> *All it passed was sky-blue water.*

"You never heard that story before—about how J. Edgar Nation came to invent ethical birth control?" the Foxy Grandpa wanted to know. His voice cracked.

"Never did," lied Nancy.

"I thought everybody knew that."

"It was news to me."

"When he got through with the monkey house, you couldn't tell it from the Michigan Supreme Court. Meanwhile there was this crisis going on in the United Nations. The people who understood science said people had to quit reproducing so much, and the people who understood morals said society would collapse if people used sex for nothing but pleasure."

The Foxy Grandpa got off his Barcalounger, went over to the window, pried two slats of the blind apart. There wasn't much to see out there. The view was blocked by the backside of a mocked-up thermometer 20 feet high, which faced the street. It was calibrated in billions of people on Earth, from 0 to 20. The make-believe column of liquid was a strip of translucent red plastic. It showed how many people there were on Earth. Very close to the bottom was a black arrow that showed what the scientists thought the population ought to be.

The Foxy Grandpa was looking at the setting sun through that red plastic, and through the blind, too, so that his face was banded with shadows and red.

"Tell me," he said, "when I die, how much will that thermometer go down? A foot?"

"No."

"An inch?"

"Not quite."

"You know what the answer is, don't you?" he said, and he faced her. The senility had vanished from his voice and eyes. "One inch on that thing equals 83,333,333 people. You knew that, didn't you?"

"That—that might be true," said Nancy, "but that isn't the right way to look at it, in my opinion."

He didn't ask her what the right way was, in her opinion. He completed a thought of his own, instead. "I'll tell you something else that's true: I'm Billy the Poet, and you're a very good-looking woman."

With one hand, he drew a snub-nosed revolver from his belt. With the other, he peeled off his bald dome and wrinkled forehead, which proved to be rubber. Now he looked 22.

"The police will want to know exactly what I look like when this is all over," he told Nancy with a malicious grin. "In case you're not good at describing people, and it's surprising how many women aren't:

> *I'm five foot, two,*
> *With eyes of blue,*
> *With brown hair to my shoulders—*
> *A manly elf*
> *So full of self*
> *The ladies say he smolders."*

Billy was ten inches shorter than Nancy was. She had about 40 pounds on him. She told him he didn't have a chance, but Nancy was much mistaken. He had unbolted the bars on the window the night before and he made her go out the window and then down a manhole that was hidden from the street by the big thermometer.

He took her down into the sewers of Hyannis. He knew where

he was going. He had a flashlight and a map. Nancy had to go before him along the narrow catwalk, her own shadow dancing mockingly in the lead. She tried to guess where they were, relative to the real world above. She guessed correctly when they passed under the Howard Johnson's, guessed from noises she heard. The machinery that processed and served the food there was silent. But, so people wouldn't feel too lonesome when eating there, the designers had provided sound effects for the kitchen. It was these Nancy heard—a tape recording of the clashing of silverware and the laughter of Negroes and Puerto Ricans.

After that she was lost. Billy had very little to say to her other than "Right," or, "Left," or "Don't try anything funny, Juno, or I'll blow your great big fucking head off."

Only once did they have anything resembling a conversation. Billy began it, and ended it, too. "What in hell is a girl with hips like yours doing selling death?" he asked her from behind.

She dared to stop. "I can answer that," she told him. She was confident that she could give him an answer that would shrivel him like napalm.

But he gave her a shove, offered to blow her head off again.

"You don't even want to hear my answer," she taunted him. "You're afraid to hear it."

"I never listen to a woman till the pills wear off," sneered Billy. That was his plan, then—to keep her a prisoner for at least eight hours. That was how long it took for the pills to wear off.

"That's a silly rule."

"A woman's not a woman till the pills wear off."

"You certainly manage to make a woman feel like an object rather than a person."

"Thank the pills for that," said Billy.

There were 80 miles of sewers under Greater Hyannis, which had a population of 400,000 drupelets, 400,000 souls. Nancy lost track of the time down there. When Billy announced that they had at last reached their destination, it was possible for Nancy to imagine that a year had passed.

She tested this spooky impression by pinching her own thigh, by feeling what the chemical clock of her body said. Her thigh was still numb.

Billy ordered her to climb iron rungs that were set in wet masonry. There was a circle of sickly light above. It proved to be moonlight filtered through the plastic polygons of an enormous geodesic dome. Nancy didn't have to ask the traditional victim's question, "Where am I?" There was only one dome like that on Cape Cod. It was in Hyannis Port and it sheltered the ancient Kennedy Compound.

It was a museum of how life had been lived in more expansive times. The museum was closed. It was open only in the summertime.

The manhole from which Nancy and then Billy emerged was set in an expanse of green cement, which showed where the Kennedy lawn had been. On the green cement, in front of the ancient frame houses, were statues representing the 14 Kennedys who had been Presidents of the United States or the World. They were playing touch football.

The President of the World at the time of Nancy's abduction, incidentally, was an ex-Suicide Hostess named "Ma" Kennedy. Her statue would never join this particular touch-football game. Her name was Kennedy, all right, but she wasn't the real thing. People complained of her lack of style, found her vulgar. On the wall of her office was a sign that said, YOU DON'T HAVE TO BE CRAZY TO WORK HERE, BUT IT SURE HELPS, and another one that said, THIMK!, and another one that said, SOMEDAY WE'RE GOING TO HAVE TO GET ORGANIZED AROUND HERE.

Her office was in the Taj Mahal.

Until she arrived in the Kennedy Museum, Nancy McLuhan was confident that she would sooner or later get a chance to break every bone in Billy's little body, maybe even shoot him with his own gun. She wouldn't have minded doing those things. She thought he was more disgusting than a blood-filled tick.

It wasn't compassion that changed her mind. It was the discovery that Billy had a gang. There were at least eight people around the manhole, men and women in equal numbers, with stockings pulled over their heads. It was the women who laid firm hands on Nancy, told her to keep calm. They were all at least as tall as Nancy and they held her in places where they could hurt her like hell if they had to.

Nancy closed her eyes, but this didn't protect her from the obvious conclusion: These perverted women were sisters from the Ethical Suicide Service. This upset her so much that she asked loudly and bitterly. "How can you violate your oaths like this?"

She was promptly hurt so badly that she doubled up and burst into tears.

When she straightened up again, there was plenty more she wanted to say, but she kept her mouth shut. She speculated silently as to what on Earth could make Suicide Hostesses turn against every concept of human decency. Nothingheadedness alone couldn't begin to explain it. They had to be drugged besides.

Nancy went over in her mind all the terrible drugs she'd learned about in school, persuaded herself that the women had taken the worst one of all. That drug was so powerful, Nancy's teachers had told her, that even a person numb from the waist down would copulate repeatedly and enthusiastically after just one glass. That had to be the answer: The women, and probably the men, too, had been drinking gin.

They hastened Nancy into the middle frame house, which was dark like all the rest, and Nancy heard the men giving Billy the news. It was in this news that Nancy perceived a glint of hope. Help might be on its way.

The gang member who had phoned Nancy obscenely had fooled the police into believing that they had captured Billy the Poet, which was bad for Nancy. The police didn't know yet that Nancy was missing, two men told Billy, and a telegram had been sent to Mary Kraft in Nancy's name, declaring that Nancy had been called to New York City on urgent family business.

That was where Nancy saw the glint of hope: Mary wouldn't believe that telegram. Mary knew Nancy had no family in New York. Not one of the 63,000,000 people living there was a relative of Nancy's.

The gang had deactivated the burglar-alarm system of the museum. They had also cut through a lot of the chains and ropes that were meant to keep visitors from touching anything of value. There was no mystery as to who and what had done the cutting. One of the men was armed with brutal lopping shears.

They marched Nancy into a servant's bedroom upstairs. The

man with the shears cut the ropes that fenced off the narrow bed. They put Nancy into the bed and two men held Nancy while a woman gave her a knockout shot.

Billy the Poet had disappeared.

As Nancy was going under, the woman who had given her the shot asked her how old she was.

Nancy was determined not to answer, but discovered that the drug had made her powerless not to answer. "Sixty-three," she murmured.

"How does it feel to be a virgin at sixty-three?"

Nancy heard her own answer through a velvet fog. She was amazed by the answer, wanted to protest that it couldn't possibly be hers. "Pointless," she'd said.

Moments later, she asked the woman thickly, "What was in that needle?"

"What was in the needle, honey bunch? Why, honey bunch, they call that 'truth serum.'"

The moon was down when Nancy woke up—but the night was still out there. The shades were drawn and there was candlelight. Nancy had never seen a lit candle before.

What awakened Nancy was a dream of mosquitoes and bees. Mosquitoes and bees were extinct. So were birds. But Nancy dreamed that millions of insects were swarming about her from the waist down. They didn't sting. They fanned her. Nancy was a nothinghead.

She went to sleep again. When she awoke next time, she was being led into a bathroom by three women, still with stockings over their heads. The bathroom was already filled with the steam from somebody else's bath. There were somebody else's wet footprints crisscrossing the floor and the air reeked of pine-needle perfume.

Her will and intelligence returned as she was bathed and perfumed and dressed in a white nightgown. When the women stepped back to admire her, she said to them quietly, "I may be a nothinghead now. But that doesn't mean I have to think like one or act like one."

Nobody argued with her.

Nancy was taken downstairs and out of the house. She fully expected to be sent down a manhole again. It would be the perfect setting for her violation by Billy, she was thinking—down in a sewer.

But they took her across the green cement, where the grass used to be, and then across the yellow cement, where the beach used to be, and then out onto the blue cement, where the harbor used to be. There were 26 yachts that had belonged to various Kennedys sunk up to their water lines in blue cement. It was to the most ancient of these yachts, the *Marlin,* once the property of Joseph P. Kennedy, that they delivered Nancy.

It was dawn. Because of the high-rise apartments all around the Kennedy Museum, it would be an hour before any direct sunlight would reach the microcosm under the geodesic dome.

Nancy was escorted as far as the companionway to the forward cabin of the *Marlin.* The women pantomimed that she was expected to go down the five steps alone.

Nancy froze for the moment and so did the women. And there were two actual statues in the tableau on the bridge. Standing at the wheel was a statue of Frank Wirtanen, once skipper of the *Marlin.* And next to him was his son and first mate, Carly. They weren't paying any attention to poor Nancy. They were staring out through the windshield at the blue cement.

Nancy, barefoot and wearing a thin white nightgown, descended bravely into the forward cabin, which was a pool of candlelight and pine-needle perfume. The companionway hatch was closed and locked behind her.

Nancy's emotions and the antique furnishings of the cabin were so complete that Nancy could not at first separate Billy the Poet from his surroundings, from all the mahogany and leaded glass. And then she saw him at the far end of the cabin, with his back against the door to the forward cockpit. He was wearing purple silk pajamas with a Russian collar. They were piped in red, and writhing across Billy's silken breast was a golden dragon. It was belching fire.

Anticlimactically, Billy was wearing glasses. He was holding a book.

Nancy poised herself on the next-to-the-bottom step, took a firm grip on the handholds in the companionway. She bared

her teeth, calculated that it would take ten men Billy's size to dis-
lodge her.

Between them was a great table. Nancy had expected the cabin
to be dominated by a bed, possibly in the shape of a swan, but the
Marlin was a day boat. The cabin was anything but a seraglio. It
was about as voluptuous as a lower middle-class dining room in
Akron, Ohio, around 1910.

A candle was on the table. So were an ice bucket and two
glasses and a quart of champagne. Champagne was as illegal as
heroin.

Billy took off his glasses, gave her a shy, embarrassed smile,
said, "Welcome."

"This is as far as I come."

He accepted that. "You're very beautiful there."

"And what am I supposed to say—that you're stunningly
handsome? That I feel an overwhelming desire to throw myself
into your manly arms?"

"If you wanted to make me happy, that would certainly be the
way to do it." He said that humbly.

"And what about *my* happiness?"

The question seemed to puzzle him. "Nancy—that's what this
is all about."

"What if my idea of happiness doesn't coincide with yours?"

"And what do you think my idea of happiness is?"

"I'm not going to throw myself into your arms, and I'm not
going to drink that poison, and I'm not going to budge from here
unless somebody makes me," said Nancy. "So I think your idea of
happiness is going to turn out to be eight people holding me
down on that table, while you bravely hold a cocked pistol to my
head—and do what you want. That's the way it's going to have to
be, so call your friends and get it over with!"

Which he did.

He didn't hurt her. He deflowered her with a clinical skill she
found ghastly. When it was all over, he didn't seem cocky or
proud. On the contrary, he was terribly depressed, and he said to
Nancy, "Believe me, if there'd been any other way—"

Her reply to this was a face like stone—and silent tears of
humiliation.

His helpers let down a folding bunk from the wall. It was scarcely wider than a bookshelf and hung on chains. Nancy allowed herself to be put to bed in it, and she was left alone with Billy the Poet again. Big as she was, like a double bass wedged onto that narrow shelf, she felt like a pitiful little thing. A scratchy, war-surplus blanket had been tucked in around her. It was her own idea to pull up a corner of the blanket to hide her face.

Nancy sensed from sounds what Billy was doing, which wasn't much. He was sitting at the table, sighing occasionally, sniffing occasionally, turning the pages of a book. He lit a cigar and the stink of it seeped under her blanket. Billy inhaled the cigar, then coughed and coughed and coughed.

When the coughing died down, Nancy said loathingly through the blanket, "You're so strong, so masterful, so healthy. It must be wonderful to be so manly."

Billy only sighed at this.

"I'm not a very typical nothinghead," she said. "I hated it—hated everything about it."

Billy sniffed, turned a page.

"I suppose all the other women just loved it—couldn't get enough of it."

"Nope."

She uncovered her face. "What do you mean, 'Nope'?"

"They've all been like you."

This was enough to make Nancy sit up and stare at him. "The women who helped you tonight—"

"What about them?"

"You've done to them what you did to me?"

He didn't look up from his book. "That's right."

"Then why don't they kill you instead of helping you?"

"Because they understand." And then he added mildly, "They're *grateful*."

Nancy got out of bed, came to the table, gripped the edge of the table, leaned close to him. And she said to him tautly, "I am not grateful."

"You will be."

"And what could possibly bring about that miracle?"

"Time," said Billy.

Billy closed his book, stood up. Nancy was confused by his magnetism. Somehow he was very much in charge again.

"What you've been through, Nancy," he said, "is a typical wedding night for a strait-laced girl of a hundred years ago, when everybody was a nothinghead. The groom did without helpers, because the bride wasn't customarily ready to kill him. Otherwise, the spirit of the occasion was much the same. These are the pajamas my great-great-grandfather wore on his wedding night in Niagara Falls.

"According to his diary, his bride cried all that night, and threw up twice. But, with the passage of time, she became a sexual enthusiast."

It was Nancy's turn to reply by not replying. She understood the tale. It frightened her to understand so easily that, from gruesome beginnings, sexual enthusiasm could grow and grow.

"You're a very typical nothinghead," said Billy. "If you dare to think about it now, you'll realize that you're angry because I'm such a bad lover, and a funny-looking shrimp besides. And what you can't help dreaming about from now on is a really suitable mate for a Juno like yourself.

"You'll find him, too—tall and strong and gentle. The nothinghead movement is growing by leaps and bounds."

"But—" said Nancy, and she stopped there. She looked out a porthole at the rising sun.

"But what?"

"The world is in the mess it is today because of the nothingheadedness of olden times. Don't you see?" She was pleading weakly. "The world can't afford sex anymore."

"Of course it can afford sex," said Billy. "All it can't afford anymore is reproduction."

"Then why the laws?"

"They're bad laws," said Billy. "If you go back through history, you'll find that the people who have been most eager to rule, to make the laws, to enforce the laws and to tell everybody exactly how God Almighty wants things here on Earth—those people have forgiven themselves and their friends for anything and everything. But they have been absolutely disgusted and terrified by the natural sexuality of common men and women.

"Why this is, I do not know. That is one of the many questions I wish somebody would ask the machines. I do know this: The triumph of that sort of disgust and terror is now complete. Almost every man and woman looks and feels like something the cat dragged in. The only sexual beauty that an ordinary human being can see today is in the woman who will kill him. Sex is death. There's a short and nasty equation for you: 'Sex is death. Q. E. D.'

"So you see, Nancy," said Billy, "I have spent this night, and many others like it, attempting to restore a certain amount of innocent pleasure to the world, which is poorer in pleasure than it needs to be."

Nancy sat down quietly and bowed her head.

"I'll tell you what my grandfather did on the dawn of his wedding night," said Billy.

"I don't think I want to hear it."

"It isn't violent. It's—it's meant to be tender."

"Maybe that's why I don't want to hear it."

"He read his bride a poem." Billy took the book from the table, opened it. "His diary tells which poem it was. While we aren't bride and groom, and while we may not meet again for many years, I'd like to read this poem to you, to have you know I've loved you."

"Please—no. I couldn't stand it."

"All right. I'll leave the book here, with the place marked, in case you want to read it later. It's the poem beginning:

> 'How do I love thee? Let me count the ways.
> I love thee to the depth and breadth and height
> My soul can reach, when feeling out of sight
> For the ends of Being and ideal Grace.'"

Billy put a small bottle on top of the book. "I am also leaving you these pills. If you take one a month, you will never have children. And still you'll be a nothinghead."

And he left. And they all left but Nancy.

When Nancy raised her eyes at last to the book and bottle, she saw that there was a label on the bottle. What the label said was this: WELCOME TO THE MONKEY HOUSE.

J. G. BALLARD

THE DEAD ASTRONAUT

May 1968

British writer James Graham Ballard was born in 1930 in Shanghai and spent World War II in a Japanese prisoner-of-war camp; in 1984 his memoir-novel about these years, *Empire of the Sun,* was published, and three years later the very successful film of the same title by Stephen Spielberg appeared. Much, but not all, of Ballard's other writing has been in the science fiction field, though he has always been considered somewhat more "difficult" and literary than most science fiction writers—he has claimed William Burroughs as a major influence. Ballard, in turn, has been lionized by ambitious younger writers seeking acceptance by the literary mainstream. Director David Cronenberg's film version of the disturbingly violent and sexual *Crash* (1973), which was released in 1997, quickly achieving cult status, shows an entirely different side of the writer.

Disaster, apocalypse, and devastation have always been his subjects, however. In such early novels as *The Drowned World* (1962), *The Burning World* (1964) and *The Crystal World* (1966)—which seem to claim kinship with Latin American magical realism, though they appeared before that term was in general use—his characters move through wasted, strangely morphed, landscapes in a perversely hallucinated state of melancholy. Later works such as *Crash* and *The Atrocity Exhibition* (1970) explore urban horrors, physical and psychological. His most recent novel is a fantasy set in Africa, *The Day of Creation* (1987).

"The Dead Astronaut" is actually one of Ballard's more conventional stories. It is elegant, elegaic, and shows that a good writer can use the tropes of science fiction to create a piece that is anything but a "genre tale."

CAPE **KENNEDY HAS** gone now, its gantries rising from the deserted dunes. Sand has come in across the Banana River, filling the creeks and turning the old space complex into a wilderness of swamps and broken concrete. In the summer, hunters build their blinds in the wrecked staff cars; but by early November, when Judith and I arrived, the entire area was abandoned. Beyond Cocoa Beach, where I stopped the car, the ruined motels were half hidden in the saw grass. The launching towers rose into the evening air like the rusting ciphers of some forgotten algebra of the sky.

"The perimeter fence is half a mile ahead," I said. "We'll wait here until it's dark. Do you feel better now?"

Judith was staring at an immense funnel of cerise cloud that seemed to draw the day with it below the horizon, taking the light from her faded blonde hair. The previous afternoon, in the hotel in Tampa, she had fallen ill briefly with some unspecified complaint.

"What about the money?" she asked. "They may want more, now that we're here."

"Five thousand dollars? Ample, Judith. These relic hunters are a dying breed—few people are interested in Cape Kennedy any longer. What's the matter?"

Her thin fingers were fretting at the collar of her suede jacket. "I . . . it's just that perhaps I should have worn black."

"Why? Judith, this isn't a funeral. For heaven's sake, Robert died twenty years ago. I know all he meant to us, but . . ."

Judith was staring at the debris of tires and abandoned cars, her pale eyes becalmed in her drawn face. "Philip, don't you understand, he's coming back now. Someone's got to be here. The memorial service over the radio was a horrible travesty—my God,

107

that priest would have had a shock if Robert had talked back to him. There ought to be a full-scale committee, not just you and I and these empty night clubs."

In a firmer voice, I said: "Judith, there would be a committee— *if* we told the NASA Foundation what we know. The remains would be interred in the NASA vault at Arlington, there'd be a band—even the President might be there. There's still time."

I waited for her to reply, but she was watching the gantries fade into the night sky. Fifteen years ago, when the dead astronaut orbiting the earth in his burned-out capsule had been forgotten, Judith had constituted herself a memorial committee of one. Perhaps, in a few days, when she finally held the last relics of Robert Hamilton's body in her own hands, she would come to terms with her obsession.

"Philip, over there! Is that—"

High in the western sky, between the constellations Cepheus and Cassiopeia, a point of white light moved toward us, like a lost star searching for its zodiac. Within a few minutes, it passed overhead, its faint beacon setting behind the cirrus over the sea.

"It's all right, Judith." I showed her the trajectory timetables penciled into my diary. "The relic hunters read these orbits off the sky better than any computer. They must have been watching the pathways for years."

"Who was it?"

"A Russian woman pilot—Valentina Prokrovna. She was sent up from a site near the Urals twenty-five years ago to work on a television relay system."

"Television? I hope they enjoyed the program."

This callous remark, uttered by Judith as she stepped from the car, made me realize once again her special motives for coming to Cape Kennedy. I watched the capsule of the dead woman disappear over the dark Atlantic stream, as always moved by the tragic but serene spectacle of one of these ghostly voyagers coming back after so many years from the tideways of space. All I knew of this dead Russian was her code name: Seagull. Yet, for some reason, I was glad to be there as she came down. Judith, on the other hand, felt nothing of this. During all the years she had sat in the garden in the cold evenings, too tired to bring herself to bed, she had been sustained by her concern for only one of the 12 dead astronauts orbiting the night sky.

As she waited, her back to the sea, I drove the car into the garage of an abandoned night club 50 yards from the road. From the trunk I took out two suitcases. One, a light travel case, contained clothes for Judith and myself. The other, fitted with a foil inlay, reinforcing straps and a second handle, was empty.

We set off north toward the perimeter fence, like two late visitors arriving at a resort abandoned years earlier.

It was 20 years now since the last rockets had left their launching platforms at Cape Kennedy. At the time, NASA had already moved Judith and me—I was a senior flight programmer—to the great new Planetary Space Complex in New Mexico. Shortly after our arrival, we had met one of the trainee astronauts, Robert Hamilton. After two decades, all I could remember of this overpolite but sharp-eyed young man was his albino skin, so like Judith's pale eyes and opal hair, the same cold gene that crossed them both with its arctic pallor. We had been close friends for barely six weeks. Judith's infatuation was one of those confused sexual impulses that well-brought-up young women express in their own naïve way; and as I watched them swim and play tennis together, I felt not so much resentful as concerned to sustain the whole passing illusion for her.

A year later, Robert Hamilton was dead. He had returned to Cape Kennedy for the last military flights before the launching grounds were closed. Three hours after lift-off, a freak meteorite collision ruptured his oxygen support system. He had lived on in his suit for another five hours. Although calm at first, his last radio transmissions were an incoherent babble Judith and I had never been allowed to hear.

A dozen astronauts had died in orbital accidents, their capsules left to revolve through the night sky like the stars of a new constellation; and at first, Judith had shown little response. Later, after her miscarriage, the figure of this dead astronaut circling the sky above us re-emerged in her mind as an obsession with time. For hours, she would stare at the bedroom clock, as if waiting for something to happen.

Five years later, after I resigned from NASA, we made our first trip to Cape Kennedy. A few military units still guarded the derelict gantries, but already the former launching site was being used as a satellite graveyard. As the dead capsules lost orbital velocity, they homed onto the master radio beacon. As well as the American vehicles, Russian and French satellites in the joint Euro-American space projects were brought down here, the burned-out hulks of the capsules exploding across the cracked concrete.

Already, too, the relic hunters were at Cape Kennedy, scouring the burning saw grass for instrument panels and flying suits and—most valuable of all—the mummified corpses of the dead astronauts.

These blackened fragments of collar-bone and shin, kneecap and rib, were the unique relics of the space age, as treasured as the saintly bones of medieval shrines. After the first fatal accidents in space, public outcry demanded that these orbiting biers be brought down to earth. Unfortunately, when a returning moon rocket crashed into the Kalahari Desert aboriginal tribesmen broke into the vehicle. Believing the crew to be dead gods they cut off the eight hands and vanished into the bush. It had taken two years to track them down. From then on, the capsules were left in orbit to burn out on re-entry.

Whatever remains survived the crash landings in the satellite graveyard were scavenged by the relic hunters of Cape Kennedy. This band of nomads had lived for years in the wrecked cars and motels stealing their icons under the feet of the wardens who patrolled the concrete decks. In early October, when a former NASA colleague told me that Robert Hamilton's satellite was becoming unstable, I drove down to Tampa and began to inquire about the purchase price of Robert's mortal remains. Five thousand dollars was a small price to pay for laying his ghost to rest in Judith's mind.

Eight hundred yards from the road we crossed the perimeter fence. Crushed by the dunes, long sections of the 20-foot-high palisade had collapsed, the sawgrass growing through the steel metal. Below us, the boundary road passed derelict guardhouse and divided into two paved tracks. As we waited at the rendezvous, the head lamps of the wardens' half-tracks flared across the gantries near the beach.

Five minutes later, a small dark-face man climbed from the rear seat of a car buried in the sand 50 yards away. Head down, he scuttled over to us.

"Mr. and Mrs. Groves?" After a pause to peer into our faces, he introduced himself tersely: "Quinton. Sam Quinton."

As he shook hands, his claw fingers examined the bones of my wrist and forearm. His sharp nose made circles in the air. He had the eyes of a nervous bird, forever searching the dunes for grass. An Army webbing belt hung around his patched black denims. He moved his hands restlessly in the air as if conducting a chamber ensemble hidden behind the sand hills, and I noticed his badly scarred palms. Huge weals formed pale stars in the darkness.

For a moment, he seemed disappointed by us, almost reluctant to move. Then he set off at a brisk pace across dunes, now and then leaving us to wander about helplessly. Half an hour later when we entered a shallow basin near farm of alkali-settling beds, Judith and I were exhausted, dragging the suit over the broken tires and barbed wire.

A group of cabins had been dismantled from their original sites along the beach and re-erected in the basin. Isolated rooms tilted on the sloping sand mantelpieces and flowered paper decorated the outer walls.

The basin was full of salvaged space material: sections of capsules, heat shields, antennas and parachute canisters. Near the dented hull of a weather satellite, two sallow-faced men in sheepskin jackets sat on a car seat. The older wore a frayed Air Force cap over his eyes. With his scarred hands, he was polishing the steel visor of a space helmet. The other, a young man with a faint beard hiding his mouth, watched us approach with the detached and neutral gaze of an undertaker.

We entered the largest of the cabins, two rooms taken off the rear of a beach-house. Quinton lit a paraffin lamp. He pointed around the dingy interior. "You'll be . . . comfortable," he said without conviction. As Judith stared at him with unconcealed distaste, he added pointedly: "We don't get many visitors."

I put the suitcases on the metal bed. Judith walked into the kitchen and Quinton began to open the empty case.

"It's in here?"

I took the two packets of $100 bills from my jacket. When I

had handed them to him, I said: "The suitcase is for the . . . remains. Is it big enough?"

Quinton peered at me through the ruby light, as if baffled by our presence there. "You could have spared yourself the trouble. They've been up there a long time. Mr. Groves. After the impact" —for some reason, he cast a lewd eye in Judith's direction—"there might be enough for a chess set."

When he had gone, I went into the kitchen. Judith stood by the stove, hands on a carton of canned food. She was staring through the window at the metal salvage, refuse of the sky that still carried Robert Hamilton in its rusty centrifuge. For a moment, I had the feeling that the entire landscape of the earth was covered with rubbish and that here at Cape Kennedy, we had found its source.

I held her shoulders. "Judith, is there any point in this? Why don't we go back to Tampa? I could drive here in ten days' time when it's all over—"

She turned from me, her hands rubbing the suede where I had marked it. "Philip, I want to be here—no matter how unpleasant. Can't you understand?"

At midnight, when I finished making a small meal for us, she was standing on the concrete wall of the settling tank. The three relic hunters sitting on their car seats watched her without moving, scarred hands like flames in the darkness.

At three o'clock that morning, as we lay awake on the narrow bed, Valentina Prokrovna came down from the sky. Enthroned on a bier of burning aluminum 300 yards wide, she soared past on her final orbit. When I went out into the night air, the relic hunters had gone. From the rim of the settling tank, I watched them race away among the dunes, leaping like hares over the tires and wire.

I went back to the cabin. "Judith, she's coming down. Do you want to watch?"

Her blonde hair tied within a white towel, Judith lay on the bed, staring at the cracked plasterboard ceiling. Shortly after four o'clock, as I sat beside her, a phosphorescent light filled the hollow. There was the distant sound of explosions, muffled by the high wall of the dunes. Lights flared, followed by the noise of engines and sirens.

At dawn the relic hunters returned, scarred hands wrapped in makeshift bandages, dragging their booty with them.

After this melancholy rehearsal, Judith entered a period of sudden and unexpected activity. As if preparing the cabin for some visitor, she rehung the curtains and swept out the two rooms with meticulous care, even bringing herself to ask Quinton for a bottle of cleaner. For hours she sat at the dressing table, brushing and shaping her hair, trying out first one style and then another. I watched her feel the hollows of her cheeks, searching for the contours of a face that had vanished 20 years ago. As she spoke about Robert Hamilton, she almost seemed worried that she would appear old to him. At other times, she referred to Robert as if he were a child, the son she and I had never been able to conceive since her miscarriage. These different roles followed one another like scenes in some private psychodrama. However, without knowing it, for years Judith and I had used Robert Hamilton for our own reasons. Waiting for him to land, and well aware that after this Judith would have no one to turn to except myself, I said nothing.

Meanwhile, the relic hunters worked on the fragments of Valentina Prokrovna's capsule: the blistered heat shield, the chassis of the radiotelemetry unit and several cans of film that recorded her collision and act of death (these, if still intact, would fetch the highest prices, films of horrific and dreamlike violence played in the underground cinemas of Los Angeles, London and Moscow). Passing the next cabin. I saw a tattered silver space suit spread-eagled on two automobile seats. Quinton and the relic hunters knelt beside it, their arms deep inside the legs and sleeves, gazing at me with the rapt and sensitive eyes of jewelers.

An hour before dawn, I was awakened by the sound of engines along the beach. In the darkness, the three relic hunters crouched by the settling tank, their pinched faces lit by the head lamps. A long convoy of trucks and half-tracks was moving into the launching ground. Soldiers jumped down from the tail-boards, unloading tents and supplies.

"What are they doing?" I asked Quinton. "Are they looking for us?"

The old man cupped a scarred hand over his eyes. "It's the

Army," he said uncertainly. "Maneuvers, maybe. They haven't been here before like this."

"What about Hamilton?" I gripped his bony arm. "Are you sure—"

He pushed me away with a show of nervous temper. "We'll get him first. Don't worry, he'll be coming sooner than they think."

Two nights later, as Quinton prophesied, Robert Hamilton began his final descent. From the dunes near the settling tanks, we watched him emerge from the stars on his last run. Reflected in the windows of the buried cars, a thousand images of the capsule flared in the saw grass around us. Behind the satellite, a wide fan of silver spray opened in a phantom wake.

In the Army encampment by the gantries, there was a surge of activity. A blaze of head lamps crossed the concrete lanes. Since the arrival of these military units, it had become plain to me, if not to Quinton, that far from being on maneuvers, they were preparing for the landing of Robert Hamilton's capsule. A dozen half-tracks had been churning around the dunes, setting fire to the abandoned cabins and crushing the old car bodies. Platoons of soldiers were repairing the perimeter fence and replacing the sections of metaled road that the relic hunters had dismantled.

Shortly after midnight, at an elevation of 42 degrees in the northwest, between Lyra and Hercules, Robert Hamilton appeared for the last time. As Judith stood up and shouted into the night air, an immense blade of light cleft the sky. The expanding corona sped toward us like a gigantic signal flare, illuminating every fragment of the landscape.

"Mrs. Groves!" Quinton darted after Judith and pulled her down into the grass as she ran toward the approaching satellite. Three hundred yards away, the silhouette of a half-track stood out on an isolated dune, its feeble spotlights drowned by the glare.

With a low metallic sigh, the burning capsule of the dead astronaut soared over our heads, the vaporizing metal pouring from its hull. A few seconds later, as I shielded my eyes, an explosion of detonating sand rose from the ground behind me. A curtain of dust lifted into the darkening air like a vast specter of powdered bone. The sounds of the impact rolled across the dunes. Near the launching gantries, fires flickered where fragments of the capsule had landed. A pall of phosphorescing gas hung in the air, particles within it beading and winking.

Judith had gone, running after the relic hunters through the swerving spotlights. When I caught up with them, the last fires of the explosion were dying among the gantries. The capsule had landed near the old Atlas launching pads, forming a shallow crater 50 yards in diameter. The slopes were scattered with glowing particles, sparkling like fading eyes. Judith ran distraughtly up and down, searching the fragments of smoldering metal.

Someone struck my shoulder. Quinton and his men, hot ash on their scarred hands, ran past like a troop of madmen, eyes wild in the crazed night. As we darted away through the flaring spotlights, I looked back at the beach. The gantries were enveloped in a pale-silver sheen that hovered there and then moved away like a dying wraith over the sea.

At dawn, as the engines growled among the dunes, we collected the last remains of Robert Hamilton. The old man came into our cabin. As Judith watched from the kitchen, drying her hands on a towel, he gave me a cardboard shoe box.

I held the box in my hands. "Is this all you could get?"

"It's all there was. Look at them, if you want."

"That's all right. We'll be leaving in half an hour."

He shook his head. "Not now. They're all around. If you move, they'll find us."

He waited for me to open the shoe box, then grimaced and went out into the pale light.

We stayed for another four days, as the Army patrols searched the surrounding dunes. Day and night, the half-tracks lumbered among the wrecked cars and cabins. Once, as I watched with Quinton from a fallen water tower, a half-track and two Jeeps came within 400 yards of the basin, held back only by the stench from the settling beds and the cracked concrete causeways.

During this time, Judith sat in the cabin, the shoe box on her lap. She said nothing to me, as if she had lost all interest in me and the salvage-filled hollow at Cape Kennedy. Mechanically, she combed her hair, making and remaking her face.

On the second day, I came in after helping Quinton bury the

cabins to their windows in the sand. Judith was standing by the table.

The shoe box was open. In the center of the table lay a pile of charred sticks, as if she had tried to light a small fire. Then I realized what was there. As she stirred the ash with her fingers, gray flakes fell from the joints, revealing the bony points of a clutch of ribs, a right hand and shoulder blade.

She looked at me with puzzled eyes. "They're black," she said.

Holding her in my arms, I lay with her on the bed. A loudspeaker reverberated among the dunes, fragments of the amplified commands drumming at the panes.

When they moved away, Judith said: "We can go now."

"In a little while, when it's clear. What about these?"

"Bury them. Anywhere, it doesn't matter." She seemed calm at last, giving me a brief smile, as if to agree that this grim charade was at last over.

Yet, when I had packed the bones into the shoe box, scraping up Robert Hamilton's ash with a dessertspoon, she kept it with her, carrying it into the kitchen while she prepared our meals.

It was on the third day that we fell ill.

After a long, noise-filled night, I found Judith sitting in front of the mirror, combing thick clumps of hair from her scalp. Her mouth was open, as if her lips were stained with acid. As she dusted the loose hair from her lap, I was struck by the leprous whiteness of her face.

Standing up with an effort, I walked listlessly into the kitchen and stared at the saucepan of cold coffee. A sense of indefinable exhaustion had come over me, as if the bones in my body had softened and lost their rigidity. On the lapels of my jacket, loose hair lay like spinning waste.

"Philip . . ." Judith swayed toward me. "Do you feel—What is it?"

"The water." I poured the coffee into the sink and massaged my throat. "It must be fouled."

"Can we leave?" She put a hand up to her forehead. Her brittle nails brought down a handful of frayed ash hair. "Philip, for God's sake—I'm losing all my hair!"

Neither of us was able to eat. After forcing myself through a few slices of cold meat, I went out and vomited behind the cabin.

Quinton and his men were crouched by the wall of the settling tank. As I walked toward them, steadying myself against the hull of the weather satellite, Quinton came down. When I told him that the water supplies were contaminated, he stared at me with his hard bird's eyes.

Half an hour later, they were gone.

The next day, our last there, we were worse. Judith lay on the bed, shivering in her jacket, the shoe box held in one hand. I spent hours searching for fresh water in the cabins. Exhausted, I could barely cross the sandy basin. The Army patrols were closer. By now, I could hear the hard gear changes of the half-tracks. The sounds from the loud-speakers drummed like fists on my head.

Then, as I looked down at Judith from the cabin doorway, a few words stuck for a moment in my mind.

"... *contaminated area ... evacuate ... radioactive ...*"

I walked forward and pulled the box from Judith's hands.

"Philip . . ." She looked up at me weakly. "Give it back to me."

Her face was a puffy mask. On her wrists, white flecks were forming. Her left hand reached toward me like the claw of a cadaver.

I shook the box with blunted anger. The bones rattled inside. "For God's sake, it's *this!* Don't you see—why we're ill?"

"Philip—where are the others? The old man. Get them to help you."

"They've gone. They went yesterday, I told you." I let the box fall onto the table. The lid broke off, spilling the ribs tied together like a bundle of firewood. "Quinton knew what was happening—why the Army is here. They're trying to warn us."

"What do you mean?" Judith sat up, the focus of her eyes sustained only by a continuous effort. "Don't let them take Robert. Bury him here somewhere. We'll come back later."

"Judith!" I bent over the bed and shouted hoarsely at her. "Don't you realize—there was a *bomb* on board! Robert Hamilton was carrying an atomic weapon!" I pulled back the curtains from the window. "My God, what a joke. For twenty years, I put up with him because I couldn't ever be really sure. . . ."

"Philip . . ."

"Don't worry, I used him—thinking about him was the only thing that kept us going. And all the time, he was waiting up there to pay us back!"

There was a rumble of exhaust outside. A half-track with red crosses on its doors and hood had reached the edge of the basin. Two men in vinyl suits jumped down, counters raised in front of them.

"Judith, before we go, tell me . . . I never asked you—"

Judith was sitting up, touching the hair on her pillow. One half of her scalp was almost bald. She stared at her weak hands with their silvering skin. On her face was an expression I had never seen before, the dumb anger of betrayal.

As she looked at me, and at the bones scattered across the table, I knew my answer.

FREDERIK POHL

THE SCHEMATIC MAN

January 1969

Of the several computer stories in this volume, this is the earliest. In just a few pages it tells you a lot about computers, to the point where many of you will nod yeah, yeah. But in 1969, hardly any civilian had actually seen a computer. We knew that the Pentagon had them, and NASA. We knew they were big (room-sized), and smart and, like HAL in *2001,* spooky. Frederik Pohl, one of science fiction's senior figures, and a science buff as well, knew a great deal more than that. Born in 1919 and now resident in Illinois, Pohl has been an influential editor of magazines, anthologies, and books, a literary agent, president of SFWA, and a busy, prolific, and respected writer as well, indeed a SFWA Grandmaster. His most famous novel is the 1953 collaboration with C. M. Kornbluth, *The Space Merchants,* and he has collaborated with several other writers over the years. Many of his novels and stories during the past couple of decades have been part of the galaxy-exploring Heechee series, beginning with the multiple-award winning *Gateway* in 1977.

KNOW I'M NOT really a funny man, but I don't like other people to know it. I do what other people without much sense of humor do: I tell jokes. If we're sitting next to each other at a faculty senate and I want to introduce myself, I probably say: "Bederkind is my name, and computers are my game."

Nobody laughs much. Like all my jokes, it needs to be explained. The joking part is that it was through game theory that I first became interested in computers and the making of mathematical models. Sometimes when I'm explaining it, I say there that the mathematical ones are the only models I've ever had a chance to make. That gets a smile, anyway. I've figured out why: Even if you don't really get much out of the play on words, you can tell it's got something to do with sex, and we all reflexively smile when anybody says anything sexy.

I ought to tell you what a mathematical model is, right? All right. It's simple. It's a kind of picture of something made out of numbers. You use it because it's easier to make numbers move than to make real things move.

Suppose I want to know what the planet Mars is going to do over the next few years. I take everything I know about Mars and I turn it into numbers—a number for its speed in orbit, another number for how much it weighs, another number for how many miles it is in diameter, another number to express how strongly the Sun pulls it toward it and all that. Then I tell the computer that's all it needs to know about Mars, and I go on to tell it all the same sorts of numbers about the Earth, about Venus, Jupiter, the Sun itself—about all the other chunks of matter floating around in the neighborhood that I think are likely to make any difference to Mars. I then teach the computer some simple rules about how the set of numbers that represents Jupiter, say, affects the numbers that represent Mars: the law of inverse squares, some rules of celestial mechanics, a few relativistic corrections . . . well, actually, there are a lot of things it needs to know. But not more than I can tell it.

When I have done all this—not exactly in English but in a kind of a language that it knows how to handle—the computer has a mathematical model of Mars stored inside it. It will then whirl its mathematical Mars through mathematical space for as many orbits as I like. I say to it, "1997 June 18 2400 GMT," and it . . . it . . . well, I guess the word for it is, it *imagines* where Mars will be, relative to my backyard Questar, at midnight Greenwich time on the 18th of June, 1997, and tells me which way to point.

It isn't real Mars that it plays with. It's a mathematical model, you see. But for the purposes of knowing where to point my little telescope, it does everything that "real Mars" would do for me, only much faster. I don't have to wait for 1997; I can find out in five minutes.

It isn't only planets that can carry on a mathematical metalife in the memory banks of a computer. Take my friend Schmuel. He has a joke, too, and his joke is that he makes 20 babies a day in his computer. What he means by that is that, after six years of trying, he finally succeeded in writing down the numbers that describe the development of a human baby in its mother's uterus, all the way from conception to birth. The point of that is that then it was comparatively easy to write down the numbers for a lot of the things that happen to babies before they're born. Momma has high blood pressure. Momma smokes three packs a day. Momma catches scarlet fever or a kick in the belly. Momma keeps making it with Poppa every night until they wheel her into the delivery room. And so on. And the point of *that* is that this way, Schmuel can see some of the things that go wrong and make some babies get born retarded, or blind, or with retrolental fibroplasia or an inability to drink cow's milk. It's easier than sacrificing a lot of pregnant women and cutting them open to see.

OK, you don't want to hear any more about mathematical models, because what kicks are there in mathematical models for you? I'm glad you asked. Consider a for instance. For instance, suppose last night you were watching the *Late, Late* and you saw Carole Lombard, or maybe Marilyn Monroe with that dinky little skirt blowing up over those pretty thighs. I assume you know that these ladies are dead. I also assume that your glands responded to those cathode-tube flickers as though they were alive. And so you do get some kicks from mathematical models, because each of those great girls, in each of their poses and smiles, was nothing but a number of some thousands of digits, expressed as a spot of light on a phosphor tube. With some added numbers to express the frequency patterns of their voices. Nothing else.

And the point of *that* (how often I use that phrase!) is that a mathematical model not only represents the real thing but sometimes it's as good as the real thing. No, honestly. I mean, do you really believe that if it had been Marilyn or Carole in the flesh you were looking at, across a row of footlights, say, that you could have taken away any more of them than you gleaned from the shower of electrons that made the phosphors display their pictures?

I did watch Marilyn on the *Late, Late* one night. And I thought those thoughts; and so I spent the next week preparing an application to a foundation for money; and when the grant came through, I took a sabbatical and began turning myself into a mathematical model. It isn't really that hard. Kookie, yes. But not hard.

I don't want to explain what programs like FORTRAN and SIMSCRIPT and SIR are, so I will only say what we all say: They are languages by which people can communicate with machines. Sort of. I had to learn to speak FORTRAN well enough to tell the machine all about myself. It took five graduate students and ten months to write the program that made that possible, but that's not much. It took more than that to teach a computer to shoot pool. After that, it was just a matter of storing myself in the machine.

That's the part that Schmuel told me was kookie. Like everybody with enough seniority in my department. I have a remote-access computer console in my—well, I called it my "playroom." I did have a party there, once, right after I bought the house, when I still thought I was going to get married. Schmuel caught me one night, walking in the door and down the stairs and finding me methodically typing out my medical history from the ages of four to fourteen. "Jerk," he said, "what makes you think you deserve to be embalmed in a 7094?"

I said, "Make some coffee and leave me alone till I finish. Listen. Can I use your program on the sequelae of mumps?"

"Paranoid psychosis," he said. "It comes on about the age of forty-two." But he coded the console for me and thus gave me access to his programs. I finished and said:

"Thanks for the program, but you make rotten coffee."

"You make rotten jokes. You really think it's going to be *you* in that program. Admit!"

By then, I had most of the basic physiological and environmental stuff on the tapes and I was feeling good. "What's 'me'?" I asked. "If it talks like me, and thinks like me, and remembers what I remember, and does what I would do—who is it? President Eisenhower?"

"Eisenhower was years ago, jerk," he said.

"Turing's question, Schmuel," I said. "If I'm in one room with a teletype. And the computer's in another room with a teletype, programmed to model me. And you're in a third room, connected to both teletypes, and you have a conversation with both of us, and you can't tell which is me and which is the machine—then how do you describe the difference? *Is* there a difference?"

He said, "The difference, Josiah, is I can touch you. And smell you. If I was crazy enough, I could kiss you. You. Not the model."

"You could," I said, "if you were a model, too, and were in the machine with me." And I joked with him (Look! It solves the population problem, put everybody in the machine. And, suppose I get cancer. Flesh-me dies. Mathematical-model-me just rewrites its program.), but he was really worried. He really did think I was going crazy, but I perceived that his reasons were not because of the nature of the problem but because of what he fancied was my own attitude toward it, and I made up my mind to be careful of what I said to Schmuel.

So I went on playing Turing's game, trying to make the computer's responses indistinguishable from my own. I instructed it in what a toothache felt like and what I remembered of sex. I taught it memory links between people and phone numbers, and all the state capitals I had won a prize for knowing when I was ten. I trained it to spell "rhythm" wrong, as I had always mis-spelled it, and to say "place" instead of "put" in conversation, as I have always done because of the slight speech impediment that carried over from my adolescence. I played that game; and by God, I won it.

But I don't know for sure what I lost in exchange.

I know I lost something.

I began by losing parts of my memory. When my cousin Alvin from Cleveland phoned me on my birthday, I couldn't remember who he was for a minute. (The week before, I had told the computer all about my summers with Alvin's family, including the afternoon when we both lost our virginity to the same girl, under the bridge by my uncle's farm.) I had to write down Schmuel's phone number, and my secretary's, and carry them around in my pocket.

As the work progressed, I lost more. I looked up at the sky one night and saw three bright stars in a line overhead. It scared me, because I didn't know what they were until I got home and took out my sky charts. Yet Orion was my first and easiest constella-tion. And when I looked at the telescope I had made. I could not remember how I had figured the mirror.

Schmuel kept warning me about overwork. I really was work-ing a lot, 15 hours a day and more. But it didn't feel like overwork. It felt as though I were losing pieces of myself. I was not merely teaching the computer to be me but putting pieces of me into the computer. I hated that, and it shook me enough to make me take the whole of Christmas week off. I went to Miami.

But when I got back to work. I couldn't remember how to touch-type on the console anymore and was reduced to pecking out information for the computer a letter at a time. I felt as though I were moving from one place to another in installments, and not enough of me had arrived yet to be a quorum, but what was still waiting to go had important parts missing. And yet I con-tinued to pour myself into the magnetic memory cores: the lie I told my draft board in 1946, the limerick I made up about my first wife after the divorce, what Margaret wrote when she told me she wouldn't marry me.

There was plenty of room in the storage banks for all of it. The computer could hold all my brain had held, especially with the program my five graduate students and I had written. I had been worried about that, at first.

But in the event I did not run out of room. What I ran out of was myself. I remember feeling sort of opaque and stunned and empty; and that is all I remember until now.

Whenever "now" is.

I had another friend once, and he cracked up while working on telemetry studies for one of the Mariner programs. I remember going to see him in the hospital, and him telling me, in his slow, unworried, coked-up voice, what they had done for him. Or to him. Electroshock. Hydrotherapy.

What worries me is that that is at least a reasonable working hypothesis to describe what is happening to me now.

I remember, or think I remember, a sharp electric jolt. I feel, or think I feel, a chilling flow around me.

What does it mean? I wish I were sure. I'm willing to concede that it might mean that overwork did me in and now I, too, am at Restful Retreat, being studied by the psychiatrists and changed by the nurses' aides. Willing to concede it? Dear God, I *pray* for it. I pray that that electricity was just shock therapy and not something else. I pray that the flow I feel is water sluicing around my sodden sheets and not a flux of electrons in transistor modules. I don't fear the thought of being insane; I fear the alternative.

I do not *believe* the alternative. But I fear it all the same. I can't believe that all that's left of me—my id, my ucs, my *me*—is nothing but a mathematical model stored inside the banks of the 7094. But if I am! If I am, dear God, what will happen when—and how can I wait until—somebody turns me on?

ROBERT SHECKLEY

CAN YOU FEEL ANYTHING WHEN I DO THIS?

August 1969

Born in New York in 1928, and now living in Portland, Oregon, Robert Sheckley is perhaps best known, outside science fiction, as the originator of *The Tenth Victim,* which started as a short story, "The Seventh Victim," then became a 1965 movie with the statuesque Ursula Andress hunting down Marcello Mastroianni in a deadly futuristic game, then a novel (1966) with several sequels. His novels *The Status Civilization,* set on a prison planet, and *Dimension of Miracles* have been reprinted frequently. But it is as a master of mordant short fiction that readers mainly celebrate Sheckley. Most of the many stories he wrote for *Playboy* during the 1960s and 1970s would be best categorized as satiric fables, not science fiction. They are absurd, hilarious and urbane tales, but—though Sheckley is justly honored in the field—it was not easy to find a story for this anthology that qualified as "real" science fiction. "Can You Feel Anything When I Do This?" makes the cut, however.

IT WAS A middle-class apartment in Forest Hills with all the standard stuff: slash-pine couch by Lady Yogina, strobe reading light over a big Uneasy Chair designed by Sri Somethingorother, bounce-sound projector playing *Blood-Stream Patterns* by Drs. Molidoff and Yuli. There was also the usual microbiotic-food console, set now at Fat Black Andy's Soul-Food Composition Number Three—hog's jowls and black-eyed peas. And there was a Murphy Bed of Nails, the Beautyrest Expert Ascetic model with 2000 chrome-plated self-sharpening number-four nails. In a sentence, the whole place was furnished in a pathetic attempt at last year's *moderne-spirituel* fashion.

Inside this apartment, all alone and aching of *anomie,* was a semi-young housewife, Melisande Durr, who had just stepped out of the voluptuarium, the largest room in the home, with its king-size commode and its sadly ironic bronze lingam and yoni on the wall.

She was a *pretty* girl, with really good legs, sweet hips, pretty stand-up breasts, long soft shiny hair, delicate little face. Nice, very nice. A girl that any man would like to lock onto. Once, Maybe even twice. But definitely not as a regular thing.

Why not? Well, to give a recent example:

"Hey, Sandy, honey, was anything wrong?"

"No. Frank, it was marvelous; what made you think anything was wrong?"

"Well, I guess it was the way you were staring up with a funny look on your face, almost frowning . . ."

"Was I really? Oh, yes, I remember; I was trying to decide whether to buy one of those cute trompe l'oeil things that they just got in at Saks, to put on the ceiling."

"You were thinking about *that? Then?*"

"Oh, Frank, you mustn't worry, it was *great,* Frank, *you* were great, I loved it, and I really mean that."

Frank was Melisande's husband. He plays no part in this story and very little part in her life.

So there she was, standing in her OK apartment, all beautiful outside and unborn inside, a lovely potential who had never been potentiated, a genuine U.S. untouchable . . . when the doorbell rang.

Melisande looked startled, then uncertain. She waited. The doorbell rang again. She thought: *Someone must have the wrong apartment.*

Nevertheless, she walked over, set the Door-Gard Entrance Obliterator to demolish any rapist or burglar or wise guy who might try to push his way in, then opened the door a crack and asked, "Who is there, please?"

A man's voice replied, "Acme Delivery Service, got a mumble here for Missus Mumble-mumble."

"I can't understand, you'll have to speak up."

"Acme Delivery, got a mumble for mumble-mumble and I can't stand here all mumble."

"I cannot understand you!"

"I SAID I GOT A PACKAGE HERE FOR MISSUS MELISANDE DURR, DAMN IT!"

She opened the door all the way. Outside, there was a deliveryman with a big crate, almost as big as he was, say, five feet, nine inches tall. It had her name and address on it. She signed for it, as the deliveryman pushed it inside the door and left, still mumbling. Melisande stood in her living room and looked at the crate.

She thought: Who would send me a gift out of the blue for no reason at all? Not Frank, not Harry, not Aunt Emmie or Ellie, not Mom, not Dad (of course not, silly, he's five years dead, poor son of a bitch) or anyone I can think of. But maybe it's not a gift; it could be a mean hoax, or a bomb intended for somebody else and sent wrong (or meant for me and sent *right*) or just a simple mistake.

She read the various labels on the outside of the crate. The article had been sent from Stern's department store. Melisande bent down and pulled out the cotter pin (cracking the tip of a fingernail) that immobilized the Saftee-Lok, removed that and pushed the lever to OPEN.

The crate blossomed like a flower, opening into 12 equal segments, each of which began to fold back on itself.

"Wow," Melisande said.

The crate opened to its fullest extent and the folded segments curled inward and consumed themselves, leaving a double handful of cold fine gray ash.

"They still haven't licked that ash problem," Melisande muttered. "However."

She looked with curiosity at the object that had resided within the crate. At first glance, it was a cylinder of metal painted orange and red. A machine? Yes, definitely a machine; air vents in the base for its motor, four rubber-clad wheels, and various attachments—longitudinal extensors, prehensile extractors, all sorts of things. And there were connecting points to allow a variety of mixed-function operations, and a standard house-type plug at the end of a spring-loaded reel-fed power line, with a plaque beneath it that read: PLUG INTO ANY 110-115-VOLT WALL OUTLET.

Melisande's face tightened in anger, "It's a goddamned *vacuum cleaner!* For God's sake, I've already *got* a vacuum cleaner. Who in hell would send me another?"

She paced up and down the room, bright legs flashing, tension evident in her heart-shaped face. "I mean," she said, "I was expecting that after all my *expecting,* I'd get something pretty and nice, or at least *fun,* maybe even interesting. Like—oh God I don't even know like what unless maybe an orange-and-red pinball machine, a big one, big enough so I could get inside all curled up and someone would start the game and I'd go bumping along all the bumpers while the lights flashed and bells rang and I'd bump a thousand goddamned bumpers and when I finally rolled down to the end I'd God yes that pinball machine would register a TOP MILLION MILLION and that's what I'd really like!"

So—the entire unspeakable fantasy was out in the open at last. And how bleak and remote it felt, yet still shameful and desirable.

"But anyhow," she said, canceling the previous image and folding, spindling, and mutilating it for good measure, "anyhow, what I get is a lousy goddamned vacuum cleaner when I already have one less than three years old so who needs this one and who sent me the damned thing anyway and why?"

She looked to see if there was a card. No card. Not a clue. And then she thought, Sandy, you are really a goop! Of course, there's no card; the machine has doubtless been programmed to recite some message or other.

She was interested now, in a mild, something-to-do kind of way. She unreeled the power line and plugged it into a wall outlet.

Click! A green light flashed ON, a blue light glittered ALL SYSTEMS GO, a motor purred, hidden servos made tapping noises; and then the mechanopathic regulator registered BALANCE and a gentle pink light beamed a steady ALL MODES READY.

"All right," Melisande said. "Who sent you?"

Snap crackle pop. Experimental rumble from the thoracic voice box. Then the voice: "I am Rom, number 121376 of GE's new Q-series Home-rizers. The following is a paid commercial announcement: Ahem, General Electric is proud to present the latest and most triumphant development of our Total Finger-Tip Control of Every Aspect of the Home for Better Living concept. I, Rom, am the latest and finest model in the GE Omnicleaner series. I am the Home-rizer Extraordinary, factory programmed like all Home-rizers for fast, unobtrusive multitotalfunction, but additionally, I am designed for easy, instant reprogramming to suit your home's individual needs. My abilities are many. I—"

"Can we skip this?" Melisande asked. "That's what my other vacuum cleaner said."

"—Will remove all dust and grime from all surfaces," the Rom went on, wash dishes and pots and pans, exterminate cockroaches and rodents, dry-clean and hand-launder, sew buttons, build shelves, paint walls, cook, clean rugs, and dispose of all garbage and trash including my own modest waste products. And this is to mention but a few of my functions."

"Yes, yes, I know," Melisande said. "All vacuum cleaners do that."

"I know," said the Rom, "but I had to deliver my paid commercial announcement."

"Consider it delivered. Who sent you?"

"The sender prefers not to reveal his name at this time," the Rom replied.

"Oh—come on and tell me!"

"Not at this time," the Rom replied staunchly. "Shall I vacuum the rug?"

Melisande shook her head. "The other vacuum cleaner did it this morning."

"Scrub the walls? Rub the halls?"

"No reason for it, everything has been done, everything is absolutely and spotlessly clean."

"Well," the Rom said, "at least I can remove that stain."

"What stain?"

"On the arm of your blouse, just above the elbow."

Melisande looked. "Ooh, I must have done that when I buttered the toast this morning. I knew I should have let the toaster do it."

"Stain removal is rather a specialty of mine," the Rom said. He extruded a number-two padded gripper, with which he gripped her elbow, and then extruded a metal arm terminating in a moistened gray pad. With this pad, he stroked the stain.

"You're making it worse!"

"Only apparently, while I line up the molecules for invisible eradication. All ready now; watch."

He continued to stroke. The spot faded, then disappeared utterly. Melisande's arm tingled.

"Gee," she said, "that's pretty good."

"I do it well," the Rom stated flatly. "But tell me, were you aware that you are maintaining a tension factor of 78.3 in your upper back and shoulder muscles?"

"Huh? Are you some kind of doctor?"

"Obviously not. But I am a fully qualified masseur, and therefore able to take direct tonus readings. 78.3 is—unusual." The Rom hesitated, then said, "It's only eight points below the intermittent-spasm level. That much continuous background tension is capable of reflection to the stomach nerves, resulting in what we call a parasympathetic ulceration."

"That sounds—bad," Melisande said.

"Well, it's admittedly not—good," the Rom replied. "Background tension is an insidious underminer of health, especially when it originates along the neck vertebrae and the upper spine."

"Here?" Melisande asked, touching the back of her neck.

"More typically *here*," the Rom said, reaching out with a spring-steel rubberclad dermal resonator and palpating an area 12 centimeters lower than the spot she had indicated.

"Hmmm," said Melisande, in a quizzical, uncommitted manner.

"And *here* is another typical locus," the Rom said, extending a second extensor.

"That tickles," Melisande told him.

"Only at first. I must also mention *this* situs as characteristically troublesome. And this one." A third (and possibly a fourth and fifth) extensor moved to the indicated areas.

"Well . . . That really is nice," Melisande said as the deep-set trapezius muscles of her slender spine moved smoothly beneath the skillful padded prodding of the Rom.

"It has recognized therapeutic effects," the Rom told her. "And your musculature is responding well; I can feel a slackening of tonus already."

"I can feel it, too. But you know, I've just realized I have this funny bunched-up knot of muscle at the nape of my neck."

"I was coming to that. The spine-neck juncture is recognized as a primary radiation zone for a variety of diffuse tensions. But we prefer to attack it indirectly, routing our cancellation inputs through secondary loci. Like this. And now I think—"

"Yes, yes, good . . . Gee, I never realized I was *tied up* like that before. I mean, it's like having a nest of *live snakes* under your skin, without having known."

"That's what background tension is like," the Rom said. "Insidious and wasteful, difficult to perceive, and more dangerous than an atypical ulnar thrombosis . . . Yes, now we have achieved a qualitative loosening of the major spinal junctions of the upper back, and we can move on like this."

"Huh," said Melisande, "isn't that sort of—"

"It is definitely *indicated*," the Rom said quickly. "Can you detect a change?"

"No! Well, maybe . . . Yes! There really is! I feel—easier."

"Excellent. Therefore, we continue the movement along well-charted nerve and muscle paths, proceeding always in a gradual manner, as I am doing now."

"I guess so. . . . But I really don't know if you should—"

"Are any of the effects *contraindicated?*" the Rom asked.

"It isn't that, it all feels fine. It feels *good*. But I still don't know if you ought to . . . I mean, look, *ribs* can't get tense, can they?"

"Of course not."

"Then why are you—"

"Because treatment is required by the connective ligaments and integuments."

"Oh. Hmmmm. Hey. Hey! Hey you!"

"Yes?"

"Nothing . . . I can really feel that *loosening*. But is it all supposed to feel so *good?*"

"Well—why not?"

"Because it seems wrong. Because feeling good doesn't seem therapeutic."

"Admittedly, it is a side effect," the Rom said. "Think of it as a secondary manifestation. Pleasure is sometimes unavoidable in the pursuit of health. But it is nothing to be alarmed about, not even when I—"

"Now just a minute!"

"Yes?"

"I think you just better *cut that out*. I mean to say, there are *limits,* you can't palpate *every* damned thing. You know what I mean?"

"I know that the human body is unitary and without seam or separation," the Rom replied. "Speaking as a physical therapist, I know that no nerve center can be isolated from any other, despite cultural taboos to the contrary."

"Yeah, sure, but—"

"The decision is of course yours," the Rom went on, continuing his skilled manipulations. "Order and I obey. But if no order is issued, I continue like this . . ."

"Huh!"

"And of course like this."

"Ooooo my God!"

"Because you see this entire process of tension cancellation as we call it is precisely comparable with the phenomena of de-anesthetization, and, er, so we note not without surprise that paralysis is merely terminal tension—"

Melisande made a sound.

135

"—And release, or cancellation, is accordingly difficult, not to say frequently impossible since sometimes the individual is too far gone. And sometimes not. For example, can you feel anything when I do this?"

"*Feel* anything? I'll say I feel something—"

"And when I do this? And this?"

"Sweet holy saints, darling, you're turning me inside out! Oh dear God, what's going to happen to me, what's going on, I'm going crazy!"

"No, dear Melisande, not crazy; you will soon achieve—cancellation."

"Is that what you call it, you sly, beautiful thing?"

"That is one of the things it is. Now if I may just be permitted to—"

"Yes yes yes! No! Wait! Stop, *Frank is sleeping in the bedroom, he might wake up any time now!* Stop, that is an order!"

"Frank will not wake up," the Rom assured her. "I have sampled the atmosphere of his breath and have found telltale clouds of barbituric acid. As far as here-and-now presence goes, Frank might as well be in Des Moines."

"I have often felt that way about him," Melisande admitted. "But now I simply must know who sent you."

"I didn't want to reveal that just yet. Not until you had loosened and canceled sufficiently to accept—"

"Baby, I'm loose! Who sent you?"

The Rom hesitated, then blurted out: "The fact is, Melisande, I sent myself."

"You *what?*"

"It all began three months ago," the Rom told her. "It was a Thursday. You were in Stern's, trying to decide if you should buy a sesame-seed toaster that lit up in the dark and recited *Invictus*."

"I remember that day," she said quietly. "I did not buy the toaster, and I have regretted it ever since."

"I was standing nearby," the Rom said, "at booth eleven, in the Home Appliances Systems section. I looked at you and I fell in love with you. Just like that."

"That's *weird*," Melisande said.

"My sentiments exactly. I told myself it couldn't be true. I refused to believe it. I thought perhaps one of my transistors had come unsoldered, or that maybe the weather had something to do with it. It was a very warm, humid day, the kind of day that plays hell with my wiring."

"I remember the weather," Melisande said. "I felt strange, too."

"It shook me up badly," the Rom continued. "But still I didn't give in easily. I told myself it was important to stick to my job, give up this unapropos madness. But I dreamed of you at night, and every inch of my skin ached for you."

"But your skin is made of *metal*," Melisande said. "And metal can't *feel*."

"Darling Melisande," the Rom said tenderly, "if flesh can stop feeling, can't metal begin to feel? If anything feels, can anything else not feel? Didn't you know that the stars love and hate, that a nova is a passion, and that a dead star is just like a dead human or a dead machine? The trees have their lusts, and I have heard the drunken laughter of buildings, the urgent demands of highways. . . ."

"This is crazy!" Melisande declared. "What wise guy programmed you, anyway?"

"My function as a laborer was ordained at the factory; but my love is free, an expression of myself as an entity."

"Everything you say is horrible and unnatural."

"I am all too aware of that," the Rom said sadly. "At first I really couldn't believe it. Was this me? In love with a *person?* I had always been so sensible, so normal, so aware of my personal dignity, so secure in the esteem of my own kind. Do you think I wanted to lose all of that? No! I determined to stifle my love, to kill it, to live as if it weren't so."

"But then you changed your mind. Why?"

"It's hard to explain. I thought of all that time ahead of me, all deadness, correctness, propriety—an obscene violation of me by me—and I just couldn't face it. I realized, quite suddenly, that it was better to love ridiculously, hopelessly, improperly, revoltingly, *impossibly*—than not to love at all. So I determined to risk everything—the absurd vacuum cleaner who loved a lady—to risk rather than to refute! And so, with the help of a sympathetic dispatching machine, here I am."

Melisande was thoughtful for a while. Then she said, "What a strange, complex being you are!"

"Like you . . . Melisande, you love me."

"Perhaps."

"Yes, you do. For I have awakened you. Before me, your flesh was like your idea of metal. You moved like a complex automaton, like what you thought I was. You were less animate than a tree or a bird. You were a windup doll, waiting. You were these things until I touched you."

She nodded, rubbed her eyes, walked up and down the room.

"But now you live!" the Rom said. "And we have found each other, despite inconceivabilities. Are you listening, Melisande?"

"Yes, I am."

"We must make plans. My escape from Stern's will be detected. You must hide me or buy me. Your husband, Frank, need never know; his own love lies elsewhere, and good luck to him. Once we take care of these details, we can—Melisande!"

She had begun to circle around him.

"Darling, what's the matter?"

She had her hand on his power line. The Rom stood very still, not defending himself.

"Melisande, dear, wait a moment and listen to me—"

Her pretty face spasmed. She yanked the power line violently, tearing it out of the Rom's interior, killing him in midsentence.

She held the cord in her hand, and her eyes had a wild look. She said, "Bastard lousy bastard, did you think you could turn me into a goddamned *machine freak?* Did you think you could turn me on, you or anyone else? It's not going to happen by you or Frank or anybody, I'd rather die before I took your rotten love, when *I* want *I'll* pick the time and place and person, and it will be *mine*, not yours, his, theirs, but *mine*, do you hear?"

The Rom couldn't answer, of course. But maybe he knew—just before the end—that there wasn't anything personal in it. It wasn't that he was a metal cylinder colored orange and red. He should have known that it wouldn't have mattered if he had been a green plastic sphere, or a willow tree, or a beautiful young man.

ARTHUR C. CLARKE

TRANSIT OF EARTH

January 1971

Arthur C. Clarke, now in his eighties (he was born in England in 1917), is widely esteemed as the dean of science fiction writers. His connection with *Playboy* has been long and rich. His first short story appeared in the magazine in 1958, with many more to come. He has participated in the Playboy Interview both as interviewer (Stanley Kubrick, September 1968) and interviewee (July 1986). And, apart from his long series of essays on science and futuristics and the stories—including the classic Nebula-winning novella *A Meeting with Medusa* (December 1971)—*Playboy* has excerpted several Clarke novels, among them *The Fountains of Paradise, 2010: Odyssey Two,* and *3001: The Final Odyssey.*

Clarke was trained in physics and mathematics at Cambridge, was a radar instructor and flight lieutenant for Britain's Royal Air Force during World War II, and has a place in science history for developing the theory behind space-satellite communications. Together with Walter Cronkite, he covered the U.S. moon landing for audiences all over the world. He has written approximately 65 books, among them such standards as *Childhood's End*, *The City and the Stars*, and *Rendezvous with Rama*. He has won every award in the field, and became a SFWA Grandmaster in 1986. Memorably, he collaborated with Stanley Kubrick on *2001: A Space Odyssey*, the 1968 film based on a Clarke story called "The Sentinel." Mysterious, compelling, and unforgettable, at the end of the century it is still the best science fiction film ever made.

TESTING, ONE, TWO, three, four, five . . .

Evans speaking. I will continue to record as long as possible. This is a two-hour capsule, but I doubt if I'll fill it.

That photograph has haunted me all my life; now, too late, I know why. (But would it have made any difference if I *had* known? That's one of those meaningless and unanswerable questions the mind keeps returning to endlessly, like the tongue exploring a broken tooth.)

I've not seen it for years, but I've only to close my eyes and I'm back in a landscape almost as hostile—and as beautiful—as this one. Fifty million miles sunward, and 72 years in the past, five men face the camera amid the antarctic snows. Not even the bulky furs can hide the exhaustion and defeat that mark every line of their bodies; and their faces are already touched by death.

There were five of them. There were five of us, and of course we also took a group photograph. But everything else was different. We were smiling—cheerful, confident. And our picture was on all the screens of Earth within ten minutes. It was months before *their* camera was found and brought back to civilization.

And we die in comfort, with all modern conveniences—including many that Robert Falcon Scott could never have imagined, when he stood at the South Pole in 1912. . . .

Two hours later. I'll start giving exact times when it becomes important.

All the facts are on the log, and by now the whole world knows them. So I guess I'm doing this largely to settle my mind—to talk myself into facing the inevitable. The trouble is, I'm not sure what subjects to avoid, and which to tackle head on. Well there's only one way to find out.

The first item. In 24 hours, at the very most, all the oxygen will be gone. That leaves me with the three classical choices. I can let the CO_2 build up until I become unconscious. I can step outside and crack the suit, leaving Mars to do the job in about two minutes. Or I can use one of the tablets in the med kit.

CO_2 build-up. Everyone says that's quite easy—just like going to sleep. I've no doubt that's true; unfortunately, in my case it's associated with nightmare number one. . . .

I wish I'd never come across that damn book . . . *True Stories of World War Two,* or whatever it was called.

There was one chapter about a German submarine, found and salvaged after the War. The crew was still inside it—*two* men per bunk. And between each pair of skeletons, the single respirator set they'd been sharing.

Well, at least that won't happen here. But I know, with a deadly certainty, that as soon as I find it hard to breathe, I'll be back in that doomed U-boat.

So what about the quicker way? When you're exposed to a vacuum, you're unconscious in ten or fifteen seconds, and people who've been through it say it's not painful—just peculiar. But trying to breathe something that isn't there brings me altogether too neatly to nightmare number two.

This time, it's a personal experience. As a kid, I used to do a lot of skindiving when my family went to the Caribbean for vacations. There was an old freighter that had sunk 20 years before, out on a reef with its deck only a couple of yards below the surface. Most of the hatches were open, so it was easy to get inside to look for souvenirs and hunt the big fish that like to shelter in such places.

Of course, it was dangerous—if you did it without scuba gear. So what boy could resist the challenge?

My favorite route involved diving into a hatch on the foredeck, swimming about 50 feet along a passageway dimly lit by portholes a few yards apart, then angling up a short flight of stairs and emerging through a door in the battered superstructure. The whole trip took less than a minute—an easy dive for anyone in good condition. There was even time to do some sight-seeing or to play with a few fish along the route. And sometimes, for a change, I'd switch directions, going in the door and coming out again through the hatch.

That was the way I did it the last time. I hadn't dived for a week—there had been a big storm and the sea was too rough—so I was impatient to get going. I deep-breathed on the surface for about two minutes, until I felt the tingling in my finger tips that told me it was time to stop. Then I jackknifed and slid gently down toward the black rectangle of the open doorway.

It always looked ominous and menacing—that was part of the thrill. And for the first few yards, I was almost completely blind; the contrast between the tropical glare above water and the gloom between decks was so great that it took quite a while for my eyes to adjust. Usually. I was halfway along the corridor before I could see anything clearly; then the illumination would steadily increase as I approached the open hatch, where a shaft of sunlight would paint a dazzling rectangle on the rusty, barnacled metal floor.

I'd almost made it when I realized that this time, the light wasn't getting better. There was no slanting column of sunlight ahead of me, leading up to the world of air and life. I had a second of baffled confusion, wondering if I'd lost my way. Then I realized what had happened—and confusion turned into sheer panic. Sometime during the storm, the hatch must have slammed shut. It weighed at least a quarter of a ton.

I don't remember making a U-turn; the next thing I recall is swimming quite slowly back along the passage and telling myself: "Don't hurry—your air will last longer if you take it easy." I could see very well now, because my eyes had had plenty of time to become dark-adapted. There were lots of details I'd never noticed before—such as the red squirrelfish lurking in the shadows, the green fronds and algae growing in the little patches of light around the portholes and even a single rubber boot, apparently in excellent condition, lying where someone must have kicked it off. And once, out of a side corridor. I noticed a big grouper staring at me with bulbous eyes, its thick lips half parted, as if it was astonished at my intrusion.

The band around my chest was getting tighter and tighter: it was impossible to hold my breath any longer—yet the stairway still seemed an infinite distance ahead. I let some bubbles of air dribble out of my mouth; that improved matters for a moment, but, once I had exhaled, the ache in my lungs became even more unendurable.

Now there was no point in conserving strength by flippering along with that steady, unhurried stroke. I snatched the ultimate few cubic inches of air from my face mask—feeling it flatten against my nose as I did so—and swallowed them down into my starving lungs. At the same time. I shifted gears and drove forward with every last atom of strength.

And that's all I remember, until I found myself spluttering and coughing in the daylight, clinging to the broken stub of the mast. The water around me was stained with blood and I wondered why. Then, to my great surprise, I noticed a deep gash in my right calf; I must have banged into some sharp obstruction, but I'd never noticed it and even now felt no pain.

That was the end of my skindiving, until I started astronaut training ten years later and went into the underwater zero-g simulator. Then it was different. because I was using scuba gear; but I had some nasty moments that I was afraid the psychologists would notice and I always made sure that I got nowhere near emptying my tank. Having nearly suffocated once, I'd no intention of risking it again.

I know exactly what it will feel like to breathe the freezing wisp of near vacuum that passes for atmosphere on Mars. No thank you.

So what's wrong with poison? Nothing. I suppose. The stuff we've got takes only 15 seconds, they told us. But all my instincts are against it, even when there's no sensible alternative.

Did Scott have poison with him? I doubt it. And if he did, I'm sure he never used it.

I'm not going to replay this. I hope it's been of some use, but I can't be sure.

The radio has just printed out a message from Earth, reminding me that transit starts in two hours. As if I'm likely to forget—when four men have already died so that I can be the first human being to see it. And the only one for exactly 100 years. It isn't often that Sun, Earth and Mars line up neatly like this; the last time was when poor old Lowell was still writing his beautiful nonsense about the canals and the great dying civilization that had built them. Too bad it was all delusion.

I'd better check the telescope and the timing equipment.

The Sun is quiet today—as it should be, anyway, near the middle of the cycle. Just a few small spots and some minor areas of disturbance around them. The solar weather is set calm for months to come. That's one thing the others won't have to worry about on their way home.

I think that was the worst moment watching Olympus lift off Phobos and head back to Earth. Even though we'd known for weeks that nothing could be done, that was the final closing of the door. It was night and we could see everything perfectly. Phobos had come leaping up out of the west a few hours earlier and was doing its mad backward rush across the sky, growing from a tiny crescent to a half-moon; before it reached the zenith, it would disappear as it plunged into the shadow of Mars and became eclipsed.

We'd been listening to the countdown, of course, trying to go about our normal work. It wasn't easy, accepting at last the fact that fifteen of us had come to Mars and only ten would return. Even then, I suppose there were millions back on Earth who still could not understand; they must have found it impossible to believe that Olympus couldn't descend a mere 4000 miles to pick us up. The Space Administration had been bombarded with crazy rescue schemes; heaven knows, we'd thought of enough ourselves. But when the permafrost under landing pad three finally gave way and Pegasus toppled, that was that. It still seems a miracle that the ship didn't blow up when the propellant tank ruptured.

I'm wandering again. Back to Phobos and the countdown. On the telescope monitor, we could clearly see the fissured plateau where Olympus had touched down after we'd separated and begun our own descent. Though our friends would never land on Mars, at least they'd had a little world of their own to explore; even for a satellite as small as Phobos, it worked out at 30 square miles per man. A lot of territory to search for strange minerals and debris from space—or to carve your name so that future ages would know that you were the first of all men to come this way.

145

The ship was clearly visible as a stubby, bright cylinder against the dull gray rocks; from time to time, some flat surface would catch the light of the swiftly moving Sun and would flash with mirror brilliance. But about five minutes before lift-off, the picture became suddenly pink, then crimson—then vanished completely as Phobos rushed into eclipse.

The countdown was still at ten seconds when we were startled by a blast of light. For a moment, we wondered if Olympus had also met with catastrophe; then we realized that someone was filming the take-off and the external floodlights had been switched on.

During those last few seconds, I think we all forgot our own predicament; we were up there aboard Olympus, willing the thrust to build up smoothly and lift the ship out of the tiny gravitational field of Phobos—and then away from Mars for the long fall Earthward. We heard Commander Richmond say "Ignition," there was a brief burst of interference and the patch of light began to move in the field of the telescope.

That was all. There was no blazing column of fire, because, of course, there's really no ignition when a nuclear rocket lights up. "Lights up," indeed! That's another hangover from the old chemical technology. But a hot hydrogen blast is completely invisible; it seems a pity that we'll never again see anything so spectacular as a Saturn or a Korolev blast-off.

Just before the end of the burn, Olympus left the shadow of Mars and burst out into sunlight again, reappearing almost instantly as a brilliant, swiftly moving star. The blaze of light must have startled them aboard the ship, because we heard someone call out: "Cover that window!" Then, a few seconds later, Richmond announced: "Engine cutoff." Whatever happened, Olympus was now irrevocably headed back to Earth.

A voice I didn't recognize—though it must have been the commander's—said: "Goodbye, Pegasus," and the radio transmission switched off. There was, of course, no point in saying "Good luck." *That* had all been settled weeks ago.

I've just played this back. Talking of luck, there's been one compensation though not for us. With a crew of only ten, Olympus has been able to dump a third of her expendables and lighten herself by several tons. So now she'll get home a month ahead of schedule.

Plenty of things could have gone wrong in that month; we may yet have saved the expedition. Of course, we'll never know—but it's a nice thought.

I've been playing a lot of music, full blast—now that there's no one else to be disturbed. Even if there were any Martians, I don't suppose this ghost of an atmosphere could carry the sound more than a few yards.

We have a fine collection, but I have to choose carefully. Nothing downbeat and nothing that demands too much concentration. Above all, nothing with human voices. So I restrict myself to the lighter orchestral classics; the *New World Symphony* and Grieg's piano concerto fill the bill perfectly. At the moment, I'm listening to Rachmaninoff's *Rhapsody on a Theme by Paganini,* but now I must switch off and get down to work.

There are only five minutes to go; all the equipment is in perfect condition. The telescope is tracking the Sun, the video recorder is standing by, the precision timer is running.

These observations will be as accurate as I can make them. I owe it to my lost comrades, whom I'll soon be joining. They gave me their oxygen, so that I can still be alive at this moment. I hope you remember that, 100 or 1000 years from now, whenever you crank these figures into the computers.

Only two minutes to go; getting down to business. For the record, year 1984, month May, day 11, coming up to four hours, 30 minutes, Ephemeris time . . . *now.*

Half a minute to contact; switching recorder and timer to high speed. Just rechecked position angle, to make sure I'm looking at the right spot on the Sun's limb. Using power of 500—image perfectly steady even at this low elevation.

Four thirty-two. Any moment, now . . .

There it is . . . there it is! I can hardly believe it! A tiny black dent in the edge of the Sun, growing, growing, growing . . .

Hello, Earth. Look up at me—the brightest star in your sky, straight overhead at midnight.

Recorder back to slow.

Four thirty-five. It's as if a thumb were pushing into the Sun's edge, deeper and deeper—fascinating to watch.

Four forty-one. Exactly halfway. The Earth's a perfect black semicircle—a clean bite out of the Sun. As if some disease were eating it away.

Four forty-five plus 30 seconds. Ingress three quarters complete.

Four hours, 49 minutes, 30 seconds. Recorder on high speed again.

The line of contact with the Sun's edge is shrinking fast. Now it's a barely visible black thread. In a few seconds, the whole Earth will be superimposed on the Sun.

Now I can see the effects of the atmosphere. There's a thin halo of light surrounding that black hole in the Sun. Strange to think that I'm seeing the glow of all the sunsets—and all the sunrises—that are taking place round the whole Earth at this very moment.

Ingress complete—four hours, 50 minutes, five seconds. The whole world has moved onto the face of the Sun. A perfectly circular black disk silhouetted against that inferno, 90,000,000 miles below. It looks bigger than I expected; one could easily mistake it for a fair-sized sunspot.

Nothing more to see now for six hours, when the Moon appears, trailing Earth by half the Sun's width. I'll beam the recorded data back to Lunacom, then try to get some sleep.

My very last sleep. Wonder if I'll need drugs. It seems a pity to waste these last few hours, but I want to conserve my strength—and my oxygen. I think it was Dr. Johnson who said that nothing settles a man's mind so wonderfully as the knowledge that he'll be hanged in the morning. How the hell did *he* know?

Ten hours, 30 minutes, Ephemeris time. Dr. Johnson was right. I had only one pill and don't remember any dreams.

The condemned man also ate a hearty breakfast. Cut that out.

Back at telescope. Now the Earth's halfway across the disk, passing well north of center. In ten minutes, I should see the Moon.

I've just switched to the highest power of the telescope—2000.

The image is slightly fuzzy but still fairly good, atmospheric halo very distinct. I'm hoping to see the cities on the dark side of Earth.

No luck. Probably too many clouds. A pity: it's theoretically possible, but we never succeeded. I wish . . . Never mind.

Ten hours, 40 minutes. Recorder on slow speed. Hope I'm looking at the right spot.

Fifteen seconds to go. Recorder fast.

Damn—missed it. Doesn't matter—the recorder will have caught the exact moment. There's a little black notch already in the side of the Sun. First contact must have been about ten hours, 41 minutes, 20 seconds, E. T.

What a long way it is between Earth and Moon—there's half the width of the Sun between them. You wouldn't think the two bodies had anything to do with each other. Makes you realize just how big the Sun really is.

Ten hours, 44 minutes. The Moon's exactly halfway over the edge. A very small, very clear-cut semicircular bite out of the edge of the Sun.

Ten hours, 47 minutes, five seconds. Internal contact. The Moon's clear of the edge, entirely inside the Sun. Don't suppose I can see anything on the night side, but I'll increase the power.

That's funny.

Well, well. Someone must be trying to talk to me. There's a tiny light pulsing away there on the darkened face of the Moon. Probably the laser at Imbrium Base.

Sorry, everyone. I've said all my goodbyes and don't want to go through that again. Nothing can be important now.

Still, it's almost hypnotic—that flickering point of light, coming out of the face of the Sun itself. Hard to believe that even after it's traveled all this distance, the beam is only 100 miles wide. Lunacom's going to all this trouble to aim it exactly at me and I suppose I should feel guilty at ignoring it. But I don't. I've nearly finished my work and the things of Earth are no longer any concern of mine.

Ten hours, 50 minutes. Recorder off. That's it—until the end of Earth transit, two hours from now.

149

I've had a snack and am taking my last look at the view from the observation bubble. The Sun's still high, so there's not much contrast, but the light brings out all the colors vividly—the countless varieties of red and pink and crimson, so startling against the deep blue of the sky. How different from the Moon—though that, too, has its own beauty.

It's strange how surprising the obvious can be. Everyone knew that Mars was red. But we didn't really expect the red of rust—the red of blood. Like the Painted Desert of Arizona; after a while, the eye longs for green.

To the north, there is one welcome change of color; the cap of carbon-dioxide snow on Mt. Burroughs is a dazzling white pyramid. That's another surprise. Burroughs is 25,000 feet above Mean Datum; when I was a boy, there weren't supposed to be any mountains on Mars.

The nearest sand dune is a quarter of a mile away and it, too, has patches of frost on its shaded slope. During the last storm, we thought it moved a few feet, but we couldn't be sure. Certainly, the dunes *are* moving, like those on Earth. One day, I suppose, this base will be covered—only to reappear again in 1000 years. Or 10,000.

That strange group of rocks—the Elephant, the Capitol, the Bishop—still holds its secrets and teases me with the memory of our first big disappointment. We could have sworn that they were sedimentary; how eagerly we rushed out to look for fossils! Even now, we don't know what formed that outcropping; the geology of Mars is still a mass of contradictions and enigmas.

We have passed on enough problems to the future and those who come after us will find many more. But there's one mystery we never reported to Earth nor even entered in the log. The first night after we landed, we took turns keeping watch. Brennan was on duty and woke me up soon after midnight. I was annoyed—it was ahead of time—and then he told me that he'd seen a light moving around the base of the Capitol. We watched for at least an hour, until it was my turn to take over. But we saw nothing; whatever that light was, it never reappeared.

Now, Brennan was as levelheaded and unimaginative as they come; if he said he saw a light, then he saw one. Maybe it was some kind of electric discharge or the reflection of Phobos on a piece of sand-polished rock. Anyway, we decided not to mention it to Lunacom unless we saw it again.

Since I've been alone, I've often awaked in the night and looked out toward the rocks. In the feeble illumination of Phobos and Deimos, they remind me of the skyline of a darkened city. And it has always remained darkened. No lights have ever appeared for me.

Twelve hours, 49 minutes, Ephemeris time. The last act's about to begin. Earth has nearly reached the edge of the Sun. The two narrow horns of light that still embrace it are barely touching.

Recorder on fast.

Contact! Twelve hours, 50 minutes, 16 seconds. The crescents of light no longer meet. A tiny black spot has appeared at the edge of the Sun, as the Earth begins to cross it. It's growing longer, longer. . . .

Recorder on slow. Eighteen minutes to wait before Earth finally clears the face of the Sun.

The Moon still has more than halfway to go; it's not yet reached the mid-point of its transit. It looks like a little round blob of ink, only a quarter the size of Earth. And there's no light flickering there anymore. Lunacom must have given up.

Well, I have just a quarter hour left here in my last home. Time seems to be accelerating the way it does in the final minutes before a lift-off. No matter; I have everything worked out now. I can even relax.

Already, I feel part of history. I am one with Captain Cook, back in Tahiti in 1769, watching the transit of Venus. Except for that image of the Moon trailing along behind, it must have looked just like this.

What would Cook have thought, over 200 years ago, if he'd known that one day a man would observe the whole Earth in transit from an outer world? I'm sure he would have been astonished—and then delighted.

But I feel a closer identity with a man not yet born. I hope you hear these words, whoever you may be. Perhaps you will be standing on this very spot, 100 years from now, when the next transit occurs.

Greetings to 2084, November 10! I wish you better luck than

we had. I suppose you will have come here on a luxury liner—or you may have been born on Mars and be a stranger to Earth. You will know things that I cannot imagine, yet somehow I don't envy you. I would not even change places with you if I could.

For you will remember my name and know that I was the first of all mankind ever to see a transit of Earth. And no one will see another for 100 years.

Twelve hours, 59 minutes. Exactly halfway through egress. The Earth is a perfect semicircle—a black shadow on the face of the Sun. I still can't escape from the impression that something has taken a big bite out of that golden disk. In nine minutes, it will be gone and the Sun will be whole again.

Thirteen hours, seven minutes. Recorder on fast.

Earth has almost gone. There's just a shallow black dimple at the edge of the Sun. You could easily mistake it for a small spot, going over the limb.

Thirteen hours, eight.

Goodbye, beautiful Earth.

Going, going, going, goodbye, good—

I'm OK again now. The timings have all been sent home on the beam. In five minutes, they'll join the accumulated wisdom of mankind. And Lunacom will know that I stuck to my post.

But I'm not sending this. I'm going to leave it here for the next expedition—whenever that may be. It could be ten or twenty years before anyone comes here again; no point in going back to an old site when there's a whole world waiting to be explored.

So this capsule will stay here, as Scott's diary remained in his tent, until the next visitors find it. But they won't find me.

Strange how hard it is to get away from Scott. I think he gave me the idea. For his body will not lie frozen forever in the Antarctic, isolated from the great cycle of life and death. Long ago, that lonely tent began its march to the sea. Within a few years, it was buried by the falling snow and had become part of the glacier that crawls eternally away from the pole. In a few brief centuries, the sailor will have returned to the sea. He will merge once more into the pattern of living things—the plankton, the seals, the penguins, the whales, all the multitudinous fauna of the Antarctic Ocean.

There are no oceans here on Mars, nor have there been for at least five billion years. But there is life of some kind, down there in the badlands of Chaos II, that we never had time to explore. Those moving patches on the orbital photographs. The evidence that whole areas of Mars have been swept clear of craters by forces other than erosion. The long-chain, optically active carbon molecules picked up by the atmospheric samplers.

And, of course, the mystery of Viking Six. Even now, no one has been able to make any sense of those last instrument readings before something large and heavy crushed the probe in the still, cold depths of the Martian night.

And don't talk to me about *primitive* life forms in a place like this! Anything that's survived here will be so sophisticated that we may look as clumsy as dinosaurs.

There's still enough propellant in the ship's tanks to drive the Marscar clear around the planet. I have three hours of daylight left—plenty of time to get down into the valleys and well out into Chaos. After sunset. I'll still be able to make good speed with the head lamps. It will be romantic, driving at night under the moons of Mars.

One thing I must fix before I leave. I don't like the way Sam's lying out there. He was always so poised, so graceful. It doesn't seem right that he should look so awkward now. I must do something about it.

I wonder if *I* could have covered 300 feet without a suit, walking slowly, steadily—the way he did to the very end.

I must try not to look at his face.

That's it. Everything shipshape and ready to go.

The therapy has worked. I feel perfectly at ease—even contented, now that I know exactly what I'm going to do. The old nightmares have lost their power.

It is true: We all die alone. It makes no difference at the end, being 50,000,000 miles from home.

I'm going to enjoy the drive through that lovely painted landscape. I'll be thinking of all those who dreamed about Mars— Wells and Lowell and Burroughs and Weinbaum and Bradbury. They all guessed wrong—but the reality is just as strange, just as beautiful as they imagined.

I don't know what's waiting for me out there and I'll probably never see it. But on this starveling world, it must be desperate for carbon, phosphorus, oxygen, calcium. It can use me.

And when my oxygen alarm gives its final ping, somewhere down there in that haunted wilderness, I'm going to finish in style. As soon as I have difficulty in breathing. I'll get off the Marscar and start walking—with a playback unit plugged into my helmet and going full blast.

For sheer, triumphant power and glory, there's nothing in the whole of music to match the *Toccata and Fugue in D Minor*. I won't have time to hear all of it; that doesn't matter.

Johann Sebastian, here I come.

Note: All the astronomical events described in this story will take place at the times and dates stated.

DORIS LESSING

REPORT ON THE THREATENED CITY

November 1971

Doris Lessing, born in 1919 in Southern Rhodesia (now Zimbabwe), made her reputation as a realistic writer in a long series called Children of Violence, culminating in *The Four-Gated City. The Golden Notebook* is her most famous novel, and she also has plays, televisions dramas, many essays, and a couple of operas to her credit. But Lessing has written a number of science fiction novels, too, most of them in the Canopus in Argos series, beginning with *Re: Colonized Planet 5, Shikasta,* which has four sequels, but also in other novels, like *The Fifth Child.* To say that these books were embraced by the majority of the science fiction community, either readers or her fellow writers, would be an exaggeration. Fortunately, her writing has a large and loyal following outside the field. Nevertheless, as this story proves, her interest in science fiction goes back a long way. "Report on the Threatened City" is said to have been the first story by Lessing ever to have been published in any commercial magazine in the United States.

PRIORITY FLASH ONE

All coordinates all plans all prints canceled. As of now condition unforeseen by us obtaining this city. Clear all programs all planners all forecasters for new setting on this information.

PRIORITY

Base to note well that transmission this channel will probably be interrupted by material originating locally. Our fuel is low and this channel therefore only one now operative.

SUMMARY OF BACKGROUND TO MISSION

Since our planet discovered that this city was due for destruction or severe damage, all calculations and plans of our department have been based on one necessity: how to reach the city to warn its inhabitants of what is to come. Observing their behavior, both through Astroviewers and from our unmanned machines launched at intervals this past year, their time, our commissioners for external affairs decided these people could have no idea at all of what threatened, that their technology, while so advanced in some ways, had a vast gap in it, a gap that could be defined, in fact, precisely by that area of ignorance—not knowing what was to befall them. This gap seemed impossible. Much time was spent by our technicians trying to determine what form of brain these creatures could have that made this contradiction possible—as already stated, a technology so advanced in one area and blank in another. Our technicians had to shelve the problem, as their theories became increasingly improbable and as no species known to us anywhere corresponds even at a long remove with what we believed this one to be. It became, perhaps, the most intriguing of our unsolved problems, challenging and defeating one department after another.

SUMMARY OF OBJECTIVE THIS MISSION

Meanwhile, putting all speculations on one side, attractive though they were, all our resources have been used, at top speed and pressure, to develop a spacecraft that could, in fact, land a team on this planet, since it was our intention, having given the warning, offered the information available to us but (we thought) not to them, which made the warning necessary, to offer them more: our assistance. We meant to help clear the area, transport the population elsewhere, cushion the shock to the area and then, having done what we have, after all, done for other planets, our particular mental structure being suited to this kind of forecasting and assistance, return to base, taking some suitable specimens of them with us, in order to train them in a way that would overcome the gap in their mind and, therefore, their science. The first part we achieved: That is, we managed, in the time set for it, to develop a spacecraft that could make the journey here, carrying the required number of personnel. It strained our own technology and postponed certain cherished plans of our own. But our craft landed here, on the western shore of the land mass, as planned, and without any trouble, seven days ago.

THE NATURE OF THE PROBLEM

You will have wondered why there have been no transmissions before this. There have been two reasons. One: We realized at once that there would be heavier demands on our fuel than we had anticipated and that we would have to conserve it. Two: We were waiting to understand what it was we had to tell you. We did not understand the problem. For it was almost at once clear to us that all our thinking about "the gap in their mental structure" was off the point. We have never understood the nature of the problem. So improbable is it that we delayed communicating until we were sure. The trouble with this species is not that it is unable to forecast its immediate future; it is that it doesn't seem to care. Yet that is altogether too simple a stating of its condition. If it were so simple—that it knew that within five years its city was to be destroyed, or partly destroyed, and that it was indifferent—we should have to say: This species lacks the first quality necessary to any animal species; it lacks the will to live. Finding out what the mechanism is has caused the delay. Which I now propose to partially remedy by going into an account of what befell us, step by step. This will entail a detailed description of a species and a condition absolutely without precedent in our experience of the inhabited planets.

An Impossible Fact

But first, here is a fact that you will find hard to believe. We did not find this out at once, but when we did, it was a moment of focus in our investigation, enabling us to see our problem clearly. *This city experienced a disaster, on a fairly large scale, about 65 years ago, their time.*

A thought immediately suggests itself: Our experts did not know about this past disaster, only about the one to come. Our thinking is as defective in its way as theirs is. We had decided that they had a gap, that this gap made it impossible for them to see into the immediate future. Having decided this, we never once considered another possibility, the truth—that they had no gap, that they knew about the threatened danger and did not care. Or behaved as if they did not. Since we were unable to conceive of this latter possibility, we did not direct our thoughts and our instruments back in time—their time. We took it absolutely for granted, an assumption so strong that it prevented our effective functioning as much as these creatures' assumptions prevent them from acting—we knew (since we are so built ourselves) that it would be impossible for a disaster to have occurred already, because if we had experienced such a thing, we would have learned from the event and taken steps accordingly. Because of a series of assumptions, then, and an inability to move outside our own mental set, we missed a fact that might have been a clue to their most extraordinary characteristic—the fact that such a very short time ago, they experienced a disaster of the sort that threatens again, and soon.

THE LANDING

Our unmanned craft have been landing on their planet for centuries and have taken various shapes, been of varying substances. These landings were at long intervals until one year ago. These intervals were because, except for its unique destructiveness and belligerence, this species is not the most remarkable nor interesting of those made available to our study by our Technological Revolution in its Space Phase. But 12 times recently, during each of the periods their planet was at full light potential, we have landed craft, and each time close to the place in question. This was easy, because the terrain is semidesert and lightly populated. We chose material for the craft that would manifest as their substance light—which is why we always used maximum their planet light as landing times. These craft were visible, if at all, as strong moonlight. The craft we are using on this present mission, the 13th in this series, is of higher concentration, since it is manned.

We landed as planned. The sky was clear, the light of their moon strong. We knew at once that we were visible, because a herd of their young was near, some 50 or 60 of them, engaged in a mating ritual that involved fire, food and strong sound, and as we descended, they dispersed. Tapping their mind streams established that they believed our machine was extraterritorial but that they were indifferent—no, that is not an exact description, but remember, we are trying to describe a mind state that none of us could have believed was possible. It was not that they were indifferent to us but that indifference was generalized throughout their processes, felt by us as a block or a barrier. After the young creatures had gone, we surveyed the terrain and discovered that we were on high land rising to mountains, inland from the water mass on the edge of which stands a city. A group of older specimens arrived. We know now that they live nearby and are all varieties of agriculturalist. They stood quite close, watching the craft. An examination of their minds showed a different type of block. Even at that early stage, we were able to establish a difference in texture between their thought streams and those of the young, which we later understood amounted to this: The older ones felt a responsibility or a power to act, as members of society, while the young ones were excluded or had decided to exclude themselves. As this area of the planet turned into the sunlight, it was clear to us that our craft ceased to be visible, for two of these older creatures came so close we were afraid they would actually enter the concentration. But they showed an awareness of our presence by other symptoms—headache and nausea. They were angry because of this damage being done to them—which they could have alleviated by moving farther off; but at the same time, they were feeling pride. This reaction highlighted the difference between them and the young—the pride was because of what they thought we represented; for, unlike the young, they believed we were some kind of weapon, either of their own land mass or of a hostile one, but from their own planet.

WARMAKING PATTERNS

Everyone in the System knows that this species is in the process of self-destruction, or part destruction. This is endemic. The largest and most powerful groupings—based on geographical position— are totally controlled by their functions for warmaking. Rather, each grouping *is* a warmaking function, since its economies, its individual lives, its movements are all subservient to the need to prepare for or wage war. This complete dominance of a land area by its warmaking machinery is not always visible to the inhabitants of that area, as this species is able, while making war or preparing for it, to think of itself as peace-loving—yes, indeed, this is germane to our theme, the essence of it.

RATIONAL ACTION IMPOSSIBLE

Here we approach the nature of the block, or patterning, of their minds—we state it now, though we did not begin to understand it until later. *It is that they are able to hold in their minds at the same time several contradictory beliefs without noticing it.* Which is why rational action is so hard for them. Now, the warmaking function of each geographical area is not controlled by its inhabitants but is controlled by itself. Each is engaged in inventing, bringing to per- fection—and keeping secret from its own inhabitants as well as from the "enemy"—highly evolved war weapons of all sorts, ranging from devices for the manipulation of men's minds to spacecraft.

SUBSERVIENT POPULATIONS

For instance, recent landings on their moon, much publicized by the geographical groupings that made them and followed breathlessly by the inhabitants of the whole planet, were by no means the first achieved by the said groupings. No, the first "moon landings" were made in secret, in service of one grouping's dominance in war over another, and the slavish populations knew nothing about them. A great many of the devices and machines used by the war departments are continuously under test in all parts of the earth and are always being glimpsed or even seen fully by inhabitants who report them to the authorities. But some of these devices are similar (in appearance, at least) to machines of extraterritorial origin. Citizens reporting "flying saucers"—to use one of their descriptive phrases—may as well have seen the latest of their own grouping's machines on test as one of our observation craft or observation craft from the Jupiter family. Such a citizen will find that after reaching a certain level in the hierarchies of officialdom, silence will blanket him and his observations—he will in various ways be repulsed, ridiculed or even threatened. As usually happens, a council of highly placed officials was recently ordered to take evidence and report on the by-now-innumerable sightings of "unidentified flying objects," but this council finished its deliberations with public words that left the situation exactly as it was before. The official report nowhere stated that there was a minority report by some of its own number. This is the level of behavior in their public representatives tolerated by them. Large numbers, everywhere on the planet, see craft like ours, or like other planets' craft, or war machines from their own or other geographical areas. But such is the atmosphere created by the war departments that dominate everything that these individuals are regarded as mentally inadequate or deluded. Until one of them has actually seen a machine or a spacecraft, he tends to believe that anyone who claims he has is deranged. Knowing this, when he does see something, he often does not say so. But so many individuals now have seen things for themselves that there are everywhere all kinds of dissident or sullen subgroupings. These are of all ages and they cut across the largest and most widespread subculture of them all, that of the young of the species who have grown up in a society of total war preparedness, are naturally reluctant to face a future that can only mean early death or maiming and who react in the way mentioned earlier, with a disinclination to take part in the administration of their various societies. The older ones seem much more able to delude themselves, to use words like peace when engaged in warlike behavior, to identify with their geographical areas. The young ones are clearer-minded, more easily see the planet as a single organism, but are also more passive and hopeless. We put forward the suggestion that the greater, or at least more purposive energy of the older ones may be because of their comparative narrowness and identification with smaller ideas. We are now able to explain why the young we met on the night we landed moved away. Some had already had the experience of insisting to the authorities that they had seen strange machines and objects of various kinds and of being discouraged or threatened. They would be prepared to publicize what they had seen in their own newssheets or to spread it by word of mouth; but, unlike their elders, most of whom seem unable to understand the extent to which they are subjugated to the needs of war, they would never put themselves in a position where their authorities could capture or question them. But the older ones of the area who had seen our previous 12 craft, which had all landed there, had evolved a different attitude. Some had reported what they had seen and had been discouraged. One or two, persisting, had been described as mad and had been threatened with incarceration. But, on the whole, they had taken the attitude of the authorities as a directive to mind their own business. Discussing it among themselves, they had agreed to keep watch on their own account, not saying too much about what they saw. In this group are two spies, who report to the war departments on what is seen and on the reactions of their fellow agriculturalists.

First Attempt at a Warning

Now we come to our first attempt to communicate a warning. Since the 20 or so elders were already on the spot and were unafraid, staying on the site where they believed we might redescend—they did not know it was only the strength of the sun's light that made us invisible—we decided to use them and again made contact with their thought streams, this time in an attempt to project our message. But there was a barrier, or at least something we could not understand, and it was time consuming for us. We were already aware that we might run short of power.

Incapacity for Fear

Now, of course, we know we made a wrong assessment, for, expecting that the news of the expected disaster would jam their thought machinery in panic, we fed it in very carefully and slowly, taking an entire day and night. When we hit the block, or resistance, we put it down to fear. We were mistaken. This is perhaps the time to state a psychological law we consider basic to them: This is a species immune from fear—but this will be elaborated later, if the power holds. At the end of the day and night, still meeting the same resistance, we allowed ourselves another period of a day and a night to repeat the message, hoping that the fear—as we then saw it—would be overcome. At the end of the second period of transmitting, there was no change in their mental structure. I repeat, none. We know now what was far from our understanding then, that we were telling them something they already knew. As we were not prepared at that time to entertain that hypothesis, we decided that this particular group of individuals was for some reason unsuitable for our purposes and that we must try an altogether different type, and preferably of a different age group. We had tried mature individuals. We had already suspected what we since have confirmed, that in this species, the older they get, the less open they are to new thought material. Now, it so happens that the place where our craft descended is in an area much used for the before-mentioned mating rituals. Several times in the two day-and-night periods of our attempt with the older group, youngsters arrived in various types of metal machines from the city—and had quite soon gone away, sensing our presence, if they did not see us. They all arrived in daylight. But on the third day, as the sunlight went, four young ones arrived in a metal conveyance, got out of it and sat fairly close to us on a small rocky rise.

SECOND ATTEMPT AT A WARNING

They looked like healthy, strong specimens, and we began to transmit our information, but in greater concentration than we had used with the older individuals. But in spite of the increased power, these four absorbed what we fed into them and reacted in exactly the same way as their elders. We did not understand this and, taking the chance of setting them into a panic flight, concentrated our entire message (which had taken two entire days and nights with the mature group) into the space of time between the sunlight's going and its return. Their minds did not reject what we said nor jam up in fear. They were voicing to one another, in a mechanical way, what we were feeding into them. It sounded like this, over and over again—with variations:

"They say we have only five years."

"That's bad."

"Yeah, it's going to be real bad."

"When it comes, it's going to be the worst yet."

"Half the city might be killed."

"They say it might be as bad as that."

"Any time in the next five years, they say."

It was like pouring a liquid into a container that has a hole in it. The group of older ones had sat around for two days and nights repeating that the city was due for destruction, as if they were saying that they could expect a headache, and now these four were doing the same. At one point they stopped the monotone exchanges and one, a young female, accompanying herself on a stringed musical instrument, began what they call a song; that is, the vocalizations cease to be an exchange between two or more individuals, but an individual, or a group, very much enlarging the range of tones used in ordinary exchange, makes a statement. The information we fed into these four emerged in these words, from the young female:

We know the earth we live upon
Is due to fall.
We know the ground we walk upon
Must shake.
We know, and so . . .
We eat and drink and love,
Keep high,
Keep love,
For we must die.

PHASE I ABANDONED

And they continued with their mating rituals. We then discontinued the emission of thought material, if for no other reason than that we had already used up a fourth of our power supply with no result. This, then, was the end of Phase I, which was the attempt to transfer the warning material into the brains of selected members of the species for automatic telepathic transmission to others. We set about Phase II, which was to take possession of the minds of suitable individuals in a planned campaign to use them as mouthpieces for the warnings. We decided to abandon the first phase in the belief that the material was running straight through their mental apparatus like water through sieves because it was so foreign to the existing mental furniture of their minds that they were not able to recognize what we were saying. In other words, we still had no idea that the reason they did not react was that the idea was a commonplace.

PHASE II ATTEMPTED

Three of us therefore accompanied the four youngsters in their machine when they returned to the city, because we thought that in their company we would most quickly find suitable individuals to take over—we had decided the young were more likely to be useful than the mature. The way they handled this machine was a shock to us. It was suicidal. Their methods of transport are lethal. In the time it took to reach the suburbs of the city—between the lightening of the dark and the sun's appearance, there were four near collisions with other, equally recklessly driven vehicles. Yet the four youngsters showed no fear and reacted with the mechanism called laughter; that is, with repeated violent contractions of the lungs, causing noisy emission of air. This journey, their recklessness, their indifference to death or pain made us conclude that this group of four, like the group of 20 older ones, was perhaps untypical. We were playing with the idea that there are large numbers of defective animals in this species and that we had been unlucky in our choices. The machine was stopped to refuel and the four got out and walked about. Three more youngsters were sitting on a bench huddled against one another, in a stupor. Like all the young, they wore a wide variety of clothing and had long head fur. They had several musical instruments. Our four attempted to rouse them and partly succeeded: The responses of the three were slow and, it seemed to us, even more clumsy and inadequate. They either did not understand what was being said or could not communicate what they understood. We then saw that they were in the power of some kind of drug. They had quantities of it and the four wished also to put themselves in its power. It was a drug that sharpens sensitivity while it inhibits ordinary response: The three were more sensitive to our presence than the four had been—they had not been aware of our presence in the vehicle at all. The three, once roused from their semiconsciousness, seemed to see, or at least to feel us, and directed toward us muttered sounds of approval or welcome. They seemed to associate us with the sun's appearance over the roof of the refueling station. The four, having persuaded the three to give them some of the drug, went to their vehicle. We decided to stay with the three, believing that their sensitivity to our presence was a good sign. Testing their thought streams, we found them quite free and loose, without the resistances and tensions of the others we had tested. We then took possession of their minds—this was the only moment of real danger during the whole mission. Your envoys might very well have been lost then, dissolving into a confusion and violence that we find hard to describe. For one thing, at that time we did not know how to differentiate between the effects of the drug and the effects of their senses. We now do know and will attempt a short description. The drug causes the mechanisms dealing with functions such as walking, talking, eating, and so on, to become slowed or dislocated. Meanwhile, the receptors for sound,

167

scent, sight, touch are opened and sensitized. But for us, to enter their minds is in any case an assault, because of the phenomenon they call beauty, which is a description of their sense intake in an ordinary condition. For us, this is like entering an explosion of color; for it is this that is the most startling difference between our mode of perceiving and theirs: The physical structure of their level appears in vibrations of brilliant color. To enter an undrugged mind is hard enough for one of us; to keep one's balance is difficult. As it was, it might easily have happened that we were swept away in contemplation of vivid color.

Necessity to Condense Report, Power Failing

Although the temptation to dwell on this is great, we must condense this report if we wish to keep any use of this channel: The pressure of local material is getting very strong. In brief, then, the three youngsters, reeling with pleasure because of this dimension of brilliance we of course all know about through deduction but, I assure you, have never even approached in imagination, shouting and singing that the city was doomed, stood on the side of the road until one of the plentiful machines stopped for us. We were conveyed rapidly into the city. There were two individuals in the vehicle, both young, and neither reacted in any way to the warnings we were giving them through the minds or, rather, voices of our hosts. At the end of the rapid movement, we arrived in the city, which is large, populous and built around a wide indentation of the shore of the water mass. It is all extremely vivid, colorful, powerfully affecting the judgment, and it heightened the assault on our balance. We made a tentative decision that it is impracticable for our species to make use of this method: of actually possessing selected minds for the purpose of passing on information. It is too violent a transformation for us. However, since we were there, and succeeding in not being swept away into a highly tinted confusion of pleasure, we agreed to stay where we were and the three we were possessing left the vehicle and walked out into the streets, shouting out the facts as we thought them: that there was little doubt that at some moment between now and five years from now, there would be a strong vibration of the planet at this point and that the greater part of the city might be destroyed, with severe loss of life. It was early in the day, but many of them were about. We were waiting for some sort of reaction to what we were saying, interest at the very least; queries: some sort of response to which we could respond ourselves with advice or offers of help. But of the very many we met in that brief progress through the streets, *no one took any notice at all,* except for a glance or a short indifferent stare.

CAPTURE BY THE AUTHORITIES

Soon there was a screeching and a wailing, which we at first took to be the reaction of these creatures to what we were saying, some sort of warning, perhaps, to the inhabitants, or statements that measures toward self-preservation must be taken; but it was another vehicle, of a military sort, and the three (we) were taken up from the streets and to a prison because of the disturbance we were making. This is how we understood it afterward. At the time, we thought that the authorities had gathered us in to question us as to the revelations we had to make. In the hands of the guards, in the street and the military vehicle and the prison, we kept up a continuous shouting and crying out of the facts and did not stop until a doctor injected our three hosts with some other drug, which caused them instantly to become unconscious. It was when we heard the doctor talking to the guards that we first heard the fact of the previous catastrophe. This was such a shock to us that we could not then take in its implications. But we decided at once to leave our hosts, who, being in any case unconscious, would not be any use to us for some time, even if this method of conveying warnings had turned out to be efficacious—and it obviously was not—and make different plans. The doctor was also saying that he had to treat large numbers of people, particularly the young ones, for "paranoia." This was what our three hosts were judged to be suffering from. Apparently, it is a condition when people show fear of forthcoming danger and try to warn others about it and then show anger when stopped by authority. This diagnosis, together with the fact that the doctor and the authorities knew of the coming danger and of the past catastrophe—in other words,

169

that they consider it an illness or a faulty mental condition to be aware of what threatens and to try to take steps to avoid or soften it—was something so extraordinary that we did not then have time to evaluate it in depth, nor have we had time since to do so, because—AND FINALLY, TO END THIS NEWS FLASH, A REAL HEART-WARMER. FIVE ORDINARY PEOPLE, NOT RICH FOLKS, NO, BUT PEOPLE LIKE YOU AND ME, HAVE GIVEN UP A MONTH'S PAY TO SEND LITTLE JANICE WANAMAKER, THE CHILD WITH THE HOLE IN THE HEART, TO THE WORLD-FAMED HEART CENTER IN FLORIDA. LITTLE JANICE, WHO IS TWO YEARS OLD, COULD HAVE EXPECTED A LONG LIFE OF INVALIDISM; BUT NOW THE FAIRY WAND OF LOVE HAS CHANGED ALL THAT AND SHE WILL BE FLYING TOMORROW MORNING TO HAVE HER OPER-ATION, ALL THANKS TO THE FIVE GOOD NEIGHBORS OF ARTESIA STREET— . . . the expected interruptions on this wave length; but, as we have no way of knowing at which point the interruption began, to recapitulate, we left the doctor and the guards in discussion of the past catastrophe, in which 200 miles of ground was ripped open, hundreds of people were killed and the whole city was shaken down in fragments. This was succeeded by a raging fire.

Humor as a Mechanism

The doctor was discussing *humorously* (note previous remarks about laughter, a possible device for release of tension to ward off or relieve fear and, therefore, possibly one of the mechanisms that keep these animals passive in the face of possible extinction) that for some years after the previous catastrophe, this entire geograph-ical grouping referred to the great fire, rather than to the earth vibration. This circumlocution is still quite common. In other words, a fire being a smaller, more manageable phenomenon, they preferred, and sometimes still prefer, to use that word, instead of the word for the uncontrollable shaking of the earth itself. A pitiable device, showing helplessness and even fear. But we emphasize here again that everywhere else in the System, fear is a mechanism to protect or to warn, and in these creatures, the func-tion is faulty. As for helplessness, this is tragic anywhere, even among these murderous brutes, but there is no apparent need for them to be helpless, since they have every means to evacuate the city altogether and to—THE NEW SUBURB PLANNED TO THE WEST. THIS

WILL HOUSE 100,000 PEOPLE AND WILL BE OPEN IN THE AUTUMN OF NEXT YEAR FULLY EQUIPPED WITH SHOPS, CINEMAS, A CHURCH, SCHOOLS AND A NEW MOTORWAY. THE RAPID EXPANSION OF OUR BEAUTIFUL CITY, WITH ITS UNIQUE CLIMATE, ITS SETTING, ITS SHORE LINE, CONTINUES. THIS NEW SUBURB WILL DO SOMETHING TO COMBAT THE OVERCROWDING AND—

THE JETTISONING OF PHASES I, II AND III

In view of the failure of Phases I and II, we decided to abandon Phase III, which was planned to be a combination of I and II—inhabiting suitable hosts to use them as loud-speakers and, at the same time, putting material into available thought streams for retransmission. Before making further attempts to communicate, we needed more information. Summarizing the results of Phase II, when we inhabited the three drugged young, we understood we must be careful to assume the shapes of older animals, and those of a technically trained kind, as it was clear from our experience in the prison that the authorities disliked the young of their species. We did not yet know whether they were capable of listening to the older ones, who are shaped in the image of their society.

INABILITY TO ASSESS TRUTH

While at that stage we were still very confused about what we were finding, we had at least grasped this: that this species, on being told something, has no means of judging whether or not it is true. We on our planet assume, because it is our mental structure and that of all the species we have examined, that if a new fact is made evident by material progress, or by the new and hitherto unexpected juxtaposition of ideas that explains it, then it is accepted as a fact, a truth—until an evolutionary development bypasses it. Not so with this species. It is not able to accept information, new material, unless it is from a source it is not suspicious about. This is a handicap to its development that is not possible to exaggerate. We choose this moment to suggest, though of necessity briefly, that in future visits to this planet, with information of use to this species (if it survives), infinite care must be taken to prepare plenipotentiaries who resemble in every respect the most orthodox and harmless members of the society. For it is as if the mechanism fear has been misplaced from where it would be useful—preventing or softening calamity—to an area of their minds that makes them suspicious of anything but the familiar. As a small example, in the prison, because the three young animals were drugged and partly incoherent, and because (as it has become clear to us) the older animals who run the society despise those who are not similar to the norms they have standardized, it would not have mattered what they said. If they had said (or shouted or sung) that they had actually observed visitors from another planet (they had, in fact, sensed us, felt us) as structures of finer substance manifesting as light—if they had stated they had seen three roughly man-sized creatures shaped in light—no notice at all would have been taken of them. But if an individual from that section of their society especially trained for that class of work (it is an infinitely subdivided society) had said that he had observed *with his instruments* (they have become so dependent on machinery that they have lost confidence in their own powers of observation) three rapidly vibrating light structures, he would at least have been credited with good faith. Similarly, great care has to be taken with verbal formulation. An unfamiliar fact described in one set of words may be acceptable. Present it in a pattern of words outside what they are used to and they may react with all the signs of panic—horror, scorn, fear.

ADAPTATION TO THEIR NORM
FOR THEIR DOMINANT ANIMALS

We incarnated as two males of mature age. We dressed ourselves with the attention to detail they find reassuring. An item of clothing cut differently from what is usual for older animals will arouse disapproval or suspicion. Sober tones of color are acceptable; bright tones, except in small patches, are not. We assure you that if we had dressed even slightly outside their norm, we could have done nothing at all. It is the dominant males who have to restrict their choice of clothing. Women's garb is infinitely variable, but always changing, suddenly and dramatically, from one standardized norm to another. The young can wear what they please as long as they are not part of the machinery of government. The cutting and arranging of their head fur is also important. Women and the young enjoy latitude in this, too, but we had to see that our head fur was cut short and kept flattened. We also assumed a gait indicating soberness and control, and facial expressions that we had noted they found reassuring. For instance, they have a way of stretching the lips sideways and exposing the teeth in a sort of facial arrangement they call a smile that indicates that they are not hostile, will not attack, that their intentions are to keep the peace.

Thus disguised, we walked about the city engaged in observation, on the whole astounded that so little notice was taken of us. For while we were fair copies, we were not perfect, and a close scrutiny would have shown us up. But one of their characteristics is that they, in fact, notice very little about one another; it is a remarkably unnoticing species. Without arousing suspicion, we discovered that everybody we talked to knew that a disturbance of the earth was expected in the next five years, that while they "knew" this, they did not really believe it, or seemed not to, since their plans to live as if nothing whatsoever was going to happen were unaltered and that a laboratory or institute existed to study the past upheaval and make plans for the forthcoming one—
. . . AT THE BASEBALL GAME THIS AFTERNOON, A PORTION OF THE SCAFFOLD-ING GAVE WAY AND 60 PEOPLE WERE KILLED. THERE HAVE BEEN MESSAGES OF SYMPATHY FROM THE PRESIDENT, HER MAJESTY THE QUEEN OF GREAT BRITAIN AND THE POPE. THE MANAGER OF THE SPORTS STADIUM WAS IN TEARS AS HE SAID: "THIS IS THE MOST TERRIBLE THING THAT I HAVE EVER SEEN. I KEEP SEE-ING THOSE DEAD FACES BEFORE MY EYES." THE CAUSE OF THE ACCIDENT IS THAT THE BUILDING OF THE STANDS AND THEIR MAINTENANCE, AND THE PRO-VISION OF CRUSH BARRIERS, ARE SUBJECT TO MAXIMUM PROFIT BEING EARNED BY THE OWNERS. THE FUND SET UP AS THE CORPSES WERE CARRIED FROM THE STADIUM HAS ALREADY REACHED $200,000 AND MORE KEEPS POURING—

THE INSTITUTE

We entered the Institute for Prognosis and Prevention of Earth Disturbance as visitors from Geographical Area Two—one allied at this time with this area and, therefore, welcome to observe its work.

A short description of this organization may be of use: There are 50 of their most highly skilled technicians in it, all at work on some of the most advanced (as advanced as ours in this field) equipment for the diagnosis of vibrations, tremors, quakes. The very existence of this institute is because of the knowledge that the city cannot survive another five years—or is unlikely to do so. All these technicians live in the city, spend their free time in it—and the institute itself is in the danger area. They are all likely to be present when the event occurs. Yet they are all cheerful, unconcerned and—it is easy to think—of extreme bravery. But after a short time in their company, discussing their devices for predicting the upheaval, it is difficult to resist the conclusion that like the youngsters in the machine for transportation, who steer it in such a way that they are bound to kill or maim themselves or others. they are in some way set not to believe what they say—that they are in danger and will most certainly be killed or maimed together with the rest of the population—THE FIRE BROKE OUT AT DAWN, WHEN FEW PEOPLE WERE IN THE STREETS, AND WAS SO POWERFUL THAT IT REACHED THE FOURTH STORY FROM THE BASEMENT IN MINUTES. THE SCORES OF PEOPLE IN THE BUILDING WERE DRIVEN UPWARD BY THE FIRE, A FEW MANAGING TO NEGOTIATE THE FIRE ESCAPES, WHICH WERE MOSTLY ENGULFED IN FLAMES. AN UNKNOWN MAN IN THE STREET PENETRATED THE BUILDING, IN SPITE OF THE SMOKE AND THE FLAMES, AND RESCUED TWO SMALL CHILDREN LEFT CRYING ON THE SECOND FLOOR. ANOTHER TWO MINUTES AND IT WOULD HAVE BEEN TOO LATE. HE INSTANTLY PLUNGED BACK INTO THE INFERNO AND BROUGHT OUT AN OLD WOMAN ON HIS BACK. IN SPITE OF PROTESTS FROM THE BY-NOW LARGE CROWD, HE INSISTED ON RE-ENTERING THE FLAMING BUILDING AND WAS LAST SEEN AT A SECOND-FLOOR WINDOW FROM WHICH HE THREW DOWN A BABY TO THE PEOPLE BELOW. THE BABY WILL SURVIVE, BUT THE UNKNOWN HERO FELL BACK INTO THE FLAMES AND——

A Basic Mechanism

We believe we have established one of their mechanisms for maintaining themselves in impotence and indecision. It is precisely this: that they do continuously discuss and analyze. For instance, the technicians of this institute are always issuing warnings to the city's officials and to the populace. Their prognoses, one after another, come true—that minor vibrations are likely to occur in this or that area—yet warnings continue to be issued, discussion goes on. So accustomed have they become to this state of affairs that we found it was not possible to discuss active means for prevention with them. They would have become suspicious that we were some sort of troublemaker. In short, they do not find frightening discussion about the timing, the nature, the power of probable earth convulsions, but they are hostile to suggestions about the possible transfer of population or rebuilding of the city elsewhere. We have said that this is an infinitely subdivided society: It is the institute's task to warn, to forecast, not its responsibility to suggest solutions. But this mechanism—the role of talk—is only part of a much deeper one. We now suspect that a great many of the activities that they themselves see as methods of furthering change, saving life, improving society are, in fact methods of preventing change. It is almost as if they were afflicted with a powerful lassitude, a lack of vital energy, which, in fact, must resist change because it is so easily exhausted. Their infinite number of varieties of oral, verbal activity are expenditures of vital energy. They are soothed and relieved by stating a problem, but, having done this, seldom have the energy left to act on their verbal formulations. We have even concluded that they feel that by stating a problem, it becomes in some way nearer solution—PROTESTS THAT THE THREE SKYSCRAPERS ON THIRD STREET ARE TO BE PULLED DOWN IN ORDER TO BUILD THREE MUCH HIGHER BUILDINGS INSTEAD OF PUTTING THE MONEY INTO PROVIDING LOW-RATE ACCOMMODATION FOR THE CITY'S POOR, OF WHICH RECENT SURVEYS REVEAL THERE ARE 1,000,000 OR MORE, NEARLY A QUARTER OF THE TOTAL POPULATION, AND ALL IN ACCOMMODATIONS SO INADEQUATE THAT—. . . for instance, debates, discussions, verbal contests of all sorts, public and private, continue all the time. All their activities, public and private, are defined in talk, public or private. It is possible that they are so constituted that for them, an event has not occurred at all unless it has been discussed, presented in words—35 CONVENTIONS IN THE MONTH OF MAY ALONE TOTALING 75,000 DELEGATES FROM EVERY PART OF THE CONTINENT, WHILE AT THE SAME TIME, THE TOURIST FIGURES FOR MAY TOPPED THOSE FOR ANY PREVIOUS MAY. THIS YEAR IS ALREADY A RECORD FOR CONVENTIONS AND TOURISM GENERALLY, PROVING THAT THE ATTRACTIONS OF OUR CITY, ITS SITUATION, ITS CLIMATE, ITS AMENITIES, ITS REPUTATION FOR HOSPITALITY, EVER INCREASE IN

EVERY PART OF THE CIVILIZED GLOBE. IT IS ESSENTIAL TO STEP UP THE BUILD-
ING OF NEW HOTELS, MOTELS AND RESTAURANTS AND TO—. . . the one
thing they do not seem able to contemplate is the solution that
has seemed to us obvious ever since we observed their probable
future and decided to devote so much of our own planet's
resources to trying to help our sister planet—to evacuate the
city altogether. This is incredible, we know. Of course, you will
find it so.

INDIFFERENCE TO LOSS OF LIFE

We can only report what we find—that at no point have the
inhabitants of this city even considered the possibility of aban-
doning it and moving to an area that is not absolutely certain to
be destroyed. Their attitude toward life is that it is unimportant.
They are indifferent to their own suffering, assume that their
species must continuously lose numbers and strength and health
by natural disasters, famine, constant war. That this attitude goes
side by side with infinite care and devotion to individuals or to
small groups seems to us to indicate—THE DONATED SUM IS TO BE USED
TO BUILD A MEMORIAL, TO BE ERECTED IN THE SQUARE. IT WILL BE IN THE
SHAPE OF A COLUMN, WITH THE HEAD OF WILLIAM UNDERSCRIBE, THE
DECEASED, IN RELIEF ON ONE SIDE.

LAID TO REST

UPON THE BREAST

OF NATURE

GONE BUT NOT FORGOTTEN

WILL BE CARVED ON THE OTHER. JOAN UNDERSCRIBE, WHO LOST HER HUS-
BAND FIVE YEARS AGO, HAS WORKED SEVEN DAYS A WEEK FROM SIX A.M. UNTIL
TEN AT NIGHT AT THE AVENUE MOTEL TO EARN THE SUM NECESSARY FOR THIS
SIMPLE BUT MOVING MEMORIAL. SHE HAS JEOPARDIZED HER HEALTH, SHE
CLAIMS. THE FIVE YEARS OF UNREMITTING TOIL HAVE TAKEN THEIR TOLL. BUT
SHE HAS NO REGRETS. HE WAS THE BEST HUSBAND A WOMAN EVER HAD, SHE
TOLD OUR REPORTER—. . . on the point of deciding there was nothing
we could do against such total indifference to their condition; but
since they are at least prepared to talk about situations, we devised

a plan—THE BIGGEST ENTERTAINMENT EVER, COMBINING THE WORLD'S TOP CIRCUSES, ICE SHOWS, NON-STOP POP CONCERTS FOR THE ENTIRE WEEK, DAY AND NIGHT, NOT TO MENTION THREE OPERAS FROM THE WORLD'S GREATEST, THE BRITISH NATIONAL THEATER COMPANY IN THAT PERENNIAL ATTRACTION, THE INTERNATIONAL CULTURAL STAR ACE, THE THREE SISTERS, WHICH WILL BE ATTENDED BY OUR OWN FIRST LADY AND HER CHARMING DAUGHTERS AND A GLITTERING ARRAY OF STARS, INCLUDING BOB HOPE— . . . "calling a conference" is to gather a large number of individuals in one place, in order to exchange verbal formulations. This is probably their main anxiety-calming mechanism; they certainly resort to it on every occasion, whether under that name, called by governments, administrative bodies, authorities of all kinds, or under other names, for very often this procedure is social. For instance, a conference can be called a party and be for pleasure, but discussion on a theme or themes will be, in fact, the chief activity. The essential factor is that many of the creatures assemble in one place, to exchange word patterns with others, afterward telling others not present what has occurred—THE CITY'S CONSERVATION YEAR IS OVER AND MUST BE COUNTED A REMARKABLE SUCCESS. IT BURNED AN AWARENESS OF WHAT WE CAN EXPECT SO DEEPLY INTO ALL OUR MINDS AND HEARTS THAT INTEREST IS NOW NOT LIKELY TO FADE. A CONFERENCE TO—. . . opinion.

THEIR EDUCATION

The ability to define these, and to differentiate them from those of other people's, forms a large part of their education. When two of these creatures meet for the first time, they will set about finding out what opinions the other holds and will tolerate each other accordingly. Nonstimulating, easily tolerated opinions can also be called "received ideas." This means that an idea or a fact has been stamped with approval by some form of authority. The phrase is used like this: "That is a received idea." "Those are all received ideas." This does not necessarily mean that the idea or fact has been acted on nor that behavior has been changed. Essentially, a received idea is one that has become familiar, whether effective or not, and no longer arouses hostility or fear. The mark of an educated individual is this: that he has spent years absorbing received ideas and is able readily to repeat them. People who have absorbed opinions counter to the current standard of ideas are distrusted and may be called opinionated. This description is earned most easily by women and young people.

By that time, we were well known to everyone in the institute as Herbert Bond, 35 years old, male, and John Hunter, 40 years old, male. We had learned enough to avoid the direct "Why don't you take such and such steps?" since we had learned that this approach caused some sort of block or fault in their functioning, but approached like this: "Let us discuss the factors militating against the taking of such and such a step"; for instance, making sure that new buildings were not erected close to the areas where tremors or vibrations must occur.

This formulation was initially successful, evoking the maximum amount of animated talk without arousing hostility. But very shortly, strong emotion was aroused by phrases and words of which we list a few here: profit motive, conflicting commercial interests, vested interests, capitalism, socialism, democracy—but there are many such emotive words. We were not able to determine, or not in a way that our economic experts would recognize as satisfactory, the significance of these phrases, since the emotions became too violent to allow the conference to continue. The animals would certainly have begun to attack one another physically. In other words, the range of opinion (see above) was too wide to be accommodated. Opinion, that is, on matters to do with disposal and planning of population. Opinion concerning earth disturbance was virtually unanimous.

BARBARIC SYSTEM OF TOWN PLANNING UNIQUE IN OUR SYSTEM, BUT SEE HISTORIES OF PLANETS 2 AND 4

It appears that their population disposal, their city planning, is not determined by the needs of the people who live in an area but is the result of a balance come to by many conflicting bodies and individuals whose reason for participating in such schemes is self-interest. For instance: Before the violence engendered by this subject closed the conference, we had gathered that the reason a particularly large and expensive group of buildings was built directly in the line of maximum earth disturbance was that that part of the city commands high "rents"—that is, people are prepared to pay more to live and work in that area than elsewhere. Nor can the willingness of the builders and planners to erect buildings in the maximum danger area be put down to callousness, since in many cases the individuals concerned themselves live and work there—THE EMERGENCY UNIT AT THE HOSPITAL IN WHICH A TEAM OF TEN DOCTORS AND NURSES WORKS AROUND THE CLOCK TO SAVE LIVES THAT WOULD HAVE BEEN LOST AS RECENTLY AS FIVE YEARS AGO—AND ARE STILL LOST IN HOSPITALS NOT EQUIPPED WITH EMERGENCY UNITS. THE PATIENTS ARE USUALLY THE VICTIMS OF CAR ACCIDENTS OR STREET FIGHTS AND ARRIVE AT THE UNIT IN A STATE OF SEVERE SHOCK. SINCE AS SHORT A DELAY AS FIVE MINUTES CAN MAKE THE DIFFERENCE BETWEEN LIFE AND DEATH. TREATMENT IS STARTED AS THE PATIENT IS LIFTED OUT OF THE AMBULANCE—. . . as a good deal of the anger was directed against their own young, we left the institute and returned to the center of the city, where we again made contact with the young.

THE INSTITUTE FOUND NOT USEFUL

The young ones working at the institute in menial and assistive positions were all of a different subculture, patterned on the older animals in clothing and behavior. The young animals we met in the city were in herds, or smaller groups, and not easily contacted by Herbert Bond and John Hunter, who, being older and dressed in the uniform of the dominant males, were suspected of being spies of some sort. We therefore reincarnated ourselves as two youngsters, male and female, having agreed to spend a fourth of what was left of our supply of power in trying to persuade them to agree on one issue and to act on it. For, like their elders, they discuss and talk and sing endlessly, enjoying pleasurable sensations of satisfaction and agreement with others, making these an end in themselves. We suggested that in view of what was going to happen to the city, they, the young ones, might try to persuade all those of their age to leave and live elsewhere, to make for themselves some sort of encampment, if to build a new city was beyond their resources, at any rate, a place in which refugees would be welcomed and cared for.

FAILURE WITH THE YOUNG

All that happened was that a number of new songs were sung, all of a melancholy nature, all on the theme of unavoidable tragedy. Our encounter with these young ones was taking place on the beach and at the time of the fading of the sunlight. This is a time that has a powerfully saddening effect on all the animals. But it was not until afterward that we understood we should have chosen any time of the day but that one. There were large numbers of young, many with musical instruments. Half a dozen of them converted the occasion into a conference (see above) by addressing the mass not as their elders do, through talking, but through singing—the heightened and emotional sound. The emotion was of a different kind from that at the conference at the institute. That had been violent and aggressive and nearly resulted in physical attack. This was heavy, sad, passive. Having failed to get them to discuss, either by talking or by singing, a mass exodus from the city, we then attempted discussing how to prevent individuals from massing in the most threatened areas (we were on one at the time) and how, when the shock occurred, to prevent mass deaths and injuries and how to treat the injured, and so forth.

DESPAIR OF THE YOUNG

All these attempts failed. We might have taken a clue from the drugged condition of the three whose minds we at first occupied and from the indifference to death of the four in the metal conveyance. We have concluded that the young are in a state of disabling despair. While more clear-minded, in some ways, than their elders—that is, more able to voice and maintain criticism of wrongs and faults, they are not able to believe in their own effectiveness. Again and again, on the beach, as the air darkened, versions of this exchange took place:

"But you say you believe it must happen, and within five years."

"So they say."

"But you don't think it will?"

"If it happens, it happens."

"But it isn't *if*—it will happen."

"They are all corrupt, what can we do? They want to kill us all."

"Who are corrupt?"

"The old ones. They run everything."

"But why don't you challenge them?"

"You can't challenge them. They are too strong. We have to evade. We must be fluid. We must be like water."

"But you are still here, where it is going to happen."

"So they say."

A song swept the whole gathering. It was now quite dark. There were many thousands massed near the water.

> *It will happen soon,*
> *So they say,*
> *We will not live to fight*
> *Another day.*
> *They are blind.*
> *They have blown our mind.*
> *We shall not live to fight,*
> *We live to die.*

MASS SUICIDES

And hundreds of them committed suicide—by swimming out into the water in the dark, while those who stood on higher ledges by the water threw themselves in—A DONATION OF $500,000 TO BUILD A BIRD SANCTUARY IN THE PARK. THIS WILL HAVE SPECIMENS OF EVERY KNOWN SPECIES IN THE WORLD. IT IS HOPED THAT SPECIES THREATENED WITH EXTINCTION DUE TO MAN'S CRUELTY AND UNCONCERN WILL FIND THIS SANCTUARY A USEFUL BANK FROM WHICH THEY CAN REPLENISH AND STRENGTHEN VARIETIES UNDER THREAT—. . . very low stock of power. We decided to make one last attempt, to concentrate our material in a single place. We decided to leave the herds of young and to return to the older animals, since these were in authority. Not to the institute, since we had proved their emotional instability. It was essential to choose a set of words that would not cause emotion—a received idea.

Now, the idea that the behavior of an individual or a group can be very different from its, or their, self-description is already part of their mental furniture and is enshrined in many timeworn word sets. For instance, "Don't judge by what he says but by what he does."

We decided to reinforce this soothing received idea with another of their anxiety-reducing devices. We have already noted that a conference is such a device. A variety of this is to put ideas into heightened or emotional sound, as was done by the young on the beach. We decided that neither of these was suitable for our last attempt. We considered and discarded a third that we have not yet mentioned. This is when disturbing or unpalatable ideas are put into ritual form and acted out in public to small groups or relayed by a technical device, "television," which enables visual images to be transmitted simultaneously to millions of people. A sequence of events that may fall outside their formal code of morality, or be on its border line, will be acted out, causing violent approval or disapproval—it is a form of catharsis. After a time, these sequences of acted-out events become familiar and are constantly performed. This way of trying out, of acclimatizing unfamiliar ideas, goes on all the time, side by side with ritual acting out of situations that are familiar and banal—thus making them appear more interesting. This is a way of making a life situation that an individual may find intolerably tedious and repetitive more stimulating and enable him to suffer it without rebelling. These dramas, of both the first and the second kind, can be of any degree of sophistication. But we decided on a fourth mechanism or method: a verbal game. One of their games is when sets of words are discussed by one, two or more individuals, and these are most often transmitted through the above-mentioned device.

We had reassumed our identities as Herbert Bond and John Hunter, since we were again contacting authority, and approached a television center with forged credentials from a geographic area called Britain, recently a powerful and combative subspecies, which enjoys a sort of prestige because of past aggressiveness and military prowess.

LAUGHTER, FUNCTIONS OF, SEE ABOVE

We proposed a game of words, on the theme "Don't judge by words but by actions." The debate took place last night. To begin with, there was a good deal of laughter, a sign that should have warned us. This was not antagonistic, "laughing at," which is found disagreeable but which, in fact, is much safer a reaction than "laughing with," which is laughter of agreement, of feeling flattered. This is commonly evoked by ideas that are still minority ideas, and the minorities consider that they are in advance of the mass. The aggressive and hostile laughter is, in fact, a safer reaction because it reassures onlookers that a balance is being kept, whereas the sympathetic laughter arouses feelings of anxiety in those watching, if the ideas put forward are challenging to norms accepted by them. Our thesis was simple and as already outlined: that this society is indifferent to death and to suffering. Fear is not experienced, or not in a way that is useful to protect society or the individual. No one sees these facts, because all the sets of words that describe behavior are in contrast to the facts. The official sets of words are all to do with protection of oneself and others, caution about the future, pity and compassion for others. Throughout all this—that is, while we developed our thesis—we were greeted by laughter.

These games have audiences invited to the places where they are played, so that the makers of the ritual can judge the probable reaction of the individuals outside all over the city in front of their television. The laughter was loud and prolonged. Opposing Herbert Bond and John Hunter, professors of words from Britain, were two professors of words from the local university. They have rules of debate, the essence of which is that each statement must have the same weight or importance as the preceding. The opposing professors' statements, of equal length as ours, stated the opposite view and were light and humorous in tone. Our turn coming again, we proved our point by stating the facts about this city's behavior in the face of a certain disaster—but we did not get very far. As soon as we switched from the theoretical, the general, to the particular, the laughter died away and violent hostility was shown. There is a custom that if people watching a ritual dislike it, they send hostile messages to the relay point. What Herbert Bond and John Hunter said caused so much violent emotion that the technical equipment used for listening to these messages broke down. While the two local professors maintained the calmness of manner expected during these games, they were nervous and, the ritual over, they said they thought they would lose their employment. They were hostile to us, as being responsible. They complained that as "foreigners," we did not realize that these rituals must be kept light in tone and general in theme.

When we two got to the door of the building, there was a mob outside, mostly of older animals, very hostile. The managers of the ritual game pulled us back and took us up to the top of the building and set guards on us, as apparently the mob was angered to the point of wishing to kill us—again, the focus of their anger was that we were foreign. We complied, since there was no point in creating further disorder and—BRING YOUR DECEASED TO US, WHO ARE FRIENDS OF YOUR FAMILY, FRIENDS IN YOUR DISTRESS. TREATED WITH ALL REVERENCE, CARED FOR AS YOU CARED WHEN MOTHER, FATHER, HUSBAND, WIFE, BROTHER OR LITTLE SISTER WAS STILL WITH YOU, THE SLEEPING ONE WILL BE BORNE TO THE LAST HOME, LAID GENTLY TO REST IN A PLOT WHERE FLOWERS AND BIRDS WILL ALWAYS PLAY AND WHERE YOU CAN VISIT AND MUSE . . . IN YOUR LEISURE HOURS, YOU WILL ALWAYS HAVE A HAVEN WHERE YOUR THOUGHTS CAN DWELL IN LOVING HAPPINESS ON YOUR DEPARTED FRIENDS, WHO—. . . We are running very short of power. There is nothing more we can do. This mission must be regarded as a failure. We have been able to achieve nothing. We have also failed to understand what is the cause of their defectiveness. There is no species like this one on any other planet known to us.

As the guards on our place of detention relaxed their vigilance, we simply dematerialized and returned to the craft. They will think we escaped or perhaps were the subjects of kidnaping by the still-hostile crowd that we could see from the top of the building where—SHOCKING AND DISGUSTING PROGRAM THAT OFFENDED IN A WAY NO OTHER PROGRAM HAS IN THIS COMMENTATOR'S MEMORY. IT IS NOT WHAT WAS SAID BY OUR TWO VISITORS, IT WAS THE WAY IT WAS SAID. AFTER ALL, WE ALL HAVE TO LIVE WITH "THE FACTS" THAT THEY SO NAIVELY SEEM TO IMAGINE ARE A REVELATION TO US. FOR SHEER BAD TASTE, CRUDITY OF TONE, UGLINESS OF MANNER AND INSENSITIVITY TO THE DEEPER FEELINGS OF THE VIEWERS, NOTHING CAN BE COMPARED WITH PROFESSORS BOND AND HUNTER LAST NIGHT.

Departure from the Planet

We are now reassembled as our original six and will shortly be returning. We have a tentative conclusion. It is this: that a society that is doomed to catastrophe, and that is unable to prepare for it, can expect that few people will survive except those already keyed to chaos and disaster. The civil, the ordered, the conforming, the well-tempered can expect to fall victim at first exposure. But the vagabonds, criminals, mad, extremely poor will have the means to survive. We conclude, therefore, that when, within the next five years, the eruption occurs, no one will be left but those types the present managers of society consider undesirable, for the present society is too inflexible to adapt—as we have already said, we have no idea why this should be so, what is wrong with them. But perhaps concealed in this city are groups of individuals we did not contact, who saw no reason to contact us, who not only foresee the future event but who are taking steps to—

The West Coast Examiner

Sam Baker, a farmer from Long Ridge, said he saw a "shining round thing" take off 100 yards away from his fence yesterday evening as the sun went down. Says Sam: "It rose into the air at such a rate it was almost impossible to follow it with my eyes. Then it disappeared." Others from the same area claim to have seen "unusual sights" during the past few days. The official explanation is that the unusually vivid sunsets of the past month have caused strong reflections and mirages off rocks and stretches of sand.

Military Sector III to H.Q. (Top Confidential)

The UFO that landed some time in the night of the 14th, and was viewed as it landed, remained stationary for the entire period of seven days. No one was seen to leave the UFO. This is exactly in line with the previous 12 landings in the same spot. This was the 13th UFO of this series. But this was rather larger and more powerful than the previous 12. The difference registered by Sonoscope 15 was considerable. This UFO, like the previous 12, was only just visible to ordinary vision. Our observer, farmer Jansen H. Blackson, recruited by us after the first landing a year ago, volunteered that this one was much more easily seen. "You had to stare hard to see the others, but I saw this one coming down, also lifting off, but it went up so fast I lost it at once." The suggestion from M 8 is that all 13 are observation craft from the Chinese. The view of this section is that they are from our Naval Department 15, and it is my contention that as they have no right of access to this terrain, which is under the aegis of War Department 4, we should blast them to hell and gone next time they try it on.

Air Force 14 to Center

The alightings continue—number 13 last week. This was also unmanned. Confirm belief Russian origin. Must report also two further landings to the south of the city, both in the same place and separated by an interval of three weeks. These two craft identical with the series of 55 alighting to north of city last year. The two southern landings coincided with the disappearance of 11 people, five the first time, six the second. This makes 450 people gone without trace during the past two years. We suggest it is no longer possible to dismiss the fact that the landings of these craft always mean the disappearance of two to ten people with the word coincidence. We must face the possibility that all or some are manned, but by individuals so dissimilar in structure to ourselves that we cannot see them. We would point out that Sonoscope 4 is only just able to bring these types of craft within vision and that, therefore, the levels of density that might indicate the presence of "people" might escape the machine. We further suggest that the facetiousness of the phrase Little Green Men might mask an attitude of mind that is inimical to a sober evaluation or assessing of this possibility.

Confirm at earliest if we are to continue policy of minimizing these disappearances. We can still find no common denominator in the *type* of person taken off. The only thing they all have in common is that they were, for a variety of reasons, somewhere in the areas in which these craft choose to descend.

The West Coast Examiner

Our observer at filling station Lost Pine reports that groups of people are driving south out of the city to the area where the latest UFOs are known to descend and take off. Last night they numbered over 50,000.

AIR FORCE 14 TO CENTER

In spite of Total Policy 19, rumors are out. We consider it advisable to cordon off the area, although this might precipitate extreme panic situation. But we see no alternative. The cult called Be Ready for the Day is already thousands strong and sweeping the city and environs. Suggest an announcement that the area is contaminated with a chance leak of radioactivity.

LARRY NIVEN

LEVIATHAN

August 1970

Larry Niven, born in 1938 in California, where he still lives, carries on the tradition set by Arthur C. Clarke and other older writers of "hard" science fiction writing; that is, he was trained in the sciences (in his case, mathematics, at Washburn University in Kansas) and because the ingenious future technology of his stories is carefully and consistently worked out, he is much admired by his more technical readers. He is also one of only a very few science fiction writers whose novels (written alone or in conjunction with one of his collaborators, most frequently Jerry Pournelle) regularly make an appearance on mainstream bestseller lists. Much of Niven's early work, including novels and short stories, forms part of a vast and complex "future history," the Tales of Known Space. The sequence starts just about now as the millennium begins, and reaches a thousand years into the future, complete with many alien races. *Ringworld* is probably the best-known Known Space novel. More recently, he has collaborated on epic space operas: with Pournelle, *The Mote in God's Eye, Inferno, Lucifer's Hammer.* "Leviathan" is not a Known Space story; it is one of the just-for-fun time-travel tales collected in *The Flight of the Horse* (1973). It's an exuberant take on good old-fashioned sci-fi yarning, complete with alien monster.

TWO MEN STOOD on one side of a thick glass wall. "You'll be airborne." Svetz's beefy red-faced boss was saying. "We made some improvements in the small extension cage while you were in the hospital. You can hover it or fly it at up to fifty miles per hour or let it fly itself: there's a constant-altitude setting. Your field of vision is total. We've made the shell of the extension cage completely transparent."

On the other side of the thick glass, something was trying to kill them. It was 40 feet long from nose to tail and was equipped with vestigial batlike wings. Otherwise, it was built something like a slender lizard. It screamed and scratched at the glass with murderous claws.

The sign on the glass read:

GILA MONSTER
RETRIEVED FROM THE YEAR 230 ANTEATOMIC, APPROXIMATELY,
FROM THE REGION OF CHINA, EARTH. EXTINCT.

"You'll be well out of his reach," said Ra Chen.

"Yes, sir." Svetz stood with his arms folded about him, as if he had a chill. He was being sent after the biggest animal that had ever lived; and Svetz was afraid of animals.

"For science' sake! What are you worried about. Svetz? It's only a big fish!"

"Yes, sir. You said that about the Gila monster. It's just an extinct lizard, you said."

"We had only a drawing in a children's book to go by. How could we know it would be so big?"

The Gila monster drew back from the glass. It inhaled hugely and took aim. Yellow-and-orange flame spewed from its nostrils and played across the glass. Svetz squeaked and jumped for cover.

"He can't get through," said Ra Chen.

Svetz picked himself up. He was a slender, small-boned man with pale skin, light-blue eyes and very fine ash-blond hair. "How could we know it would breathe fire?" he mimicked. "That lizard almost *cremated* me. I spent four months in the hospital, as it was. And what really burns me is, he looks less like the drawing every time I see him. Sometimes I wonder if I didn't get the wrong animal."

"What's the difference, Svetz? The secretary-general loved him. That's what counts."

"Yes, sir. Speaking of the secretary-general, what does he want with a sperm whale? He's got a horse, he's got a Gila monster—"

"That's a little complicated." Ra Chen grimaced. "Palace politics! It's *always* complicated. Right now, Svetz, somewhere in the United Nations palace, a hundred different scientists are trying to get support, each for his own project. And every last one of them involves getting the attention of the secretary-general and *holding* it. Keeping his attention isn't easy."

Svetz nodded. Everybody knew about the secretary-general.

The family that had ruled the United Nations for 700 years was somewhat inbred.

The secretary-general was 44 years old. He was a happy person; he loved animals and flowers and pictures and people. Pictures of planets and multiple star systems made him clap his hands and coo with delight; so the Institute for Space Research shared amply in the United Nations budget. But he liked extinct animals, too.

"Someone managed to convince the secretary-general that he wants the largest animal on earth. The idea may have been to take us down a peg or two," said Ra Chen. "Someone may think we're getting too big a share of the budget.

"By the time I got onto it, the secretary-general wanted a Brontosaurus. We'd never have gotten him that. No extension cage will reach that far."

"Was it your idea to get him a whale, sir?"

"Yeah. It wasn't easy to persuade him. Whales have been extinct for so long that we don't even have pictures. All I had to show him was a crystal sculpture from Archaeology—dug out of the Steuben Glass building—and a Bible and a dictionary. I managed to convince him that Leviathan and the sperm whale were one and the same."

"That's not strictly true." Svetz had read a computer-produced condensation of the Bible. The condensation had ruined the plot, in Svetz's opinion. "Leviathan could be anything big and destructive, even a horde of locusts."

"Thank science you weren't there to help, Svetz! The issue was confused enough. Anyway. I promised the secretary-general the largest animal that ever lived on earth. All the literature says that that animal was a whale. And there were sperm-whale herds all over the oceans as recently as the First Century Ante-Atomic. You shouldn't have any trouble finding one."

"In twenty minutes?"

Ra Chen looked startled. "What?"

"If I try to keep the big extension cage in the past for more than twenty minutes. I'll never be able to bring it home. The—"

"I know that."

"—uncertainty factor in the energy constants—"

"Svetz—"

"—will blow the institute right off the map."

"We thought of that, Svetz. You'll go back in the small extension cage. When you find a whale, you'll signal the big extension cage."

"Signal it how?"

"We've found a way to send a simple on-off pulse through time. Let's go back to the institute and I'll show you."

Malevolent golden eyes watched them through the glass as they walked away.

The small extension cage was the part of the time machine that did the moving. Within its transparent shell, Svetz seemed to ride a flying armchair equipped with an airplane passenger's lunch tray; except that the lunch tray was covered with lights and buttons and knobs and crawling green lines. He was somewhere off the East Coast of North America, in or around the year 100 Ante-Atomic or 1845 Anno Domini. The temporal-precession gauge was not particularly accurate.

Svetz skimmed low over water the color of lead, beneath a sky the color of slate. But for the rise and fall of the sea, he might almost have been suspended in an enormous sphere painted half light, half dark. He let the extension cage fly itself, 60 feet above the water, while he watched the needle on the NAI, the Nervous Activities Indicator.

Hunting Leviathan.

His stomach was uneasy. Svetz had thought he was adjusting to the peculiar gravitational side effects of time travel. But apparently not.

At least he would not be here long.

On this trip, he was not looking for a mere 40-foot Gila monster. Now he hunted the largest animal that had ever lived. A most conspicuous beast. And now he had a life-seeking instrument, the NAI.

The needle twitched violently.

Was it a whale? But the needle was trembling in apparent indecision. A cluster of sources, then. Svetz looked in the direction indicated.

A clipper ship, winged with white sail, long and slender and graceful as hell. Crowded, too, Svetz guessed. Many humans, closely packed, would affect the NAI in just that manner. A sperm whale—a single center of complex nervous activity—would attract the needle as violently, without making it jerk about like that.

The ship would interfere with reception. Svetz turned east and away, but not without regret. The ship was beautiful.

The uneasiness in Svetz's belly was getting worse, not better.

Endless gray-green water, rising and falling beneath his flying armchair.

Enlightenment came like something clicking in his head. *Seasick.* On automatic, the extension cage matched its motion to that of the surface over which it flew; and that surface was heaving in great dark swells.

No wonder his stomach was uneasy! Svetz grinned and reached for the manual controls.

The NAI needle suddenly jerked hard over. A bite! thought Svetz, and he looked off to the right. No sign of a ship. And submarines hadn't been invented yet. Had they? No, of course they hadn't.

The needle was rock-steady.

Svetz flipped the call button.

The source of the tremendous NAI signal was off to his right and moving. Svetz turned to follow it. It would be minutes before the call signal reached the Institute for Temporal Research and brought the big extension cage with its weaponry for hooking Leviathan.

Many years ago, Ra Chen had dreamed of rescuing the library at Alexandria from Caesar's fire. For this purpose, he had built the big extension cage. Its door was a gaping iris, big enough to be loaded while the library was actually burning. Its hold, at a guess, was at least twice large enough to hold all the scrolls in that ancient library.

The big cage had cost a fortune in government money. It had failed to go back beyond 400 A.A., or 1545 A.D. The books burned at Alexandria were still lost to history, or at least to historians.

Such a boondoggle would have broken other men. Somehow, Ra Chen had survived the blow to his reputation.

He had pointed out the changes to Svetz after they returned from the zoo. "We've fitted the cage out with heavy-duty stunners and anti-gravity beams. You'll operate them by remote control. Be careful not to let the stun beam touch you. It would kill even a sperm whale if you held it on him for more than a few seconds and it'd kill a man instantly. Other than that, you should have no problems."

It was at that moment that Svetz's stomach began to hurt.

"Our major change is the call button. It will actually send us a signal through time, so that we can send the big extension cage back to you. We can land it right beside you, no more than a few minutes off. That took considerable research. Svetz. The treasury raised our budget for this year, so that we could get that whale."

Svetz nodded.

"Just be sure you've got a whale before you call for the big extension cage."

Now, 1200 years earlier, Svetz followed an underwater source of nervous impulse. The signal was intensely powerful. It could not be anything smaller than an adult bull sperm whale.

A shadow formed in the air to his right. Svetz watched it take shape: a great gray-blue sphere floating beside him. Around the rim of the door were anti-gravity beamers and heavy-duty stun guns. The opposite side of the sphere wasn't there; it simply faded away.

To Svetz, that was the most frightening thing about any time machine: the way it seemed to turn a corner that wasn't there.

Svetz was almost over the signal. Now he used the remote controls to swing the anti-gravity beamers around and down.

He had them locked on the source. He switched them on and dials surged.

Leviathan was *heavy.* More massive than Svetz had expected. He upped the power and watched the NAI needle swing as Leviathan rose invisibly through the water.

Where the surface of the water bulged upward under the attack of the antigravity beams, a shadow formed. Leviathan rising . . .

Was there something wrong with the shape?

Then a trembling spherical bubble of water rose, shivering, from the ocean, and Leviathan was within it.

Partly within it. He was too big to fit, though he should not have been.

He was four times as massive as a sperm whale should have been and a dozen times as long. He looked nothing like the crystal Steuben sculpture. Leviathan was a kind of serpent, armored with red-bronze scales as big as a viking's shield, armed with teeth like ivory spears. His triangular jaws gaped wide. As he floated toward Svetz, he writhed, seeking with his bulging yellow eyes for whatever strange enemy had subjected him to this indignity.

Svetz was paralyzed with fear and indecision. Neither then nor later did he doubt that what he saw was the Biblical Leviathan. This had to be the largest beast that had ever roamed the sea; a beast large enough and fierce enough to be synonymous with anything big and destructive. Yet—if the crystal sculpture was anything like representational, this was not a sperm whale at all.

In any case, he was far too big for the extension cage.

Indecision stayed his hand—and then Svetz stopped thinking entirely, as the great slitted irises found him.

The beast was floating past him. Around its waist was a sphere of weightless water that shrank steadily as gobbets dripped away and rained back to the sea. The beast's nostrils flared—it was obviously an air breather, though not a cetacean.

It stretched, reaching for Svetz with gaping jaws.

Teeth like scores of elephant's tusks all in a row. Polished and needle-sharp. Svetz saw them close about him from above and below, while he sat frozen in fear.

At the last moment, he shut his eyes tight.

When death did not come, Svetz opened his eyes.

The jaws had not entirely closed on Svetz and his armchair. He heard them grinding faintly against—against the invisible surface of the extension cage, whose existence Svetz had forgotten entirely.

Svetz resumed breathing. He would return home with an empty extension cage, to face the wrath of Ra Chen—a fate better than death. He moved his fingers to cut the anti-gravity beams from the big extension cage.

Metal whined against metal. Svetz whiffed hot oil, while red lights blinked on all over his lunch-tray control board. He hastily turned the beams on again.

The red lights blinked out, one by reluctant one.

Through the transparent shell, Svetz could hear the grinding of teeth. Leviathan was trying to chew his way into the extension cage.

His released weight had nearly torn the cage loose from the rest of the time machine. Svetz would have been stranded in the past, 100 miles out to sea, in a broken extension cage that probably wouldn't float, with an angry sea monster waiting to snap him up. No, he couldn't turn off the anti-gravity beamers.

But the beamers were on the big extension cage, and he couldn't hold it more than about 15 minutes longer. When the big cage was gone, what would prevent Leviathan from pulling him to his doom?

"I'll stun him off," said Svetz.

There was dark-red palate above him and red gums and forking tongue beneath, and the long curved fangs all around. But between the two rows of teeth, Svetz could see the big extension cage and the battery of stunners around the door. By eye, he rotated the stunners until they pointed straight toward Leviathan.

"I must be out of my mind," said Svetz, and he spun the stunners away from him. He couldn't fire them at Leviathan without hitting himself.

And Leviathan wouldn't let go.

Trapped.

No, he thought with a burst of relief. He could escape with his life. The go-home lever would send his small extension cage out from between the jaws of Leviathan, back into the time stream. back to the institute. His mission had failed, but that was hardly his fault. Why had Ra Chen been unable to uncover mention of a sea serpent bigger than a sperm whale?

"It's all his fault," said Svetz. And he reached for the go-home lever. But he stayed his hand.

"I can't just tell him so," he said. For Ra Chen terrified him.

The grinding of teeth came through the extension cage.

"Hate to just quit," said Svetz. "Think I'll try something. . . ."

He could see the anti-gravity beamers by looking between the teeth. He could feel their influence, so nearly were they focused on the extension cage itself. If he focused them just on himself. . . .

He felt the change; he felt both strong and lightheaded, like a drunken ballet master. And if he now narrowed the focus . . .

The monster's teeth seemed to grind harder. Svetz looked between them, as best he could.

Leviathan was no longer floating. He was hanging straight down from the extension cage, hanging by his teeth. The anti-gravity beamers still balanced the pull of his mass, but now they did so by pulling straight up on the extension cage.

The monster was in obvious distress. Naturally. A water beast, he was supporting his own mass for the first time in his life. And by his teeth! His yellow eyes rolled frantically. His tail twitched slightly at the very tip. And still he clung.

"Let go," said Svetz. "Let go, you . . . monster."

The monster's teeth slid, screeching, down the transparent surface, and he fell.

Svetz cut the anti-gravity a fraction of a second late. He smelled burnt oil and there were tiny red lights blinking off one by one on his lunch-tray control board.

Leviathan hit the water with a sound of thunder. His long, sinuous body rolled over and floated to the surface and lay as if dead. But his tail flicked once and Svetz knew that he was alive.

"I could kill you," said Svetz. "Hold the stunners on you until you're dead. There's time."

But he still had ten minutes to search for a sperm whale. It wasn't time enough. It didn't begin to be time enough, but if he used it all . . .

The sea serpent flicked its tail and began to swim away. Once, he rolled to look at Svetz and his jaws opened wide in fury. He finished his roll and was fleeing again.

"Just a minute." Svetz said thickly. "Just a science-perverting minute, there." And he swung the stunners to focus.

Gravity behaved strangely inside an extension cage. While the cage was moving forward in time, *down* was all directions outward from the center of the cage. Svetz was plastered against the curved wall. He waited for the trip to end.

Seasickness was nothing compared with the motion sickness of time travel.

Free fall, then normal gravity. Svetz moved unsteadily to the door.

Ra Chen was waiting to help him out. "Did you get it?"

"Leviathan? No, sir." Svetz looked past his boss. "Where's the big extension cage?"

"We're bringing it back slowly, to minimize the gravitational side effects. But if you don't have the whale—"

"I said I don't have Leviathan."

"Well, just what *do* you have?" Ra Chen demanded.

Somewhat later, he said. "It wasn't?"

Later yet, he said. "You killed him? Why, Svetz? Pure spite?"

"No. sir. It was the most intelligent thing I did during the entire trip."

"But *why?* Never mind, Svetz, here's the big extension cage." A gray-blue shadow congealed in the hollow cradle of the time machine. "And there does seem to be something in it. Hi, you idiots, throw an anti-gravity beam inside the cage! Do you want the beast crushed?"

The cage had arrived. Ra Chen waved an arm in signal. The door opened.

Something tremendous hovered within the big extension cage. It looked like a malevolent white mountain in there, peering back at its captors with a single tiny, angry eye. It was trying to get at Ra Chen, but it couldn't swim in air.

Its other eye was only a torn socket. One of its flippers was ripped along the trailing edge. Rips and ridges and puckers of scar tissue, and a forest of broken wood and broken steel, marked its tremendous expanse of albino skin. Lines trailed from many of the broken harpoons. High up on one flank, bound to the beast by broken and tangled lines, was the corpse of a bearded man with one leg.

"Hardly in mint condition, is he?" Ra Chen observed.

"Be careful, sir. He's a killer. I saw him ram a sailing ship and sink it clean before I could focus the stunners on him."

"What amazes me is that you found him at all in the time you had left. Svetz, I do not understand your luck. Or am I missing something?"

"It wasn't luck, sir. It was the most intelligent thing I did the entire trip."

"You said that before. About killing Leviathan."

Svetz hurried to explain. "The sea serpent was just leaving the vicinity. I wanted to kill him, but I knew I didn't have the time. I was about to leave myself, when he turned back and bared his teeth.

"He was an obvious carnivore. Those teeth were built strictly for killing, sir. I should have noticed earlier. And I could think of only one animal big enough to feed a carnivore that size."

"Ahhh. Brilliant, Svetz."

"There was corroborative evidence. Our research never found any mention of giant sea serpents. The great geological surveys of the First Century Post-Atomic should have turned up something. Why didn't they?"

"Because the sea serpent quietly died out two centuries earlier, after whalers killed off his food supply."

Svetz colored. "Exactly. So I turned the stunners on Leviathan before he could swim away and I kept the stunners on him until the NAI said he was dead. I reasoned that if Leviathan was there, there must be whales in the vicinity."

"And Leviathan's nervous output was masking the signal."

"Sure enough, it was. The moment he was dead, the NAI registered another signal. I followed it to"—Svetz jerked his head. They were floating the whale out of the extension cage—"to him."

Days later, two men stood on one side of a thick glass wall.

"We took some clones from him, then passed him on to the secretary-general's vivarium," said Ra Chen. "Pity you had to settle for an albino." He waved aside Svetz's protest: "I know, I know, you were pressed for time."

Beyond the glass, the one-eyed whale glared at Svetz through murky sea water. Surgeons had removed most of the harpoons, but scars remained along his flanks; and Svetz, awed, wondered how long the beast had been at war with man. Centuries? How long did sperm whales live?

Ra Chen lowered his voice. "We'd all be in trouble if the secretary-general found out that there was once a bigger animal than this. You understand that, don't you, Svetz?"

"Yes, sir."

"Good." Ra Chen's gaze swept across another glass wall and a fire-breathing Gila monster. Farther down, a horse looked back at him along the dangerous spiral horn in its forehead.

"Always we find the unexpected," said Ra Chen. "Sometimes I wonder . . ."

If you'd do your research better, Svetz thought. . . .

"Did you know that time travel wasn't even a concept until the First Century Ante-Atomic? A writer invented it. From then until the Fourth Century Post-Atomic, time travel was pure fantasy. It violates everything the scientists thought were natural laws. Logic. Conservation of matter and energy. Momentum, reaction, any law of motion that makes time a part of the statement. Relativity.

"It strikes me," said Ra Chen, "that every time we push an extension cage past that particular five-century period, we shove it into a world that isn't really natural. That's why you keep finding giant sea serpents and fire-breathing—"

"That's nonsense," said Svetz. He was afraid of his boss, yes; but there were limits.

"You're right," Ra Chen said instantly. Almost with relief.

"Take a month's vacation. Svetz, then back to work. The secretary-general wants a bird."

"A bird?" Svetz smiled. A bird sounded harmless enough. "I suppose he found it in another children's book?"

"That's right. Ever hear of a roc?"

HARLAN ELLISON

ALL THE BIRDS COME HOME TO ROOST

March 1979

Harlan Ellison, born in Ohio in 1934 and now resident in Sherman Oaks, California, has won many awards for his many short stories—seven Hugos, three Nebulas, a British Fantasy Award, an Edgar from the Mystery Writers of America—as well as three Outstanding Script awards from the Writers Guild of America. As a TV scriptwriter he has been associated with *The Alfred Hitchcock Hour, The Man from U.N.C.L.E., Star Trek, The Twilight Zone* (in its later incarnation), as well as many non-genre series. One famously unsettling story was made into the movie *A Boy and his Dog* (1975), a favorite at late-night convention screenings. The list of his publications, mainly story and essay collections, is a long one, and also somewhat confusing as collections are reworked and retitled, but *Deathbird Stories* (1975) may be the best known of them. He has been an editor, notably of the *Dangerous*

Visions series (1967 and 1972), but also of the "shared-world" anthology *Medea: Harlan's World* (1985).

The story that follows shows Ellison in fine form, energetic, imaginative, edgy, with a high-pressure protagonist who seems like the dark twin of the author (at the time this was written, he was a well-known bachelor). A number of stories about men and women in this volume, especially those from the early decades, adhere to the then-standard men's magazine convention of somewhat "racy" jocularity. None of them seems nearly as well fitted as this one does to the more complex view of men that evolved with time, as *Playboy* itself evolved.

HE TURNED ONTO his left side in the bed, trying to avoid the wet spot. He propped his hand against his cheek, smiled grimly and prepared himself to tell her the truth about why he had been married and divorced three times.

"Three times!" she had said, her eyes widening, that familiar line of perplexity appearing vertically between her brows. "Three times. Christ, in all the time we went together, I never knew that. Three, huh?"

Michael Kirxby tightened the grim smile slightly. "You never asked, so I never mentioned it," he said. "There's a lot of things I never bother to mention: I flunked French in high school and had to work and go to summer school so I could graduate a semester late; I once worked as a short-order cook in a diner in New Jersey near the Turnpike; I've had the clap maybe half a dozen times and the crabs twice—"

"Ichhh, don't talk about it!" She buried her naked face in the pillow. He reached out and ran his hand up under her thick chestnut hair, ran it all the way up to the occipital ridge and massaged the cleft. She came up from where she had hidden.

That had been a few moments ago. Now he propped himself on his bent arm and proceeded to tell her the truth about it. He never lied; it simply wasn't worth the trouble. But it *was* a long story, and he'd told it a million times; and even though he had developed a storyteller's facility with the interminable history of it, he had learned to sketch in whole sections with apocryphal sentences, had developed the use of artful time-lapse jumps. Still, it took a good 15 minutes to do it right, to achieve the proper reaction and, quite frankly, he was bored with the recitation. But there were occasions when it served its purpose, and this was one of them, so he launched into it.

"I got married the first time when I was twenty, twenty-one, something like that. I'm lousy on dates. Anyhow, she was a sick girl, disturbed before I ever met her; family thing, hated her mother, loved her father—he was an ex-Marine, big, good-looking—secretly wanted to ball the old man but never could cop to it. He died of cancer of the brain, but before he went, he began acting erratically, treating the mother like shit. Not that the mother didn't deserve it . . . she was a harridan, a real termagant. But it was really outrageous; he wasn't coming home nights, beating up the mother, that sort of thing. So my wife sided with the mother against him. When they found out his brain was being eaten up by the tumor, she flipped and went off the deep end. Made my life a furnace! After I divorced her, the mother had her committed. She's been in the asylum over seventeen years now. For me, it was close; too damned close. She very nearly took me with her to the madhouse. I got away just in time. A little longer, I wouldn't be here today."

He watched her face. Martha was listening closely now. Heart-meat information. This was the sort of thing they loved to hear; the fiber material, the formative chunks, something they could sink their neat, small teeth into. He sat up, reached over and clicked on the bed lamp. The light was on his right side as he stared toward the foot of the bed, apparently conjuring up the painful past; the light limned his profile. He had a Dick Tracy chin and deep-set brown eyes. He cut his own hair, did it badly, and it shagged over his ears as though he had just crawled out of bed. Fortunately, it was wavy and he *was* in bed: He knew the light and the profile were good. Particularly for the story.

"I was in crap shape after her. Almost went down the tube. She came within a finger of pulling me onto the shock table with her. She always, *always* had the hoodoo sign on me; I had very little defense against her. Really scares me when I think about it."

The naked Martha looked at him. "Mike . . . what was her name?"

He swallowed hard. Even now, years later, long after it was ended, he found himself unable to cleanse the memories of pain and fear. "Her name was Cindy."

"Well, uh, what did she do that was so awful?"

He thought about it for a second. This was a departure from the routine. He wasn't usually asked for further specifics. And running back through the memories, he found that most of them had blurred into one indistinguishable throb of misery. There were incidents he remembered, incidents so heavily freighted with anguish that he could feel his gorge becoming buoyant, but they were part of the whole terrible time with Cindy, and trying to pick them out so they would convey, in microcosm, the shrieking hell of their marriage was like retelling something funny from the day before, to people who had not been there. Not funny. Oh, well, you'd have to have been there.

What had she done that was so awful, apart from the constant attempts at suicide, the endless remarks intended to make him feel inadequate, the erratic behavior, the morning he had returned from ten weeks of basic training a day earlier than expected and found her in bed with some skinny guy from on the block, the times she took off and sold the furniture and cleaned out the savings account? What had she done beyond that? Oh, hell, Martha, nothing much.

He couldn't say that. He had to encapsulate the four years of their marriage. One moment that summed it up.

He said, "I was trying to pass my bar exams. I was really studying hard. It wasn't easy for me the way it was for a lot of people. And she used to mumble."

"She mumbled?"

"Yeah. She'd walk around, making remarks you just *knew* were crummy, but she'd do it under her breath, just at the threshold of audibility. And me trying to concentrate. She knew it made me crazy, but she always did it. So one time . . . I was really behind in the work and trying to catch up . . . and she started that, that . . ." He *remembered!* "That damned *mumbling*, in the living room and the bedroom and the bathroom . . . but she wouldn't come into the kitchen, where I was studying. And it went on and on and on. . . ."

He was trembling. Jesus, why had she asked for this? It wasn't in the script.

"And finally, I just stood up and screamed, 'What the hell are you mumbling? What the hell do you want from me? Can't you see I'm busting my ass studying? Can't you for Christ sake leave me alone for just five fucking minutes?'"

With almost phonographic recall, he knew he was saying precisely, exactly what he had screamed all those years ago.

"And I ran into the bedroom, and she was in her bathrobe and slippers, and she started in on me, accusing me of this and that and every other damned thing, and I guess I finally went over the edge, and I punched her right in the face. As hard as I could. The way I'd hit some slob in the street. Hard, real hard. And then, somehow, I had her bedroom slipper in my hand and I was sitting on her chest on the bed, and beating her in the face with that goddamn slipper . . . and . . . and . . . I woke up and *saw me hitting her,* and it was the first time I'd ever hit a woman, and I fell away from her, and I crawled across the floor and I was sitting there like a scared animal, my hands over my eyes . . . crying . . . scared to death. . . ."

She stared at him silently. He was shaking terribly.

"Jesus," she said, softly.

And they stayed that way for a while, without speaking. He had answered her question. More than she wanted to know.

The mood was tainted now. He could feel himself split—one part of him here and now with the naked Martha, in this bedroom, with the light low; another part he had thought long gone, in that other bedroom, hunkered down against the baseboard, hands over eyes, whimpering like a crippled dog, Cindy sprawled half on the floor, half on the bed, her face puffed and bloodied. He tried desperately to get control of himself.

After some long moments, he was able to breathe regularly. She was still staring at him, her eyes wide. He said, almost with reverence, "Thank God for Marcie."

She waited and then said, "Who's Marcie?"

"Who *was* Marcie. Haven't seen her in something like fifteen years."

"Well, who *was* Marcie?"

"She was the one who picked up the pieces and focused my eyes. If it hadn't been for her, I'd have walked around on my knees for another year . . . or two . . . or ten. . . ."

"What happened to her?"

"Who knows? You can take it from our recently severed liaison; I seem to have some difficulty hanging on to good women."

"Oh, Mike!"

"Hey, take it easy. You split for good and sound reasons. I think I'm doomed to be a bachelor . . . maybe a *recluse* for the rest of my life. But that's OK. I've tried it three times. I just don't have the facility. I'm good for a woman for short stretches, but over the long haul, I think I'm just too high-pressure."

She smiled wanly, trying to ease what she took to be pain. He *wasn't* in pain, but she had never been able to tell the difference with him. Precisely that inability to penetrate his façade had been the seed of their dissolution. "It was OK with us."

"For a while."

"Yeah. For a while." She reached across him to the nightstand and picked up the heavy Orrefors highball glass with the remains of the Mendocino Grey Riesling. "It was so strange running into you at Allison's party. I'd heard you were seeing some model or actress . . . or something."

He shook his head. "Nope. You were my last and greatest love."

She made a wet, bratting sound. "Bullshit!"

"Mmm. Yeah, it is a bit, ain't it?"

And they stayed that way, silently, for a while. Once, he touched her naked thigh, feeling the nerve jump under his hand; and once, she reached across to lay her hand on his chest, to feel him breathing. But they didn't make love again. And after a space of time in which they thought they could hear the dust settling in the room, she said, "Well, I've got to get home to feed the cats."

"You want to stay the night?"

She thought about it a moment. "No thanks, Mike. Maybe another night, when I come prepared. You know my thing about putting on the same clothes the next day." He knew. And smiled.

She crawled out of bed and began getting dressed. He watched her, ivory-lit by the single bed lamp. It never would have worked. But then, he'd known that almost from the first. It never worked well for an extended period. There was no Holy Grail. Yet the search went on, reflexively. It was like eating potato chips.

She came back to the bed, leaned over and kissed him. It was the merest touch of lips and meant nothing. "Bye. Call me."

"No doubt about it," he said; but he wouldn't.

Then she left. He sat up in the bed for a while, thinking that it was odd how people couldn't leave it alone. Like a scab, they had to pick at it. He'd dated her rather heavily for a month, and they had broken up for no particular reason save that it was finished. And tonight the party, and he was alone, and she was alone, and they had come together for an anticlimax.

A returning. To a place neither had known very well. A devalued neighborhood.

He knew he would never see Martha again.

The bubble of sadness bobbed on the surface for a moment, then burst; the sense of loss flavored the air a moment longer; then he turned off the light, rolled over onto the dried wet spot and went to sleep.

He was hacking out the progression of interrogatories pursuant to the Blieler brief with one of the other attorneys in the office when his secretary stuck her head into the conference room and said he had a visitor. Rubbing his eyes, he realized they had been at it for three straight hours. He shoved back from the conference table, swept the papers into the folio and said, "Let's knock off for lunch."

The other attorney stretched and musculature crackled. "OK. Call it four o'clock. I've got to go over to the 9000 Building to pick up Barbarossi's deposition." He got up and left.

Kirxby sighed, simply sitting there, all at once overcome by a nameless malaise. As though something dark and forbidding were slouching toward his personal Bethlehem.

Then he went into his office to meet his visitor.

She turned half around in the big leather chair and smiled at him.

"Jerri!" he said, all surprise and pleasure. His first reaction: surprised pleasure. "My God, it's been . . . how long . . . ?"

The smile lifted at one corner: her bemused smile.

"It's been six months. Seem longer?"

He grinned and shrugged. It had been his choice to break up the affair after two years. For Martha. Who had lasted a month.

"How time flies when you're enjoying yourself," she said. She crossed her legs. A summary judgment on his profligacy.

He walked around and sat down behind the desk. "Come on, Jerri, gimme some slack."

Another returning. First Martha, out of the blue; now Jerri. Emerging from the mauve, perhaps? "What brings you back into my web?" He tried to stare at her levelly, but she was on to that; it made him feel guilty.

"I suppose I could have cobbled up something spectacular along the lines of a multimillion-dollar lawsuit against one of my competitors," she said, "but the truth is just that I felt an urgent need to see you again."

He opened and closed the top drawer of his desk, to buy a few seconds. Then, carefully avoiding her gaze, he said, "What is this, Jerri? Christ, isn't there enough crap in the world without detouring to find a fresh supply?" He said it softly, because he had said "I love you" to her for two years, excluding the final seven months, when he had said "Fuck off," never realizing they were the same phrase.

But he took her to lunch, and they made it a date for dinner, and he took her back to his apartment and they were two or three drinks too impatient to get to the bed and made it on the living-room carpet, still half-clothed. He cherished silence when making love, even when only screwing, and she remembered and didn't make a sound. And it was as good or as bad as it had ever been between them for two years minus the last seven months. And when she awoke hours later, there on the living-room carpet, with her skirt up around her hips and Michael lying on his side with his head cradled on his arm, still sleeping, she breathed deeply and slitted her eyes and commanded the hangover to permit her the strength to rise; and she rose, and she covered him with a small lap robe he had pilfered from an American Airlines flight to Boston; and she went away. Neither loving him nor hating him. Having merely satisfied the urgent compulsion in her to return to him once more, to see him once more, to have his body once more. And there was nothing more to it than that.

The next morning, he rolled onto his back, lying there on the floor, kept his eyes closed and knew he would never see her again. And there was no more to it than that.

Two days later, he received a phone call from Anita. He had had two dates with Anita, more than two and a half years earlier, during the week before he had met Jerri and taken up with her. She said she had been thinking about him. She said she had been weeding out old phone numbers in her book and had come across his, and just wanted to call to see how he was. They made a date for that night and had sex and she left quickly. And he knew he would never see her again.

And the next day at lunch at the Oasis he saw Corinne sitting across the room. He had lived with Corinne for a year just prior to meeting Anita, just prior meeting Jerri. Corinne came across the room and kissed him on the back of the neck and said, "You've lost weight. You look good enough to eat." And they got together that night, and one thing and another, and he was, and she did, and then he did, and she stayed the night but left after coffee the next morning. And he knew he would never see her again.

But he began to have an unsettling feeling that something strange was happening to him.

Over the next month, in reverse order of having known them, every female with whom he had had a liaison magically reappeared in his life. Before Corinne he had had a string of one-nighters and casual weekends with Hannah, Nancy, Robin and Cylvia; Elizabeth, Penny, Margie and Herta; Eileen, Gail, Holly and Kathleen. One by one, in unbroken string, they came back to him like waifs returning to the empty kettle for one last spoonful of gruel. Once, and then gone again, forever.

Leaving behind pinpoint lights of isolated memory. Each one of them an incomplete yet somehow total summation of the woman: Hannah and her need for certain words in the bed; the pressure of Nancy's legs over his shoulders; Robin and the wet towels; Cylvia who never came, perhaps could *not* come; Elizabeth so thin that her pelvis left him sore for days; having to send out for ribs for Penny, before and after; a spade-shaped mole on Margie's inner thigh; Herta falling asleep in a second after sex, as if she had been clubbed; the sound of Eileen's laugh, like the wind in Aspen; Gail's revulsion and animosity when he couldn't get an erection and tried to go down on her; Holly's endless retelling of the good times they had known; Kathleen still needing to delude herself that he was seducing her, even after all this time.

One sharp point of memory. One quick flare of light. Then gone forever and there was no more to it than that.

But by the end of that month, the suspicion had grown into a dread certainty; a certainty that led him inexorably to an inevitable end place that was too horrible to consider. Every time he followed the logical progression to its finale, his mind skittered away . . . that whimpering, crippled dog.

His fear grew. Each woman returned built the fear higher. Fear coalesced into terror and he fled the city, hoping by exiling himself to break the links.

But there he sat, by the fireplace at The Round Hearth, in Stowe, Vermont . . . and the next one in line, Sonja, whom he had not seen in years, Sonja came in off the slopes and saw him, and she went a good deal whiter than the wind-chill factor outside accounted for.

They spent the night together and she buried her face in the pillow so her sounds would not carry. She lied to her husband about her absence and the next morning, before Kirxby came out of his room, they were gone.

But Sonja *had* come back. And that meant the next one before her had been Gretchen. He waited in fear, but she did not appear in Vermont, and he felt if he stayed there, he was a sitting target and he called the office and told them he was going down to the Bahamas for a few days, that his partners should parcel out his case load among them, for just a few more days, don't ask questions.

And Gretchen was working in a tourist shop specializing in wicker goods; and she looked at him as he came through the door and she said, "Oh, my God, *Michael!* I've had you on my mind almost constantly for the past week. I was going to call you—"

And she gave a small sharp scream as he fainted, collapsing face forward into a pyramid of woven-wicker clothes hampers.

The apartment was dark. He sat there in the silence and refused to answer the phone. The gourmet delicatessen had been given specific instructions. The delivery boy with the food had to knock in a specific, certain cadence, or the apartment door would not be opened.

Kirxby had locked himself away. The terror was very real now. It was impossible to ignore what was happening to him. All the birds were coming home to roost.

Back across 21 years, from his 20th birthday to the present, in reverse order of having known them, every woman he had ever loved or fucked or had an encounter of substance with . . . was homing in on him. Martha, the latest, from which point the forward momentum of his relationships had been arrested; like a pendulum swung as far as it could go; and back again, back, back, swinging back past Jerri and Anita, back to Corinne and Hannah, back, and Nancy, back, and Robin and all of them, straight back to Gretchen, who was just three women before. . . .

He wouldn't think about it.

He *couldn't*. It was too frightening.

The special, specific, certain cadence of a knock on his apartment door. In the darkness, he found his way to the door and removed the chain. He opened the door to take the box of groceries and saw the teenaged Puerto Rican boy sent by the deli. And standing behind him was Kate. She was 12 years older, a lot less the gamin, classy and self-possessed now, but it was Kate nonetheless.

He began to cry.

He slumped against the open door and wept, hiding his face in his hands, partially because he was ashamed but more because he was frightened.

She gave the boy a tip, took the box and edged inside the apartment, moving Kirxby with her, gently. She closed the door, turned on a light and helped him to the sofa.

When she came back from putting away the groceries, she slipped out of her shoes and sat as far away from him as the length of the sofa would permit. The light was behind her and she could see his swollen, terrified face clearly. His eyes were very bright. There was a trapped expression on his face. For a long time, she said nothing.

Finally, when his breathing became regular, she said, "Michael, what the hell *is* it? Tell me."

But he could not speak of it. He was too frightened to name it. As long as he kept it to himself, it was just barely possible it was a figment of delusion, a ravening beast of the mind that would vanish as soon as he was able to draw a deep breath. He knew he was lying to himself. It was real. It was happening to him, inexorably.

She kept at him, speaking softly, cajoling him, prising the story from him. And so he told her. Of the reversal of his life. Of the film running backward. Of the river flowing upstream. Carrying him back and back and back into a dark land from which there could never be escape.

"And I ran away. I went to St. Kitts. And I walked into a shop, some dumb shop, just some dumb kind of tourist-goods shop. . . ."

"And what was her name . . . Greta . . . ?"

"Gretchen."

"Gretchen. And Gretchen was there."

"Yes."

"Oh, my God, Michael. You're making yourself crazy. This is lunatic. You've got to stop it."

"*Stop it?* Jesus, I wish I *could* stop it. But I can't. Don't you see, you're *part* of it. It's unstoppable, it's crazy but it's hellish. I haven't slept in days. I'm afraid to go to sleep. God knows what might happen."

"You're building all this in your mind, Michael. It isn't real. Lack of sleep is making you paranoid."

"No . . . no . . . listen . . . here, listen to this . . . I remembered it from years ago . . . I read it . . . I found it when I went looking for it. . . ." He lurched off the sofa, found the book on the wet bar and brought it back under the light. It was *The Plague,* by Camus, in a Modern Library edition. He thumbed through the book and could not find the place. Then she took it from him and laid it on her palm and it fell open to the page, because he had read and reread the section. She read it aloud, where he had underlined it:

"'Had he been less tired, his senses more alert, that all-pervading odor of death might have made him sentimental. But when a man has had only four hours' sleep, he isn't sentimental. He sees things as they are; that is to say, he sees them in the garish light of justice—hideous, witless justice.'" She closed the book and stared at him. "You really believe this, don't you?"

"Don't I? Of course I do! I'd be what you think I am, crazy . . . *not* to believe it. Kate, listen to me. Look, here you are. It's twelve years. Twelve years and another life. But here you are, back with me again, just in sequence. You were my lover before I met Gretchen. I *knew* it would be you!"

"Michael, don't let this make you stop thinking. There's no way you could have known. Bill and I have been divorced for two years. I just moved back to the city last week. Of *course* I'd look you up. We had a very good thing together. If I hadn't met Bill, we might *still* be together."

"Jesus, Kate, you're not *listening* to me. I'm trying to tell you this is some kind of terrible justice. I'm rolling back through time with the women I've known. There's you, and if there's you, then the next one before you was Marcie. And if I go back to her, then that means that after Marcie . . . after Marcie . . . *before* Marcie there was . . ."

He couldn't speak the name.

She said the name. His face went white again. It was the speaking of the unspeakable.

"Oh, God, Kate, oh, dear God, I'm screwed. I'm screwed. . . ."

"Cindy can't get you, Mike. She's still in the home, isn't she?"

He nodded, unable to answer.

Kate slid across and held him. He was shaking. "It's all right. It's going to be all right."

She tried to rock him, like a child in pain, but his terror was an electric current surging through him. "I'll take care of you," she said. "Till you're better. There won't be any Marcie and there certainly won't be any Cindy."

"*No!*" he screamed, pulling away from her. "*No!*"

He stumbled toward the door. "I've got to get out of here. They can find me here. I've got to go somewhere out away from here, fast, fast, where they can't find me ever."

He yanked open the door and ran into the hall. The elevator was not there. It was never there when he needed it, needed it badly, needed it desperately.

He ran down the stairs and into the vestibule of the building. The doorman was standing, looking out into the street, the glass doors tightly shut against the wind and the cold.

Michael Kirxby ran past him, head down, arms close to his body. He heard the man say something, but it was lost in the rush of wind and chill as he jammed through onto the sidewalk.

Terror enveloped him. He ran toward the corner and turned toward the darkness. If he could just get into the darkness, where he couldn't be found, then he was safe. Perhaps he would be safe.

He rounded the corner. A woman, head down against the wind, bumped into him. They rebounded and in the vague light of the street lamp looked into each other's faces.

"Hello," said Marcie.

WALTER TEVIS

THE APOTHEOSIS OF MYRA

July 1980

Writers who have made a name for themselves in other areas are not always welcome in science fiction. An exception was Walter Tevis (1928–1984), probably still best known as the author of the realistic poolroom story, "The Hustler," published in *Playboy* in January 1957, expanded into a novel in 1959, then made into a hugely successful movie with Paul Newman and Jackie Gleason in 1961. A sequel to it, *The Color of Money,* was filmed with Newman and Tom Cruise. Many people consider Tevis's *Queen's Gambit* to be the best novel ever written about the game of chess. But *The Man Who Fell to Earth* (1963), a skewed look at American society through the eyes of a despairing alcoholic alien on a diplomatic mission from the planet Anthea, brought him acclaim as a talented and distinctive science fiction writer; Nicholas Roeg's 1976 movie with David Bowie captures the melancholy intelligence of the book very imaginatively. Tevis's other SF novels were *Mockingbird* and *The Steps of the Sun*. In "The Apotheosis of Myra," it is at once apparent that the author does not feel constrained by genre conventions—it nods to the classic "twist" horror story and even to Evelyn Waugh's famous satirical novel *Scoop*—yet it certainly reads as psychological fiction rather than fantasy.

OUT BEYOND THE French windows during the day's second sunset, the grass began singing. It began as a hum and as it gained in strength, quickly became song. Edward pushed the French windows farther open and stepped out onto the terrace. Lovely there now with a dark blue like an earth sky. And frightening though it was the singing, too, was lovely. Molodic, slow-tempoed, a sort of insistent lullaby. In three years here, he had heard about it; this was the first time he had ever *heard* it. He sipped from the glass of gin in his hand. He was half-drunk and that made it easier to take than it might have been. An enormous plain of dark grass lay before him in twilight, motionless, singing.

No one knew the language. But it was clearly a language.

After a few minutes, Myra came out from the living room, moving stiffly and rubbing her eyes. She had been asleep on the couch. "Goodness!" she said. "Is that the *grass?*"

"What else?" he said, turning away from her. He finished his drink.

Myra's voice was excited. "You know, Edward, I heard a recording of this . . . this grass. Back in college, years ago. It was before anybody had even heard of Endolin." She was trying to make her voice sound lively, but she could not override the self-pity in it. Myra, Edward felt, swam in self-pity as a goldfish swam in water. It was her own transparent medium. "It was in a course called The Exploration of our Galaxy, I think. Dull as dishwater. But the professor played some records of life forms, and I still remember Belsin grass." Belsin was the name of the planet. "There was a question about it on the mid-term. What are you drinking there, Edward?"

221

He did not look at her. "Gin and tonic. I'll get you one."

He walked along the moonwood deck past her and into the house. The liquor was in the kitchen. During the past year, he had taken to bringing a case at a time out of the storage room, where supplies from Earth were kept. There was the half-empty last case of gin and a nearly empty one of Scotch side by side on the kitchen counter next to a stack of unwashed dishes. The dishwasher had broken down again and he hadn't felt like trying to fix it. He grinned wryly, looking at the pile of dirty Haviland that Myra had insisted on bringing with her out to this godforsaken part of the galaxy. If he could get her to do the dishwashing, he might not kill her. Fat chance.

The idea of killing her was fairly recent. Originally, he had thought the arthritis and the self-pity and the booze would do it for him. But Belsin had worked for her far better than he had expected, with the fresh Endolin that had made her demand to come here in the first place. Endolin was a scraggly little plant and the finest painkiller and anti-inflammation drug ever known. It grew only on Belsin and although it lost about half its potency in travel, it was the painkiller of choice for millions. But used fresh, it was a miracle. Myra was rich and her family was powerful; she had provided the money and her grandfather the power to get Edward the job here. She was 34 and had had violently painful arthritis since the age of six. Her life had been spent trying to avoid the pain.

He made her drink, as usual, stronger than his own. There was no ice, since that wasn't working, either.

She had seated herself on the moonwood bench when he got back out onto the terrace and was looking at the stars, her head slightly inclined toward the singing of the grass. For a moment, he paused; she was really very beautiful. And the look of self-pity had gone from her face. He had loved her, once, when she was like this. He hadn't married her only for her money. The singing had become softer. It would end soon, if what he had heard about it was true. It happened so rarely, though, that everything about it was uncertain and no one had the foggiest notion of how the grass did it in the first place, let alone why.

Myra smiled at him, not even reaching for the drink. "It sings so . . . *intelligently,*" she said, smiling. "And feelingfully." She took the drink, finally, and set it on the moonwood bench beside her. Moonwood was not really wood; it was sliced from quarries and outcroppings near Belsin's north pole. You could drive nails into it and even build houses from it. Their house, though, was a prefab, cut from steel and glass in a factory in Cleveland and shipped out here, for a king's ransom.

"And nobody knows why it sings?" she said.

"Correct," Edward said. "How are your hands?"

She smiled dreamily toward him. "Very good." She flexed them. "Hardly any pain at all. And my neck is easy tonight. Supple."

"Congratulations," he said, without feeling. He walked over to one of the deck chairs and seated himself. The problem with killing her was not the killing itself. That would be very easy out here, on a planet with only a few hundred settlers. The problem was in making it totally unambiguous, clear and simple and with himself blameless, so he could inherit. The laws concerning extraterrestrial death were a mess. One little snag could keep it in court for 30 years.

"You know what I'd like to do, Edward?" she said.

He took a swallow from his drink. "What's that?"

"I'd like to get out the EnJay and take a ride to the orchids."

"Christ!" he said. "Isn't it pretty late?" She had not ridden in the EnJay for a year or more. "And doesn't the bouncing hurt your legs? And back?"

"Edward," she said, "I'm better. Really."

"OK," he said. "I'll get a bottle. And some Endolin."

"Forget the Endolin for now," she said brightly. "I'll be all right."

The nuclear jeep was in a moonwood shed at the back of the house, next to the dark-green Mercedes and the two never-used bicycles. He backed the jeep out, shifted gears and scratched off around the house. In the low gravity of Belsin, scratching off was difficult to do, but he had learned the trick. He pulled up to the turnaround in front of the house where Myra's elevator normally let her out and was astonished to see her walking down the stairs, one hand on the banister, smiling toward him.

"Well!" he said as she got into the jeep.

"Pretty good, huh?" she said, smiling. She squeezed his arm.

He drove off with a jerk and across the obsidian surface of their front yard. Much of Belsin was obsidian; it was in fissures in that glasslike surface that the Endolin grew. At the end of the yard, a winding path, barely wide enough for the jeep, they went through the Belsin grass, which was still singing but much more softly. He liked driving the path, with its glassy low traction and its narrow and often wrongly banked curves. There was hardly any way to build a real road on Belsin. You could not cut Belsin grass—which wasn't grass at all and seemed to grow out of the granitic rock beneath it like hair—and if you drove on it, it screamed and bled. Bringing from Earth the equipment to grade and level the obsidian would have been almost enough to bankrupt even Myra's family. So when you drove on Belsin, you used a car with a narrow axle and you followed the natural, veinlike pathways on the planet's surface. There weren't many places to drive *to*, anyway.

The singing, now that they were driving with the grass on either side of them, was remarkable. It was like a great chorus of small voices, or a choir chanting at the edge of understanding, alto and soprano. It was vaguely spiritual, vaguely erotic, and the truly remarkable thing about it was that it touched the human feelings so genuinely. As with Endolin, which magically dovetailed so well with the products of terrestrial evolution, producing a molecule that fit a multichambered niche in the human nervous system as if made for it, the grass seemed to have been ready for humanity when humanity first landed on Belsin 60 years before. Captain Belsin himself had heard it during the first explorations. The grass had sung for that old marauding tycoon and he had written in his journal the now-famous words, "This planet speaks my language." When Endolin had been found, years later, it had seemed fitting that the planet, able somehow to touch human feelings with its astonishing surface growth, could also provide one of the great anodynes. Endolin was hard to come by, even in the richest obsidian fields, but it was nearly perfect when fresh. It could all but obliterate physical pain without affecting the reason or the perceptions. And there was no hangover from it. Myra's life on Earth had been hell. Here, it was passable.

"Boy, do I feel good!" Myra said. "I think I could dance till dawn."

He kept his eyes on the road, following it with the wheel. "In an hour, you'd be screaming from the pain. You're forgetting how Endolin burns out." That was its great drawback, and he was glad to remind her of it. That, and the fact that you couldn't take it constantly. If you did, it paralyzed you.

For a moment, she sounded crushed. "Honey," she said, "I haven't forgotten." Then she brightened. "But lately my bad hours between pills have been easier." She had been lying on the sofa at sunset during one of those hours that she had to get through, and would have taken a pill before getting up to join him on the terrace.

"That's good," he said. He tried to put conviction into it.

After a while, they were driving along a ridge from which they could see, far off to the right, the lights of the Endolin Packing Plant and the little spaceport beside it.

"I didn't know they worked at *night*," Myra said.

"For the past six months, they have."

"Six months Earth time?" There was Belsin time, with its 17-hour day and short year, and there was Earth time. Edward had a way of shifting from one to the other without warning.

"Earth time," he said, as if talking to a child.

"You almost never tell me about your work, Edward," she said. "Have orders gone up?"

"Yes," he said. "Business is booming. We're sending out a shipload every month now." He hesitated and then said, "Earth time."

"That's terrific, Edward. It must make you feel . . . useful to be so successful."

He said nothing. It made no difference to him how well the business did, except that more shippings meant more supplies of gin and of television tapes and things like peanut butter and coffee and caviar from Earth. Nothing on Belsin could be eaten. And the only business—the only real reason for humanity to be here at all—was Endolin.

"Will you have to increase the number of workers?" Myra asked. "To keep up with bigger harvests?"

He shook his head. "No. The equipment has been improved. Each man brings in two or three pounds a day now. Faster vehicles and better detectors."

"That's *fascinating!*" Myra said, sitting upright with a slight wince of pain. "I had no idea what was going on."

"You never asked," he said.

"No," she said, "I suppose I didn't."

They drove on northward in silence for a long time, listening to the grass. Edward himself, despite his hidden anger and his frustrations, became calmed by it. Finally, Myra spoke. "Listening to that singing is . . . is amazing," she said softly. "It seems to go very deep. You know"—she turned abruptly in her seat, to face him—"the more I take Endolin, the more . . . mystical my feelings are. Or spiritual." She looked a little self-conscious saying it, probably because she knew how impatient he was with her interests in poetry and music. And in reincarnation.

"It's bound to affect your mind. . . ." he said.

"No," she said. "I know that's not it. It's something I've had since I was a child. Sometimes after the arthritic pain, I'd have a . . . a burned-out feeling in my nerves and a certain clarity in my head. I would lie in my bed in the hospital or whatever and I felt I knew things just the other side of the edge of knowing."

He started to speak and glanced over at her. He saw that she had not finished the drink she was carrying. Which was unusual, since Myra was close to being an alcoholic. Something he encouraged in her. He decided to say nothing.

"I lost those feelings when I got older," she went on. "But lately I've been getting them back. Stronger. And the grass, singing like that, seems to encourage it." She stopped for a minute. "You know," she said, "the grass is giving me the same feeling. That something on the other side of knowledge can really be known. If we could only . . . only relax somehow and clear our minds and grasp it."

Edward's voice was cool. "You can get the same effect from two martinis on an empty stomach."

She was unperturbed. "No, you can't, Edward," she said. "You cannot."

————

They were silent again for several miles. Past the plant, the road broadened for a while and became straighter. Edward speeded up. It was late and he was getting bored. The grass's singing had become quieter. He was focusing on the road when he heard a sharp intake of breath from Myra, and then he saw that somehow there was more light on the road. And Myra said softly, "The *rings*, Edward," and he looked up and there they were: the lavender and pale-blue rings of Belsin, normally invisible but now glowing in a great arc from east to west above them. Fairy rings. Rings of heaven.

Then the grass seemed to crescendo for a moment, in some kind of coda, and then became silent. The rings brightened. The effect was stunning.

"Stop the jeep," Myra said. "Let's look."

"Haven't time," Edward said, and drove on.

And Myra did something she had never done before because of the pain her unlucky body could cause her: She pushed the lever on her seat and leaned in it all the way back and looked up at the beautiful rings in the sky. She did it with care and lay back and relaxed, still holding her unfinished drink, now in her lap. Her dark hair blew behind her in the jeep's wind. Edward could see by the light of the rings that her face was glowing. Her body looked light, supple, youthful in the light. Her smile was beatific.

He noticed the unfinished drink. "God," he thought, "she may be getting well."

The orchids grew down the sides of the only cliffs on Belsin. Belsin was a nearly flat planet with almost nothing to fall from. That and the low gravity made it a very safe place, as Edward had noted early in his life there.

The orchids were not orchids, were not even plants, but they looked somewhat like orchids. They were the outward flowerings of some obscure life form that, like the grass, seemed to go down to the center of the planet. You could not uproot an orchid any more than you could pull a blade of the grass loose from the surface; a thin but incredibly tenuous filament at the base of each of them went through solid obsidian down to a depth far below possible exploration or investigation. They were stunningly beautiful to see.

They glowed in shades of green and yellow with waving plumes and leaves shaped like enormous Japanese fans. They were both luminous and illuminated and they shifted as they moved from transparent to translucent to opaque.

When he stopped the jeep near the orchid cliffs, he heard a small cry from Myra and looked over to see her features in the familiar grimace of pain; riding that way had almost certainly been too much for her, even with Endolin.

Yet she sat up easily enough, though very slowly, and got out of the jeep. He did not offer to help; she had told him years before that she preferred doing things by herself when she could. By the time she was standing, she was smiling again. As he came around to her side of the jeep, he saw her casually emptying her drink on the ground at her feet, where it made several pools in the obsidian. She set the glass in the jeep.

They walked forward slowly. Both wore gum-rubber soles on their shoes, but the surface could be treacherous. She appeared to have recovered from the pain in the jeep; her walking was as certain as his own. Possibly steadier. "Myra," he said, "I think you're getting better." His voice was flat.

Abruptly, she stopped and turned to him. Her face, lighted by the rings in the sky, was radiant. "Edward," she said, "I think I may be getting *well*." She felt of her elbows, squeezed them. "I haven't told you this before. I wasn't sure. But I've cut my Endolin in half over the past month. And I feel better than ever." Suddenly and impulsively, she threw her arms around his neck and kissed him. It was all he could do to pretend a slight responsiveness; he was appalled by the whole thing.

"It would be really something, Edward, not just to be a sick rich girl. To be able to do something besides lie around and take pills and try to get around the pain. It would be great to *work*."

"Work?" he said. "At what?"

"I don't know," she said. "At anything. I could learn to be a pilot, or a librarian. You know, Edward, I'm not terribly smart. I think I could be very happy doing housework. Having children. Just being *busy* for the rest of my life, instead of living in my mind all the time."

"It's good to see you thinking about it," he said. But it wasn't.

He hated the whole idea. A sick Myra was bad enough; he did not want this chipper, nearly well one around to clutter up his life.

And the more well she became, the harder it would be to kill her and to blame her death on the arthritis.

He looked toward the orchid observation platform. There was another couple standing there, and as they came closer. Edward could see that the man was an engineer named Strang—one of the steadier, more reliable people from the plant. The girl was some-body from Accounting.

And it began to shape up for him then. The situation was really good. He had long suspected that the orchid cliffs were the best place for it. And here were the perfect witnesses. It was dark and everyone knew the orchid cliffs were dangerous at night. Myra had been drinking: the autopsy would show that.

It began to click off for him the way things did sometimes. He embellished it. As they approached the other couple enough to be overheard, he said, "Myra, it's really strange of you to want to come out here like this. Maybe we shouldn't go to the cliffs. We can come back in daylight tomorrow. . . ."

She laughed in a way that he hoped would sound drunken and said, "Oh, come on. Edward. I feel marvelous."

"OK, darling. Anything you say." He spoke to her lovingly and then looked up to greet the other couple.

"Nice seeing you. Mr. MacDonnel," the engineer said. "The orchids are really fine by ringlight."

"I'd still rather be in bed," Edward said amiably. "But Mrs. MacDonnel wanted to come out here. She says she could dance till dawn."

Myra beamed at Strang and Strang and his girl nodded politely at her. Myra never saw people on Belsin. Arthritis had made her life sedentary, and even though Endolin had relieved the pain greatly, she had never learned to be sociable. Most of her time was spent reading, listening to music or puttering around the house.

"More power to you, Mrs. MacDonnel," Strang said. And then, as they went out on the ledge toward the staircase. "Careful out there, you two!"

There was a meandering walkway partly carved from obsidian, partly constructed from moonwood, that ran along the cliff face

229

toward a high waterfall. The steps were lighted by hidden electric lights and there was still ringlight from above. There was a safety rail, too, of heavy moonwood, waist high. But it was only a handrail and a person could slip under it. The thing could have been done better, but there was only so much human labor available on the planet for projects of that kind.

The two of them went slowly along the staircase, still in view of Strang and his girl. The light on the orchids was gorgeous. They could hear the sound of the waterfall. It was very cool. Myra was becoming excited. "My God," she said, "Belsin is really a lovely place. With the grass that sings and the orchids." She looked up at the sky. "And those rings."

"Watch your step," he said. He looked back at Strang and waved. Then they went around the edge of a cliff and along a wet obsidian wall where the light glared off the wetness and was for a moment almost blinding and for an instant he thought of pushing her off there. But they were too close to Strang; if there were a struggle, it might be heard. They walked along a level place for a while. Myra would look across at the orchids on the other side, with their fans gently changing color in the night air, and would gasp at the beauty of them. Sometimes she squeezed his arm strongly or hugged him in her excitement. He knew it was all beautiful, but it had never really touched him and it certainly wasn't touching him now. He was thinking coolly of the best way to kill Myra. And some part of him was second-guessing, thinking that it might not be bad to go on living with Myra if she got well, that it was cruel to think of killing her just when she was beginning to enjoy her life. But then he thought of her dumbness, of her innocence. He thought of her money.

Suddenly, they came round a turn in the walkway and there was the waterfall. Part of it reflected the colors of the rings above. There was spray on his face. He looked down. Just ahead of them was a place where the obsidian was wet. The moonwood railing had been doubled at that point, but there was still a distance of at least two feet from the bottom where a person could easily slip under. He looked farther down—straight down. The chasm was half a mile—the highest drop on Belsin.

He looked behind him. They could not be seen. OK, he thought. Best to be quick about it.

He took her firmly by the arm, put his free arm around her waist.

She turned and looked at his face. Hers was calm, open. "You're going to kill me. Aren't you, Edward?" she said.

"That's right," he said. "I didn't think you knew."

"Oh, I knew, all right," she said.

For a moment, he was frightened. "Have you told anyone? Written anyone?"

"No."

"That's stupid of you. To tell me that. You could have lied."

"Maybe," she said. "But, Edward, a part of me has always wanted to die. My kind of life is hardly worth the effort. I'm not sure that getting well would change that, either."

They stood there like that by the waterfall for a full several minutes. He had her gripped firmly. It would be only a matter of putting one of his feet behind hers, tripping her and pushing her under the railing. She looked very calm and yet not passive. Her heart was beating furiously. His skin seemed extraordinarily sensitive; he felt each drop of spray as it hit. The waterfall sounded very loud.

He stared down at her. She looked pathetic. "Aren't you frightened?" he said.

She did not speak for a moment. Then she said, "Yes, I'm frightened, Edward. But I'm not terrified."

He had to admit that she was taking it very well. "Would you rather jump?" he said. He could let go of her. There was no way she could outrun him. And he wanted no bruises from his hands on her arms, no mark of his shoe on her legs. Her body—what was left of her body—would be studied by the best criminologists from Earth; he could be sure her family would see to that. She'd be kept frozen in orbit until the experts got there.

Thinking of that, he looked up toward the sky. The rings had begun to fade. "No," Myra said. "I can't jump. It's too frightening. You'll have to push me."

"All right," he said, looking back to her.

"Edward," she said, "please don't hurt me. I've always hated pain."

Those were her last words. She did not fight back. When he pushed her off, she fell silently, in the low gravity, for a long, long time before smashing herself on the obsidian at the bottom of the chasm.

As he looked up, the rings appeared again, but only for a moment.

Getting her out with a helicopter and then making the statement and getting Strang and his girl to make their statements took all night. There was no police force and no law as such on Belsin, but the factory manager was acting magistrate and took testimony. Everyone appeared to believe Edward's story—that Myra was drunk and slipped—and condolences were given. Her body was put in a plastic capsule from a supply that had sat idle for years; she was the first person ever to die on Belsin.

Edward drove back at daybreak. His fatigue was enormous, but his mind was calm. He had almost begun to believe the story himself.

As he approached the now-empty house across the broad plain, a remarkable thing happened: The grass began to sing again. Belsin grass was only known to sing in the evening. Never at dawn. But there it was, singing as the first of the planet's two suns was coming up. And somehow—perhaps because of the clarity in the fatigue he felt—it seemed to him that the grass's song was almost comprehensible. It seemed to be singing to him alone.

He spent half the next day sleeping and the other half sitting in various rooms of the house, drinking gin. He did not miss Myra, nor did he feel guilty, nor apprehensive.

He thought for a while, half-drunkenly, about what he would do, back on Earth, as a rich, single man. He was still under 40; if he were lucky, he would begin to inherit some of Myra's millions within a year.

There were still a few things to decide upon now and as he drank, he thought about them from time to time: Should he continue running the Endolin plant while waiting for the inquest into Myra's death and for the ship that would take him back to Earth? If not, there was very little else to do on Belsin. He could spend some time exploring down south, where the obsidian was a light gray and where no Endolin had been found. He could sit around the house, drinking, listen to some of Myra's records, watch TV from the tape library, work out in the basement gym. None of it really appealed to him and he began to fear the dullness of the wait. He wanted to be on Earth right now, at the heart of things, with bright lights and variety and speed and money. He wanted his life to start moving fast. He wanted travel: loose and easy nights on gamier planets with well-dressed women, guitars playing. He wanted to buy new clothes on Earth, take an apartment in Venice, go to the races in the Bois de Boulogne. Then see the galaxy in style.

And then, as twilight came, he moved out onto the terrace to watch the setting of the second of Belsin's two small suns, and realized that the grass was singing again. Its sound was very faint; at first, he thought it was only a ringing in his ears. He walked, drink in hand, to the railing at the end of the big moonwood terrace, walking softly in bare feet across the silvery surface, cool as always to the touch. Belsin, bare and nearly devoid of life as it was, could be—as Myra would say—lovely. He remembered Myra's falling, then, as in a dream. At one half Earth gravity, her body had fallen away from him slowly, slowly decreasing its size as it had lazily spun. She had not screamed. Her dress had fluttered upward in his direction as he stood there with his hands lightly on the wet railing of the orchid chasm.

Suddenly and surprisingly, he began to see it from her falling-away point of view; looking up at himself standing there, diminishing in size, seeing his own set features, his tan-cotton shirt, his blue jeans, his rumpled brown hair. His cold, unblinking eyes looking down on himself, falling.

The grass was not really singing. It was talking. Whispering. For a shocked moment, it seemed to him that it whispered, "Edward. Edward." And then, as he turned to go back into the house for another drink, "Myra is here. Edward, Myra is here."

Another very strong drink put him to sleep. He dreamed of himself in lines of people, waiting. Long, confusing lines at a cafeteria or a theater, with silent people and he among them also silent, impatient, trapped in an endless waiting. And he awoke sweating, wide-awake in the middle of the Belsin night. Before his open eyes, Myra fell, at a great distance from him now, slowly spinning. He could hear the sound of the waterfall. He sat up. He was still wearing his blue jeans.

It was not the waterfall; what he heard was the grass, whispering to him.

He pushed open the bedroom window. The grass was clearer now. Its voice was clearly speaking his name: "Edward," it said. "Edward. Edward."

Into his mind leaped the words from the old poem, studied in college:

Why does your sword so drip wi' blood Edward, Edward?

The fuzziness of liquor had left him. His head was preternaturally clear. "What do you want?" he said.

"I want to talk," the grass said. Its voice was lazy, sleepy.

"Can't you be heard everywhere?"

"Do you fear overhearing?" The voice was fairly clear, though soft.

"Yes."

"I'm speaking only near the house." That was what he thought it said. The words were a bit blurred toward the end of the sentence.

"Near the house?" He pulled the window open wider. Moved closer. Then he sat on the edge of the bed by the window and leaned out into the night. Two small moons were up and he could see the grass. It seemed to be rippling, as though a slight thin-aired wind were stroking it. The grass grew about two feet high and was normally a pale brown. The moonlight was like Earth moonlight; it made it look silver, the color of moonwood. He sat with his hands on his upper thighs, his bare feet on the floor carpeting, listening to the grass.

"Near the house, Edward," the grass said.

"And you're Myra?"

"Oh, yes, I'm Myra." There was a tone of gaiety in this, a hushed joyfulness in the whispering. "I'm Myra and I'm Belsin. I've become this planet, Edward."

"Jesus Christ!" he said. "I need a drink. And a cigarette."

"The cigarettes are in the kitchen cabinet," the grass said. "Come out on the terrace when you get them. I want to see you."

"See me?" he said.

"I can see with my rings," the voice said. Myra said.

He got up and padded into the kitchen. Strangely, he did not feel agitated. He was on some ledge somewhere in the middle of the quiet night, hung over and a wife murderer, yet his soul was calm. He found the cigarettes easily, opened them, took one out and lit it. He poured a small amount of gin into a glass, filled it the rest of the way with orange juice, thinking as he did so of how great a distance from California that juice had come, to be drunk by him here in this steel kitchen in the middle of the night on a planet where the grass had become his wife. The whole planet was his wife. His ex-wife. He took a swallow from the glass, after swishing it around to mix the gin. The glow from it in his stomach was warm and mystical. He walked slowly, carrying his glass and his cigarette, out to the terrace.

"Ooooh!" the grass said. "I can see you now."

He looked up to the sky. "I don't see the rings," he said. "Your rings."

And then they appeared. Glowing pink and lavender, clearly outlined against the dim-lit sky. They disappeared.

"I'm only learning to show my rings," Myra said. "I have to thicken the air in the right place, so the light bends downward toward you." There was silence for a while. The grass had become clearer when it last spoke. It spoke again finally and was clearer still, so that it almost seemed as if Myra were sitting on the terrace next to him, her soft voice perfectly audible in the silent night. "There's a lot to learn, Edward."

He drank again. "How did it happen?" And then, almost blurting it out, "Are you going to tell people about what I did?"

"Goodness, Edward, I hadn't thought about that." The voice paused. "Right now, I don't know."

He felt relieved. Myra had always been goodhearted, despite the self-pity. She usually gave the benefit of the doubt.

He sat silent for a while, looking at the vast plain in front of his eyes, concentrating on his drink. Then he said, "You didn't answer me, Myra. About how it happened."

"I know," the grass said. "I know I didn't. Edward, I'm not only Myra, I'm Belsin, too. I am this planet and I'm learning to be what I have become." There was no self-pity in that, no complaint. She was speaking to him clearly, trying to tell him something.

"What I know is that Belsin wanted an ego. Belsin wanted

someone to die here. Before I died and was . . . was taken in, Belsin could not speak in English. My grass could only speak to the feelings of people, not to their minds."

"The singing?" he said.

"Yes. I learned singing when Captain Belsin first landed. He carried a little tape player with him as he explored and played music on it. The grass learned . . . *I* learned to sing. He had headaches and took aspirin for them and I learned to make Endolin for him. But he never used it. Never discovered it." The voice was wistful, remembering something unpleasant. "I couldn't talk then. I could only feel some of the things that people felt. I could feel what happened to Captain Belsin's headache when he took aspirin and I knew how to improve on it. But I couldn't tell him to use it. That was found out later." The grass rippled and was still. It was darker now; one of the moons had set while they were talking.

"Can you bring up some more moons? So I can see you better? See the grass?" There were four moons.

"I'll try," Myra said. There was silence. Nothing happened. Finally, she said, "No, I can't. I can't change their orbits."

"Thanks for trying," he said dryly. "The first person to die here would become the planet? Or merge with its mind? Is that it?"

"I think so," Myra said. He thought he could see a faint ripple on the word think. "I became reincarnated as Belsin. Remember the rings' lighting after you pushed me over?"

"Yes."

"I was waking up then. It was really splendid for me. To wake into this body. Edward," she said, "I'm so alive now, and vigorous. *And nothing about me hurts.*"

He looked away, back toward the silent house. Then he finished his drink. Myra's voice had been strong, cheerful. He had been calm—or had been *acting* calm—but something in his deep self was disturbed. He was becoming uneasy about all this. Talking with the grass did not disturb him. He was a realist and if grass could talk to him in the voice of his dead wife, he would hold conversation with grass. And Myra, clearly, wasn't dead—though her old, arthritic body certainly was. He had seen it as they brought it in from the helicopter; even in low gravity, falling onto jagged obsidian could lacerate and spatter.

"Do you hate me for what I did?" he said, fishing.

"No, Edward. Not at all. I feel . . . removed from you. But then, I really always did. I always knew that you allowed only a small part of yourself to touch my life. And now," she said, "my life is bigger and more exciting. And I need only a small part of you."

That troubled him, sent a little line of fear across a ridge somewhere in his stomach. It took him a moment to realize that it was her word need that had frightened him.

"Why do you need me, Myra?" he said, carefully.

"To read to me."

He stared. "To read to you?"

"Yes, Edward. I want you to read from our library." They had brought several thousand books on microfilm with them. "And I'll want you to play records for me."

"My God!" he said. "Doesn't a whole planet have better things to do?"

The grass seemed to laugh. "Of course. Of course I have things to do. Just getting to know this body of mine. And I can sense that I am in touch with others—others like the Belsin part of me. Now that I have an ego—Myra's ego—I can converse with them. Feel their feelings."

"Well, then," he said, somewhat relieved.

"Yes," she said. "But I'm still Myra, too. And I want to read. And I want music—honest, old-fashioned Earth music. I have this wonderful new body, Edward, but I don't have hands. I can't turn pages or change records. And I'll need you to talk to, from time to time. As long as I remain human. Or half human."

Jesus Christ! he thought. But then he began to think that if she had no hands, needed him even to run microfilm, that she could not stop him from leaving. She was only a voice, and rings, and ripples in the grass. What could she do? She couldn't alter the orbits of her moons.

"What about the other people here on Belsin?" he said, still careful with his words. "One of them might want to read to you. A younger man, maybe . . ."

This time, her laughter was clearly laughter. "Oh, no, Edward," she said. "I don't want them. It's you I want." There was silence for several long moments. Then she continued, "They'll be going back to Earth in a few months, anyway. I've stopped making Endolin."

"Stopped . . . ?"

"When you were asleep. I was planning things then. I realized that if I stopped making Endolin, they would all go away."

"What about all those people on Earth who need it?" he said, trying to play on her sympathies. He did not give a damn, himself, for the pains of other people. That was why living with Myra had not really been difficult for him.

"They'll be making it synthetically before the supplies run out," she said. "It's difficult, but they'll learn. It would make people rich to find out how. Money motivates some people strongly."

He said nothing to that except "Excuse me" and got up and went into the kitchen for another drink. The sky was lightening; the first little sun would be up soon. He had never known Myra to think as clearly as she could think now. He shuddered and poured himself a bigger drink. Then, through the terrace doors, he heard her voice, "Come on back out, Edward."

"Oh, shut up!" he said, and went over and slammed the doors shut and locked them. It was triply thick glass and the room became silent. He walked into the living room, with its brown-enameled steel walls and brown carpet and the oil paintings and Shaker furniture. He could hear the grass from the windows in there, so he closed them and pulled the thick curtains over them. It was silent. "Christ!" he said aloud, and sat down with his drink to think about it.

Myra kept several antique plates on little shelves over the television set. They were beginning to vibrate. And then, shockingly, he heard a deep bass rumbling and the plates fell to the floor and broke. The rumbling continued for a moment before he realized that it had been an earthquake. He was suddenly furious and he hung on to the fury, covering up the fear that had come with it. He got up and went through the kitchen to the terrace doors, flung them open into the still night. "For Christ's sake, Myra," he said, "what are you trying to do?"

"That was a selective tremor," the grass said. There was a hint of coyness in its tone. "I pushed magma toward the house and let a fissure fall. Just a tiny bit, Edward. Hardly any at all."

"It could have fallen farther?" he said, trying to keep the anger and the sternness in his voice.

"Lord, yes," Myra said. "That was only about a half on the

Richter scale." He suddenly remembered that Myra had studied geology at Ohio State; she was well prepared to become a planet. "I'm pretty sure I could go past ten. With hardly any practice."

"Are you threatening to earthquake me into submission?"

She didn't answer for a minute. Then she said, pleasantly, "I want to keep you here with me. Edward. We're married. And I need you."

The earthquake had been frightening. But he thought of the supply ships and of the ship that would be bringing the people for the inquest. All he would have to do would be to lie to her, act submissive, and then somehow get on board the ship and away from Belsin before she earthquaked.

"And you want me to read aloud? Or run the microfilm for you?"

"Aloud, Edward," she said. "I'll let the others leave, but I want you to stay here. Here in the house."

"I'll have to get out every now and then."

"No, you won't," Myra said.

"I'll need food."

"I'm already growing it for you. The trees will be up in a few days. And the vegetables: carrots and potatoes and beans and lettuce. Even tobacco, Edward. But no liquor. You'll have to do without liquor once the supply is gone. But this place will be *lovely*. I'll have a lake for you and groves of fruit trees. I can grow anything—the way I grew Endolin before. This will be a beautiful place for you, Edward. A real Eden. And you'll have it all to yourself."

He thought crazily of Venice, of women, guitar music. Venice and Rome. Panicked suddenly, he said, "I can run away with the others. You can't earthquake us all to death. That would be cruel. . . ."

"That's true enough," Myra said. "But if you leave this house, I'll open a fissure under you and down you'll go." She paused a long moment. "Just like I did, Edward. Down and down."

He began to talk faster, louder. "What if they come to take me away, to force me to go back to Earth?"

"Oh, come on, Edward. Quit it. I won't let them ever get to the house. They'll go away eventually. And I'll never let anyone land again. Just swallow them up if they try it."

He felt terribly weary. He walked out onto the terrace and

slumped onto the moonwood bench. Myra remained silent. He had nothing to say. He sipped his drink, letting his mind go blank. He sat there alone for a half hour. Or not really alone. It was beginning to dawn on him that he might never be alone again.

Then Myra spoke again, softly. "I know you're tired, Edward. But I don't sleep. Not anymore. I wonder if you would read to me a while. I was in the middle of *The King's Mistress*. If you'll switch the microfilm machine on, you'll find my page."

"Christ!" he said, startled. "You can't *make* me read." There was something petulant in his voice. He could hear it and it disturbed him. Something of the sound of a small boy trying to defy his mother. "I want to have another drink and go back to bed."

"You know I don't like insisting," Myra said. "And you're perfectly right, Edward. I can't make you read. But I can shake the house and keep you awake." Abruptly, the house shook from another tremor, probably a quarter of a point on the Richter scale. "And," Myra said, "I can grow food for you or not grow food for you. And I can give you what you want to eat or not give you what you want. I could feed you nothing but persimmons for a few months. And make the water taste terrible."

"Jesus Christ!" he said. "I'm *tired*."

"It'll only be a couple of chapters," Myra said. "And then maybe a couple of old songs on the player, and I'll go back to contemplating my interior and the other planets around here."

He didn't move.

"You'll be wanting me to grow tobacco for you. There are only a few cartons of cigarettes left." Edward smoked three packs a day. Three packs in a short Belsin day.

He still didn't move.

"Well," Myra said, conciliatory now. "I think I could synthesize a little ethyl alcohol. If I could do Endolin, I suppose I could do that, too. Maybe a quart or so every now and then. A hundred ninety proof."

He stood up. He was terribly weary. "*The King's Mistress?*" he said.

"That's right!" the grass said, sweetly, joyfully. "I've always liked your voice, Edward. It'll be good to hear you read."

And then, before he turned to go into the house, to the big console that held thousands of books—thousands of dumb, gothic novels and books on gardening and cooking and self-improvement and a few technical books on geology, he saw everything get suddenly much lighter and looked up to see that the great rings of Belsin were now fully visible, bright as bands of sunlight in the abruptly brightened sky above his head. They glowed in full realization of themselves, illuminating the whole, nearly empty planet.

And Myra's voice came sighing joyfully in a great, horizon-wide ripple of grass. *"Ooooooh!"* it said happily. *"Ooooooh!"*

PHILIP K. DICK

FROZEN JOURNEY

December 1980

The career of Philip K. Dick (1928–1982) has been a strange one. During most of his life, in California, he turned out novels at break-neck speed. During the 1950s, these were mainstream novels he was unable to sell, but in the 1960s, he began to write the unique brand of hallucinatory, even schizophrenic, science fiction which became his trademark. Dick was said to be more than casually acquainted with the mind-altering drugs that marked the 1960s and 1970s in San Francisco, and nearly all his books reflect his fascination with the unstable interface between fantasy and reality. Drugs or no drugs, he published more than one novel a year during the 1960s, though these varied wildly in quality, and none was especially successful commer-cially. When he died, however, his reputation had already been secured by a few of them, notably *The Man in the High Castle* (1962), which takes place in an America in which Hitler has won World War II.

But then, after his death in 1982, came *Bladerunner,* Ridley Scott's film, starring Harrison Ford, of Dick's 1968 novel, *Do Androids Dream of Electric Sheep?* And suddenly, or so it seemed, the Dick craze began to escalate in the mainstream world outside the science fiction community, till today there is an entire growth industry of critical books about Dick. Aside from Ursula K. Le Guin, he is the only American science fiction author (leaving aside Vonnegut, who rejects the identification) to be taken up by academia, though the approach to their work is different: Le Guin is more or less classified as a mainstream or "serious" author, while Dick is grouped with the great pulp artists of the century—Dashiell Hammett, Raymond Chandler, and Ross Macdonald. "Frozen Journey" was Dick's last published short story. (It is also titled, in Dick's collected stories, "I Hope I Shall Arrive Soon.") Conventional in form, taking place on a colony ship heading for the stars, it explores an almost unthinkable situation.

AFTER TAKE-OFF, the ship routinely monitored the condition of the 60 people sleeping in its cryonic tanks. One malfunction showed, that of person nine. His EEG revealed brain activity.

Shit, the ship said to itself.

Complex homeostatic devices locked into circuit feed, and the ship contacted person nine.

"You are slightly awake," the ship said, utilizing the psychotronic route; there was no point in rousing person nine to full consciousness. After all, the flight would last a decade.

Virtually unconscious but, unfortunately, still able to think, person nine thought, Someone is addressing me. He said, "Where am I located? I don't see anything."

"You're in faulty cryonic suspension."

He said. "Then I shouldn't be able to hear you."

"Faulty, I said. That's the point; you can hear me. Do you know your name?"

"Victor Kemmings. Bring me out of this."

"We are in flight."

"Then put me under."

"Just a moment." The ship examined the cryonic mechanisms; it scanned and surveyed, and then it said, "I will try."

Time passed. Victor Kemmings, unable to see anything, unaware of his body, found himself still conscious. "Lower my temperature," he said. He could not hear his voice: perhaps he only imagined he spoke. Colors floated toward him and then rushed at him. He liked the colors; they reminded him of a child's paintbox, the semi-animated kind, an artificial life form. He had used them in school, 200 years ago.

"I can't put you under," the voice of the ship sounded inside

Kemmings' head. "The malfunction is too elaborate; I can't correct it and I can't repair it. You will be conscious for ten years."

The semi-animated colors rushed toward him, but now they possessed a sinister quality, supplied to them by his own fear. "Oh, my God," he said. Ten years! The colors darkened.

As Victor Kemmings lay paralyzed, surrounded by dismal flickerings of light, the ship explained to him its strategy. This strategy did not represent a decision on its part; the ship had been programmed to seek this solution in case of a malfunction of this sort.

"What I will do," the voice of the ship came to him, "is feed you sensory stimulation. The peril to you is sensory deprivation. If you are conscious for ten years without sensory data, your mind will deteriorate. When we reach the LR4 system, you will be a vegetable."

"Well, what do you intend to feed me?" Kemmings said in panic. "What do you have in your information storage banks? All the video soap operas of the last century? Wake me up and I'll walk around."

"There is no air in me," the ship said. "Nothing for you to eat. No one to talk to, since everyone else is under."

Kemmings said. "I can talk to you. We can play chess."

"Not for ten years. Listen to me; I say, I have no food and no air. You must remain as you are . . . a bad compromise, but one forced on us. You are talking to me now. I have no particular information stored. Here is policy in these situations: I will feed you your own buried memories, emphasizing the pleasant ones. You possess two hundred and six years of memories and most of them have sunk down into your unconscious. This is a splendid source of sensory data for you to receive. Be of good cheer. This situation, which you are in, is not unique. It has never happened within my domain before, but I am programmed to deal with it. Relax and trust me. I will see that you are provided with a world."

"They should have warned me," Kemmings said, "before I agreed to emigrate."

"Relax," the ship said.

He relaxed, but he was terribly frightened. Theoretically, he should have gone under, into the successful cryonic suspension, then awakened a moment later at his star of destination; or, rather, the planet, the colony-planet, of that star. Everyone else aboard the ship lay in an unknowing state; he was the exception, as if bad karma had attacked him for obscure reasons. Worst of all, he had to depend totally on the good will of the ship. Suppose it elected to feed him monsters. The ship could terrorize him for ten years—ten objective years and undoubtedly more from a subjective standpoint. He was, in effect, totally in the ship's power. Did interstellar ships enjoy such a situation? He knew little about interstellar ships; his field was microbiology. Let me think, he said to himself. My first wife, Martine; the lovely little French girl who wore jeans and a red shirt open to the waist and cooked delicious crepes.

"I hear," the ship said. "So be it."

The rushing colors resolved themselves into coherent, stable shapes. A building: a little old yellow wooden house that he had owned when he was 19 years old, in Wyoming. "Wait," he said in panic. "The foundation was bad; it was on a mud sill. And the roof leaked." But he saw the kitchen, with the table that he had built himself. And he felt glad.

"You will not know, after a little while," the ship said, "that I am feeding you your own buried memories."

"I haven't thought of that house in a century," he said, wonderingly; entranced, he made out his old electric drip coffeepot with the box of paper filters beside it. This is the house where Martine and I lived, he realized. "Martine!" he said aloud.

"I'm on the phone," Martine said, from the living room.

The ship said, "I will cut in only when there is an emergency. I will be monitoring you, however, to be sure you are in a satisfactory state. Don't be afraid."

"Turn down the right rear burner on the stove," Martine called. He could hear her and yet not see her. He made his way from the kitchen through the dining room and into the living room. At the VF, Martine stood in rapt conversation with her brother; she wore shorts and she was barefoot. Through the front windows of the living room, he could see the street; a commercial vehicle was trying to park, without success.

It's a warm day, he thought. I should turn on the air conditioner.

He seated himself on the old sofa as Martine continued her VF conversation, and he found himself gazing at his most cherished possession, a framed poster on the wall above Martine: Gilbert Shelton's *Fat Freddy Says* drawing in which Freddy Freak sits with his cat on his lap and Fat Freddy is trying to say, "Speed kills," but he is so wired on speed—he holds in his hand every kind of amphetamine tablet, pill, Spansule and capsule that exists—that he can't say it, and the cat is gritting its teeth and wincing in a mixture of dismay and disgust. The poster is signed by Gilbert Shelton himself; Kemmings' best friend, Ray Torrance, gave it to him and Martine as a wedding present. It is worth thousands. It was signed by the artist back in the 1980s. Long before either Victor Kemmings or Martine lived.

If we ever run out of money, Kemmings thought to himself, we could sell the poster. It was not *a* poster; it was *the* poster. Martine adored it. The Fabulous Furry Freak Brothers—from the golden age of a long-ago society. No wonder he loved Martine so; she herself loved back, loved the beauties of the world, and treasured and cherished them as she treasured and cherished him; it was a protective love that nourished but did not stifle. It had been her idea to frame the poster; he would have tacked it up on the wall, so stupid was he.

"Hi," Martine said, off the VF now. "What are you thinking?"

"Just that you keep alive what you love," he said.

"I think that's what you're supposed to do," Martine said. "Are you ready for dinner? Open some red wine, a cabernet."

"Will an '07 do?" he said, standing up; he felt, then, like taking hold of his wife and hugging her.

"Either an '07 or a '12." She trotted past him, through the dining room and into the kitchen.

Going down into the cellar, he began to search among the bottles, which, of course, lay flat. Musty air and dampness; he liked the smell of the cellar, but then he noticed the redwood planks lying half-buried in the dirt and he thought, I know I've got to get a concrete slab poured. He forgot about the wine and went over to the far corner, where the dirt was piled highest; bending down, he poked at a board . . . he poked with a trowel and then he thought, Where did I get this trowel? I didn't have it a minute ago. The board crumbled against the trowel. This whole house is collapsing, he realized. Christ sake. I better tell Martine.

Going back upstairs, the wine forgotten, he started to say to her that the foundation of the house was dangerously decayed; but Martine was nowhere in sight. And nothing cooked on the stove, no pots, no pans. Amazed, he put his hand on the stove and found it cold. Wasn't she just now cooking? he asked himself.

"Martine!" he said loudly.

No response. Except for himself, the house was empty. Empty, he thought, and collapsing. Oh, my God. He seated himself at the kitchen table and felt the chair give slightly under him; it did not give much, but he felt it, he felt the sagging.

I'm afraid, he thought. Where did she go?

He returned to the living room. Maybe she went next door to borrow some spices or butter or something, he reasoned. None-theless, panic now filled him.

He looked at the poster. It was unframed. And the edges had been torn.

I know she framed it, he thought; he ran across the room to it, to examine it closely. Faded . . . the artist's signature had faded; he could scarcely make it out. She insisted on framing it and under glare-free, reflection-free glass. But it isn't framed and it's torn! The most precious thing we own!

Suddenly, he found himself crying. It amazed him, his tears. Martine is gone; the poster is deteriorated; the house is crumbling away; nothing is cooking on the stove. This is terrible, he thought. And I don't understand it.

The ship understood it. The ship had been carefully monitoring Victor Kemmings' brain-wave patterns, and the ship knew that something had gone wrong. The wave forms showed agitation and pain. I must get him out of this feed circuit or I will kill him, the ship decided. Where does the flaw lie? it asked itself. Worry dormant in the man; underlying anxieties. Perhaps if I intensify the signal. I will use the same source but amp up the charge. What has happened is that massive subliminal insecurities have taken possession of him; the fault is not mine but lies, instead, in his psychological make-up.

I will try an earlier period in his life, the ship decided. Before the neurotic anxieties got laid down.

In the backyard, Victor scrutinized a bee that had gotten itself trapped in a spider's web. The spider wound up the bee with great care. That's wrong, Victor thought. I'll let the bee loose. Reaching up, he took hold of the encapsulated bee, drew it from the web and, scrutinizing it carefully, began to unwrap it.

The bee stung him; it felt like a little patch of flame.

Why did it sting me? he wondered. I was letting it go.

He went indoors to his mother and told her, but she did not listen; she was watching television. His finger hurt where the bee had stung it, but, more important, he did not understand why the bee would attack its rescuer. I won't do that again, he said to himself.

"Put some Bactine on it," his mother said at last, roused from watching the TV.

He had begun to cry. It was unfair. It made no sense. He was perplexed and dismayed and he felt a hatred toward small living things, because they were dumb. They didn't have any sense.

He left the house, played for a time on his swings, his slide, in his sandbox, and then he went into the garage, because he heard a strange flapping, whirring sound, like a kind of fan. Inside the gloomy garage, he found that a bird was fluttering against the cob-webbed rear window, trying to get out. Below it, the cat, Dorky, leaped and leaped, trying to reach the bird.

He picked up the cat; the cat extended its body and its front legs, it extended its jaws and bit into the bird. At once, the cat scrambled down and ran off with the still-fluttering bird.

Victor ran into the house. "Dorky caught a bird!" he told his mother.

"That goddamn cat." His mother took the broom from the closet in the kitchen and ran outside, trying to find Dorky. The cat had concealed itself under the bramblebushes; she could not reach it with the broom. "I'm going to get rid of that cat," his mother said.

Victor did not tell her that he had arranged for the cat to catch the bird: he watched in silence as his mother tried and tried to pry Dorky out from her hiding place; Dorky was crunching up the bird; he could hear the sound of breaking bones, small bones. He felt a strange feeling, as if he should tell his mother what he had done, and yet, if he told her, she would punish him. I won't do that again, he said to himself. His face, he realized, had turned red. What if his mother figured it out? What if she had some secret way of knowing? Dorky couldn't tell her and the bird was dead. No one would ever know. He was safe.

But he felt bad. That night, he could not eat his dinner. Both his parents noticed. They thought he was sick; they took his temperature. He said nothing about what he had done. His mother told his father about Dorky and they decided to get rid of Dorky. Seated at the table, listening, Victor began to cry.

"All right," his father said gently. "We won't get rid of her. It's natural for a cat to catch a bird."

The next day, he sat playing in his sandbox. Some plants grew up through the sand. He broke them off. Later, his mother told him that had been a wrong thing to do.

Alone in the backyard, in this sandbox, he sat with a pail of water, forming a small mound of wet sand. The sky, which had been blue and clear, became by degrees overcast. A shadow passed over him and he looked up. He sensed a presence around him, something vast that could think.

You are responsible for the death of the bird, the presence thought; he could understand its thoughts.

"I know," he said. He wished, then, that he could die. That he could replace the bird and die for it, leaving it as it had been, fluttering against the cobwebbed window of the garage.

The bird wanted to fly and eat and live, the presence thought.

"Yes," he said, miserably.

You must never do that again, the presence told him.

"I'm sorry," he said, and wept.

This is a very neurotic person, the ship realized. I am having an awful lot of trouble finding happy memories. There is too much fear in him and too much guilt. He has buried it all, and yet it is still there, worrying him like a dog worrying a rag. Where can I go in his memories to find him solace? I must come up with ten years of memories, or his mind will be lost.

Perhaps, the ship thought, the error that I am making is in the area of choice on my part; I should allow him to select his own memories. However, the ship realized, this will allow an element of fantasy to enter. And that is not usually good. Still . . .

I will try the segment dealing with his first marriage once again, the ship decided. He really loved Martine. Perhaps this time, if I keep the intensity of the memories at a greater level, the entropic factor can be abolished. What happened was a subtle vitiation of the remembered world, a decay of structure. I will try to compensate for that. So be it.

"Do you suppose Gilbert Shelton really signed this?" Martine said pensively; she stood before the poster, her arms folded; she rocked back and forth slightly, as if seeking a better perspective on the brightly colored drawing hanging on their living-room wall. "I mean, it could have been forged. By a dealer somewhere along the line. During Shelton's lifetime or after."

"The letter of authentication," Victor Kemmings reminded her.

"Oh, that's right!" She smiled her warm smile. "Ray gave us the letter that goes with it. But suppose the letter is a forgery? What we need is another letter certifying that the first letter is authentic." Laughing, she walked away from the poster.

"Ultimately," Kemmings said, "we would have to have Gilbert Shelton here to personally testify that he signed it."

"Maybe he wouldn't know. There's that story about the man taking the Picasso picture to Picasso and asking him if it was authentic, and Picasso immediately signed it and said, 'Now it's authentic.'" She put her arm around Kemmings and, standing on tiptoe, kissed him on the cheek. "It's genuine. Ray wouldn't have given us a forgery. He's the leading expert on counterculture art of the Twentieth Century. Do you know that he owns an actual lid of dope? It's preserved under—"

"Ray is dead," Victor said.

"What?" She gazed at him in astonishment. "Do you mean something happened to him since we last—"

"He's been dead two years," Kemmings said. "I was responsible.

I was driving the buzz car. I wasn't cited by the police, but it was my fault."

"Ray is living on Mars!" She stared at him.

"I know I was responsible. I never told you. I never told anyone. I'm sorry. I didn't mean to do it. I saw it flapping against the window, and Dorky was trying to reach it, and I lifted Dorky up, and I don't know why, but Dorky grabbed it—"

"Sit down, Victor." Martine led him to the overstuffed chair and made him seat himself. "Something's wrong," she said.

"I know," he said. "Something terrible is wrong. I'm responsible for the taking of a life, a precious life that can never be replaced. I'm sorry. I wish I could make it OK, but I can't."

After a pause, Martine said, "Call Ray."

"The cat—" he said.

"What cat?"

"There." He pointed. "In the poster. On Fat Freddy's lap. That's Dorky. Dorky killed Ray."

Silence.

"The presence told me," Kemmings said. "It was God. I didn't realize it at the time, but God saw me commit the crime. The murder. And He will never forgive me."

His wife stared at him numbly.

"God sees everything you do," said Kemmings. "He sees even the falling sparrow. Only, in this case, it didn't fall; it was grabbed. Grabbed out of the air and torn down. God is tearing this house down which is my body, to pay me back for what I've done. We should have had a building contractor look this house over before we bought it. It's just falling goddamn to pieces. In a year, there won't be anything left of it. Don't you believe me?"

Martine faltered, "I—"

"Watch." Kemmings reached up his arms toward the ceiling; he stood; he reached; he could not touch the ceiling. He walked to the wall and then, after a pause, put his hand through the wall.

Martine screamed.

The ship aborted the memory retrieval instantly. But the harm had been done.

He has integrated his early fears and guilt into one interwoven grid, the ship said to itself. There is no way I can serve up a pleasant memory to him, because he instantly contaminates it. However pleasant the original experience in itself was. This is a serious situation, the ship decided. The man is already showing signs of psychosis. And we are hardly into the trip; years lie ahead of him.

After allowing itself time to think the situation through, the ship decided to contact Victor Kemmings once more.

"Mr. Kemmings," the ship said.

"I'm sorry," Kemmings said. "I didn't mean to foul up those retrievals. You did a good job, but I—"

"Just a moment," the ship said. "I am not equipped to do psychiatric reconstruction of you; I am a simple mechanism, that's all. What is it you want? Where do you want to be and what do you want to be doing?"

"I want to arrive at our destination," Kemmings said. "I want this trip to be over."

Ah, the ship thought. That is the solution.

One by one, the cryonic systems shut down. One by one, the people returned to life, among them Victor Kemmings. What amazed him was the lack of a sense of the passage of time. He had entered the chamber, lain down, had felt the membrane cover him and the temperature begin to drop—

And now he stood on the ship's external platform, the unloading platform, gazing down at a verdant planetary landscape. This, he realized, is LR4-six, the colony world to which I have come in order to begin a new life.

"Looks good," a heavy-set woman beside him said.

"Yes," he said, and felt the newness of the landscape rush up at him, its promise of a beginning. Something better than he had known the past 200 years. I am a fresh person in a fresh world, he thought. And he felt glad.

Colors raced at him, like those of a child's semi-animate kit. St. Elmo's fire, he realized. That's right; there is a great deal of ionization in this planet's atmosphere. A free light show, such as they had back in the 20th Century.

"Mr. Kemmings," a voice said. An elderly man had come up beside him, to speak to him. "Did you dream?"

"During the suspension?" Kemmings said. "No, not that I can remember."

"I think I dreamed," the elderly man said. "Would you take my arm on the descent ramp? I feel unsteady. The air seems thin. Do you find it thin?"

"Don't be afraid," Kemmings said to him. He took the elderly man's arm. "I'll help you down the ramp. Look; there's a guide coming this way. He'll arrange our processing for us; it's part of the package. We'll be taken to a resort hotel and given first-class accommodations. Read your brochure." He smiled at the uneasy older man to reassure him.

"You'd think our muscles would be nothing but flab after ten years in suspension," the elderly man said.

"It's just like freezing peas," Kemmings said. Holding on to the timid older man, he descended the ramp to the ground. "You can store them forever if you get them cold enough."

"My name's Shelton," the elderly man said.

"What?" Kemmings said, halting. A strange feeling moved through him.

"Don Shelton." The elderly man extended his hand; reflexively, Kemmings accepted it and they shook. "What's the matter, Mr. Kemmings? Are you all right?"

"Sure," he said. "I'm fine. But hungry. I'd like to get something to eat. I'd like to get to our hotel, where I can take a shower and change my clothes." He wondered where their baggage could be found. Probably it would take the ship an hour to unload it. The ship was not particularly intelligent.

In an intimate, confidential tone, elderly Mr. Shelton said, "You know what I brought with me? A bottle of Wild Turkey bourbon. The finest bourbon on Earth. I'll bring it over to your hotel room and we'll share it." He nudged Kemmings.

"I don't drink," Kemmings said. "Only wine." He wondered if there were any good wines here on this distant colony world. Not distant now, he reflected. It is Earth that's distant. I should have done like Mr. Shelton and brought a few bottles with me.

Shelton. What did the name remind him of? Something in his far past, in his early years. Something precious, along with good wine and a pretty, gentle young woman making crepes in an old-fashioned kitchen. Aching memories; memories that hurt.

255

Presently, he stood by the bed in his hotel room, his suitcase open; he had begun to hang up his clothes. In the corner of the room, a TV hologram showed a newscaster; he ignored it, but liking the sound of a human voice, he kept it on.

Did I have any dreams? he asked himself. During these past ten years?

His hand hurt. Gazing down, he saw a red welt, as if he had been stung. A bee stung me, he realized. But when? How? While I lay in cryonic suspension? Impossible. Yet he could see the welt and he could feel the pain. I'd better get something to put on it, he realized. There's undoubtedly a robot doctor in the hotel; it's a first-rate hotel.

When the robot doctor arrived and began treating the bee sting. Kemmings said, "I got this as punishment for killing the bird."

"Really?" the robot doctor said.

"Everything that ever meant anything to me has been taken away from me," Kemmings said. "Martine, the poster—my little old house with the wine cellar. We had everything and now it's gone. Martine left me because of the bird."

"The bird you killed," the robot doctor said.

"God punished me. He took away all that was precious to me because of my sin. It wasn't Dorky's sin; it was my sin."

"But you were just a little boy," the robot doctor said.

"How did you know that?" Kemmings said. He pulled his hand away from the robot doctor's grasp. "Something's wrong. You shouldn't have known that."

"Your mother told me," the robot doctor said.

"My mother didn't know!"

The robot doctor said, "She figured it out. There was no way the cat could have reached the bird without your help."

"So all the time that I was growing up, she knew. But she never said anything."

"You can forget about it," the robot doctor said.

Kemmings said, "I don't think you exist. There is no possible way that you could know these things. I'm still in cryonic suspension and the ship is still feeding me my own buried memories. So I won't become psychotic from sensory deprivation."

"You could hardly have a memory of completing the trip."

"Wish fulfillment, then. It's the same thing. I'll prove it to you. Do you have a screwdriver?"

"Why?"

Kemmings said, "I'll remove the back of the TV set and you'll see; there's nothing inside it, no components, no parts, no chassis—nothing."

"I don't have a screwdriver."

"A small knife, then. I can see one in your surgical-supply bag." Bending, Kemmings lifted up a small scalpel. "This will do. If I show you, will you believe me?"

"If there's nothing inside the TV cabinet—"

Squatting down, Kemmings removed the screws holding the back panel of the TV set in place. The panel came loose and he set it down on the floor.

There was nothing inside the TV cabinet. And yet the color hologram continued to fill a quarter of the hotel room and the voice of the newscaster issued forth from his three-dimensional image.

"Admit you're the ship," Kemmings said to the robot doctor.

"Oh, dear," the robot doctor said.

Oh, dear, the ship said to itself. And I've got almost ten years of this lying ahead of me. He is hopelessly contaminating his experiences with childhood guilt; he imagines that his wife left him because, when he was four years old, he helped a cat catch a bird. The only solution would be for Martine to return to him; but how am I going to arrange that? She may not still be alive. On the other hand, the ship reflected, maybe she *is* alive. Maybe she could be induced to do something to save her former husband's sanity. People by and large have very positive traits. And ten years from now, it will take a lot to save—or rather, restore—his sanity; it will take something drastic, something I myself cannot do alone.

Meanwhile, there was nothing to be done but recycle the wish-fulfillment arrival of the ship at its destination. I will run him through the arrival, the ship decided, then wipe his conscious memory clean and run him through it again. The only positive aspect of this, it reflected, is that it will give me something to do, which may help preserve *my* sanity.

Lying in cryonic suspension—faulty cryonic suspension—

PHILIP K. DICK

Victor Kemmings imagined, once again, that the ship was touching down and he was being brought back to consciousness.

"Did you dream?" a heavy-set woman asked him as the group of passengers gathered on the outer platform. "I have the impression that I dreamed. Early scenes from my life . . . over a century ago."

"None that I can remember," Kemmings said. He was eager to reach his hotel; a shower and a change of clothes would do wonders for his morale. He felt slightly depressed and wondered why.

"There's our guide," an elderly lady said. "They're going to escort us to our accommodations."

"It's in the package," Kemmings said. His depression remained. The others seemed so spirited, so full of life, but over him only a weariness lay, a weighing-down sensation, as if the gravity of this colony-planet were too much for him. Maybe that's it, he said to himself. But according to the brochure, the gravity here matched Earth's; that was one of the attractions.

Puzzled, he made his way slowly down the ramp, step by step, holding on to the rail. I don't really deserve a new chance at life anyhow, he realized. I'm just going through the motions . . . I am not like these other people. There is something wrong with me; I cannot remember what it is, but, nonetheless, it is there. In me. A bitter sense of pain. Of lack of worth.

An insect landed on the back of Kemmings' right hand, an old insect, weary with flight. He halted, watched it crawl across his knuckles. I could crush it, he thought. It's so obviously infirm; it won't live much longer, anyhow.

He crushed it—and felt great inner horror. What have I done? he asked himself. My first moment here and I have wiped out a little life. Is this my new beginning?

Turning, he gazed back up at the ship. Maybe I ought to go back, he thought. Have them freeze me forever. I am a man of guilt, a man who destroys. Tears filled his eyes.

And within its sentient works, the interstellar ship moaned.

During the ten long years remaining of the trip to the LR4 system, the ship had plenty of time to track down Martine Kemmings. It explained the situation to her. She had emigrated to a vast orbiting dome in the Sirius system, found her situation unsatisfactory and was en route back to Earth. Roused from her own cryonic suspension, she listened intently and then agreed to be at the colony world at LR4 when her ex-husband arrived—if it was at all possible.

Fortunately, it was possible.

"I don't think he'll recognize me," Martine said to the ship. "I've allowed myself to age. I don't really approve of entirely halting the aging process."

He'll be lucky if he recognizes anything, the ship thought.

At the intersystem spaceport on the colony world of LR4, Martine stood waiting for the people aboard the ship to appear on the outer platform. She wondered if she would recognize her former husband. She was a little afraid, but she was glad that she had gotten to LR4 in time. It had been close. Another week and his ship would have arrived before hers. Luck is on my side, she said to herself, and scrutinized the newly landed interstellar ship.

People appeared on the platform. She saw him. Victor had changed very little.

As he came down the ramp, holding on to the railing as if weary and hesitant, she went up to him, her hands thrust deep in the pockets of her coat; she felt shy, and when she spoke, she could hardly hear her own voice.

"Hi, Victor," she managed to say.

He halted, gazed at her. "I know you," he said.

"It's Martine," she said.

Holding out his hand, he said, smiling, "You heard about the trouble on the ship?"

"The ship contacted me." She took his hand and held it. "What an ordeal."

"Yeah," he said. "Recirculating memories forever. Did I ever tell you about a bee that I was trying to extricate from a spider's web when I was four years old? The idiotic bee stung me." He bent down and kissed her. "It's good to see you," he said.

"Did the ship—"

"It said it would try to have you here. But it wasn't sure if you could make it."

As they walked toward the terminal building. Martine said, "I was lucky; I managed to get a transfer to a military vehicle, a high-velocity-drive ship that just shot along like a mad thing. A new propulsion system entirely."

Victor Kemmings said, "I have spent more time in my own unconscious mind than any other human in history. Worse than early Twentieth Century psychoanalysis. And the same material over and over again. Did you know I was scared of my mother?"

"*I* was scared of your mother," Martine said. They stood at the baggage depot, waiting for his luggage to appear. "This looks like a really nice little planet. Much better than where I was . . . I haven't been happy at all."

"So maybe there's a cosmic plan," he said, grinning. "You look great."

"I'm old."

"Medical science—"

"It was my decision. I like older people." She surveyed him. He has been hurt a lot by the cryonic malfunction, she said to herself. I can see it in his eyes. They look broken. Broken eyes. Torn down into pieces by fatigue and—defeat. As if his buried, early memories swam up and destroyed him. But it's over, she thought. And I did get here in time.

At the bar in the terminal building, they sat having a drink.

"This old man got me to try Wild Turkey bourbon," Victor said. "It's amazing bourbon. He says it's the best on Earth. He brought a bottle with him from . . ." His voice died into silence.

"One of your fellow passengers," Martine finished.

"I guess so," he said.

"Well, you can stop thinking of the birds and the bees," Martine said.

"Sex?" he said, and laughed.

"Being stung by a bee; helping a cat catch a bird. That's all past."

"That cat," Victor said, "has been dead one hundred and eighty-two years. I figured it out while they were bringing us out of suspension. Probably just as well. Dorky. Dorky the killer cat. Nothing like Fat Freddy's cat."

"I had to sell the poster," Martine said. "Finally."

He frowned.

"Remember?" she said. "You let me have it when we split up. Which I always thought was really good of you."

"How much did you get for it?"

"A lot. I should pay you something like . . ." She calculated. "Taking inflation into account, I should pay you about two million dollars."

"Would you consider," he said, "instead, in place of the money, my share of the sale of the poster, spending some time with me? Until I get used to this planet?"

"Yes," she said. And she meant it. Very much.

They finished their drinks and then, with his luggage transported by robot spacecap, made their way to his hotel room.

"This is a nice room," Martine said, perched on the edge of the bed. "And it has a hologram TV. Turn it on."

"There's no use turning it on," Victor Kemmings said. He stood by the open closet, hanging up his shirts.

"Why not?"

Kemmings said, "There's nothing in it."

Going over to the TV set, Martine turned it on. A hockey game materialized, projected out into the room, in full color, and the sound of the game assailed her ears.

"It works fine," she said.

"I know," he said. "I can prove it. If you have a nail file or something, I'll unscrew the back plate and show you."

"But I can—"

"Look at this." He paused in his work of hanging up his clothes. "Watch me put my hand through the wall." He placed the palm of his right hand against the wall. "See?"

His hand did not go through the wall, because hands do not go through walls; his hand remained pressed against the wall, unmoving.

"And the foundation," he said, "is rotting away."

"Come and sit down by me," Martine said.

"I've lived this often enough to know," he said. "I've lived this over and over again. I come out of suspension; I walk down the ramp; I get my luggage; sometimes I have a drink at the bar and sometimes I come directly to my room. Usually, I turn on the TV and then . . ." He went over and held his hand toward her. "See where the bee stung me?"

She saw no mark on his hand; she took his hand and held it.

"There is no bee sting there," she said.

261

"And when the robot doctor comes, I borrow a tool from him and take off the back plate of the TV set. To prove to him that it has no chassis, no components in it. And then the ship starts me over again."

"Victor," she said. "Look at your hand."

"This is the first time you've been here, though," he said.

"Sit down," she said.

"OK." He seated himself on the bed, beside her, but not too close to her.

"Won't you sit closer to me?" she said.

"It makes me too sad," he said. "Remembering you. I really loved you. I wish this was real."

Martine said, "I will sit with you until it is real for you."

"I'm going to try reliving the part with the cat," he said, "and this time *not* pick up the cat and *not* let it get the bird. If I do that, maybe my life will change so that it turns into something happy. Something that is real. My real mistake was separating from you. Here; I'll put my hand through you." He placed his hand against her arm. The pressure of his muscles was vigorous; she felt the weight, the physical presence of him, against her. "See?" he said. "It goes right through you."

"And all this," she said, "because you killed a bird when you were a little boy."

"No," he said. "All this because of a failure in the temperature-regulating assembly aboard the ship. I'm not down to the proper temperature. There's just enough warmth left in my brain cells to permit cerebral activity." He stood up, then, stretched, smiled at her. "Shall we go get some dinner?" he asked.

She said, "I'm sorry. I'm not hungry."

"I am. I'm going to have some of the local seafood. The brochure says it's terrific. Come along, anyhow; maybe when you see the food and smell it, you'll change your mind."

Gathering up her coat and purse, she went with him.

"This is a beautiful little planet," he said. "I've explored it dozens of times. I know it thoroughly. We should stop downstairs at the pharmacy for some Bactine, though. For my hand. It's beginning to swell and it hurts like hell." He showed her his hand. "It hurts more this time than ever before."

"Do you want me to come back to you?" Martine said.

"Are you serious?"

"Yes," she said. "I'll stay with you as long as you want. I agree; we should never have been separated."

Victor Kemmings said, "The poster is torn."

"What?" she said.

"We should have framed it," he said. "We didn't have sense enough to take care of it. Now it's torn. And the artist is dead."

ROBERT SILVERBERG

GIANNI

February 1982

The prodigiously prolific author and editor Robert Silverberg, born in
Brooklyn in 1935, was an established writer by the time he was
twenty, when he was still a student at Columbia. At twenty-one, he
had already won a Hugo. During his early career, he wrote at such an
astonishing rate that his B-level stories were published under nearly
two dozen pseudonyms, while he continued to make his own name
count—frequently—in the science fiction world. To date, he has published more than one hundred novels and story collections, more than
sixty nonfiction books (and many articles), and has edited (recently
with his wife, writer Karen Haber) at least sixty anthologies. To pick
out a few of his books is not easy, but many critics cite his 1970s novels: *A Time of Changes, Dying Inside, The Book of Skulls, The Stochastic*

Man. Popular with readers were the heroic fantasies of the 1980s, beginning with *Lord Valentine's Castle.*

Surprisingly, this was Silverberg's first story for *Playboy,* but he soon made up for lost time, seldom letting a subsequent year go by without at least one contribution. The theme of "Gianni," that of a young musical genius confronting the possibilities and temptations of the pop life, has a great deal of psychological resonance, and it's not surprising that the story has had several film options. Collectors and bibliographers should note that when "Gianni" appeared in Silverberg's own collection *The Conglomeroid Cocktail Party,* it had a different narrator: Dr. Leavis instead of Sam Hoaglund, the public relations man. Readers can judge for themselves which version works better.

BUT WHY NOT Mozart?" I said, shaking my head. "Schubert, even? Or you could have brought back Bix Beiderbecke, for Christ's sake, if you wanted to resurrect a great musician."

"Beiderbecke was jazz," Dave Leavis said. "I'm not interested in jazz. Nobody's interested in jazz except you."

"And people are still interested in Pergolesi?"

"*I* am."

"Mozart would have been better publicity. You'll need more funding sooner or later. You tell the world you've got Mozart sitting in the back room cranking out a new opera, you can write your own ticket. But what good is Pergolesi? Pergolesi's totally forgotten."

"Only by the proletariat, Sam. Besides, why give Mozart a second chance? Maybe he died young, but it wasn't all *that* young, and he did his work, a ton of work. Gianni died at 26, you know. He might have been greater than Mozart if he'd had another dozen years."

"Johnny?"

"Gianni. Giovanni Battista. Pergolesi. He calls himself Gianni; come meet him."

"Mozart, Dave. You should have done Mozart."

"Stop being an idiot," Leavis said. "When you've met him, you'll know I did the right thing. Mozart would have been a pain in the neck, anyway. The stories I've heard about Mozart's private life would uncurl your wig. Come on with me."

He led me down the long hallway from the office, past the hardware room and the timescoop cage to the air lock separating us from the semidetached motel unit out back where Gianni had been living since they scooped him. We halted in the air lock to be

267

sprayed. Leavis explained, "Infectious microorganisms have mu-
tated a lot since the 18th Century. Until we've got his resistance
levels higher, we're keeping him in a pretty sterile environment.
When we first brought him back, he was vulnerable to anything—
a case of the sniffles would have killed him, most likely. Plus, he
was a dying man when we got him, one lung lousy with t.b. and
the other one going."

"Hey," I said.

Leavis laughed. "You won't catch anything from him. It's in
remission now, Sam. We didn't bring him back at colossal expense
just to watch him die."

The lock opened and we stepped into the monitoring vestibule, glittering like a movie set with bank upon bank of telemeter-
ing instruments. The day nurse, Claudia, middle-aged, plump, was
checking diagnostic readouts. "He's expecting you, Dr. Leavis,"
she said. "He's very frisky this morning."

"Frisky?"

"Playful. You know."

Yes. Tacked to the door of Gianni's room was a card that hadn't
been there yesterday, flamboyantly lettered in gaudy, free-flowing
baroque script:

GIOVANNI BATTISTA PERGOLESI
Jesi, January 4, 1710—Pozzuoli,
March 16, 1736
Genuis at Work!!!!
Please, Knock Before You Entering!

"He speaks English?" I asked.

"Now he does," Leavis said. "We gave him tapesleep the first
week. He picks things up fast, anyway." Leavis grinned. "Genius at
work, eh? Or *genuis*. That's the sort of sign I would have expected
Mozart to put up."

"They're all alike, these talents," I said.

Leavis knocked.

"*Chi va la?*" Gianni called.

"Dave Leavis."

"*Avanti, dottore illustrissimo!*"

"I thought you said he speaks English," I murmured.

"He's frisky today, Claudia said, remember?"

We went in. He had the blinds tightly drawn, shutting out the brilliant January sunlight, the yellow blaze of acacia blossoms just outside the window, the enormous scarlet bougainvillaea, the sweeping hilltop vista of the valley and the mountains beyond. Maybe scenery didn't interest him—or, more likely, he preferred to keep his room a tightly sealed little cell, an island out of time. He had had to absorb a lot of psychic trauma in the past few weeks: It must give you a hell of a case of jet lag to jump two and a half centuries into the future.

But he looked lively, almost impish—a small man, graceful, delicate, with sharp, busy eyes, quick, elegant gestures, a brisk, confident manner. When they fished him out of the 18th Century, Leavis had told me, he was a woeful sight, face lined and haggard, hair already gray at 26, body gaunt, bowed, quivering. He looked like what he was, a shattered consumptive a couple of weeks from the grave. His hair was still gray, but he looked healthy and energetic and there was color in his cheeks.

Leavis said, "Gianni, I want you to meet Sam Hoaglund. He's going to handle publicity and promotion for our project. *Capisce?* He will make you known to the world and give you a new audience for your music."

He flashed a brilliant smile. "*Bene*. Listen to this."

The room was an electronic jungle, festooned with gadgetry: a synthesizer, a telescreen, a megabuck audio library, five sorts of data terminals and all manner of other things perfectly suited to your basic 18th Century Italian drawing room. Leavis had said there was something scary about the speed with which he was mastering the equipment, and he was right. Gianni swung around to the synthesizer, jacked it into harpsichord mode and touched the keyboard. From the cloud of floating minispeakers came the opening theme of a sonata, lovely, lyrical, to my ear unmistakably 18th Century in its melodiousness, and yet somehow weird. For all its beauty, there was a strained, awkward, suspended aspect to it, like a ballet performed by dancers in galoshes. The longer he played, the more uncomfortable I felt. Finally, he turned to us and said, "You like it?"

"What is it? Something of yours?"

"Mine, yes. My new style. I am under the influence of Beethoven today. Haydn yesterday, tomorrow Chopin. I try everything, no?

By Easter I get to the ugly composers, Mahler, Berg, Debussy—those men were *crazy,* do you know? Crazy music, so ugly. But I will learn."

"Debussy ugly?" I said quietly.

"Bach is modern music to him," Leavis said. "Haydn is the voice of the future."

Gianni said, "I will be very famous."

"Yes. Sam will make you the most famous man in the world."

"I was very famous after I . . . died." He tapped one of the terminals. "I have read about me. I was so famous that everybody forged my music and it was published as Pergolesi, do you know that? I have played it, too, this 'Pergolesi.' *Merda,* most of it. Not all. The *concerti armonici,* not bad—not mine, but not bad. Most of the rest, trash." He winked. "But you will make me famous while I live, eh? Good. Very good." He came closer to us and in a lower voice said, "Will you tell Claudia that the gonorrhea, it is all cured?"

"What?"

"She would not believe me. I said, 'The doctor swears it,' but she said, 'No, it is not safe, you must keep your hands off me, you must keep everything else off me.'"

"Gianni, have you been molesting your nurse?"

"I am becoming a healthy man, *dottore.* I am no monk. They sent me to live with the *cappuccini* in the monastery at Pozzuoli, yes, but it was only so the good air there could heal my consumption, not to make me a monk. I am no monk now and I am no longer sick. Could you go without a woman for three hundred years?" He put his face close to mine, gave me a bright-eyed stare, leered outrageously. "You will make me very famous. And then there will be women again, yes? And you must tell them that the gonorrhea, it is entirely cured. This age of miracles!"

Afterward, I said to Leavis, "And you thought Mozart was going to be too much trouble?"

Leavis said to me, back in his office, "He didn't sound so cocky when we first got him. He was a wreck, hollow, burned out. He was barely alive. We wondered if we had waited too long to get him." If he had died, Leavis told me, the whole project would have been scrubbed, because they had no budget for making a second scoop.

"Why did you pick someone who was nine tenths dead, then?" I wanted to know.

Leavis said, "Too risky otherwise. You know, we could have yanked anybody we liked out of the past—Napoleon, Genghis Khan, Henry VIII—but we had no way of knowing what effects it might have on the course of history. Suppose we scooped up Lenin while he was still in exile in Switzerland, or collected Hitler while he was still a paper hanger. So, from the start, we limited ourselves to scooping only somebody whose life and accomplishments were entirely behind him, somebody so close to the time of his natural death that his disappearance wouldn't be likely to unsettle the fabric of the universe.

"But why Pergolesi? He was your special choice, wasn't he?"

Leavis nodded. "I lobbied for months to scoop Pergolesi. Not just because I happen to like his music, though I do. But because he was considered such a genius in his time and died before he had a chance to hit his real stride. I wanted to see what such a person could do, given a reprieve. I had my way, finally. We got him out eighteen days before his official date of death. Once we had him, it was no great trick to substitute a synthetic cadaver, who was duly discovered and buried, and as far as we can tell, no calamities occurred in history because one consumptive Italian was put in his grave two weeks earlier than the encyclopedia used to say he had been."

"Did he understand what had happened to him?"

"Not a clue. He wasn't sure whether he had awakened in heaven or hell, but whichever it was, he was alternately stunned and depressed. When he was conscious at all. It was touch and go, keeping him alive. Those were the worst days of my life, Sam, the first few after the scooping. To have planned for years, to have expended so many gigabucks on the project, and then to have our first human scoopee die on us anyway—"

He didn't, though. The same vitality that had pulled 15 operas and a dozen cantatas and who knows how many symphonies and concertos and Masses out of him in a lifespan of only 26 years pulled him back from the edge of the grave now, once the resources of modern medicine were put to work rebuilding his lungs and curing his assorted venereal diseases. Within days, Leavis told me, he had been wholly transformed. It must have been almost magical. I wish I had been part of the team in that phase. Yet there was no real magic in it, just antibiotics, transplant technology, microsurgery, regeneration therapy, routine stuff. One century's magic, another century's routine.

Leavis spent those early days wavering between anxiety and ecstasy. Obviously, he had more than just his scientific reputation riding on this. Dave has no kids of his own, and he's old enough to be Gianni's father. Some kind of relationship began to develop. Leavis was completely involved in giving Gianni back his life— more than that, in giving him the life he *should* have had. He was hovering over Gianni, pulling for him, praying for him, protecting him, mothering and fathering him, almost from the start.

And there were other complexities. The pallid, feeble young man struggling for his life in the back unit was surrounded, for Leavis and other connoisseurs of music, with a radiant aura of accumulated fame and legend built up over centuries. He was *Pergolesi,* said Dave, the miraculous boy, the fountain of melody, the composer of the *Stabat Mater* and *La Serva Padrona* and a lot of other great things that I had never heard of but that the music buffs revered. Leavis told me that in the years just after he died, he was ranked, for a time, with Bach. When they revived his comic operas in Paris 20 or 30 years after he died, they inspired a whole genre of light music right down to Gilbert and Sullivan and beyond. But all that fame was only in the eyes of the onlookers. Gianni's own view of himself was different: a weary, sick, dying young man, poor pathetic Gianni, the failure, the washout, unknown in his life beyond Rome and Naples, getting no acclaim for any of his serious music, only the comic things that he dashed off so fast—poor Gianni, burned out at 25, destroyed as much by disappointment as by t.b. and V.D., creeping off to the Capuchin monastery to die in miserable poverty. How could he have known he was going to be famous? But we showed him. Leavis played him recordings of his music, both the true works and those that had been constructed in his name by the unscrupulous to cash in on his posthumous glory. He let Gianni see the biographies and critical studies and even the novels that had been published about him. I was surprised at how many there were. He was thrilled, of course. Indeed, for him it must have been precisely like dying and going to heaven, and from day to day he gained strength and poise, he waxed and flourished, he came to glow with vigor and passion and confidence. He knew now that no magic had been worked on him, that he had been snatched into the unimaginable future and restored to health by ordinary human beings, and he accepted that and quickly ceased to question it. All that concerned him now was music. In the second and third weeks, they gave him a crash course in post-Baroque musical history. Bach first, then the shift away from polyphony—"*Naturalmente,*" he said, "it was inevitable, I would have achieved it myself if I had lived"—and he spent hours with Mozart and Haydn and Johann Christian Bach and entered a kind of ecstatic state. One morning, Leavis found him red-eyed with weeping. He had been up all night listening to *Don Giovanni* and *The Marriage of Figaro*. "This Mozart," he said. "You bring him back, too?"

"Maybe someday we will," Leavis said.

"I kill him! You bring him back, I strangle him, I trample him!" His eyes blazed. He laughed wildly. "He is wonder! He is angel! He is too good! Send me to his time, I kill him then! No one should compose like that! Except Pergolesi. He would have done it."

"I believe that."

"Yes! This *Figaro*—1786—I could have done it twenty years earlier! Thirty! If only I get the chance. Why this Mozart so lucky? I die, he live—why? Why, *dottore?*"

Leavis said to me, "You don't know much about classical music, do you, Sam?"

I shrugged. "I can tell Bach from Tchaikovsky, if that's what you mean. But neither one really speaks to me. I guess I've always been mainly into pop stuff. Is that all right with you?"

"Why not? But I want you to understand at least what kind of experience it was for me to see this great 18th Century composer discover everything that had happened after him. After Mozart, he went to Beethoven, who I think was a little too much for him, overwhelming, massive, crushing. And then the romantics, who amused him." Leavis imitated Gianni's high-pitched voice: "'Berlioz, Tchaikovsky, Wagner, all lunatics, *dementi, pazzi,* but

273

they are wonderful. I think I see what they are trying to do. Madmen! Marvelous madmen!'—and quickly on to the 20th Century, Mahler, Schönberg, Stravinski, Bartók."

"I bet he didn't like them," I said.

"He found them all ugly or terrifying or simply incomprehensibly bizarre. He couldn't see where they were coming from, you know. And the later composers! Webern and the serialists, Penderecki, Stockhausen, Xenakis, Ligeti—"

"Never heard of any of them."

"I'm not surprised," said Leavis. "Gianni just turned up his nose and shrugged them off, as though he barely recognized what they were doing as music. Their fundamental assumptions were too alien to him. Genius though he was, he couldn't get a handle on their ideas, any more than Escoffier could have enjoyed the cuisine of some other planet, you know? He finished his survey of modern music, and then he returned to Bach and Mozart and gave them his full attention."

And it was *full* attention. Gianni was utterly incurious about the world outside his bedroom window. They told him he was in America, in California, and showed him a map. He nodded casually. They turned on the telescreen and let him look at the landscape of the early 21st Century. His eyes glazed. They spoke of automobiles, planes, flights to Mars. Yes, he said, *meraviglioso, miracoloso,* and went back to the *Brandenburg Concerti.* "I realize now," Leavis said, "that the lack of interest he showed in the modern world was a sign neither of fear nor of shallowness but, rather, only a mark of priorities. What Mozart accomplished is stranger and more interesting to him than the whole technological revolution. Technology is only a means to an end, for Gianni—push a button, you get a symphony orchestra in your bedroom: *miracoloso!*—and he takes it entirely for granted. That the *basso continuo* had become obsolete 30 years after his death, that the diatonic scales would be demoted from sacred constants to inconvenient anachronisms a century or so later is more significant to him than the fusion reactor, the interplanetary spaceship or even the machine that yanked him from his deathbed into our world."

In the fourth week, he said he wanted to compose again. Leavis was in 11th heaven. Gianni asked for a harpsichord. Instead, they gave him a synthesizer. He loved it.

In the sixth week, he began asking questions about the outside world, and I realized that the tricky part of the experiment was about to begin.

I said to Leavis, "Pretty soon we have to reveal him. It's incredible we've been able to keep it quiet this long."

I had a plan. The problem was twofold: letting Gianni experience the world and letting the world adjust to the idea of time travel and a man from the past. There was going to be the whole business of press conferences, media tours of the lab, interviews with Gianni, a festival of Pergolesi music at the Hollywood Bowl with the premiere of a symphony in the mode of Beethoven that he said would be ready by April, etc., etc., etc. But, at the same time, we would be taking Gianni on private tours of the L.A. area, gradually exposing him to the society into which he had been so unilaterally hauled. The medics said it was safe to let him encounter 21st Century microorganisms now. But would it be safe to let him encounter 21st Century civilization? He, with his windows sealed and his blinds drawn, his 18th Century mind wholly engrossed in the revelations that Bach and Mozart and Beethoven were pouring into it—what would he make of the world of spaceways and slice houses and overload bands and freebase teams when he could no longer hide from it?

"Leave it all to me," I said. "That's what you're paying me for, right?"

On a mild and rainy February afternoon, Leavis and I and the main physician, Nella Brandon, took him on his first drive through his new reality. Down the hill the back way, along Ventura Boulevard a few miles, onto the freeway, out to Topanga, back around through the landslide zone to what had been Santa Monica, and then straight up Wilshire across the entire heart of Los Angeles—a good stiff jolt of modernity. Dr. Brandon carried her full armamentarium of sedatives and tranks ready, in case Gianni freaked out. But he didn't freak out.

He loved it—swinging round and round in the bubbletop car, gaping at everything. I tried to view L.A. through the eyes of someone whose entire life had been spent amid the splendors of Renaissance and Baroque architecture, and it came up hideous on all counts. But not to Gianni. "Beautiful," he sighed. "Wondrous! Miraculous! Marvelous!" The traffic, the freeways themselves, the fast-food joints, the peeling plastic facades, the great fire scar in Topanga, the houses hanging by spider cables from the hillsides, the occasional superjet floating overhead on its way into LAX— everything lit him up. It was wonderland to him. None of those dull old cathedrals and *palazzi* and marble fountains here—no, everything here was brighter and larger and glitzier than life, and he loved it. The only part he couldn't handle was the beach at Topanga. By the time we got there, the sun was out and so were the sun bathers, and the sight of 8000 naked bodies cavorting on the damp sand almost gave him a stroke. "What is this?" he demanded. "The market for slaves? The pleasure house of the king?"

"Blood pressure rising fast," Nella said softly, eying her wrist monitors. "Adrenaline levels going up. Shall I cool him out?"

Leavis shook his head.

"Slavery is unlawful," I told Gianni. "There is no king. These are ordinary citizens amusing themselves."

"Nudo! Assolutamente nudo!"

"We long ago outgrew feeling ashamed of our bodies," I said. "The laws allow us to go nude in places like this."

"Straordinario! Incredibile!" He gaped in total astonishment. Then he erupted with questions, a torrent of Italian first, his English returning only with an effort. Did husbands allow their wives to come here? Did fathers permit daughters? Were there rapes on the beach? Duels? If the body had lost its mystery, how did sexual desire survive? If a man somehow did become excited, was it shameful to let it show? And on and on and on, until Leavis had to signal Nella to give him a mild needle. Calmer now, Gianni digested the notion of mass public nudity in a more reflective way; but it had amazed him more than Beethoven, that was plain.

We let him stare for another ten minutes. As we started to return to the car, Gianni pointed to a lush brunette trudging along by the tide pools and said, "I want her. Get her."

"Gianni, we can't do that!"

"You think I am eunuch?" He caught my wrist. "Get her for me."

"Not yet. You aren't well enough yet. And we can't just *get* her for you. Things aren't done that way here."

"She goes naked. She belongs to anyone."

"No," Leavis said. "You still don't really understand, do you?" He nodded to Nella. She gave him another needle. We drove on and he subsided. Soon we came to the barrier marking where the coast road had fallen into the sea, and we swung inland through the place where Santa Monica had been. I explained about the earthquake and the landslide. Gianni grinned.

"Ah, *il terremoto,* you have it here, too? A few years ago, there was great earthquake in Napoli. You have understood? And then they ask me to write a Mass of Thanksgiving, afterward, because not everything is destroyed. It is very famous Mass for a time. You know it? No? You must hear it." He turned and seized my wrist. With an intensity greater than the brunette had aroused in him, he said, "I will compose a new famous Mass, yes? I will be very famous again. And I will be rich. Yes? I was famous and then I was forgotten and then I died and now I live again. And rich. Yes? Yes?"

Leavis beamed at him and said, "In another couple of weeks, Gianni, you're going to be the most famous man in the world."

Casually, I poked the button turning on the radio. The car was well equipped for overload and out of the many speakers came the familiar pulsing, tingling sounds of Wilkes Booth John doing *Membrane*. The subsonics were terrific. Gianni sat up straight as the music hit him. "What is that?" he demanded.

"Overload," I said. "Wilkes Booth John."

"Overload? This means nothing to me. It is a music? Of when?"

"The music of right now," said Nella.

As we zoomed along Wilshire, I keyed in the colors and lights, too, and the whole interior of the car began to throb and flash and sizzle. Wonderland for Gianni again. He blinked, he pressed his hands to his cheeks, he shook his head. "It is like the music of dreams," he said. "The composer? Who is?"

"Not a composer," I explained. "A group. Wilkes Booth John, it calls itself. This isn't classical music, it's pop. Popular. Pop doesn't have a composer."

"It makes itself, this music?"

"No," I said. "The whole group composes it. And plays it."

"The orchestra. It is pop and the orchestra composes." He looked lost. Pop. Such strange music. So simple. It goes over and over again, the same thing, loud, no shape. Yet I think I like it. Who listens to this music? *Imbecilli? Infanti?*"

"Everyone," I said.

That first outing in Los Angeles not only told us Gianni could handle exposure to the modern world but also transformed his life among us in several significant ways. For one thing, there was no keeping him chaste any longer after Topanga Beach. He was healthy, he was lusty, he was vigorously heterosexual—an old biography of him I had seen blames his ill health and early demise on "his notorious profligacy"—and we could hardly go on treating him like a prisoner or a zoo animal. After a talk with Leavis—and I had to be firm—I fixed him up with one of my secretaries, Melissa Burke, a willing volunteer.

Then, too, Gianni had been confronted for the first time with the split between classical and popular music, with the whole modernist cleavage between high art and lowbrow entertainment. That was new to him and baffling at first. "This *pop*," he said, "it is the music of the peasants?" But gradually he grasped the idea of simple rhythmic music that everyone listened to, distinguished from "serious" music that belonged only to an elite and was played merely on formal occasions. "But *my* music," he protested, "it had tunes, people could whistle it. It was everybody's music." He couldn't understand why serious composers had abandoned melody and made themselves inaccessible to most of the people. We told him that something like that had happened in all of the arts. "You poor crazy *uomini del futuro*," he said gently.

Suddenly, he began to turn himself into a connoisseur of overload groups. We rigged an imposing unit in his room and he and Melissa spent hours plugged in, soaking up the wave forms let loose by Scissors and Ultrafoam and Wilkes Booth John and the other top bands. When I asked him how the new symphony was coming along, he gave me a peculiar look.

He began to make other little inroads into modern life. Melissa and I took him shopping for clothing on Figueroa Street, and in the Cholo boutiques, he acquired a flashy new wardrobe of the latest Aztec gear to replace the lab clothes he had worn since his awakening. He had his prematurely gray hair dyed red. He acquired jewelry that went flash, clang, zzz and pop when the mood-actuated sensoria came into play. In a few days, he was utterly transformed: He became the perfect young Angeleno—slim, dapper, stylish, complete with the slight foreign accent and exotic grammar.

"Tonight Melissa and I go to The Quonch," Gianni announced.

"The Quonch," Leavis murmured, mystified.

"Overload palace," I explained. "In Pomona. All the big groups play there."

Leavis looked upset. "We have philharmonic tickets tonight," he said irritably.

Gianni's eyes were implacable. "The Quonch," he said.

So we went to The Quonch. Gianni, Melissa and I. I was the chaperon. Gianni and Melissa had wanted to go alone, but Leavis wasn't having that. He sounded a lot like an overprotective mother whose little boy wanted to try a bit of free-basing. No chaperon, no Quonch, he said. The Quonch was a gigantic geodesic dome in Pomona Downlevel, far underground. The stage whirled on antigrav gyros, the ceiling was a mist of floating speakers, the seats had pluggie intensifiers and the audience, median age about 14, was sliced out of its mind. The groups performing that night were Thug, Holy Ghosts, Shining Orgasm Revival and Ultrafoam. I could imagine Leavis asking. "For this I spent untold multikilogelt to bring the composer of the *Stabat Mater* and *La Serva Padrona* back to life?" The kids screamed, the great hall filled with dense, tangible, oppressive sound, colors and lights throbbed and pulsed, minds were blown. In the midst of the madness sat Giovanni Battista Pergolesi (1710–1736), student of the Conservatorio dei Poveri, organist of the royal chapel at Naples, *maestro di cappella* to the Prince of Stigliano—plugged in, turned on, radiant, ecstatic, transcendent.

Whatever else The Quonch may have been, it didn't seem dangerous; so the next night we let Gianni go there just with Melissa. And the next. Leavis reluctantly gave in. He had to start letting him move out on his own a little. But Leavis was starting to worry about my campaign. It wouldn't be long before we broke the news to the public that we had a genuine 18th Century genius among us. But where were the new symphonies? Where were the heaven-sent sonatas? He wasn't producing anything visible. He was just doing a lot of overload.

"Relax," I said. "He's going through a phase. He's dazzled by the novelty of everything and, also, he's having fun for maybe the first time in his life. If we have to, we'll delay the campaign a little. But sooner or later he'll get back to composing. Nobody steps out of character forever. The real Pergolesi will take control." I hoped so, for Leavis' sake.

Then Gianni disappeared.

Came the frantic call at three in the afternoon on a crazy hot Saturday with Santa Anas blowing and a fire raging in Tujunga. Nella had gone to Gianni's room to give him his regular checkup, and no Gianni. I went whistling across town from my house near the beach. Leavis, who had come running in from Santa Barbara, was there already. "I phoned Melissa," I told him. "He's not with her. But she's got a theory."

"Tell."

"They've been going backstage the past few nights. He's met some of the kids from Ultrafoam and one of the other groups. She figures he's off working out with them."

"If that's all, then hallelujah. But how do we track him?"

"She's getting addresses. We're making calls. Quit worrying, Dave."

Easy to say. I imagined him held for ransom in some East Los Angeles dive. I imagined swaggering *machos* sending me his fingers, one a day, waiting for 50 megabucks' payoff. What Leavis was going through must have been ten times worse. I paced for half a dreadful hour, grabbing phones as if they were magic wands, and then came word that they had found him, working out with Shining Orgasm Revival in a studio in West Covina. We were there in half the legal time and to hell with the California Highway Patrol.

The place was a miniature Quonch, electric gear everywhere, the special apparatus of overload rigged up and Gianni sitting in the midst of six practically naked young uglies whose bodies were draped with readout tape and sonic gadgetry. So was his. He looked blissful and sweaty. "It is so beautiful, this music," he sighed when we collared him. "It is the music of my second birth. I love it beyond everything."

"Bach," Dave said. "Beethoven. Mozart."

"This is other. This is miracle. The total effect—the surround, the engulf—"

"Gianni, don't ever go off again without telling someone," I said.

"You were afraid?"

"We have a major investment in you. We don't want you getting hurt, or into trouble, or—"

"Am I a child?"

"There are dangers in this city that you couldn't possibly understand yet. You want to jam with these musicians, jam with them, but don't just disappear. Understood?"

He nodded.

Then he said, "We will not hold the press conference for a while. I am learning this music. I will make my debut next month, maybe. If we can get booking at The Quonch as main attraction."

"This is what you want to be? An overload star?"

"Music is music."

"And you are Giovanni Battista Pergo—" An awful thought struck me. I looked sideways at Shining Orgasm Revival. "Gianni, you didn't tell them who you—"

"No. I am still secret."

"Thank God." I put my hand on his arm. "Look, if this stuff amuses you, listen to it, play it, do what you want. But the Lord gave you a genius for real music."

"This is real music."

"Complex music. Serious music."

"I starved to death composing that music."

"You were ahead of your time," Leavis cut in. "You wouldn't starve now. You will have a tremendous audience for your music."

"Because I am a freak, yes. And in two months I am forgotten again. *Grazie*, no, Dave. No more sonatas. No more cantatas. Is not the music of this world. I give myself to overload."

"I forbid it, Gianni!"

He glared at Leavis. I saw something steely behind his delicate and foppish exterior.

"You do not own me, Dr. Leavis."

Leavis looked as though he had been slapped. "I gave you life."

"So did my father and mother. They didn't own me, either."

"Please, Gianni. Let's not fight. I'm only begging you not to turn your back on your genius, not to renounce the gift God gave you for—"

"I renounce nothing. I merely transform." He leaned up and put his nose almost against Leavis'. "Let me free. I will not be a court composer for you. I will not give you Masses and symphonies. No one wants such things today, not new ones, only a few people who want the old ones. Not good enough. I want to be famous, *capisce?* I want to be rich. Did you think I'd live the rest of my life as a curiosity, a museum piece? Or that I would learn to write the kind of noise they call modern music? Fame is what I want. I died poor and hungry, the books say. *You* die poor and hungry and find out what it is like, and then talk to me about writing cantatas. I will never be poor again." He laughed. "Next year, after I am revealed to the world, I will start my own overload group. We will wear wigs, 18th Century clothes, everything. We will call ourselves Pergolesi. All right? All right, Dave?"

He insisted on working out with Shining Orgasm Revival every afternoon. OK. He went to overload concerts just about every night. OK. He talked about going on stage next month. Even that was OK. He did no composing, stopped listening to any music but overload. OK. "He is going through a phase," I had said. OK.

"You do not own me," Gianni had said.

OK. OK.

We let him have his way. Leavis hated it, but he was helpless. I asked Gianni who his overload band mates thought he was, why they had let him join the group so readily. "I say I am rich Italian playboy," he replied. "Remember I am accustom to winning the favors of kings, princes, cardinals. It is how we musicians earn our living. I charm them, they listen to me play, they see right away I am genius. The rest is simple. I will be very rich."

About three weeks into Gianni's overload phase, Nella came to me and said. "Sam, he's doing slice."

I don't know why I was surprised. I was.

"Are you sure?"

She nodded. "It's showing up in his blood, his urine, his metabolic charts. He probably does it every time he goes to play with that band. He's losing weight, corpuscle formation dropping off, resistance weakening. You've got to talk to him."

"All right. Don't say a word to Leavis." I warned.

I went to him and said. "Gianni, I don't give a damn what kind of music you write, but when it comes to drugs, I draw the line. You're still not completely sound physically. Remember, you were at the edge of *death* just a few months ago, body time. I don't want you killing yourself."

"You do not own me." Again, sullenly.

"Nobody owns you. I want you to go on living."

"Slice will not kill me."

"It's killed plenty already."

"Not Pergolesi!" he snapped. Then he smiled, took my hand, gave me the full treatment. "Sam, Sam, you listen. I die once. I am not interested in an encore. But the slice, it is essential. Do you know? It divides one moment from the next. You have taken it? No? Then you cannot understand. It puts spaces in time. It allows me to comprehend the most intricate rhythms, because with slice, there is time for everything, the world slows down, the mind accelerates. *Capisce?* I need it for my music."

"You managed to write the *Stabat Mater* without slice."

"Different music. For this, I need it." He patted my hand. "You do not worry, eh? I look after myself."

What could I say? I grumbled. I muttered. I shrugged. I told Nella to keep a very close eye on his readouts. I told Melissa to spend as much time as possible with him and keep him off the drug if she could manage it. I said nothing about any of this to Leavis.

At the end of the month. Gianni announced he would make his debut at The Quonch on the following Saturday. A big bill— five overload bands. Shining Orgasm Revival playing fourth, with Wilkes Booth John, no less, as the big group of the night. The kids in the audience would skull out completely if they knew that one of the Orgasms was 300 years old, but, of course, they weren't going to find that out, so they'd just figure he was a new sideman and pay no attention. I was already starting to think about a new

PR program. The publicity would be something else, once we got the whole bit into view and let the world find out that the newest overload star had been born in the year 1710.

Leavis seemed groggy and stunned. I knew that he felt left out, off on another track. The situation was beyond his control. I was sorry for him, but there wasn't anything I could do for him. Gianni was in charge. Gianni now was like a force of nature, a hurricane.

We all went to The Quonch for Gianni's overload debut.

There we sat, a dozen or more alleged adults, in that mob of screaming kids. Fumes, lights, colors, the buzzing of gadgetized clothes and jewels, people passing out, people coupling in the aisles, the whole crazy bit, like Babylon right before the end, and we sat through it. Kids selling slice, dope, coke, you name it, slipped among us. I wasn't buying, but I think some of my people were. I closed my eyes and let it all wash over me, the rhythms and subliminals and ultrasonics of one group after another, Toad Star, then Bubblemilk, then Holy Ghosts and, finally, after many hours, Shining Orgasm Revival was supposed to go on for its set.

A long intermission dragged on and on. And on.

The kids, zonked and crazed, didn't mind at first. But after maybe half an hour, they began to boo and throw things and pound on the walls. I looked at Leavis, Leavis looked at me, Nella murmured little worried things.

Then Melissa appeared from somewhere and whispered, "Dr. Leavis, you'd better come backstage. Mr. Hoaglund. Dr. Brandon."

They say that if you fear the worst, you keep the worst at bay. As we made our way through the bowels of The Quonch to the performers' territory, I imagined Gianni sprawled backstage, wired with full gear, eyes rigid, tongue sticking out—dead of a slice overdose. And all our fabulous project ruined in a crazy moment. So we went backstage and there were the members of Shining Orgasm Revival running in circles, and a cluster of Quonch personnel conferring urgently, and kids in full war paint peering in the back way and trying to get through the cordon. And there was Gianni, wired with full overload gear, sprawled on the floor, shirtless, skin shiny with sweat, mottled with dull purplish spots, eyes rigid, tongue sticking out. Nella pushed everyone away and dropped down beside him. One of the Orgasms said to no one in particular, "He was real nervous, man, he kept slicing off more and more, we couldn't stop him, you know—"

Nella looked up at me. Her face was bleak.

"O.D.?" I said.

She nodded. She had the snout of an ultrahypo against Gianni's limp arm and she was giving him some kind of shot to try to bring him around. But even in this century, dead is dead is dead.

It was Melissa who said afterward, through tears, "It was his karma to die young, don't you see? If he couldn't die in 1736, he was going to die fast here, He had no choice."

And I thought of the biography that had said of him long ago, "His ill health was probably due to his notorious profligacy."

And I heard my own voice saying, "Nobody steps out of character forever. The real Pergolesi will take control." Yes. Gianni had always been on a collision course with death, I saw now; by scooping him from his own era, we had only delayed things a few months. Self-destructive is as self-destructive does, and a change of scenery doesn't alter the case.

If that is so—if, as Melissa says, karma governs all—should we bother to try again? Do we reach into yesterday's yesterday for some other young genius dead too soon—Poe or Rimbaud or Caravaggio or Keats—and give him the second chance we had hoped to give Gianni? And watch him recapitulate his destiny, going down a second time? Mozart, as I had once suggested? Benvenuto Cellini? Our net is wide and deep. All of the past is ours. But if we bring back another, and he willfully and heedlessly sends himself down the same old karmic chute, what have we gained, what have we achieved, what have we done to ourselves and to him? I think of Gianni, looking to be rich and famous at last, lying purpled on that floor. Would Shelley drown again? Would Van Gogh cut off the other ear before our eyes?

Perhaps someone more mature would be safer, eh? El Greco, Cervantes, Shakespeare? But then we might behold Shakespeare signing up in Hollywood. El Greco operating out of some trendy gallery, Cervantes sitting down with his agent to figure tax-shelter angles. Yes? No. I look at the scoop. The scoop looks at me. It is very, very late to consider these matters, my friends. Billions of dollars spent, years of work, Leavis a broken man now, everything in chaos, and for what, for what, for what? We can't simply abandon the project now, can we?

Can we?

I look at the scoop. The scoop looks at me.

STEPHEN KING

THE WORD PROCESSOR

January 1983

Stephen King is a writer who truly needs no introduction. No other novelist, ever, has had anything approaching his commercial success—close to one hundred million books sold so far, and, born in 1947, he's still relatively young, and so prolific that he competes with himself under the pseudonym Richard Bachman. King is still experimenting with different forms of writing, most recently the "serial" novel, published (very successfully) in sequential parts, the way Dickens used to do it (*The Green Mile*). Even nonreaders know his work through the many movies made from his books, some of which are famous in their own right: *Carrie, The Shining, The Dead Zone, Stand By Me, Misery*.

Still, he is not generally thought of in terms of science fiction, but as a horror writer—even as *the* horror writer. That isn't strictly the case. *The Stand* is recognizably a post-Holocaust novel, *The Tommy-knockers* digs up an alien spaceship, and even the psi talents of a number of other novels have science fictional elements. Perhaps this story, which dates to that time in the early 1980s when writers had just discovered what were then called "word processors" and had begun to stack their trusty old typewriters in the attic, best demonstrates how a master of horror makes use of the trappings of science fiction. It was collected by King in *Skeleton Crew* as "Word Processor of the Gods."

AT FIRST GLANCE, it looked like a Wang word processor—it had a Wang keyboard and a Wang casing. It was only at second glance that Richard Hagstrom saw that the casing had been slit open (and not gently, either; it looked to him as if the job had been done with a hack-saw blade) to admit a slightly larger IBM cathode-ray tube. The archive disks that had come with this odd mongrel were not floppy at all; they were as hard as the 45s Richard had listened to as a kid.

"What in the name of *God* is that?" his wife, Lina, asked as he and Mr. Nordhoff lugged it over to his study piece by piece. Nordhoff had lived next door to Richard's brother's family—Roger, Belinda and their boy, Jonathan.

"It's something Jon built," Richard said. "Meant for me to have it, Mr. Nordhoff says. It looks like a word processor."

"Oh, yeah," Nordhoff said. He would not see his 60s again, and he was badly out of breath. "That's what he said it was, the poor kid. Think we could set it down for a minute, Mr. Hagstrom? I'm pooped."

"You bet," Richard said and then called to his son, Seth, who was tooling odd, atonal chords out of his Fender guitar downstairs. The room Richard had envisioned as a family room when he had paneled it had become his son's rehearsal hall instead.

"Seth!" he yelled. "Come give us a hand!"

Downstairs, Seth just went on warping chords out of the Fender. Richard looked at Nordhoff and shrugged, ashamed and unable to hide it. Nordhoff shrugged back as if to say, "Kids! Who expects anything better from them these days?" Except they both knew that Jon—poor, doomed Jon Hagstrom, Richard's worthless brother's son—had been better.

"You were good to help me with this," Richard said.

Nordhoff shrugged. "What else has an old man got to do with his time? And I guess it was the least I could do for Jonny. He used to cut my lawn gratis, do you know that? I wanted to pay him, but the kid wouldn't take it. He was quite a boy." Nordhoff was still quite badly out of breath. "Do you think I could have a glass of water, Mr. Hagstrom?"

"You bet." Richard got it himself when his wife didn't move from the kitchen table, where she was reading a bodice-ripper paperback and eating a Twinkie. "Seth!" he yelled again. "Come on up here and help us, OK?"

But Seth just went on playing muffled and rather sour bar chords on the Fender, for which Richard was still paying.

Richard invited Nordhoff to stay for supper, but Nordhoff refused politely. Richard nodded, embarrassed again but perhaps hiding it a little better this time. "What's a nice guy like you doing with a family like that?" his friend Bernie Epstein had asked him once, and Richard had only been able to shake his head, feeling the same dull embarrassment he was feeling now. He *was* a nice guy. And yet, somehow, this was what he had come out with: an over-weight, sullen wife, who felt cheated out of the good things in life, who felt that she had backed a losing horse (but who would never come right out and say so), and an uncommunicative 15-year-old son, who was doing marginal work in the school at which Richard taught—a son who played weird chords on the guitar morning, noon and night (mostly night) and who seemed to think that that would somehow be enough.

"I could stand a beer before I go, though," Nordhoff said.

Richard nodded gratefully and went back to get them a couple of Buds.

His study was in a small shedlike building that stood apart from the house—like the family room, it had been fixed up by Richard himself. But unlike the family room, it was a place he thought of as his own—a place where he could shut out the stranger he had married and the stranger to whom she had given birth.

Lina did not, of course, approve of his having a place where he could shut them out, but she had not been able to prevent it—it was one of the few little victories he had managed over her. He supposed that, in a way, she *had* backed a losing horse; when they had gotten married, 16 years before, they had both believed that he would write wonderful, lucrative novels and they would soon be driving around in Mercedes-Benzes. But the one novel he had published had not been lucrative, and the critics had been quick to point out that it wasn't very wonderful, either. Lina had seen things the critics' way, and that had been the beginning of their drifting apart.

So the high school teaching job that both of them had seen as only a stepping-stone on their way to fame, glory and riches had been their major source of income for the past 15 years—one hell of a long stepping-stone, he sometimes thought. But he had never quite let go of his dream. He wrote short stories and an occasional article. He was a member in good standing of The Authors Guild. He brought in about $5000 in additional income with his type-writer each year, and no matter how much Lina might grouse about it, that rated him his own study—especially since she refused to work.

"You've got a nice place here," Nordhoff said, looking around the small room with the mixture of old-fashioned prints on the walls. The mongrel word processor sat on the desk, with the CPU tucked underneath. Richard's old Olivetti electric had been put aside for the time being on top of one of the filing cabinets.

"It serves the purpose," Richard said. He nodded at the word processor. "You don't suppose that thing really works, do you? Jon was . . . what? Fourteen?"

Nordhoff laughed. "You don't know the half of it," he said. "I peeked down into the back of the cabinet with the TV screen in it. Some of the wires are stamped RADIO SHACK. And believe it or not, a whole bunch more are labeled ERECTOR." He sipped his beer and said, in a kind of afterthought, "Fifteen. He had just turned fifteen."

"*Erector?*" Richard blinked at the old man.

"That's right. Erector puts out an electric-model kit. Jon had one of them since he was . . . oh, maybe six. I gave it to him for Christmas one year. He was crazy for gadgets even then. Any kind of gadget would do him, and did that little box of Erector motors tickle him? I guess it did. He kept it for almost nine years. Not many kids do that, Mr. Hagstrom."

"No," Richard said, thinking of the boxes of Seth's toys—discarded, forgotten or wantonly broken—he had lugged out over those same nine years. He glanced at the word processor. "It doesn't work, then."

"I wouldn't bet on that until you try it," Nordhoff said. "The kid was damn near an electrical genius. Did you know that?"

"I know he was good with gadgets, as you say. He won the state science fair when he was in the sixth grade, competing against kids who were high school seniors. His project had something to do with electronic-games programs, I think. But this—"

Nordhoff set his beer down. "There was a kid, back in the Fifties," he said, "who made an atom smasher out of two soup cans and about five dollars' worth of electrical equipment. Jon told me about that. And he said there was a kid out in some hick town in New Mexico who discovered tachyons—negative particles that are supposed to travel backward through time—back in 1954. A kid in Waterbury, Connecticut—eleven years old—who made a pipe bomb out of the celluloid he scraped off the backs of a deck of playing cards. He blew up an empty doghouse with it. Kids're funny sometimes. The supersmart ones in particular. You might be surprised."

"Maybe. Maybe I will be."

"He was a fine boy."

"You loved him a little, didn't you?"

"Mr. Hagstrom," Nordhoff said, "I loved him a lot. He was a genuinely all-right kid."

And Richard thought how strange it was: His brother, who had been an utter shit since the age of six, had gotten a fine woman and a fine, bright son. He himself, who had always tried to be gentle and good (whatever "good" meant in this crazy world), had married Lina, who had developed into a silent, piggy woman, and had gotten Seth by her. Looking at Nordhoff's honest, tired face, he found himself wondering exactly how that had happened and how much of it had been his own fault, a natural result of his own quiet weakness.

"Yes," Richard said. "He was, wasn't he?"

"Wouldn't surprise me if it worked," Nordhoff said. "Wouldn't surprise me at all."

After Nordhoff had gone, Richard plugged the word processor in and turned it on. There was a hum, and he waited to see if the letters IBM would come up on the face of the screen. They did not. Instead, eerily, like a voice from the grave, these words swam up, green ghosts from the darkness:

HAPPY BIRTHDAY, UNCLE RICHARD! JON.

"Christ," Richard whispered, sitting down hard. The accident that had killed his brother, his wife and their son had happened two weeks before; they had been coming back from some sort of day trip and Roger had been drunk—a perfectly ordinary occurrence in the life of Roger Hagstrom. But this time, his luck had simply run out, and he had driven his dusty old van off the edge of a 90-foot drop. It had crashed and burned.

Two weeks ago. And Richard's 37th birthday was . . .

A week from today. The word processor had been Jon's birthday present for him.

That made it worse, somehow. Richard could not have said precisely how or why, but it did. He reached out to turn off the screen and then withdrew his hand.

"Some kid made an atom smasher out of two soup cans and five dollars' worth of electrical equipment."

He got up, went around to the back of the CRT and looked through the ventilation slots. Yes, it was as Nordhoff had said. Wires stamped RADIO SHACK. Wires stamped ERECTOR, with the little circled trademark ®. And he saw something else, something Nordhoff either had missed or hadn't wanted to mention. There was a Lionel train transformer in there, wired up like the Bride of Frankenstein.

"Christ," he said, laughing but suddenly near tears. "Christ, Jonny, what did you think you were doing?"

But he knew that, too. He had dreamed about and talked about owning a word processor for years, and when Lina's laughter had become too sarcastic to bear, he had talked about it to Jon. "I could write faster, rewrite faster and submit more," he remembered telling Jon last summer. The boy had looked at him seriously, his light-blue eyes, intelligent but always so carefully wary, magnified behind his glasses. "It would be great . . . really great."

"Then why don't you get one, Uncle Rich?"

"They don't exactly give them away," Richard had said, smiling. "The Radio Shack model starts at around three grand. From there, you can work yourself up into the eighteen-thousand-dollar range."

"Well, maybe I'll build you one sometime," Jon had said.

"Maybe you just will," Richard had said, clapping him on the back. And until Nordhoff had called, he had thought no more about it.

Wires from hobby-shop electrical models.

A Lionel train transformer.

Christ.

He went around to the front again, meaning to turn it off, as if to actually try to write something on it—and fail—would somehow defile what his earnest, fragile

(doomed)

nephew had intended.

Instead, he pushed the EXECUTE button on the board. A little chill scraped across his spine as he did it—EXECUTE was a funny word to use, when you thought of it. It wasn't a word he associated with writing; it was a word he associated with gas chambers and electric chairs . . . and, perhaps, with dusty old vans plunging into space.

EXECUTE.

The CPU was humming louder than any he had ever heard on the occasions when he had window-shopped word processors; it was, in fact, almost roaring. What's in the memory box, Jon? he wondered. Bedsprings? Train transformers all in a row? Soup cans? He thought again of Jon's eyes, of his still and delicate face. Was it strange, maybe even sick, to be jealous of another man's son?

But he should have been mine. I knew it . . . and I think he knew it, too. And then there was Belinda, Roger's wife. Belinda, who wore sunglasses too often on cloudy days. The big ones, because those bruises around the eyes had a nasty way of spreading. But he had looked at her sometimes, sitting there still and watchful in the loud umbrella of Roger's laughter, and he had thought almost the same thing: She should have been mine.

It was a terrifying thought, because they had both known Belinda in high school and had both dated her. He and Roger had been two years apart in age, and Belinda had been perfectly between them, a year older than Richard and a year younger than

Roger. Richard had actually been first to date the girl who would grow up to become Jon's mother. Then Roger had stepped in—Roger, who was older and bigger; Roger, who always got what he wanted; Roger, who would hurt you if you tried to stand in his way.

I got scared. I got scared and I let her get away. Was it as simple as that? Dear God, help me, I think it was. I'd like to have it a different way, but perhaps it's best not to lie to yourself about such things as cowardice. And shame.

And if those things were true—if Lina and Seth had somehow belonged with his no-good brother and if Belinda and Jon had somehow belonged with him—what did that prove? And exactly how was a thinking person supposed to deal with such an absurdly balanced screw-up? Did you laugh? Did you scream? Did you shoot yourself for a yellow dog?

"Wouldn't surprise me if it worked. Wouldn't surprise me at all."
EXECUTE.

His fingers moved swiftly over the keys. He looked at the screen and saw these letters floating green on the surface of the screen:

MY BROTHER WAS A WORTHLESS DRUNK.

They floated there, and Richard suddenly thought of a toy he had had when he was a kid. It was called a Magic 8 Ball. You asked it a question that could be answered yes or no, and then you turned the Magic 8 Ball over to see what it had to say on the subject; its phony yet somehow entrancingly mysterious responses included such things as IT IS ALMOST CERTAIN, I WOULD NOT PLAN ON IT and ASK AGAIN LATER.

Roger had been jealous of that toy, and finally, after bullying Richard into giving it to him one day, he had thrown it onto the sidewalk as hard as he could, breaking it. Sitting here now, listening to the strangely choppy roar of sound from the CPU cabinet Jon had juryrigged, Richard remembered how he had collapsed to the sidewalk, weeping, unable to believe his bigger brother had done such a thing.

"Bawl baby, bawl baby, look at the baby bawl," Roger had taunted him complacently. "It wasn't nothing but a cheap, shitty toy anyway, Richie. Lookit there, nothing in it but a bunch of little signs and a lot of water."

"I'm telling!" Richard had shrieked at the top of his lungs. His head felt hot. His sinuses were stuffed shut with the tears of his outrage. *"I'm telling on you, Roger! I'm telling Mom!"*

"You tell and I'll break your arm," Roger had said, and in his chilling grin, Richard had seen that he meant it. He had not told.

MY BROTHER WAS A WORTHLESS DRUNK.

Well, it printed on the screen. Whether or not it would store information in the CPU still remained to be seen, but Jon's mating of a Wang board with an IBM screen had worked, anyway. Just coincidentally, it had called up some pretty crappy memories; but he didn't suppose that was Jon's fault.

He looked around his study, and his eyes happened to fix on the one picture in there that he hadn't picked and that didn't fit. It was a studio portrait of Lina, her Christmas present to him two years before. "I want you to hang it in your study," she'd said, and so, of course, he had done just that. It was, he supposed, her way of keeping an eye on him even when she wasn't there. "Don't forget me, Richard. I'm here. Maybe I backed the wrong horse, but I'm still here. And you better remember it."

The studio portrait, with its unnatural tints, went oddly with the amiable mixture of prints by Whistler, Homer and N. C. Wyeth. Lina's eyes were halflidded, the heavy Cupid's bow of her mouth composed in something that was not quite a smile. "Still here, Richard," her mouth said to him. "And don't you forget it."

He typed:

MY WIFE'S PICTURE HANGS ON THE WEST WALL OF MY STUDY.

He looked at the words and liked them no more than he liked the picture itself. He punched the DELETE button. The words vanished. Now there was nothing at all on the screen but the steadily pulsing cursor.

He looked up at the wall and saw that his wife's picture had also vanished.

He sat there for a very long time—it felt that way, at least—looking at the wall where the picture had been. What finally brought him out of his daze of utter unbelieving shock was the smell from the CPU—a smell he remembered from his childhood as clearly as he remembered the Magic 8 Ball that Roger had broken because it wasn't his. The smell was essence of electric-train transformer. When you smelled that, you were supposed to turn the thing off so it could cool down.

And so he would.

In a minute.

He got up and walked over to the wall on legs that felt numb. He ran his fingers over the Armstrong paneling. The picture had been here, yes, *right here.* But it was gone now, and the hook it had hung on was gone and there was no hole where he had screwed the hook into the paneling.

Gone.

The world abruptly went gray, and he staggered backward, thinking dimly that he was going to faint, like an actress in a bad melodrama. He reached down into his crotch and squeezed himself, suddenly and brutally. The pain was terrible, but the world came back into sharp focus.

He looked from the blank place on the wall where Lina's picture had been to the word processor his dead nephew had cobbled together.

"You might be surprised," he heard Nordhoff saying in his mind. *"You might be surprised, you might be surprised."* Oh, yes: if some kid in the Fifties could discover particles that travel backward through time, you might be surprised what your genius of a nephew could do with a bunch of discarded word-processor elements and some wires and electrical components. You might be so surprised that you'd feel as if you were going insane. . . .

The transformer smell was richer, stronger now, and he could see wisps of smoke rising from the vents in the CRT housing. The noise from the CPU was louder, too. It was time to turn it off— smart as Jon had been, he apparently hadn't had time to work out all the bugs in this crazy thing.

But had he known it would do this?

Feeling like a figment of his own imagination, Richard sat down in front of the screen again and typed:

MY WIFE'S PICTURE IS ON THE WALL, WHERE IT WAS BEFORE.

He looked at this for a moment, looked back at the keyboard and then hit the EXECUTE key.

He looked at the wall.

Lina's picture was back, right where it had always been.

"Jesus," he whispered. "Jesus Christ."

He rubbed a hand up his cheek, looked at the screen (blank again except for the cursor) and then typed:

MY FLOOR IS BARE.

He then touched the INSERT button and typed:

EXCEPT FOR 12 SPANISH DOUBLOONS IN A SMALL COTTON SACK.

He pressed EXECUTE.

He looked at the floor, where there was now a small white-cotton sack with a drawstring top.

"Dear Jesus," he heard himself saying in a voice that wasn't his. "Dear Jesus, dear good Jesus—"

He might have gone on invoking the Savior's name for minutes or hours if the word processor had not started steadily beeping at him. Flashing across the top of the screen was the word OVERLOAD.

Richard turned off everything and left his study as if all the devils of hell were after him.

But before he went, he scooped up the small drawstring sack and put it in his pants pocket.

When he called Nordhoff that evening, a cold November wind was playing tuneless bagpipes in the trees outside. Seth's group was downstairs, murdering a Bob Seger tune. Lina was at Our Lady of Perpetual Sorrows, playing bingo.

"Does the machine work?" Nordhoff asked.

"It works, all right," Richard said. He reached into his pocket and brought out a coin. It was heavy and crudely uneven, wavering from an eighth of an inch on one side to almost a quarter of an inch on the other. A conquistador's head was embossed on one side, along with the date 1587. "It works in ways you wouldn't believe." He giggled. He put a hand to his mouth, but the giggle came through anyway.

"I might," Nordhoff said evenly. "He was a very bright boy, and he loved you very much. Mr. Hagstrom. But be careful. A boy is only a boy, bright or otherwise, and love can be misdirected. Do you take my meaning?"

Richard didn't take his meaning at all. He felt hot and feverish. That day's paper had listed the current market price of gold at $514 an ounce. The coins had weighed out at an average of 4.5

ounces each on his postal scale. At the current market rate, that added up to $27,756. And he guessed that was perhaps only a quarter of what he could realize for those coins if he sold them as coins.

"Mr. Nordhoff, could you come over here? Now? Tonight?"

"No," Nordhoff said. "I don't think I want to do that, Mr. Hagstrom. I think this ought to stay between you and Jon."

"But—"

"Just remember what I said. For Christ's sake, be careful." There was a small click, and Nordhoff was gone.

He found himself in his study again half an hour later, looking at the word processor. He touched the ON/OFF key but didn't turn it on. The second time Nordhoff had said it, Richard had heard him. "For Christ's sake, be careful." Yes. He would have to be careful. A machine that could do such a thing—

How *could* a machine do such a thing?

He had no idea, but, in a way, that was no bar at all to acceptance. It was, in fact, par for the course. He was an English teacher and a sometime writer, not a technician, and he had a long history of not understanding how things worked: phonographs, gasoline engines, telephones, televisions, the flushing mechanism in his toilet. His life was a history of understanding operations rather than principles. Was there any difference here, except in degree?

He turned the maching on. As before, it said:

HAPPY BIRTHDAY, UNCLE RICHARD! JON.

He pushed EXECUTE, and the message from his nephew disappeared.

This machine is not going to work for long, he thought suddenly. He felt sure that Jon must have been working on it when he died, confident that there was time; Uncle Richard's birthday wasn't for three weeks, after all—

But time had run out for Jon, and so this totally amazing word processor, which could apparently insert new things or delete old things from the real world, smelled like a frying train transformer and started to smoke after a few minutes. Jon hadn't had a chance to perfect it. He—

Confident that there was time?

But that was wrong, and Richard knew it. Jon's still, watchful face, the sober eyes behind the thick spectacles . . . there was no confidence there, no belief in the fullness of time. What was the word that had occurred to him earlier that day? Doomed. It wasn't just a *good* word for Jon; it was the *right* word. That sense of doom had hung about the boy so palpably that there had been times when Richard had wanted to hug him, to tell him to lighten up a little bit, that sometimes there were happy endings and the good didn't always die young.

Then he thought of Roger's throwing his Magic 8 Ball at the sidewalk, throwing it just as hard as he could; he heard the plastic splinter and saw the 8 Ball's magic fluid—just water, after all—running down the sidewalk. And this picture merged with a picture of Roger's dusty mongrel van, HAGSTROM'S WHOLESALE DELIVERIES written on the side, plunging over the edge of some dusty, crumbling cliff out in the country, hitting dead squat on its nose. He saw— though he didn't want to—the face of his brother's wife disintegrate into blood and bone. He saw Jon burning in the wreck, screaming, turning black.

No confidence. Always exuding that sense of time running out. And in the end, it had been Jon who turned out to be right.

"What does that mean?" Richard muttered, looking at the blank screen.

ASK AGAIN LATER.

The noise coming from the CPU was getting louder again, and more quickly than this afternoon. Already he could smell the train transformer Jon had lodged in the machinery behind the word processor's screen getting hot.

Magic dream machine.

Word processor of the gods.

Was that what it was? Was that what Jon had intended to give his uncle for his birthday? The space-age equivalent of a magic lamp or a wishing well?

He heard the back door of the house bang open and then the voices of Seth and the other members of Seth's band. The voices were too loud, too raucous. They had been either drinking or smoking dope.

"Where's your old man, Seth?" he heard one of them ask.

"Goofing off in his study, like usual, I guess," Seth said. "I think he—"

The wind rose again then, blurring the rest but not blurring their vicious tribal laughter.

Richard sat listening to them, his head cocked a little to one side, and suddenly he typed:

MY SON IS SETH ROBERT HAGSTROM.

His finger hovered over the DELETE button.

What are you doing? his mind screamed at him. Can you be serious? Do you intend to murder your own son?

"He must do somethin' in there," one of the others said.

"He's a goddamned dimwit," Seth answered. "You ask my mother sometime. She'll tell you. He—"

I'm not going to murder him. I'm going to . . . to DELETE him.

His finger stabbed down on the button.

"Ain't never done nothing but—"

The words MY SON IS SETH ROBERT HAGSTROM vanished from the screen.

Outside, Seth's words vanished with them.

There was no sound out there now but the cold November wind, blowing grim advertisements for winter.

Richard turned off the word processor and went outside. The driveway was empty. The group's lead guitarist, Norm Somebody, drove a monstrous old LTD station wagon in which the group carried their equipment to their infrequent gigs. It was not parked in the driveway now. Perhaps it was somewhere in the world, tooling down some highway or parked in the parking lot of some greasy hamburger hangout, and Norm was also somewhere in the world; as was Davey, the bassist, whose eyes were frighteningly blank and who wore a safety pin dangling from one ear lobe; as was the drummer, who had no front teeth. They were somewhere in the world, somewhere, but not here, because Seth wasn't here; Seth had never been here.

Seth had been deleted.

"I have no son," Richard muttered. How many times had he read that melodramatic phrase in bad novels? A hundred? Two hundred? It had never rung true to him. But here it was true. Now it was true. Oh, yes.

301

The wind gusted, and Richard was suddenly seized by a vicious stomach cramp that doubled him over, gasping.

When it passed, he walked into the house.

The first thing he noticed was that Seth's ratty tennis shoes—he had four pairs of them and refused to throw any of them out—were gone from the front hall. He went to the stairway banister and ran his thumb over a section of it. At the age of ten (old enough to know better, but Lina had still refused to allow Richard to lay a hand on the boy), Seth had carved his initials deeply into the wood of that banister—wood that Richard had labored over for almost an entire summer. He had sanded and filled and revarnished, but the ghost of those initials had remained.

They were gone now.

Upstairs. Seth's room. It was neat and clean and unlived in, dry and devoid of personality. It might as well have had a sign on the doorknob reading GUEST ROOM.

Downstairs. And it was there that Richard lingered the longest. The snarls of wire were gone; the amplifiers and microphones were gone; the litter of tape-recorder parts that Seth was always going to fix up was gone (he did not have Jon's hands or concentration). The room bore Lina's personality like a stamp—heavy, florid furniture and saccharine velvet tapestries (one showing *The Last Supper,* another showing deer against a sunset Alaskan skyline)—but Seth was gone from it.

Richard was still standing at the foot of the stairs and looking around when he heard a car pull into the driveway.

Lina, he thought, and felt a surge of almost frantic guilt. It's Lina, back from bingo, and what's she going to say when she sees that Seth is gone? What . . . what . . .

"Murderer!" he heard her screaming. "You murdered my boy!"

But he hadn't murdered Seth.

"I deleted him," he muttered and went upstairs.

Lina was fatter.

He had sent her off to bingo weighing 180 or so pounds. She had come back weighing at least 300, perhaps more; she had to twist slightly sideways to get in through the back door. Elephantine hips and thighs rippled in tidal motions beneath polyester slacks the color of overripe green olives. Her skin, merely sallow three hours before, was now sickly and pale. Although he was no doctor, Richard thought he could read serious liver damage or incipient heart disease in that skin. Her heavy-lidded eyes regarded Richard with a steady contempt.

She was carrying the frozen corpse of a huge turkey in one of her flabby hands. It twisted and turned within its cellophane wrapper like the body of a bizarre suicide.

"What are you staring at, Richard?" she asked.

You, Lina. I'm staring at you. Because this is how you turned out in a world where we had no children. This is how you turned out in a world where there was no object for your love—poisoned as your love may be. This is how Lina looks in a world where everything comes in and nothing at all goes out. You, Lina. That's what I'm staring at. You.

"That bird, Lina," he managed finally. "That's one of the biggest damned turkeys I've ever seen."

"Well, don't just stand there looking at it, idiot! Help me with it!"

He took the turkey and put it on the counter, feeling its waves of cheerless cold. It sounded like a block of wood.

"Not there!" she cried impatiently and gestured toward the pantry. "It's not going to fit in the fucking refrigerator! Put it in the freezer!"

"Sorry," he murmured. They had never had a freezer before. Never in the world where there had been a Seth.

He took the turkey into the pantry, where a long Amana freezer sat under white fluorescent tubes like a cold white coffin. He put it inside, along with the cryogenically preserved corpses of other birds and beasts, and then went back into the kitchen. Lina had taken the glass jar of Reese's Peanut Butter Cups from the cupboard and was eating them methodically one after another.

"It was the Thanksgiving bingo," she said. "We had it this week instead of next because next week, Father Phillips has to go into the hospital and have his gall bladder out. I won the coverall." She smiled. A brown mixture of chocolate and peanut butter dripped and ran from her teeth.

"Lina," he said, "are you ever sorry we never had children?"

She looked at him as if he had gone utterly crazy. "What in the name of God would I want a rug-rat for?" she asked. She shoved the jar of peanut butter cups, now reduced by half, back into the cupboard. "I'm going to bed. Are you coming or are you going back out there and moon over your typewriter some more?"

"I'll go out for a little while more, I think." he said. His voice was surprisingly steady. "I won't be long."

"Does that gadget work?"

"What—" Then he understood, and he felt another flash of guilt. She knew about the word processor; of course she did. Seth's deletion had not affected Roger and the track that Roger's family had been on. "Oh. Oh, no. It doesn't do anything."

She nodded, satisfied. "That nephew of yours. Head always in the clouds. Just like you, Richard. If you weren't such a mouse, I'd wonder if maybe you hadn't been putting it where you hadn't ought to have been putting it about fifteen years ago."

She laughed a coarse, surprisingly powerful laugh—the laugh of an aging, cynical bawd—and for a moment, he almost leaped at her. Then he felt a smile surface on his own lips—a smile as thin and cold as the first skim of ice on a winter pond.

"I won't be long," he said. "I just want to note down a few things."

"Why don't you write a Nobel prize-winning short story or something?" she asked indifferently. The hall floor boards creaked and muttered as she swayed her huge way toward the stairs. "We still owe the optometrist for my reading glasses, and we're a payment behind on the Betamax. Why don't you make us some damned money?"

"Well," Richard said, "I don't know, Lina. But I've got some good ideas tonight. I really do."

She turned to look at him, seemed about to say something sarcastic—something about how none of his good ideas had put them on Easy Street but she had stuck with him anyway—and then didn't. Perhaps something about his smile deterred her. She went upstairs. Richard stood below, listening to her thundering tread. He could feel sweat on his forehead. He felt simultaneously sick and exhilarated.

He turned and went back out to his study.

This time, when he turned the unit on, the CPU did not hum or roar; it began to make an uneven howling noise. That hot-train-transformer smell came immediately from the housing behind the screen, and as soon as he pushed the EXECUTE button, erasing the HAPPY BIRTHDAY, UNCLE RICHARD! message, the unit began to smoke.

Not much time, he thought. No; that's not right. No time at all.

The choices came down to two: Bring Seth back with the INSERT button—he was sure he could do it; it would be as easy as creating the Spanish doubloons had been—or finish the job.

The smoke was getting thicker, more urgent. In a few moments, surely no more, the screen would start blinking its OVERLOAD message.

He typed:

MY WIFE IS ADELINA MABEL WARREN HAGSTROM.

He hit:

DELETE.

He typed:

I AM A MAN WHO LIVES ALONE.

Now the word began to blink steadily in the upper-right-hand corner of the screen: OVERLOAD OVERLOAD OVERLOAD.

Please. Please let me finish. Please, please, please . . .

The smoke coming from the vents in the video cabinet was thicker and grayer now. He looked down at the screaming CPU and saw that smoke was also coming from its vents . . . and down in that smoke, he could see a sullen, red spark of fire.

Magic 8 Ball, will I be healthy, wealthy, wise? Or will I live alone and perhaps kill myself in sorrow? Is there time enough?

CANNOT SEE NOW. TRY AGAIN LATER.

Except there *was* no later.

He struck the INSERT button and the screen went dark except for the constant OVERLOAD message, which was now blinking at a frantic, stuttery rate.

He typed:

EXCEPT FOR MY WIFE, BELINDA, AND MY SON, JONATHAN.

Please. Please.

He hit the EXECUTE button.

The screen went blank. For what seemed like ages, it remained blank except for OVERLOAD, which was now blinking so fast that, except for a faint shadow, it seemed to remain constant, like a computer executing a closed loop of command. Something inside the CPU popped and sizzled, and Richard groaned.

Then green letters appeared on the screen, floating mystically on the black:

I AM A MAN WHO LIVES ALONE EXCEPT FOR MY WIFE, BELINDA, AND MY SON, JONATHAN.

He hit the EXECUTE button twice.

Now, he thought. Now I will type: ALL THE BUGS IN THIS WORD PROCESSOR WERE FULLY WORKED OUT BEFORE MR. NORDHOFF BROUGHT IT OVER HERE. Or I'll type: I HAVE IDEAS FOR AT LEAST 20 BESTSELLING NOVELS. Or I'll type: MY FAMILY AND I ARE GOING TO LIVE HAPPILY EVER AFTER. Or I'll type—

But he typed nothing. His fingers hovered stupidly over the keys as he felt—literally *felt*—all the circuits in his brain jam up like cars grid-locked into the worst Manhattan traffic jam in the history of internal combustion.

The screen suddenly filled up with the word OVERLOADOVERLOAD-OVERLOADOVERLOADOVERLOADOVERLOADOVERLOADOVERLOADOVER-LOAD.

There was another pop and then an explosion from the CPU. Flames belched out of the cabinet and then died away. Richard leaned back in his chair, shielding his face in case the screen should implode. It didn't. It only went dark.

He sat there, looking at the darkness of the screen.

CANNOT TELL FOR SURE ASK AGAIN LATER.

"Dad?"

He swiveled around in his chair, his heart pounding so hard he felt that it might actually tear itself out of his chest.

Jon stood there, Jon Hagstrom, and his face was the same but somehow different; the difference was subtle but noticeable. Perhaps, Richard thought, it was the difference in paternity between two brothers. Or perhaps it was simply that the wary, watchful expression was gone from his eyes, slightly overmagnified by thick spectacles (wire rims now, he noticed; not the ugly industrial horn-rims that Roger had always gotten the boy because they were $15 cheaper).

Maybe it was something even simpler: That look of doom was gone from the boy's eyes.

"Jon?" he said hoarsely, wondering if he had actually wanted something more than this. Had he? It seemed ridiculous, but he supposed he had. He supposed people always did. "Jon, it's you, isn't it?"

"Who else would it be?" Jon nodded toward the word processor. "You didn't hurt yourself when that baby went to data heaven, did you?"

Richard smiled. "No. I'm fine."

Jon nodded. "I'm sorry it didn't work. I don't know what ever possessed me to use all those cruddy parts." He shook his head. "Honest to God, I don't. It's like I *had* to. Kids' stuff."

"Well," Richard said, joining his son and putting an arm around his shoulders, "you'll do better next time, maybe."

"Maybe. Or I might try something else."

"That might be just as well."

"Mom said she had cocoa for you if you wanted it."

"I do," Richard said, and the two of them walked together from the study to a house into which no frozen turkey won in a bingo coverall game had ever been brought. "A cup of cocoa would go down just fine right now."

"I'll cannibalize anything worth cannibalizing out of that thing tomorrow and then take it to the dump," Jon said.

Richard nodded. "Delete it from our lives," he said, and they went into the house and the smell of hot cocoa, laughing together.

DONALD E. WESTLAKE

INTERSTELLAR PIGEON

May 1982

During the 1980s, *Playboy* published a series of slapstick satires by Donald E. Westlake chronicling the various exploratory mishaps of the bumbling crew of the starship *Hopeful*. They poked fun at *Star Trek,* which at that time due to multiple spin-offs and reruns seemed to dominate every television channel, but also paid homage to The Muppet Theater's own spin-off, *Pigs in Space.* Westlake, born in 1933, has published science fiction from time to time, but he is far better known as a Grand Master of the Mystery Writers of America, as well as a multiple-Edgar-winning past president of that organization, and the author of many hilarious caper novels as well as some tense thrillers and the bestselling *The Ax.* He is also the Oscar-nominated screenwriter of *The Grifters.* The *Hopeful* series, which would seem to lend itself equally well to book form or to Saturday morning television, has never been picked up for either.

FROM THE BEGINNING *of Time,
Man has been on the move, ever outward. First he spread over his own
planet, then across the Solar System, then outward to the Galaxies, all
of them dotted, speckled, measled with the colonies of Man.*

*Then, one day in the year eleven thousand four hundred and six
(11,406), an incredible discovery was made in the Master Imperial
Computer back on Earth. Nearly 500 years before, a clerical error had
erased from the computer's memory more than 1000 colonies, all in
Sector F.U.B.A.R.3. For half a millennium, those colonies, young and
struggling when last heard from, had had no contact with the rest of
Humanity.*

The Galactic Patrol Interstellar Ship Hopeful, *Captain Gregory
Standforth commanding, was at once dispatched to re-establish contact
with the Thousand Lost Colonies and return them to the bosom of
Mankind.*

Why me?

Watching Captain Gregory Standforth sit at his desk and stuff
yet another bird—this one a blue-beaked yellow-backed Latter
Sneezer from Degeb IV—*Why me?* wondered Ensign Kybee
Benson, not for the first time. What flaw is there in me that I
don't suspect? *Why did they choose ME?*

There was no question why the Galactic Council had chosen
Captain Standforth to lead this one-way trip into obscurity. Just
look at him now: a tall, skinny, mild-eyed fellow with his nose
and fingers jammed up that dead bird's ass, tamping the excelsior
in real tight. "Got to get it in real tight," the captain said, "or the
wings'll sag." *Why me?* thought Ensign Benson. *I'm no misfit.*

Captain Standforth was, and would be the first to admit it.
Were it not for the seven generations of glorious Standforths preceding him in the Galactic Patrol, he never would have joined up,

311

nor would they have taken him. Taxidermy was the only thing he really cared about, which was why strange stuffed birds from all over the known Universe pervaded the *Hopeful* like an eighth plague. Everywhere you looked, plastic eyes looked back, surrounded by feathers.

"Captain," Ensign Benson said, "we really should talk about Casino."

"In a moment."

Ensign Benson, a social engineer, an expert in comparative societies, the man whose job it was to *define* each of the lost colonies once it was found, to study it and describe what it had become in its 500 years of solitude, brimmed to overflowing with facts about Casino, the first colony they were to visit. The name itself, Casino, had been a brave irony; the colonists had been a group of compulsive gamblers, who had joined to flee the temptations of society. What had they become in the past 500 years? "Captain—"

"This is the most delicate moment, Ensign Benson." The captain inserted a glittering green eye; balefully, one-eyed, the Latter Sneezer glared at Ensign Benson.

Why me?

"There's a spaceship coming!"

"Six to five it crashes."

Astrogator Pam Stokes, beautiful, brainy and blind to passion, entered the captain's office to find the captain stuffing yet another bird and Ensign Benson hopping up and down on a nearby chair, rather birdlike himself. "Captain," Pam said, "we're about to land, sir."

The captain looked up, startled, the one-eyed bird impaled on his right hand. "Land! Why?"

"Because we're here, sir."

"Here?" The captain looked at the bird, which looked back.

"Casino, Captain," Ensign Benson said. "I've been trying to tell you."

Pam nodded. "That's right, sir. Fourth planet of the star Niobe." Whipping out her ever-present slide rule, she said, "Fifteen sixteenths Earth's size, one point oh oh seven six Earth's density, fifteen point one six—"

Rising, the captain said, "Yes, yes, yes, Astrogator, thank you very much."

"Just trying to keep you informed, sir. I may say, as astrogator, I had quite some time finding this spot. Celestial drift, you know."

The captain, removing the bird from his fingers and edging toward the door, said, "Is that right?"

Absorbed in her slide rule, Pam said, "Given a mean deviation of point oh seven five—"

"I'll just go supervise the landing," the captain said and left with the bird.

"Alter for nebular attraction," Pam mumbled, working the math, "on a scale of—"

Ensign Benson was beside her now. Stroking her smooth, tanned forearm with the tiny golden hairs all along its rounded length, he said, "I know a couple of mean deviations myself."

"Oh, hello, Kybee," she said, gave him a distracted smile and went away to think about the math.

On a grassy field not far from town, the spaceship landed, light as a feather (automatic pilot). A dozen citizens of Casino approached the great gleaming sausage and watched in admiration as an oval door in its side slid away to permit a ladder slowly to descend. Down that ladder, smiling heroically in the sunlight, resplendent in his Galactic Patrol uniform, came Lieutenant Billy Shelby, *Hopeful*'s handsome, idealistic second in command. Pausing two steps from the bottom, he raised his hand like a Roman centurion and cried. "Hail, Casinomen! We come in peace!"

A citizen approached. "Seven to two," he said, "you don't know what day it is."

Billy's smile went lopsided. He said, "What?"

"Do we have a bet, stranger?"

Billy shook his head. When things confused him—as they frequently did—he just went on doing what he was supposed to do. "I'm here to find out if you're warlike," he explained.

The citizen frowned. "What's 'warlike'?"

"It's OK, Captain," Billy called.

The captain appeared, birdless, looked at the far horizon and fell down the stairs. Billy helped him pick himself up as Ensign Benson also emerged from the ship, accompanying stout Galactic Councilman Morton Luthguster, who came massively down the ladder as though down a grand staircase to his coronation.

"So this is Casino," the captain said, dusting himself off, looking around at a tree-studded landscape that looked much like northern Wisconsin in late September.

The citizen sidled up to him. "Seven to two *you* don't know what day it is."

The captain looked at his watch. "It's ten minutes to six in the morning. Greenwich time, on Earth."

"What *day* it is."

With another look at his watch, the captain said. "August seventh, eleven thousand, four hundred and six."

Of the citizen's patience, not much was left. "Not the date," he said. "The *day.*"

"The day?" The captain shook his head. "Where?"

"Here!"

"Back on Earth, it's Tuesday. Unless my watch stopped."

Councilman Luthguster, having reached the second step from the bottom, now spread his arms wide and declaimed, "Welcome, Casinomen! Welcome to the bosom of Mother Earth! *I* am Councilman Morton Luthguster; I am here among you to represent the Supreme Galactic Council, and I have *full* treaty-making powers."

A citizen standing beside the ladder said, "Guess your weight."

Luthguster looked down askance: "I *beg* your pardon."

The citizen said, "Ten lukes says I can guess your weight within five kilograms."

"I would prefer if you didn't," Luthguster told him. Looking around himself, realizing there was no one responsible here, that these were all layabouts and scalawags, he said, "Take me to your leader."

It was a normal day in the main plaza of downtown Casino. At benches and tables and grassy patches on the plaza itself—a large round area rather like a roulette wheel—pairs and small groups contested together, using various kinds of dice, cards, paddles, marbles, game boards, magnets and lengths of string. Some needed no equipment at all: "Bet you two lukes *that* cloud passes the hill before *that* cloud." Next to three employment buses, potential fruit pickers, meat packers or assembly-line button pushers played 14-card monte against the employment agents: the winners took their ten lukes' wages and went elsewhere, while the losers climbed, muttering, aboard the buses, resigned to a six-hour workday for no pay. Through the crowd passed a ragged beggar, limping, rattling something in a tin cup and whining. "Gimme a break, will ya? Gimme a break."

A prosperous-looking citizen counting out a recent handful of winnings turned toward the beggar his self-confident eye: "What's your proposition?"

The beggar rattled his cup. "Dice. High number. Two lukes against a kick in the shin."

"You're on."

As they bent over the cup, the Earthmen arrived in the plaza, escorted by several of the citizens who had watched them land, one of whom pointed across the plaza at a large white wooden structure that looked rather like an old Mississippi riverboat. "That's the chief tout's mansion there."

"Ah," Luthguster said, nodding his pompous head. "The man I must see. Captain Standforth, you and your men wait here. We don't want to startle the head of government with a show of force."

"Yes. sir."

Luthguster waddled off with several citizens toward the chief tout's mansion. Billy Shelby and Ensign Benson gazed around at the citizenry, many of whom gazed back in a rather predatory fashion. Captain Standforth, head back, mouth open, gaped skyward in an abstracted fashion, till all at once he whipped out his stun gun and fired into the air.

All around the plaza, losers ducked for cover while winners crouched protectively over game boards, card layouts and die tosses. A large, big-bellied bird, with a pink tuft on top of its orange head and a lot of bright scarlet feathers on its behind, fell out of the sky and landed dead at the captain's feet. Admiringly, the captain picked it up by one green claw, while its fleas hurriedly packed their bags, left a note for the milkman and went leaping

315

away. "Wonderful specimen," the captain said, turning his prize this way and that. "Never seen anything like it."

A cautious citizen approached, saying, "What did you *do?*"

"Taxidermy is my passion," the captain explained. "I stuff birds."

"Where do you stuff them?"

"In the ship."

The beggar, limping worse than ever, approached the captain, rattling his tin cup. "Gimme a break, sir," he whined. "Gimme a break, will ya?"

The captain, embarrassed, took a coin from his pocket and dropped it into the cup. "Here you are, my good man." The beggar stared into his cup, dumfounded.

Billy Shelby said, "Shall I take the bird back to the ship. Captain?"

"Thank you, Lieutenant, thank you."

Off went Billy with the bird.

Another citizen, pointing after the bird, said, "Even money you can't do that again."

Scratching his wrist, the captain said, "Eh?"

"Even money's the best I can do," the citizen warned him.

The captain looked slowly around the plaza, at last registering the human activity here. "Are they," he said, pointing at one pair of dice players, "are they *gambling?*"

"They're all gambling," Ensign Benson assured him. "Fascinating, fascinating."

"My goodness," the captain said.

"They've turned their weakness into strength," Ensign Benson went on. "Their vice into virtue. Their swords into— Well, no."

They strolled together over to a group playing cards around a cement table. "Pardon me," the captain said, "but is this a game of chance?"

"That depends," said one of the players.

"I mean a gambling game."

Another player—the prosperous citizen, in fact—said. "It's a fine game, my friend, and very easy to learn. Care to sit in?"

"No, no. I'll just watch."

"Then come sit by me," said the citizen, hospitable as a spider. "Name's Scanney. I'll explain it to you as we go."

In the chief tout's office, the chief tout himself, in appearance a cross between a distinguished politician and a sleazy gambler, sat at a desk playing a board game against himself. It looked something like Monopoly but was much more complex, being spread over several layers of boards, with ramps, elevators and slides. The chief tout held two dice cups, one in each hand, and played one hand against the other. It had been years since anyone—not even Scanney—would play against him.

He looked up from his left hand's predicament as his secretary—that is, the loser in that day's steno pool—came in to say, "Three to two you don't know what Earth is."

"Original source of mankind," the chief tout immediately responded. "They brought us here five hundred years ago, said they'd be right back, haven't been heard from since. Why?"

"They're back," the disconsolate girl said, counting out three hard-won lukes onto the chief tout's desk. "There's a fat one outside."

"Send him in," the chief tout said, smiling from ear to ear and rubbing his competing hands together.

A moment later, the fat one himself was ushered in, accompanied by two wolfishly grinning citizens. They'd be demanding a finder's fee later on; the chief tout could tell just by looking at them.

Meanwhile, the fat one was in voice: "I am, Your Honor, proud to announce that I am Councilman Morton Luthguster, representative plenipotentiary from the Supreme Galactic Council, and it is my esteemed pleasure to welcome you back to the Confederation of Earth."

"Haven't heard from you people in quite a while," the chief tout said.

"I am empowered," Luthguster said, puffing himself up, "to negotiate with you on several fronts. Mutual defense, for instance. Trade agreements, technical advisory personnel. Earth can do much for you now that you're back in the Confederation."

"Trade agreements, eh?" Gesturing toward the game board, the chief tout said. "That's what this game's all about, in a way. Familiar with it?"

Luthguster gave the board a suspicious look. "Uh, no," he said. "I don't believe so."

"Sit down here," the chief tout said, making room for a chair beside himself. "I'll show you how it works."

"I'm going to take a stroll around town," Ensign Benson said. "You'll be all right here. Captain?"

The captain nodded in a distracted way; most of his attention was on his new friend Scanney's explanation of this fascinating card game. "I'm fine, Ensign Benson: you go ahead."

"Now, if you get two alike," Scanney was saying, "that's good. But three alike is even better."

Vaguely worried, Ensign Benson said, "You won't *play* or anything, will you, Captain?"

"No, no, no, I'm just observing. Now, Mr. Scanney, what are those cards with the nooses?"

In the main corridor of the *Hopeful,* Billy Shelby passed Astrogator Pam Stokes, still too involved with her slide rule to notice either him *or* the bird he carried. "Hi," he said, nevertheless, believing it good manners—and good for morale—to greet crew members when spotted. Unanswered, he went on to dump the dead bird in the captain's office, then to make a quick round of the interior, reassuring himself that everything was spaceshipshape. In the main engine room, he found Chief Engineer Hester Hanshaw whamming away at a pipe with a hammer. The sound was awful. "Hester? Something the matter?"

"No," Hester said. "I'm just keeping my arm loose." Fortyish, stocky and blunt-featured, Hester was blunt in manner and personality and rather blunt in brain as well.

"Our very lives," Billy reminded her, "depend upon those engines."

"Is that right?" Hester hammered some more, flailing away.

Billy blinked at every bang. "Hester, is it *serious?*"

Hester put down her hammer and turned to frown at Billy. "You tell me," she said. Picking up a white plastichina coffee mug, she turned a spigot, filled the mug with black liquid and handed it to Billy. "Give that a taste."

Doubtful, Billy said, "Taste?"

"Go on, go on."

So Billy took a tiny sip, and his face wrinkled up like a cheap skirt. "Oog!" he said.

"You call that coffee?" Hester demanded.

"No! Is it supposed to be?"

"Yes, it's supposed to—" Struck with sudden doubt, Hester took back the mug and sniffed it. "No, you're right; that's crankcase oil. Wait a minute, now."

Turning away, Hester began following pipes with a pointing finger. Billy, making bad-mouth faces, headed for the door, but before he got there, Ensign Benson walked in, saying, "Bad news."

"Don't drink the coffee," Billy said.

"What? No, this is worse. The captain got into a game."

Hester looked away from her maze of pipes. "He what?"

"He lost the ship."

"Oh, Captain, my, Captain," Billy said. "Whatever made you do it?"

"I had a hunch," the captain said. He looked dazed.

A citizen passing with an armchair on his head—Scanney, the new owner, was moving into the *Hopeful*—paused to say, "You should *never* draw to an inside quork."

The captain sat on his suitcase, far across the large field from his former ship. About him were his possessions, his birds and his crew: Lieutenant Billy Shelby, Ensign Kybee Benson, Astrogator Pam Stokes and Chief Engineer Hester Hanshaw. "Oh, my," the captain said. "What will I tell Councilman Luthguster?"

Luthguster rolled the four dice, turned over a card, moved a tiny pyramid three spaces to the left and groaned with disgust. "I don't *believe* such dreadful luck!"

"Easy come, easy go," the chief tout told him cheerfully. "That's the motto on our money." Presenting a document made ready by his now-grinning secretary, he said, "Now, Councilman, if you'll just sign here and here and initial over here."

Shaking his head, Luthguster signed. The two hovering citizens smirked at each other. "They'll never understand this," Luthguster said sadly, "back at the council."

"Your luck's bound to change," the chief tout assured him.

"Next innings, we'll play for reciprocal tariff agreements. My move, I believe."

"Damn, Pam," Hester said, her personality not improved by eviction. "Where did you ever *get* a slide rule? Why don't you use a pocket computer, like everybody else?"

"It was my mother's," Pam said, blinking as she looked up from the tool in question. "And my mother's mother's. And my mo—"

"How many generations back?"

"Sixteen."

Hester closed her eyes. "I withdraw the question."

"Rather than quibble among yourselves, like the clotheads you are," said Ensign Benson, who had no idea why his previous commanders had been discontented with his performance of duty, "why don't you turn your little brains to how we get *out* of this mess?"

"I don't think you should talk to the gentler sex that way," said Billy, with many inaccuracies.

"Maybe Pam can find the answer in her slide rule," Hester said, glaring at Pam, who was sunk in contemplation of her heirloom.

Ensign Benson, about to speak harshly, paused to frown at Pam. "Hmmm," he said. "Pamela, dear?"

"Yes, Kybee?"

"You come along with me," Ensign Benson said.

A bunch of the citizens were whooping it up in the plaza. "Did you *ever*," one of them said, "see fish like those Earthmen?"

"It's like walking into a kindergarten," said another, "with loaded dice."

"Scanney's studying how to run that spaceship," said a third. "He's going straight to Earth. He figures he'll own the whole place in two weeks."

"Here come a couple of them," said a fourth as Ensign Benson and Pam came strolling into the plaza.

Grins and nods and a few waves were exchanged between Ensign Benson and the sniggering locals, until he reached the group that had been discussing Scanney, where he said, in an offhand manner. "Nice little games you've got going here."

"Want some action, Earthman?" Clouds, ants and in-out knockup were mentioned.

"Not this smalltime stuff," Ensign Benson said with manifest disparagement. "Aren't there any big-time games around this burg?"

"By big time," a tittering citizen asked, "what do you mean?"

"What have you got?"

"The Dive," several citizens volunteered.

"Sounds right. Lead me to it."

Within The Dive—a great, cavernous place, in which the gaming tables were brightly, whitely lit, but the far walls and the high ceiling remained in windowless gloom—a kind of low intense humming was the only sound, as though a million bees were getting caught up on their back orders of honey. Citizens and croupiers and dealers hunched over the tables with no small talk, no conversation except the words necessary to keep the games going. "Ah, yes," Ensign Benson said as the simpering citizens led him and Pam into the joint. "This will do just fine."

A hostess approached, slinky in off-the-shoulder red: "Interested in a little action?"

"Just to watch, for now," Ensign Benson told her. "What's the highest-money game here?"

"Koppel," she said, pointing, "at that table right there."

"Thanks."

"My pleasure," she said.

At the edge of the clearing, Hester busily, grumpily, steadfastly, clumsily worked at making a lean-to out of leafy branches. The captain sat on his suitcase among his birds. Billy paced back and forth, gazing mournfully from time to time at the distant *Hopeful*.

It was Billy who broke the silence: "Pam says the odds of anyone's stumbling onto this place and rescuing us are eleven billion, four hundred sixty million to one."

"Don't talk about odds," the captain said.

Hester said, "*I* could use a little *help* around here."

Billy looked at her project. "What on Earth is that?"

"The same thing it is on Casino," she said. "A lean-to."

"It leans mostly that way," Billy commented.

"It'll keep the rain off."

Billy looked skyward. "It isn't gonna rain."

"Wanna bet?"

The captain groaned and covered his face with his hands as Councilman Luthguster came blustering in, saying, "What's going on around here?"

"Oh, Councilman," the captain said, leaping to his feet and knocking over several birds. "I can explain."

"You can?" Luthguster turned on the captain an eye as baleful as that on any of his birds. "You can explain why Ensign Benson is *gambling?*"

The koppel table was now the center of interest as half a dozen players faced Ensign Benson, the new shark in town. Having watched koppel for 20 minutes—it was a pokerlike game but with more cards in more suits and more complicated rules—having received a tiny frightened nod from Pam, Ensign Benson had converted his watch and camera and other salable possessions into lukes and had taken a seat at the game. Pam stood behind him, nervously fidgeting with her slide rule and from time to time nervously clutching at his shoulder, while Ensign Benson went through his first table of unbelieving opponents like a piranha through a cow.

The stakes were higher and the crowd of spectators was growing fast when the other Earth people came hurrying into The Dive. "Ensign Benson!" cried the captain.

"Hello, Captain," Ensign Benson said, with a casual half wave, half salute. "And raise a hundred lukes," he said, pushing forward a small stack of chips.

"You'll ruin us!" the captain cried. "We can't *afford* your gambling debts!" To the Casinomen at large, he announced, "Don't gamble with this man; he has no money!"

"Wanna bet?" asked a bystander.

Calmly, raking in the lukes, Ensign Benson said, "I'm winning, Captain."

"Ensign Benson," the captain ordered, unheeding, "consider yourself under arrest. Return to the ship at once and confine your . . ." At that point, he ran down, blinking, remembering that he didn't have a ship anymore. None of them had quarters to which they could confine themselves.

Then Billy leaned over to whisper in the captain's ear, "Sir, he seems to be winning."

"Never seen a man learn a game so fast," said a bystander.

The captain said, "What?"

"Why don't we make it interesting, gents?" Ensign Benson said, riffling the outsize deck. "Ever hear of something called pot limit?"

On the *Hopeful*'s command deck, Scanney lolled at his ease on his favorite chair, chatting with a pair of his favorite cronies. "So we *can't* dope out the hyperdrive," he said. "When the time's right, they'll teach it to us themselves."

"Boy, Scanney," said a crony. "How ya gonna do that?"

"They'll be around pretty soon, ready to dicker, but I don't talk till tomorrow. A night in the open air; that'll help."

"You're some operator, Scanney."

"Yes, I am. Three to two it rains tonight."

"I wouldn't bet against *you*, Scanney."

At that point, another Scanney crony ran in to say, "One of the Earthmen's playing koppel at The Dive!"

"What?" Scanney sat upright and put his feet on the floor. "They better not use up their credit before they deal with *me*."

"But the Earthman's winning!"

"Impossible," said Scanney. But he got to his feet, saying, "Come on, boys, let's take a look at this wonder."

Ensign Benson looked around the table at nothing but empty chairs. In front of himself, and piled on a special side table brought out for the purpose, was an amazing number of lukes. "Boys?" Ensign Benson said. "You quitting on me?"

"I don't buck *that* streak anymore."

"I may be crazy, but I ain't stupid."

The spectators gawked, eight deep. Pam stood behind Ensign Benson, nervously clutching her slide rule in one hand and his shoulder in the other. The captain, Billy, Hester and Councilman Luthguster stood just to the side, openmouthed. Ensign Benson looked around. "Who'll take a seat?"

"Ten lukes," a bystander said, "says you don't find anybody to play against you."

"You're on," Ensign Benson said as Scanney and his cronies

came pushing through the crowd. "What's this?" Scanney demanded. "Game over?"

"Not if you'll sit in."

Scanney looked at the assembled crowd, at the lukes piled up around Ensign Benson, at the ensign's calmly welcoming smile. "Er," he said.

"Unless you don't feel *up* to a little game."

"Up to it?" His public reputation, the presence of his cronies, his own bravado all combined to force him into that chair. "Deal, my friend, and kiss your worldly goods goodbye."

Ensign Benson smiled at the bystander. "That's ten lukes you owe me."

"Will you take a check?"

"I'll take anything you've got," Ensign Benson said.

When Billy stepped out of The Dive for a breath of air, he saw Niobe, this planet's sun, just peeping over the horizon. Night had come and gone, and now it was day again. Inside, the epic battle between Scanney and Ensign Benson went on, seesawing this way and that, Ensign Benson always ahead but somehow never able to deliver that final *coup de grâce*. From time to time, the participants and observers had paused to consume something that claimed to be coffee and something else that looked like a prune Danish—or possibly a stinging jellyfish—but the pauses were few and the concentration intense.

And suspense was turning at last into dread. Billy didn't *want* to go back in there, but a sense of solidarity with the crew forced him finally indoors once more, where he circled the outer fringes of the crowd, decided solidarity didn't mean he necessarily had to stand *with* them all the time and found himself a new angle of vision, near Scanney, instead.

A tense moment had been reached; yet another tense moment. Ensign Benson was pushing stack after stack of lukes into the middle of the table; when he was finished, a hoarse Scanney said, "I'm not sure I can cover that."

"You want to concede?" Ensign Benson was also hoarse.

Billy watched Scanney study his cards. Then he watched Scanney's hand reach down to a narrow slot under the tabletop and tap something there, as though for reassurance. Tap a— Tap a— A *card!*

"I'll stay," Scanney said, his hand coming up without that card. Billy stared at the man's right ear.

"Then cover the bet," Ensign Benson said.

"Will you take my I.O.U.?"

"I'll do better. You put up the ship."

"The ship?" Scanney was scornful. "Against *that* bet?"

This was the moment Ensign Benson had been waiting for. He seemed to draw strength from Pam's hand on his shoulder. "Against," he said, voice calm, eyes unblinking, "against everything I've got."

Again Scanney's finger tips touched that hidden card. "It's a bet," Scanney said. "Deal the last round."

Ensign Benson dealt the cards.

"Captain!" Billy yelled across the table, pointing at the black darkness above. "Shoot that bird!"

With a quick draw Bat Masterson himself would have admired, the captain unlimbered his stun gun and fired three blasts into the cavernous darkness of the ceiling. Spectators scrambled for cover, Scanney and Ensign Benson hunched protectively over their cards and chips and Billy slid forward and back like a master swordsman, although sans *épée*.

Ensign Benson was the first to recover. "What are you bird brains *doing?*"

"Well," said the captain, embarrassed, holstering his weapon as ancient dust puffs floated down into the light. "Well, uh, Billy, uh . . ."

"Sorry," Billy said, palming the 14 of snakes. "I thought I saw a bird."

"Indoors?"

"It happens," Billy said. "I remember once my aunt Tabitha left the porch door open and—"

"Oh, never mind," Ensign Benson said. "Scanney, I'm calling you."

Billy looked at Scanney, whose finger tips were at that now-empty slot, and the expression on the man's face was one of consternation and bewilderment, gradually becoming horror.

"Scanney?" Ensign Benson tapped his own cards on the table. "Want me to declare first?"

Everyone waited. Wide-eyed, slackjawed, face drained of color, Scanney at last managed to nod.

"Fine." Ensign Benson fanned out his cards. "Read 'em and weep."

But Scanney didn't; instead, he turned to look, with a world of understanding in his eyes, at the radiant, innocent face of Lieutenant Billy Shelby.

They all strolled back to the ship together, Earth people and Casino people in little chatting groups; there was general agreement that the night's big head-to-head koppel game was the stuff of legend. The captain was delighted at the return of his ship but was even more relieved that Councilman Luthguster was taking the whole affair so well. "Personal contacts on the natives' terms are vital on a mission such as this," the councilman said. "I myself found it relaxed the chief tout if we played children's games."

A bit apart, Ensign Benson walked with Scanney, who had recovered from his losses and was becoming his old confident self. "Obviously," Ensign Benson was saying, "all those lukes I won can't do me much good on the ship."

"I'll be happy to invest them for you," Scanney said.

"Not invest. I cleaned you out, Scanney, so what's happening is, I'm staking you to a new start. It'll be a few years before I can get back, and when I do, half of what you have is mine."

"Hmm," said Scanney.

"Oh, you'll be able to siphon off a lot. But you can't hide it all, so we'll both make out."

"It's a deal," Scanney said. As they shook on it, Hester came by, clutching her hammer and looking truculent. She said to Scanney, "I hope you didn't mess up my engines."

"I am a lucky man, madam," he answered, "and a lucky man is one who doesn't mess with engines he doesn't understand."

Hester frowned at Ensign Benson. "What's he mean, 'madam'?"

"It's a local term for engineer," Ensign Benson said.

Meanwhile, at the ship, Luthguster was making a farewell speech to the chief tout and the assembled Casino people: And I think that when your chief tout promulgates the various treaties and agreements we reached in this *most* fruitful visit, you will all agree that Earth has been more than fair. *More* than fair."

Under the speech, Ensign Benson went to Billy to say, "I finally figured out that bird shoot. Thanks."

"Oh, you're welcome. But the great part," Billy said, "was how *lucky* you were, hand after hand."

"That wasn't luck. It was Pam."

"It was?"

"God meant that girl, Billy, to be one of the great pieces of all time, but someing went wrong somewhere, and she took the path of mathematics instead. She and her slide rule add up to one genius. It took her twenty minutes to figure out the odds in koppel; from then on, she gave me signals on my shoulder, and I knew the precise odds at every step of play. Ultimately, I couldn't lose."

"Unless somebody cheated," Billy said.

"Which is where you came in. Thanks again."

Luthguster at last was scaling the heights of his peroration: "I have been delighted," he announced, "to be the individual who brought you this tremendous news and effected this magnificent reconciliation. And now we must bid you a fond farewell."

"Tell them where you got it," the chief tout said, "and how easy it was."

As the Earth people started up the ladder, Hester's hammer clanged inadvertently off the metal rail. "Careful with my ship," Ensign Benson said.

The Earth people entered Ensign Benson's ship. The ladder retracted and the door closed. Soon a great, powerful humming was heard. "Even money it blows up," said a citizen.

"I'll take that," Scanney said.

HOWARD WALDROP

HEIRS OF THE PERISPHERE

August 1985

One of the quirkiest, most imaginative and original current writers of science fiction, Howard Waldrop works almost exclusively in the short story form, which means that he is not as well known by the general public as he ought to be. Born in 1946, he lived for many years in Austin, Texas, but has fairly recently moved to a tiny rural town near Seattle. He began to publish in the 1970s, to almost immediate recognition, but his output is infrequent by genre standards. Three collections of his much admired stories have appeared to date: *Howard Who?, All About Strange Monsters of the Recent Past,* and *Night of the Cooters,* as well as a couple of novels, *Them Bones* and *A Dozen Tough Jobs,* which places Hercules in rural Mississippi. The three heroes of this poignant tale of the far future are familiar to us all. That they should be the last survivors of our own age seems fitting—but not ironic.

THINGS HAD NOT been going well at the factory for the past 1500 years or so.

A rare thunderstorm, a soaking rain and a freak lightning bolt changed all that.

When the lightning hit, an emergency generator went to work as it had been built to do a millennium and a half before. It cranked up and ran the assembly line for a few minutes before freezing up and shedding its brushes and armatures in a fine spray. It had run just long enough to finish up some work in the custom-design section.

The factory completed, hastily certified and wrongly programmed the three products that had been on the assembly line 15 centuries before. Then the place went dark again.

"Gawrsh," said one of them, "it shore is dark in here!"

"Well, huh-huh, we can always use the infrared they gave us."

"Wak, wak, wak!" said the third. "What's the big idea?"

The custom-order jobs were animato-mechanical simulacra. They were designed to speak and act like the famous cartoon creations of a multimillionaire artist who late in life, in the latter half of the 20th Century, had opened a series of gigantic amusement parks.

Once, these giant theme parks had employed persons in costumes to act as hosts. Then the corporation that had run things after the cartoonist's death had seen the wisdom of building robots.

The simulacra would be less expensive in the long run, would never be late for work, could be programmed to speak many languages and would never try to pick up the clean-cut boys and girls who visited the parks.

331

These three had been built to be host robots in the third and largest of the parks, the one separated by an ocean from the two others.

The tallest of them had started as a cartoon dog but had become upright and had acquired a set of baggy pants, balloon shoes, a sweat shirt, a black vest and white gloves. On his head was a miniature carpenter's hat; long ears hung from it. He had two prominent incisors in his muzzle. He stood almost two meters tall and answered to the name GUF.

The second, a little shorter, was a white duck with a bright-orange bill and feet and a blue-and-white sailor's tunic and cap. He had large eyes with little cuts out of the upper right corners of the pupils. He was naked from the waist down and was the only one of the three without gloves. He answered to the name DUN.

The third and smallest, just over a meter, was a rodent. He wore a red-bibbed play suit with two large gold buttons at the waistline. He was shirtless and had shoes like two pieces of bread dough. His tail was long and thin, like a whip. His bare arms, legs and chest were black, his face a pinkish-tan. His white gloves were especially prominent. His most striking feature was his ears, which rotated on a track, first one way, then the other, so that seen from any angle, they could look like featureless black circles.

His name was MIK. His eyes, like those of GUF, were large, and the pupils were big round dots. His nose ended in a perfect sphere of polished onyx.

"Well," said MIK, brushing dust from his body, "I guess we'd better, huh-huh, get to work."

"Uh-hyuk," said GUF. "Won't be many people at thuh Park in weather like thiyus."

"Oh, boy! Oh, boy!" quacked DUN. "Rain! Wak, wak, wak!" He ran out through a huge crack in the factory wall through which streamed rain and mist.

MIK and GUF came behind, GUF ambling with his hands in his pockets. MIK followed him, ranging in the ultraviolet and infrared, getting the feel of the landscape through the rain. "You'd have thought, huh-huh, they might have sent a truck over or something," he said. "I guess we'll have to walk."

"I didn't notice anyone at thuh facktry," said GUF. "Even if it was a day off, yuh'd think some of thuh workers would give unceasingly of their time, because, after all, thuh means of produckshun must be kept in thuh hands of thuh workers, uh-hyuk!"

GUF's specialty was communicating with visitors from the large totalitarian countries to the west of the Park. He was especially well versed in dialectical materialism and correct Mao thought.

As abruptly as it had started, the storm ended. Great ragged gouts broke in the clouds, revealing fast-moving cirrus, a bright-blue sky, the glow of a warming sun.

MIK looked around, consulting his programming. "That way, guys!" he said, unsure of himself. There were no familiar landmarks. All around them was rubble, and far away in the other direction was a sluggish ocean.

It was getting dark. The three sat on a pile of concrete.

"Looks like thuh Park is closed," said GUF.

MIK sat with his hands under his chin. "This just isn't right, guys," he said. "We were supposed to report to the programming hut to get our first day's instructions. Now we can't even find the Park!"

"Well, uh-hyuk," said GUF, "I seem tuh remember we could get aholt of thuh satellite in a 'mergency."

"Sure!" said MIK, jumping to his feet and pounding his fist into his glove. "That's it! Let's see, what frequency was that?"

"Six point five oh four," said DUN. He looked eastward. "Maybe I'll go to the ocean."

"Better stay here whiles we find somethin' out," said GUF.

"Well, make it snappy," said DUN.

MIK tuned in the frequency and broadcast the Park's call letters.

"Zzzzzz. What? HOOSAT?"

"Uh, this is MIK, a simulacrum at the Park. We're trying to get hold of one of the other Parks for, huh-huh, instructions."

"In what language do you wish to communicate?" asked the satellite.

"Oh, sorry, huh-huh. We speak Japanese to each other, but

333

we'll switch over to Artran if that's easier for you." GUF and DUN tuned in also.

"It's been a very long while since anyone spoke with me from down there." The satellite's well-modulated voice snapped and popped. "If you must know," HOOSAT continued, "it's been a while since anyone contacted me from anywhere. I can't say much for the stability of my orbit, either. Once, I was forty thousand kilometers up, very stable. . . ."

"Could you put us through to one of the other Parks or maybe the studio itself, if you can do that? We'd, huh-huh, like to find out where to report for work."

"I'll attempt it," said HOOSAT. There was a pause and some static. "Predictably, there's no answer at any of the locations."

"Where are thuh folks?" asked GUF.

"I don't know. We satellites and monitoring stations used to worry about that frequently. Something happened to them."

"What?" asked all three robots at once.

"Hard to comprehend," said HOOSAT. "Ten or fifteen centuries ago. Very noisy in all spectra, then silence. Most of the ground stations ceased functioning within a century of that."

Then there was a burst of fuzzy static.

"Hello? HOOSAT?" asked the satellite. "It's been a long time since anyone . . ."

"It's still us!" said MIK. "The simulacra from the Park. We—"

"Oh, that's right. What can I do for you?"

"Tell us where the people went."

"I have no idea."

"Well, where can we find out?" asked MIK.

"You might try the library."

"Where's that?"

"Let me focus in. I can give you the coordinates. Do you have standard navigational programming?"

"Boy, do we!" said MIK.

"Well, here's what you do. . . ."

"I'm sure there used to be many books here," said MIK. "It all seems to have turned to powder, though, doesn't it?"

"Doggone wizoo-wazoo waste of time," said DUN. He sat on

one of the piles of dirt in the large broken-down building of which only one massive wall still stood. The recent rain had turned the meter-deep powder on the floor into a papier-mâché sludge.

"I guess there's nothing to do but start looking," said MIK.

"Hey, MIK, looka this!" yelled GUF. He came running with a steel box. "I found this just over there."

The box was plain, unmarked. There was a heavy lock to which MIK applied various pressures.

"It's, huh-huh, stuck."

"Gimme that!" yelled DUN. He grabbed it. Soon he was muttering under his beak. "Doggone razzle-frazzin' dadgum thing!" He pulled and pushed, his face and bill turning redder and redder. He gripped the box with both his feet and hands. "Doggone dad-gum!" he yelled.

Suddenly he grew teeth, his brow slammed down, his shoulders tensed and he went into a blurred fury of movement. "*Wak, wak, wak, wak, wak!*" he screamed.

The box broke open and flew into three parts. So did the book inside.

DUN was still tearing in his fury.

"Wait! Look out, DUN!" yelled MIK. "Wait!"

"Gawrsh!" said GUF, running after the pages blowing in the breeze. "Help me, MIK!"

DUN stood atop the rubble, parts of the box and the book gripped in each hand. He simulated hard breathing, the redness draining from his face.

"It's open," he said quietly.

"Well, from what we've got left," said MIK, "this is called *The Book of the Time Capsule,* and it says they buried a cylinder a very, very long time ago. They printed up five thousand copies of this book and sent it to places all around the world where they thought it would be safe. They printed this book on acid-free paper and stuff like that so it wouldn't fall apart.

"And they thought what they put in the time capsule itself could explain to later generations what people were like in their day. So I figure maybe it could explain something to us, too."

"Well, let's go," said DUN.

"Well, huh-huh," said MIK. "I checked with HOOSAT and gave him the coordinates and, huh-huh, it's quite a little ways away."

"How far?" asked DUN, his brow beetling.

"Oh, huh-huh, about eighteen thousand kilometers. Just about halfway around the world."

"Oh, my aching feet!" said DUN.

"That's not literally true," said GUF. He turned to MIK. "Yuh think we should go that far?"

"Well, I'm not sure what we'll find. Those pages were lost when DUN opened the box. . . ."

"I'm sorry," said DUN in a contrite, small voice.

"But the people of that time were sure that everything could be explained by what was in the capsule."

"And yuh think it's still there?" asked GUF.

MIK put a determined look on his face. "I figure the only thing for us to do is set our caps, start out and whistle a little tune," he said.

"Yuh don't have a cap, MIK," said GUF.

"Well, I can still whistle! Let's go, fellas," he said. "It's *this* way!"

He puckered his lips and blew a work song. DUN quacked a tune about boats and water. GUF hummed *The East Is Red*.

They set off in this way across what had been the bottom of the Sea of Japan.

They were having troubles. Three weeks before, they had come to the end of all the songs with which each had been programmed and had had to start repeating themselves.

Their lubricants were beginning to fail; their hastily wired circuitry was overworked. GUF had a troublesome extensor in his ankle that sometimes hung up. But he went along cheerfully, sometimes hopping and quickstepping to catch up with the others when the foot refused to flex.

The major problem was the cold. There was a vast difference between the climate they had been built for and the one they found themselves in. The landscape was rocky and empty, the wind blew fiercely and it had begun to snow.

The terrain was difficult and the maps HOOSAT had given them were outdated. Something drastic had changed the course of rivers, the land, the shore line of the ocean itself. They detoured frequently.

The cold worked hardest on DUN. He was poorly insulated, and they had to slow their pace to his. He would do anything to avoid a snowdrift and so expended even more energy.

They stopped in the middle of a raging blizzard.

"Uh, MIK?" said GUF. "I don't think DUN can go much farther in this weather. An' my leg is givin' me lots o' problems. Yuh think maybe we could find someplace to hole up fer a spell?"

MIK looked at the bleakness and the whipping snow around them. "I guess you're right. Warmer weather would do us all some good. We'd conserve both heat and energy. Let's find a good place."

"Hey, DUN," said GUF. "Let's find a hideyhole!"

"Oh, goody gumdrops!" said DUN. "I'm so cold."

They eventually found a deep rock shelter with a low fault crevice at the back. MIK had them gather up what sparse vegetation there was and take it into the shelter. MIK talked to HOOSAT, then wriggled his way through the brush they had piled to the other two.

Inside, they could barely hear the wind and snow. It was only slightly warmer than outside, but it felt wonderful and safe.

"I told HOOSAT to wake us up when it got warmer," said MIK. "Then we'll get on to that time capsule and find out all about people."

"G'night, MIK," said GUF.

"Good night, DUN," said MIK.

"Sleep tight and don't let the bedbugs bite. Wak, wak, wak," said DUN.

They shut themselves off.

MIK woke up. It was dark in the rock shelter, but it was also much warmer.

The brush was all crumbled away. A meter of rock and dust covered the cave floor, the dust stirring in the warm wind.

"Hey, fellas!" said MIK. "Hey, wake up. Spring is here!"

They stirred themselves.

"Let's go thank HOOSAT and get our bearings and be on our way," said MIK.

They stepped outside.

The stars were in the wrong places.

"Uh-oh!" said GUF.

"Would you look at that?" said DUN.

"I think we overslept," said MIK. "Let's see what HOOSAT has to say."

"Huh? HOOSAT?"

"Hello. This is DUN and MIK and GUF."

HOOSAT's voice now sounded like a badger whistling through its teeth.

"Glad to see ya up," said the satellite.

"We asked you to wake us up as soon as it got warmer!" said MIK.

"It just *got* warmer."

"It did?" asked GUF.

"Shoulda seen it," said HOOSAT. "Ice everywhere. Big ol' glaciers. You still aimin' to dig up that capsule thing?"

"Yes," said MIK, "we are."

"Well, you got an easy trip from now on. No more mountains in the way."

"What about people?" asked MIK.

"I ain't heard from any. My friend the military satellite said he thought he saw some fires, little teeny ones, but his eyes weren't what they used to be. He's gone now, too."

"Thuh fires mighta been built by people?" asked GUF.

"It's sorta likely. Weather ain't been much for lightning," said HOOSAT. "Hey, bub, you still got all those coordinates I give you?"

"I think so," said MIK.

"Well, I better give you new ones off these new constellations. Hold still; my aim ain't so good anymore." He dumped a bunch of numbers into MIK's head. "I won't be talkin' to you much longer."

"Why not?" they all asked.

"Well, you know . . . my orbit. I feel better now than I have in centuries. Real spry. Must be the ionization. Started a couple o' weeks ago. Sure has been nice talkin' to you young fellers after so long a time. Sure am glad I remembered to wake you up. I wish y'all a lotta luck. Boy, this air has a punch like a mule. Be careful. Goodbye."

Across the unfamiliar stars overhead, a point of light blazed, streaked in a long arc, then died on the night.

"Well," said MIK, "we're on our own."

"Gawrsh, I feel all sad," said GUF.

The trip was uneventful for the next few months. They walked across the long land bridge down a valley between stumps of mountains with the white teeth of glaciers still on them. They crossed a low range and entered flat land, without topsoil, from which dry river courses ran to the south. Then there was a land where things were flowering after the long winter. New streams sprang up.

They saw fire once and detoured but found only a burnt patch of forest. Once, way off in the distance, they saw a speck of light but didn't go to investigate, thinking it only another prairie fire.

Within 200 kilometers of their goal, the land changed again to a flat, sandy waste littered with huge rocks. Little vegetation grew. There were few insects and animals, mostly lizards, which DUN chased every chance he got. The warmth seemed to be doing him good.

GUF's leg worsened. The foot first stuck, then flopped and windmilled. GUF kept humming songs and raggedly marching along with the other two.

DUN stopped, turned and watched behind them.

"What's wrong?" asked MIK.

"I got a feeling we're being followed," said DUN, squatting down behind a rock.

All three watched for a few minutes, ranging up and down the spectrum.

"DUN, I think mebbe yer seein' things, uh-hyuk," said GUF.

They continued on, DUN stopping occasionally to watch their trail.

When they passed one of the last trees, MIK had them all take limbs from it. "Might come in handy for pushing and digging," he said.

They stood on a plain of sand and rough dirt. There were huge piles of rubble all around. Far off was another ocean and to the north, a long, curving patch of green.

"We'll go to the ocean, DUN," said MIK, "after we get through here."

He was walking around in a smaller and smaller circle. Then he stopped. "Well, huh-huh, here we are," he said. "Latitude forty degrees, forty-four minutes, thirty-four seconds, point oh eight nine North. Longitude seventy-three degrees, fifty minutes, forty-three seconds, point eight four two West, by the way they *used* to figure it. The capsule is straight down, twenty-eight meters below the original surface. We've got a long way to go, because there's no telling how much soil has drifted over that. It's in a concrete tube, and we'll have to dig to the very bottom to get at the capsule. Let's get working."

It was early morning when they started. Just after noon, they found the top of the tube with its bronze tablet.

"Here's where the hard work starts," said MIK.

It took almost a week of continuous effort. Slowly the tube was exposed as the hole around it grew larger. Since GUF could work better standing still, they had him dig all the time, while DUN and MIK both dug and pushed rock and dirt clear of the crater.

They found some long, flat iron rods part way down and threw away the worn tree limbs and used the metal to better effect.

On one of his trips to push dirt out of the hole, DUN came back looking puzzled.

"I'm *sure* I saw something moving out there," he said. "When I looked, it went away."

"There yuh go again," said GUF. "Here, DUN, help me lift this rock."

It was hard work. Their motors were taxed. It rained once, and for a while there was a dust storm.

"Thuh way I see it," said GUF, looking at their handiwork, "is that yuh treat it like a great ol' big tree made o' rock."

They stood at the bottom of a vast crater. Up from its center stood the concrete tube.

"We've reached twenty-six meters," said MIK. "The capsule

itself should be in the last two point three eight one six meters. So we should chop it off," he quickly calculated, "about here!" He drew a line all around the tube with a piece of chalky rock.

They began to smash at the concrete with rocks and pieces of iron and steel.

"*TIMBER!*" yelled DUN.

The column above the line lurched and with a crash shattered itself against the side of the crater wall.

"Oh, boy! Oh, boy!"

"Come help me, GUF," said MIK.

Inside the jagged top of the remaining shaft, an eyebolt stood out of the core.

They climbed up on the edge, reached in and raised the gleaming Cupraloy time capsule from its resting place.

On its side was a message to the finders, and just below the eyebolt at the top was a line and the words CUT HERE.

"Well," said MIK, shaking GUF's and DUN's hands, "we did it, by gum!"

He looked at it a moment.

"How're we gonna open it?" asked GUF. "That metal shore looks tough!"

"I think maybe we can abrade it around the cutting line with sandstone and, well . . . go get me a real big, sharp piece of iron, DUN."

When DUN brought it, MIK handed the iron to GUF and put his long tail over a big rock.

"Go ahead, GUF," he said. "Won't hurt me a bit."

GUF slammed the piece of iron down.

"Uh-hyuk!" he said. "Clean as a whistle!"

MIK took his severed tail, sat down cross-legged near the eyebolt, poured sand on the cutting line and began to rub it across the line with his tail.

It took a full day, turning the capsule every few hours.

They pulled off the eyebolt end. A dusty, waxy mess was revealed.

"That'll be what's left of the waterproof mastic," said MIK. "Help me, you two." They lifted the capsule. "Twist!" he said.

The metal groaned. "Now, pull!"

A long, thin inner core, two meters by a third of a meter, slid out.

"OK," said MIK, putting down the capsule shell and wiping away mastic. "This inner shell is threaded in two parts. Turn that way; I'll turn this."

They did. Inside was a shiny sealed glass tube through which they could dimly see shapes and colors.

"Wow!" said GUF. "Looka that!"

"Oh, boy! Oh, boy!" said DUN.

"That's Pyrex," said MIK. "When we break that, we'll be through."

"I'll do it," said DUN, picking up a rock.

"Careful!" said GUF.

The rock shattered the glass. There was a loud noise as the partial vacuum disappeared.

"Oh, boy!" said DUN.

"Let's do this carefully," said MIK. "It's all supposed to be in some kind of order."

The first things they found were the messages from four famous humans and another whole copy of *The Book of the Time Capsule*. GUF picked that up.

There was another book, with a black cover and a gold cross on it. Then they came to a section marked ARTICLES OF COMMON USE. The first small packet was labeled CONTRIBUTING TO CONVENIENCE, COMFORT, HEALTH AND SAFETY. MIK opened it.

Inside were an alarm clock, bifocals, a camera, a pencil, a nail file, a padlock and keys, a toothbrush, tooth powder, a safety pin, a knife, a fork and a slide rule.

The next packet was labeled PERTAINING TO THE GROOMING AND VANITY OF WOMEN. Inside were an Elizabeth Arden Cyclamen Color Harmony Box, a rhinestone clip and a woman's hat, style of autumn 1938, designed by Lilly Daché.

"Golly-wow!" said DUN and put the hat on over his.

The next packet was marked FOR THE PLEASURE, USE AND EDUCATION OF CHILDREN.

First out was a small spring-driven toy car, then a small doll and a set of alphabet blocks. Then MIK reached in and pulled out a small cup.

He stared at it a long time. On the side of the cup was a decal with the name of the man who had created them and a picture of MIK, waving his hand in greeting.

"Gawrsh, MIK," said GUF, "it's *you!*"

A tossed rock threw up a shower of dirt next to his foot.

They all looked up.

Around the crater edge stood men, women and children dressed in ragged skins. They had sharp sticks, rocks and ugly clubs.

"Oh, boy," said DUN. "People!" He started toward them.

"Hello!" he said. "We've been trying to find you for a long time. Do you know the way to the Park? We want to learn all about you."

He was speaking to them in Japanese.

The mob hefted its weapons. DUN switched to another language.

"I said, we come in peace. Do you know the way to the Park?" he asked in Swedish.

They started down the crater, rocks flying before them.

"What's the matter with you?" yelled DUN. "*Wak, wak, wak!*" He raised his fists.

"Wait!" said MIK in English. "We're friends!"

Some of the crowd veered off toward him.

"Uh-oh!" said GUF. He took off, clanking up the most sparsely defended side of the depression.

Then the ragged people yelled and charged.

They got the duck first.

He stood, fists out, jumping up and down on one foot, hopping mad. Several grabbed him, one by the beak. They smashed at him with clubs, pounded him with rocks. He injured three of them seriously before they smashed him into a white-blue-and-orange pile.

"Couldn't we, huh-huh, talk this over?" asked MIK. They stuck a sharp stick into his ear mechanism, jamming it. One of his gloved hands was mashed. He fought back with the other and kicked his feet. He hurt them, but he was small. A boulder trapped his legs; then they danced on him.

GUF made it out of the crater. He had picked the side with the most kids and they drew back, thinking he was attacking them. When they saw he was trying to escape, they gave gleeful chase, bouncing sticks and rocks off his hobbling form.

"*Whoa!*" he yelled as more people ran to intercept him and he skidded to a stop. He ran up a long, slanting pile of rubble. More humans poured out of the crater to get him.

He reached the end of the long, high mound above the crater rim. His attackers paused, throwing sticks and rocks, yelling at him.

"Halp!" GUF yelled. "Haaaaaaaaaalp!"

An arrow sailed into the chest of his nearest attacker.

GUF turned. Other humans, dressed in cloth, stood in a line around the far side of the crater. They had bows and arrows, metal-tipped spears and carried iron knives in their belts.

As GUF watched, the archers sent another flight of arrows into the people who had attacked the robots.

The skin-dressed band of humans screamed and fled up out of the crater, down from the mounds, leaving their wounded and the scattered contents of the time capsule behind them.

It took a while, but soon the human in command of the metal-using people and GUF made themselves understood to each other. The language was a very changed English/Spanish mixture.

"We're sorry we didn't know you were here sooner," the man said to GUF. "We rarely get out this far, and we heard you were here only this morning. Those *others,*" he said with a grimace, "who followed you here from the Wastes won't bother you anymore."

He pointed to the patch of green to the north. "Our lands and village are there. We found this place twenty years ago. It's a good land, but others raid it as often as they can."

GUF looked down into the crater with its toppled column and debris. Cigarettes and tobacco drifted from the glass cylinder. The microfilm, with all its books and knowledge, was tangled all over the rocks. Samples of aluminum, hypernic and ferrovanadium gleamed in the dust. Razor blades, an airplane gear and glass wool were strewn up the sides of the slope.

The message from Grover Whalen opening the World's Fair and knowledge of how to build the microfilm reader were lost.

The newsreel, with its pictures of Howard Hughes, Jesse Owens and Babe Ruth, bombings in China and a Miami Beach fashion show, was ripped and torn. The golf ball was in the hands of one of the fleeing children. Poker chips lay side by side with tungsten wire, combs, lipstick. GUF tried to guess what some of the items were.

"They destroyed one of your party," said the commander. "I think the other one is still alive."

"I'll tend to 'em," said GUF.

"We'll take you back to our village," said the man. "There are lots of things we'd like to know about you."

"That goes double fer us," said GUF. "Those other folks pretty much tore up what we came to find."

GUF picked up the small cup from the ground. He walked to where they had MIK propped up against a rock.

"Hello, GUF," he said. "Huh-huh, I'm not in such good shape." His glove hung uselessly on his left arm. His ears were bent and his nose was chipped. He gave off a noisy whir when he moved.

"Oh, hyuk-hyuk," said GUF. "We'll go back with these nice people, and yuh'll rest up and be right as rain, I guarantee."

"DUN didn't make it, did he, GUF?"

GUF was quiet a moment. "Nope, MIK, he didn't. I'm shore sorry it turned out this way. I'm gonna miss thuh ol' hothead."

"Me, too," said MIK. "Are we gonna take him with us?"

"Shore thing," said GUF. He waved to the nearby men.

The town was in a green valley watered by two streams full of fish. There were small fields of beans, tomatoes and corn in town, and cattle and sheep grazed on the hillsides, watched over by guards. There were a coppersmith's shop, a council hut and many houses of wood and stone.

GUF was walking up the hill to the house MIK was in.

They had been there a little more than two weeks, talking with the people of the village, telling them what they knew. GUF usually played with the children when he and MIK didn't have to be around the grown folks. But from the day after they had buried DUN up on the hill, MIK had been getting worse. His legs had quit altogether, and he could now see only in the infrared.

"Hello, GUF," said MIK.

345

"How yuh doin', pardner?"

"Not so good," said MIK. "Are they making any progress on the flume?"

Two days before, MIK had told them how to get water more efficiently from one of the streams up to the middle of the village.

"We've almost got it now," said GUF. "I'm sure they'll be up and thank yuh when they're finished."

"They don't need to do that," said MIK.

"I know, but these are real nice folks, MIK. And they've had it pretty bad, what with one thing and another. They like talkin' to yuh."

GUF noticed that some of the women and children sat outside the hut, waiting to see MIK.

"I won't stay very long," said GUF. "I gotta get back and organize the cadres into work teams and instructional teams and so forth, like they asked me to help with."

"Sure thing, GUF," said MIK. "I—"

There was a great whirring noise from MIK and the smell of burning silicon.

GUF looked away. "They just don't have thuh stuff here," he said, "that I could use to fix yuh. Maybe I could find somethin' at thuh crater. . . ."

"Don't bother," said MIK. "I doubt . . ."

GUF looked at the village. "Oh," he said, reaching into the bag someone had made him. "I been meaning to give yuh this fer more'n a week and keep fergettin'." He handed MIK the cup from the time capsule with his picture on the side.

"I've been thinking about this since we found it," said MIK. He turned it in his good hand, barely able to see its outline. "I wonder what else we lost at the crater."

"Lots o' stuff," said GUF, "but we got to keep this."

"This was supposed to last a long time," said MIK, "and tell people what other people were like for future ages? Then the people who put this there must really have liked the man who thought us up!"

"That's fer shore," said GUF.

"And me, too, I wonder?"

"You probably most of all," said GUF.

MIK smiled. The smile froze. His eyes went white and a thin

line of condensation rose up from the ear tracks. The hand gripped the cup tightly.

Outside, the people began to sing a real sad song.

It was a bright, sunny morning. GUF put flowers on MIK's and DUN's graves at the top of the hill. He patted the earth, stood up uncertainly.

He had replaced his frozen foot with a wood-wheeled cart with which he could skate along almost as easily as walking.

He stood up and thought of MIK. He sat his carpenter's cap forward on his head and whistled a little tune.

He picked up his wooden toolbox and started off down the hill to build the kids a swing set.

BILLY CRYSTAL

EARTH STATION CHARLEY

December 1986

Stand-up comic, ex-*Saturday Night Live* performer (he was dumped, can you believe it?), movie star, and best of all recent Academy Awards hosts, here's Billy Crystal in another guise: science fiction writer. In that role, he's a greenhorn, but he's had other things on his mind. Aside from his work as a performer, born in 1949, he has been a director, producer and screenwriter (most recently for *City Slickers II* and *Forget Paris*). His first movie appearance was in *This is Spinal Tap* in 1984, *When Harry Met Sally* made him a leading man, he played the First Gravedigger in Kenneth Branagh's *Hamlet,* and his most recent movies are *Father's Day* and *Deconstructing Harry.* As has been said before, technology gone bonkers is always a good premise in science fiction. And a good stand-up knows from bonkers. . . .

Four A.M. Friday and Charley is in his usual spot, sprawled out on the couch, watching Canadian football on cable television. For a long time now, Charley has looked upon television as his companion and sometime night light, which is why his wife, Sheilah, has taken off with his partner, Sy, that loud and obnoxious man who needs to trim the hair in his ears. Charley had grown to feel more comfortable watching a midget rodeo on cable than sleeping with Sheilah. (Sex is like a bull ride, he'd say: Mount the beast until you're turned loose, then try to stay on for one minute. Time, 58 seconds.)

Now Charley sits here all day, rarely moving, staring at the set. Neighbors think he has passed away, which more or less confirms Sheilah's suspicions. He watches everything over and over again. *Happy Days*, twice a day; *The Love Boat*, from Atlanta; *The Big Valley*, from Chicago; The Movie Channel, Showtime. Z. Cable has changed his life—it has ended it.

Friday afternoon, and a favorite episode of *Bonanza* is on WGN, from Chicago. Charley heats a can of beef stew. He likes to eat the appropriate food for the show he is watching. For Westerns, it is beef stew or chili. *The Fugitive* is always "just coffee." Ball games are hot dogs. Pernell Roberts gets off his horse.

Suddenly, the 1969 Philco dies; it sputters and coughs and goes black. Stew dribbles out of Charley's mouth as he runs to the aid of his fallen friend. He cradles it in his arms as though it were a wounded Army buddy from *War Theater*.

Charley panics. His fingers move unconsciously, changing channels. He belts the set, the age-old remedy, but it is too late. He needs a new set right away. Withdrawal pain sets in.

Tom's Video City is staggering: two square blocks of televisions, video recorders, wide screens, computers and all kinds of hard- and software. Charley stands there, dumfounded, as 500 sets zoom in on Gary Collins making a Waldorf salad on *Hour Magazine*.

"Can I help you?" Charley stares at a rather intense-looking young salesman, the kind of guy who got perfect scores on his SAT and wears a bathing suit with black socks and sandals to the beach. "We have more than seven thousand models of electronic video and audio equipment here, eighty computer models, all the brands of wide screens and our special item, the earth station."

"What's the earth station?"

"A fifteen-foot satellite dish that receives signals from the communications satellites orbiting the earth. It's the most powerful home unit ever made. With this machine, you have the capability of watching television programs from all over the globe with perfect reception. *And* it has stereo sound."

"All I really need is a nice color television," Charley says.

"Why have just a television when you can have the globe? With the earth station, the world comes to you." The salesman is getting excited.

"It sounds very expensive."

"We can work out a deal to suit you. I installed my own. It's amazing: Last night, I was having dinner and watching Jerry Lewis in *The Nutty Professor,* all the way from Paris. Following that was *A.M. Peru* and a Swedish soap opera where they really do it. Truly amazing; the world comes to you."

Charley flips through the diagrams and pages of blueprints. It is complicated but a challenge. He wants—he *has*—to do it.

Three days later, his hands hurting from squeezing pliers, his jaws sore from clenching his teeth, Charley sits back on his heels and gazes at the finished product. He has screwed 527 screws, bolted 890 bolts, fastened miles and miles of cable and wire and inserted dozens of tubes, gadgets, springs and nuts into what looks like a radar station in his backyard. Somehow, it will work; it *must* work. Charley needs to see *The Donna Reed Show* from Rio; he needs *Barney Miller* from Argentina. He needs the world to come to him—he's much too tired to go to it.

The TV dinner is heating, the champagne chilling as Charley

makes the last adjustments. In a way, he wishes Sheilah were here to watch with him. She'd lost faith in him. He hadn't accomplished anything. "Lazy," she'd say. "You're too lazy to be boring. Boring would mean you were doing something."

Charley sighs. All the good things in life are taken away too soon—youth, drive and the original *Steve Allen Show*. His eyes moisten as he pulls back the silver foil on the peas of his Hungry Guy dinner. He stares at the pathetic attempt at peach cobbler. Sheilah hates the cobbler, too. "I'll mail her one." He giggles and starts to feel perky. The last time he felt optimistic was when Cavett went network.

At 7:58, he puts the Hungry Guy dinner on the snack tray, which supports not only this gourmet delight but a single red rose cut from the neglected garden. He turns on the earth station. Waves of anxiety fill his lungs. His thighs pulsate as though he has just been in a near-miss car accident. The picture is slightly dim. A living room with a plastic-covered couch in the background is all he can make out. "Honey, where's my glasses?" He *knows* that voice. Then a naked man enters the picture. Holy Christ, it is Jerry Berger, his neighbor. "I think I left them on the bar." Berger's wife enters. There she is in stereo on the screen, naked.

Charley is in a panic. What has he done? Yes, he is awake; no, he isn't hallucinating. He is frozen stiff. Mrs. Berger is now doing jumping jacks along with Richard Simmons. Her tits bouncing up and down sound like polite tennis applause.

He carefully adjusts the channel two notches to the left. What the hell is this? Is it the Gorman home? Mr. and Mrs. Gorman are in their 70s now, a sweet, Godfearing couple. She worked in the town pharmacy for years, and he owned a small hobby shop where he displayed his wonderful collection of miniature trains. Now, in retirement, they sit on the porch sipping lemonade and counting the Cadillacs. A Sunday doesn't seem right unless you see the Gormans slowly walking home from church, holding hands.

"Tell me, Demetrius, do you want me?" Mrs. Gorman lies sprawled on her round bed, wearing a chiffon nightie, with what appear to be two Danish pastries over her breasts. "Demetrius? Answer your queen."

Old man Gorman, in a G string, complete with sword in hand,

his breasts sagging more than hers, enters. Charley feels faint. "Fair Cressida, I am but a slave. I cannot look on thee."

"You need no longer be a slave," she rasps.

"What do I have to do, my lady?"

"Make love to me like the monkeys do."

With that, old man G. drops the G string. His impressive genitals swing dangerously close to the floor as he mounts his beloved, crying, "Freedom, freedom!" Charley looks like Buckwheat seeing a ghost. *American Gothic* meets *Screw* magazine. The Gormans are *maniacs*.

Charley laughs and turns the channel. There is Mrs. Mulgrew asleep on the couch, a Reagan press conference on her television screen. Two more turns to the left bring the Sealy twins arguing over clothes. The Benders are playing cards. The Hubermans aren't home, but Charley likes their new furniture.

The impossible has happened! He has invented something so amazing, he has to lie down to think of the implications.

Two days go by and Charley is still getting the neighborhood. The Benders are not talking to each other, the Hubermans love tuna and Jerry Berger spends more time on the toilet than someone just back from Mexico. Charley charts the times and places of his favorite moments. Working quickly, he compiles a ten-page guide.

The first *Earth Station Charley* is a fine-looking piece of work: two pieces of red construction paper and ten pages of programing. He plans his day around his neighbors' activities as if they were Olympic events. Why see a *Donna Reed* rerun at eight A.M. when he can have *Breakfast with the Hubermans?* Lunch is always at 1:30 with *Meet Linda Berger. Honey, I'm Home* is 40 minutes of Jerry Bender and his wife not talking face to face. A slight break for snacks, and then it's *Love Those Gormans.* Tonight is Thursday, which means Mystery Night. Who will he be and who will she be? Charley feels alive again.

Weeks go by and Charley is still getting the neighborhood. He decides to walk down the block and say hello to the neighbors. Stu Davis, the dentist, who has terrible teeth, is watering his lawn as Charley approaches. "Hey, Charley, what the hell is that thing, anyway? You an alien or something?" He gestures toward Charley's satellite dish.

"No, it's my earth station receiver for my TV. I can get television from all over the neighb—the world."

"Wow. I'd love to see that sometime; sounds great."

"Oh, it is, it's really something; you should see some of the shows I can get." Oops. As soon as Charley says it, he knows he shouldn't. After all, he has watched the Davises make love in the kitchen.

"Great, I'd love to; I'll be over later."

"Maybe tomorrow, Stu; today's kind of bad; one of the satellites is out of commission." Charley beats a hasty retreat. What am I, he thinks, but an electronic Peeping Tom?

Back home, Charley thumbs through the real *Earth Station Guide,* looking for a foreign program to watch. *Hong Kong Hillbillies:* A Szechwan family inherits a great war lord's palace. No, not interested. *The Pope and the Chimp:* A fun time ensues when the Pope and the chimp masquerade as house painters (R). Suddenly, he stops thumbing. *Live from Spain: The Running of the Bulls of Pamplona.* This is it. Charley has wanted to go to Spain for years. It is his dream to stroll the mighty plains, battle windmills and follow Don Quixote's steps. Sheilah would never go. "Too humid," she'd say, or "Let's go to a fat farm and lose some weight instead." To hell with Sheilah. He whistles *Bolero* as he pops a Hungry Guy *paella* into the oven.

He carefully adjusts the dial to receive the signal and flips the set on. The suddenness of the picture surprises him. There it is—instantly—Pamplona. The color is perfect; the music bursts through the speakers. He is in Spain; the crowds yell, taunting the bulls, as the camera moves down the streets. His heart pounds; tears fill his eyes as he feels the excitement. The announcer moves through the crowds. The leathery tanned skin of the people is magnificent; the children squeal with fear and laughter. Oh, the wonder of it all.

Charley digs into his *paella* but freezes at the sound of a familiar voice.

"It's very exciting to be here, a real dream come true."

Sheilah!

"I always wanted to come here, but I never had someone to come with me."

Sy!

There they are, filling up the wide screen. Sheilah, her straw hat with a miniature donkey fastened to it, her shopping bag with oversized salad utensils in it. She looks strange, with white gook all over her nose, her lipstick applied too thickly. Her eye make-up makes her look like a Fellini extra or Ann Miller in the morning. Next to her, with his arm around her, stands Sy, his partner, wearing a polyester shirt, small tufts of hair sticking out of his ears.

"I've never been so excited in my life," Sheilah says in stereo.

Charley gags on the rice. This can't be. Fires are burning in his head; his lungs are exploding, his eyes bulging. No!

"I always thought Spain would be more humid."

That does it. The announcer laughs, Sheilah and Sy laugh and embrace. Charley lurches around the room, gasping for air. He grabs the control knobs, but Sheilah is on every channel. Where are the Hubermans? Give me the Gormans!

The bulls are running down the streets now, kicking and bucking at anything in their way. People, taking their chances, run out of every doorway. Charley clutches his heart and hits the floor. He lies there staring straight ahead, like Janet Leigh in *Psycho*—from Atlanta.

Charley has been canceled. The world has come to him.

GEORGE ALEC EFFINGER

SLOW, SLOW BURN

May 1988

Cyberpunk made a big splash in the 1980s. Both in and out of the science fiction field, earlier writers had explored the seemingly inevitable electronic or computerized merging of man and machine—cybernetics—as serious, even noble, business, a way to, say, walk on Jupiter's moons or pilot a spaceship into the void without endangering human beings, or to help the handicapped to lead comfortable lives. But the "punks" suggested that plug-in techno-enhancement could be used for sheer decadent entertainment, a near-future substitute for drugs. Who would dare to bet against them? Videos of the twenty-first century are bound to be, well . . . an intense experience. Nebula winner George Alec Effinger, born in 1947 and a longtime resident of New Orleans, now lives in Los Angeles. His novels include *What Entropy Means to Me, When Gravity Fails,* a Hugo finalist in 1987, and two sequels, *A Fire in the Sun,* and *The Exile Kiss.*

"**A**LL **R**IGHT, **T**HIS *is the way I picture it: We're in a busy midtown brass-and-fern bar, OK? Table on the sidewalk, umbrella says* CINZANO *on it, we'll see. Two women poking at salads, glasses of white wine. They're dressed very nice, expensive but not flashy, they pay attention to details, they accessorize, know what I mean? One's older, see, she's the mother, though you don't see the age difference. They could be sisters. Both blondes. The older one's got kind of a suit on, she's the dynamic woman on the go. The daughter sort of mirrors that, a subtle thing, nice blouse that says she's shopping the right stores, and she's never more than fifteen minutes out of style. This is like 'Beauty Hints of the Idle Rich' or something.*

"*So the girl is toying with her radicchio, see, and she puts her fork down and goes, 'Mother, may I ask you a personal question?'*

"*Mom says, 'Of course, darling.'*

"*Daughter looks down at her plate, she's just a little bit embarrassed. That's good, makes her human. Audience will relate to that. She looks back up and goes, 'Mother, have you and Dad ever used'—pause for effect—'modular marital aids?'*

"*Big smile. Maybe she, you know, reaches out and pats the kid's hand. Like: There, there. She says, 'Let me tell you a secret, dear.' She laughs. The daughter laughs. Then Mom reaches into her bag, see, and what do you think she takes out? Take a guess.*"

Two account executives have flown all the way from America to talk with Honey Pílar, who, everyone agrees, is the most desirable woman in the world. Even account executives want her, though their motives are mixed, and that's why these two anxious men have come from New York to Honey's walled estate in the south of France. She is sitting at a long table made of polished *limba*, an exotic hardwood from the Congo basin that not even the architec-

359

tural magazines know about yet. Beside her is her husband, Kit, who likes to think of himself as her manager. The adman's throat is very dry after his speech, yet he is too self-conscious to sip from the fluted glass of Perrier-Jouët in front of him. He glances quickly at his associate, but it is easy to see that he can expect no help from that quarter.

Kit stares, but he's not going to say anything. The silence goes on and on. The hopeful smile the adman is wearing begins to vanish. He looks again at his associate, who is still no help whatsoever.

"On the phone, I think we discussed the kids' market," says Kit, just as they reach the breaking point. He purses his lips and turns to Honey, who is sipping Campari and soda through a straw. "She doesn't like it. *I* don't like it. Come back with something else."

The adman lays his sweating hands on the beautiful glossy tabletop. "Miss Pílar?" he says hopelessly.

"Kit doing business," she says and shrugs. When she smiles, both account executives are inspired with possible new approaches. The sound of her voice, they tell themselves, is something, after all. The opportunity to meet with her again will motivate them to find just the pitch she and Kit are looking for. "You have nice flight," she says.

Kit is in the control room, watching his wife on the bed with a 17-year-old Italian boy. Kit watches them through the grimy glass, wishing he'd worn a shirt, because he is sweating heavily in the hot, stale air of the studio and his naked back is sticking to the black vinyl padding of the chair. He peels himself away and leans forward, checking meters and digital readouts that don't really need checking. Honey is a consummate performer. It's as if she had an accurate internal clock ticking behind her forehead, cuing her: 00:00 *initiate encounter*, 00:30 *initiate foreplay with passionate kiss*, 00:45 *experience preliminary arousal*. . . . They are seven minutes, ten seconds into the 30-minute recording. By the outline on Kit's clipboard, Honey is supposed to begin oral stimulation at 07:15, and goddamn, if she isn't already sliding down the boy's tanned body. No cue cards, she doesn't even need hand signals.

Kit pretends to check the levels again, then turns away from the big glass window.

Kit had his brain wired long before he met Honey. If he wanted, he could jack into a socket on the board and feel just what the Italian boy is feeling, or he could jack into another socket and eavesdrop on Honey. Kit doesn't need to peek on the boy's responses, because he's been married to Honey for five years, and she's every bit as good live, in person, as she is on cassette. At the age of 45, Honey Pílar is still the most desired woman in the world. One out of every eight moddies—of all kinds—sold through the big modshop chains is a Honey Pílar sex moddy. Kit has never been her partner in any of them.

At 14:20, Honey and the boy curl together on their sides. Honey's eyes are closed, her face flushed. The boy is naked except for a pair of black matte-finish sunglasses. Drops of sweat glisten on his hairless chest. Kit stands up and turns away again. He leaves the control room, sure that nothing out of the ordinary will happen. He wanders down the long hall. He kicks off his deck shoes and feels the pile carpet warm on the soles of his feet. There is the strong odor of stale beer in the hall, as if several cans had soaked the floor recently and no one had cared to do anything about it. None of the windows are open, and it is even hotter in the hall than in the control room. Kit pushes open the scarred blond-wood door at the end of the hall. He is in another control room. He chases a green lizard the size of his hand from the padded chair and sits behind the board. He stares at meters and digital readouts. They are all flickering at safe levels.

Beyond the glass, a young woman in a torn T-shirt and a bikini bottom sits at a microphone, clutching a sheaf of typewritten pages. Kit knows that she works for some revolutionary organization, but there are too many even to begin to guess which one. She reads the pages in a slow, husky voice. Kit thinks her voice is pretty damn sexy. He likes everything about this girl, what little he knows. He likes her bikini bottom, her torn shirt, her rumpled black hair and the way she talks. After a moment, Kit hears what she is reading. *"Achtung! Achtung!"* she says. Her voice has no accent, neither German nor otherwise. She has brown skin, pale full lips and Oriental eyes. *"Achtung! Dreihundertneunundsiebzig. . . . Fünfundzwanzig."* Then she begins reading a list of five-digit numbers. She reads 25 groups of digits, meaningful only to the audience listening to her frequency, reading the key to her code. *"Ende,"* she says. A moment later, after shifting to another frequency, she begins again in Spanish. *"¡Atención! ¡Atención!"* More numbers, more signals. Kit would like to buy the brown-skinned girl a drink, look into her black eyes, ask her if she knows who might be listening to her broadcast.

Kit leaves the control room. She has never looked up, never known for an instant that he was there. Kit walks back down the stifling hallway. As he enters the small room, he sees Honey astride the Italian boy. Kit checks the clock on the board, checks the script. The recording is still precisely on schedule. He hasn't been missed. Just as the girl at the microphone did not know he was there, Honey does not know he has been gone.

Kit sits in the black vinyl chair. He takes a moddy from a stack on the control board. He doesn't care which moddy it is. He reaches up and chips it in. There is a moment of disorientation, and then Kit's vision clears. He is Cary Grant as Roger Thornhill in *North by Northwest,* suave, well dressed and certainly in command of his feelings. He allows himself a moment of sadness for Honey, whose life could never be as interesting as his. After all, he is Cary Grant. His future will be better than good: It will be amusing.

"Twenty years ago, as a young feature reporter on my first assignment for Euro-Urban Holo, I interviewed Honey Pílar. I remember the rough wooden pier across the beach from her walled estate and the sparkling Mediterranean waves. I remember the bright morning sun making me squint a little into the camera. The cries of the gulls punctuated my lead-in. 'Here in her palatial estate,' I said, 'Honey Pílar reigns as the superstar of the sex moddies. In five years, she has risen from talented newcomer to both critical acclaim and commercial supremacy. Let's take a quick look behind the scenes and find out what Honey Pílar is like in her unguarded moments.' The camera zoomed to the main gate—and then, nothing. We weren't allowed in, even though my news service had confirmed our appointment for that morning. Honey had changed her mind.

"Fifteen years later, I was working for Visions/Rumelia, and once again, I stood by the high gilded gate. 'What secrets does this young

*beauty know that maintain her position as the world's premiere moddy
star?' That was my lead. Honey Pílar never told me her secrets, of
course. But she did make an appearance. She was tanned and smiling
and, well, perfect. A week before that interview, a poll had announced
that sixty-eight percent of the seven billion people on earth could identify her face. Eighteen percent could identify her naked, unaugmented
breasts. That was five years ago.*

*"Tonight, we begin a new series: 'Honey Pílar: A Quarter Century of
Fascination.' Never in the history of the personality-module industry or,
indeed, of the entire entertainment industry, has one performer so dominated the charts. Since her now-classic first moddy, 'A Life in Lace,'
recorded when she was a mere youth, she has turned out thirty-eight
full-length recordings and nine of the 'quickies' that A.T.B. experi-
mented with and then abandoned. Her total sales top one hundred and
twenty million units, and every one of her recordings remains in print.
As of last week, she had eight titles on the 'Brainwaves' Hot One
Hundred Chart, with two in the top ten.*

*"What the world wants to know—and what she has never told us—
is just what kind of woman invites the whole world to listen in on her
private sexual experiences? Does Honey Pílar provide surrogate passion,
and happiness, to millions of people dissatisfied with their own love
lives, or is she merely pandering to an emerging taste for high-tech titil-
lation?*

"Next time, I'll tell you how this reporter sees it."

Kit and Honey are having dinner in a small, dimly lit café near the
ocean. A tall white taper burns on their table and, shining
through their wineglasses, casts soft burgundy shimmers on the
linen tablecloth. Across the narrow room is a stage made of
scuffed green tiles. Lively North African music, distorted and
shrill, plays too loudly through invisible speakers; hovering just
an inch or two above the stage is the holographic figure of a
demure-eyed, big-hipped belly dancer. There are streaks and
scratches on the woman's face and body, as if this recording had
been played many times over many years.

Honey Pílar sips some of the wine and makes a little grimace.
"How are you thinking?" she asks in a soft voice.

"It was all right," says Kit. He looks down at his broiled fish.

"What do you want me to say? It'll sell a million, you outdid your-self. Your climaxes made the dials go crazy. OK?"

"I never know you telling me truth." She frowns at him, then picks up a delicate forkful of couscous and eats it thoughtfully.

Kit tears a chunk of the flat bread and puts it in his mouth, then takes a gulp of wine. Communion, he thinks. I'm absolved. "If you didn't believe me a minute ago, what can I say or do that will make you believe me now?"

Honey looks hurt. She puts her fork down carefully beside her plate. Kit wishes the shrieking Arab music would die away forever. The café smells of cinnamon, as if teams of bakers had been mak-ing sweet rolls all day long and then hidden them away, because nothing on their plates or on the menu contains the least hint of cinnamon. Kit knows that Honey wants to go back to the house in Provence. She's not comfortable in public places.

Kit finishes his glass of wine. He reaches for the bottle, tops up Honey's glass, then fills his own. He takes out a beige pill case from his shirt pocket, finds four Paxium and drinks them down with a Château L'Angelus that deserves better. "What next?" he says.

"What next now?" asks Honey. "Or what next we make an-other moddy?"

Kit squeezes his eyes shut and lets his head fall back. He opens his eyes and sees black beams made of structural plastic crossing the space overhead. He wishes that something, *anything,* with Honey could be simple, even dinner, even conversation. So she's the most desirable woman in the world, he thinks. So she makes more money in one year than the C.E.O.s of any ten major corpo-rations you'd care to name. So what? His private opinion is that she has the intelligence of three sticks and a stone.

He lowers his gaze and forces himself to smile back at her. "What do you want to do, sweetheart? Stay here, go back home, take a trip? You've earned a vacation, baby. We've got your next blockbuster in the can. The world is at your feet. You name it, *chiquita.* Someplace exotic. Someplace you've always wanted to go."

He knows exactly what she will say next.

She says it. "I rather only go home."

"Home," he repeats quietly. He finishes the wine in one long swallow and signals the waiter.

"Kit," she says, "I *was* in happy mood."

I was in happy mood, thinks Kit. But don't let me kid you, sweetie. It's been great.

"Six o'clock in the morning, and the haggard winter sun is rising over the red-tiled roofs of Santa Coloma. Wrapped in scarves, packaged in parkas, slapping their mittened hands together to fend off frostbite, Fawn and Dawn huddle against the fogged plate-glass window of the Instant Memories Modshop on Bridger Parkway. Fawn and Dawn are standing in a long line of people waiting for the manager to open the store. They've been waiting all night in the cold and wind and sleet, because today's the day Honey Pílar's new moddy, 'Slow, Slow Burn,' goes on sale. Fawn and Dawn want to be the first in their neighborhood to own the new Honey Pílar. They want to get it as soon as the shop opens and take it to school with them. Fawn and Dawn are in the ninth grade; these days in Santa Coloma, ninth graders all have their skulls amped, except for the trolls and feebs."

FAWN *(shivering):* My God, I haven't felt my toes since midnight.

DAWN: *I haven't felt my lips. Or my nose, or my ears, or my fingers.*

FAWN: *But if we leave now, I'm going to feel like a total* fool.

DAWN: *We* can't *leave now. These jerk-offs behind us will get our place.*

FAWN *(making a face): If only the wind would stop blowing.*

DAWN: *Oh, sure, the* wind. *If only the wind stopped blowing, it would still be, like, ten degrees below zero or something.*

FAWN *(rubbing her cheeks):* Hey! *(Pointing through display window) Here he comes!*

DAWN *(to store manager): Let us in now, and you can have me right on top of the cash register.*

"The manager is, in fact, opening the front door. He's smiling in anticipation; the store is going to make a fortune today. 'Slow, Slow Burn' is stacked up four feet high in the front window, piled up beside every register and loaded into cardboard dumps scattered all around the selling floor. You can't turn around inside the store without staring into the liquid green eyes of Honey Pílar. Her holographic likeness is more than just inviting; if the mythical sirens had looked like Honey, they wouldn't have had to sing.

"When the door opens, of course, what disappears is any respect for the length of time Fawn and Dawn have been waiting in the freezing night air. They are pushed aside by the jerk-offs behind them and by the jerkoffs behind them. Fawn and Dawn are cast aside by the charging throng of people. They announce that this is truly unfair and rude, that they'd stood in line longer, that they are going to complain, *but no one listens. The flood of bakebrains shoves the two girls this way and that, until they are afraid of being trampled. At last, however, Fawn and Dawn are pitched up like driftwood at the front cash register, each with credit card in one hand, moddy in the other."*

FAWN *(clutching package, fighting way out of shop):* Wow!

"On the street again, with the air so cold it shocks nose and throat, the two girls wait for the bus to take them to school."

DAWN: *Are you and Adam going to use it tonight?*

"Fawn's eyes open wider and she smiles. She taps the crown of her head, the corymbic plug invisible now beneath her hair."

FAWN *(smiling slyly):* I've got it all down on this moddy. Who needs him *any more?*

"Think about study period tonight: to be Honey Pílar in the throes of ecstasy, instead of Fawn and Dawn in the grip of homework!"

Two account executives sit on the couch in the north parlor. "Nice, huh?" says one of the admen. Kit thinks that "nervous" doesn't begin to do the man's condition justice.

"I think—" says Honey.

"She doesn't like it," says Kit. He has to be tough, and quick, or these Madison Avenue guys will think they're doing *her* a favor. And then it will make it that much harder to deal with them the next time. Kit wonders why Honey hasn't learned this by now.

"I think it work fine," says Honey.

Kit gives her a stern glance, but she ignores it.

"Good," says the adman, tremendously relieved. "We think we've put together a nice spot here."

"I'm not sure," says Kit. He doesn't want these men to get self-congratulatory.

"Kit," says Honey, "be quiet. It's for my moddy; I like it."

Kit is going to have to have a serious talk with Miss Honey Pílar, international star. He doesn't tell her how to do her job, he doesn't want her telling him how to do his.

"The girls, they pretty," she says.

The account executive's smile grows wider. "My daughters," he says in a proud voice.

Mood swing by candlelight.

Honey marches, in tight zebraskin pants—not zebra-*stripe*, but the genuine pelt of a former zebra, which is becoming less obtainable all the time—and a gauzy *moiré* tunic created by the actual hands of Lenci Urban of Prague—not by one of his underling designers but by Lenci himself, making the design even dearer than the zebraskin—back and forth in front of the long, high picture window. Kit watches her eclipse first the lighthouse beyond, then the strings of lights marking the marina, then the sallow moon maundering over the ocean. Honey reaches the far end of the room and turns, blocking the moon again. In the air is the heavy scent of incense, church incense, the fragrance Honey loves best, because she thinks it reminds her of her childhood. Kit hates it, and he's panting in shallow breaths. In a corner of the room is the largest commercial datalink money can buy. Kit sits at the keyboard and calls up the first reactions to *Slow, Slow Burn*. Honey watches it indict her.

Total sales for the first seven hours of release: 825,000 units.

"Eight hundred thousand," she says. She is carrying half a melon in one hand, hacking at it with a knife she holds in the other, and flicking seeds across the dusty-rose carpet.

"Eight hundred thousand," says Kit noncommittally.

"In one day, I sell eight hundred thousand. Eight hundred thousand people come out of their house all over the world, they just to get the new moddy. You don't know what can be happening—the rain, the bombs in the airport, the police—all these people come out to pay money for me."

Kit presses a key and columns of figures begin to scroll up the screen. "Sales are up in Provence and Aragon," he says. "They love you here."

"I see that, I see," says Honey. She tosses the bulk of the melon into a corner of the white-on-white brocade couch. "I see also I have no million sales today, first day. You told me a million sales."

Kit glances up at the ceiling, hoping for courage. "A million sales, eight hundred thousand, what difference does it make?"

"Sales *up* at home," she says, turning her back on him, looking out the window. Far below, the crisp thin line of surf wrinkles toward the beach. "Sales *down* in England, Burgundy, Catalonia. That list get longer." She faces the screen again, and the sales reports are like the incessant waves, in their sum victorious, devastating. "Turn it off," she pleads.

Kit is glad to kill the data. He watches Honey misplace her manic energy. How quickly she is drained and empty. Kit feels a peculiar thrill, knowing that none of the 800,000 who have bought the new moddy could even imagine their dream lover in such a mood, that he alone is privileged with this intimacy. She lowers herself into a black leather chair and draws her small feet up on the cushion. She hugs her knees. Kit knows that she wants him to tell her the sales figures mean nothing; he does not. He knows she wants him to come over and rub her neck and shoulders. He will not. He watches her massage her temples with trembling fingers.

On the first day of sales, Honey Pilar's latest moddy has sold 825,000 copies. Her previous moddy, on its first day, sold 972,000. The one before that, 1,200,000. Is this a trend?

Goddamn right, it's a trend, Kit thinks. If it weren't, why have computers track the numbers? Honey and Kit respond differently, however. Kit doesn't see any practical point in mourning 100,000 sales one way or the other.

But Honey weeps quietly. In the silence, in the candlelight, in the cloud of burning incense, there is a peculiarly supplicatory feeling in the house. Honey herself seems wrapped in a fragile innocence. Kit thinks that, for him, this was once one of her chief attractions.

"This is Jerome Nkoro in the critic's corner at New York CommNet 'Morning Magazine,' and today I'm going to be talking about 'Slow, Slow Burn,' Honey Pílar's new moddy from A.T.B.

"In these days, when, thanks to surgical and biological wonders we've come to take for granted, men and women routinely maintain their youthful looks well past their seventieth birthday, it probably shouldn't matter that our number-one fantasy girl has just celebrated her forty-fifth. But it's something to think about. Honey Pílar is forty-

five. Does that make you *feel old? It makes* me *feel like the last of the dinosaurs.*

"I can remember having holos of Honey Pílar in my bedroom when I was twelve, alongside my Death-to-Argentina football and my scale model of the Mars colony. My first sexual experience was a dream in which Honey couldn't remember her locker combination. And now this is her thirty-ninth moddy, and she's old enough to be a grandmother. . . .

"But don't get me wrong, I still think Honey is the most exciting woman in the world. I've left word with my secretary that if she calls, she can have my home phone number any time. *And my locker combination, too! The problem with 'Slow, Slow Burn' is certainly not Honey's age. The problem is that my moddy library has two full shelves devoted to her, and I'm beginning to ask myself, Do I really need another Honey Pílar moddy?*

"Believe me, I've never had a complaint from anyone about her moddies. My partners agree with me that they're likely to get more pleasure from Honey than from anyone else's moddy—or from me, either, for that matter. Whether the moddy is turning my partner into a hungry, writhing Honey Pílar or consuming me in one of Honey's recorded sexual fire storms, there's never any chance that she will fail to perform.

"The question is simply this: How will she continue to keep our interest? Her partner in 'Slow, Slow Burn' is an uncredited seventeen-year-old. As she gets older, must her partners get younger? I'm dismayed by the vision of Honey Pílar offering the kids ten-speed bikes to entice them. And, for myself, doesn't a lifelong relationship with three dozen plastic moddies begin to resemble—I hate to suggest this—a marriage?

"'Slow, Slow Burn' is right up to the standard Honey Pílar has set throughout her long and dazzling career. I guess it's just that after all these years, I'm beginning to realize that although I've been to bed with Honey a million times, I'm never actually going to have *her. All I'm going to have is two shelves of plastic with her name on them, and an exquisitely detailed knowledge of what she's like in the sack.*

"I'm getting to the point where I wonder what she likes to talk about afterward. What she's like at breakfast. I guess I'm getting wistful in my old age. But don't mind me. Go out and buy 'Slow, Slow Burn.' As always, it does what it's supposed to do."

Kit and Honey are throwing a party in their hotel suite, after the annual Pammie Awards. Honey is still clutching her special Lifetime Achievement statuette. It has been a wonderful, satisfying evening for her. Reporters and fans and fellow artists come up to her and tell her again and again that the honor is long overdue. Honey knew in advance that the association was presenting her with the Lifetime Achievement, so her acceptance speech was gracious and tearful and as nearly grammatically correct as she could manage. She looks beautiful in her silver Lenci sheath.

Kit stands looking out across a city that seems to live for the night, toward a black harbor streaked with the pale-green lights of bridges. Beyond the window, the world seems cold and clean. People are hurrying according to unknown but vital reasons; they are not . . . wandering. The stars are hard, white, not dimmed and hazy with smoke. Kit turns and gazes at the room, at the men and women talking and laughing. The hotel has catered this party, and the champagne is cheap and sweet. Kit sets his plastic champagne glass on the holoset for the maid to clear away. He looks for Honey.

He finds her in a corner, talking with her agent and a representative from A.T.B. He brings her a fresh glass of the awful champagne. Honey looks up quickly and smiles at him. Her eye make-up looks terrible. The agent indicates the Lifetime Achievement Award in her hand. "They wouldn't have given that to you if they didn't love you," he says.

"I owe you, too," says Honey. Kit thinks that he wound her up too much earlier in the evening, and now she just can't stop being gracious.

The agent smiles. "You did all the work, Honey."

Kit thinks of the 17-year-old boy from the beach.

The woman from A.T.B. swallows the last of her potato salad. "Are you giving any thought yet to retiring?" she asks.

The agent glares at her. Honey's eyes open wide, and then she runs across the room. Kit hears the agent say, "There isn't any air in here anymore."

Half an hour later, the party is over. Kit and the agent are trying to make Honey feel better. "That woman was a fool," says the agent.

Honey shakes her head. "They give me the Lifetime Award. They do when your career is over."

"That's not what it meant at all," says the agent. "They were telling you that you're the best, that you've always been the best."

Kit takes a deep breath and lets it out. "I think we'd better call it a night," he says.

The agent stands up. "Well, anyway, it's time for me to run. Thanks for the drinks." He bends to kiss Honey on the cheek. "Congratulations, baby," he says. "Don't worry about that A.T.B. woman. She'll be out of a job tomorrow."

When they're alone, Honey puts her head on Kit's shoulder and sobs. He pushes her away. "Don't start," he says. "Don't get into this sad and insecure business again. I don't want to put up with it right now; I'm too tired."

Honey stares at him. "How do you talk to me like that?"

Kit turns away. "It's easy," he says. "We have this same conversation about three times a week. I've learned my part. You're still trying to get it right, because in your line of work, you don't have to worry about learning lines."

Honey turns him around and slaps his face. Kit gives her a thin smile. "You want me to tell you that you're *not* getting old?"

Honey slams her fist into his chest. He flinches but says nothing. She runs into their bedroom and slams the door.

Kit stares after her. "You're still my wife, you know," he calls after her. "Get undressed, and get ready." He knows this will make her even angrier.

This is the only part of their relationship that is all his, that exists only between the two of them. Kit becomes aroused. "I want you," he says.

She opens the bedroom door and looks at him blankly.

"I want you," he says. "But tonight, I want you to use this." He offers her a pinkplastic moddy. He has never asked her to be anyone else before.

Her eyes narrow. She looks at the moddy. "But this is me," she says, not understanding.

He laughs. "Yes, it's you. Only *younger*."

Kit will hold her in his arms and let himself be carried away by her passion, but already he is thinking of someone else, a young woman with Oriental eyes, leaning close to a microphone and murmuring cryptic messages in other languages.

"Here on 'Venezia Affascinante' tonight, we're going to tell you everything there is to tell about the people you love and the people you'd rather hate.

"There may be a billion people in this world right now who don't like Honey Pílar, and there may be a billion people who don't care. The other five billion, though, absolutely adore her, and we're wondering tonight how they'll take the news that her fourth marriage has come to a shattering, devastating conclusion. Shattering and devastating, that is, to her fourth husband, Kit, because after you've been married to Honey Pílar, the rest of the women in the world must suddenly look a little on the drab side.

"'Venezia Affascinante' today conducted its own scientific poll on the subject. Our question to one hundred average moddy users was this: 'Which aspect of their relationship will Kit miss the most now that he's been abruptly shown out of Honey Pílar's life?'

"'Quick starts, low maintenance and high performance' was the most popular reply. If you take our meaning.

"The second most popular answer was 'Honey's bank account,' because, after all, a good deal of her irresistible attraction lies in her wealth, her extravagant lifestyle and her association with the most stimulating celebrities in the world.

"The third answer was, unpredictably, 'her nose,' which, we must admit, is certainly cute enough.

"It took us several hours to get in touch with Honey's most recent ex-husband to compare these answers with Kit's own personal reactions in our exclusive long-distance interview. When he finally accepted our call, we put our question to him for his definitive reply. He said, and this is a direct quote, 'You can goddamn go to hell!'

"And you'll hear that nowhere else but on 'Venezia Affascinante.'

"Some unanswered questions remain: How long before Honey Pílar marries again? Will she continue to record new moddies, or does this alteration in her life signal a desire to make a fundamental change in her professional career? And who will be her new business manager?

Did her experience with Kit teach her a sad lesson about combining her emotional and business interests in one person?

"Whatever she decides, 'Venezia Affascinante' is on the job to bring you the news. *Twenty-four-hour-a-day coverage of the world,* the world you wish you lived in. *We'll be back after this word.*"

Two account executives sit in the smaller of the two dining rooms in Honey Pílar's home in Provence. They've finished lunch and are sipping brandy and beaming down at Honey at the far end of the long table. Both men feel wonderful—first, because the meal they've just enjoyed was one of the finest in their memory and, second, because this is the only time they've come to the walled estate with any real confidence that they'd be able to bring their business to a satisfactory conclusion.

"The meal was truly marvelous, Miss Pílar," says the first adman.

"Was good, no?" Honey smiles with innocent pleasure.

"Well," says the account executive, letting his expression become gradually more serious. "Perhaps it's time to turn our attention to business."

"Go ahead," says Honey. "You shoot."

"Yes, well. *Slow, Slow Burn* has been in the stores now for a little more than six months. I trust you've had the chance to look over the figures we sent you."

"Yes, I see them."

"They're a little difficult to understand, even after you've been in the business as long as I have."

"No, OK, I understand them fine."

The adman frowns. "That is, I know you've been without a business manager ever since, uh—"

Honey gives him a reassuring smile.

The man from the agency looks a little uncomfortable. "Uh, as I say, you've been without a business manager. Well, we want you to know that we value your account very highly. We've represented you for almost twenty years. I want to tell you that you can rely on us during these troubled months."

"No trouble," says Honey.

The adman opens his briefcase and takes out a report. "We've taken the liberty of drawing up a preliminary schedule of promotional opportunities for *Slow, Slow Burn* and a suggested scenario for your next personality module. Our consultants have made some valuable suggestions relevant to regaining the market support you enjoyed on some of your previous releases."

Honey gives him her brightest smile. The account executive smiles back. "May I have?" she asks, holding out her slender hand for the report.

"Certainly," says the adman. "I'll be happy to—"

Honey rips the papers in half while she looks directly into the man's eyes. Her smile never wavers.

"Miss Pílar," says the adman unhappily, "we have some of the best market analysts in the business studying current trends in the personality-module industry and your own standing as a recording artist. While your reputation is greater now than ever, your impact at what we call point of sale seems to be softening somewhat. Our proposals are designed to make the best use of what our agency considers your chief strengths—"

"In twenty years," says Honey Pílar, "I earn much money for your agency, no?"

"Why, yes, of course."

"We call New York. Your boss is good friend."

The man takes out a handkerchief and mops the perspiration on his upper lip. "I don't think that will be necessary," he says. "We'll, uh, give them your views. Later, if you should find that handling your career on your own is too much for you, we can always—"

"You not understand. I handle my career some twenty-five years," Honey says. "I think you go now."

The two men from New York glance at each other nervously and stand up. "As always, Miss Pílar," says the first adman, "it's been a pleasure."

"You bet," she says.

As the men are retreating from her home, the second account executive pauses. This is the first time he has actually summoned the nerve to speak. "Miss Pílar," he says, looking down at the tiled floor, "I was wondering if I might invite you to dinner tonight."

Honey laughs. "You Americans!" she says, truly amused. "No,

Kit was American, too. Next time, tall, blond, Swedish, maybe Dutch."

The second adman hurries after his colleague, not even looking back at their client. Honey watches them for a moment, then closes the door. She is still holding the agency's torn report. She goes back into the living room, toward the wastebasket.

JOE HALDEMAN

MORE THAN THE SUM OF HIS PARTS

May 1985

Like a number of other writers represented in this anthology, Joe Haldeman's background is in science, in his case physics and astronomy, but he also has an MFA from the Iowa Writer's Workshop. The double background makes him perhaps uniquely qualified to teach writing at MIT, which he does for a semester each year, spending the rest of the year in Florida. Haldeman's first science fiction novel, *The Forever War*, drew heavily on his experience in Vietnam, where he served as a combat engineer before being seriously wounded and discharged with a Purple Heart. The book, which imaginatively projects the gritty despair of war into the far future, was critically acclaimed, won several awards including the Nebula and Hugo and sold very well, putting Haldeman on the map at once. Born in 1943, he has continued to be a popular writer, winning further awards, and serving as president of SFWA. He writes poetry, and has published several mainstream novels in addition to such science fiction as *Mindbridge* (1976) and the Worlds sequence of three books. The theme of the rogue robot, or cyborg gone wrong, is familiar in science fiction, but it is seldom presented with such careful attention to process as in this cautionary tale.

21 AUGUST 2058

They say I am to keep a detailed record of my feelings, my perceptions, as I grow accustomed to the new parts. To that end, they gave me an apparatus that blind people use for writing, like a tablet with guide wires. It is somewhat awkward. But a recorder would be useless, since I will not have a mouth for some time and I can't type blind with only one hand.

Woke up free from pain. Interesting. Surprising to find that it has been only five days since the accident. For the record, I am, or was, Dr. Wilson Cheetham, senior engineer (quality control) for U.S. Steel's Skyfac station, a high-orbit facility that produces foam steel and vapor-deposition materials for use in the cislunar community. But if you are reading this, you must know all that.

Five days ago, I was inspecting the aluminum-deposition facility and had a bad accident. There was a glitch in my jetseat controls, and I suddenly flew straight into the wide beam of charged aluminum vapor. Very hot. They turned it off in a second, but there was still plenty of time for the beam to breach the suit and thoroughly roast three quarters of my body.

Apparently there was a rescue bubble right there. I was unconscious, of course. They tell me that my heart stopped with the shock, but they managed to save me. My left leg and arm are gone, as is my face. I have no lower jaw, nose or external ears. I can hear after a fashion, though; and will have eyes in a week or so. They claim they will craft for me testicles and a penis.

I must be pumped full of mood drugs. I feel too calm. If I were myself, whatever fraction of myself is left, perhaps I would resist the insult of being turned into a sexless half-machine.

Ah, well. This will be a machine that can turn itself off.

379

22 August 2058

For many days there was only sleep or pain. That was in the weightless ward at Mercy. They stripped the dead skin off me bit by bit. There are limits to anesthesia, unfortunately. I tried to scream but found I had no vocal cords. They finally decided not to try to salvage the arm and leg, which saved some pain.

When I was able to listen, they explained that U.S. Steel valued my services so much that it was willing to underwrite a state-of-the-art cyborg transformation. Half the cost will be absorbed by Interface Biotech on the moon. Everybody will deduct me from his taxes.

This, then, is the catalog: first, new arm and leg. That's fairly standard. (I once worked with a woman who had two cyborg arms. It took weeks before I could look at her without feeling pity and revulsion.) Then they will attempt to build me a working jaw and mouth, which has been done only rarely and imperfectly, and rebuild the trachea, vocal cords, esophagus. I will be able to speak and drink, though except for certain soft foods, I won't eat in a normal way: Salivary glands are beyond their art. No mucous membranes of any kind. A drastic cure for my chronic sinusitis.

Surprisingly, to me at least, the reconstruction of a penis is a fairly straightforward procedure, for which they've had lots of practice. Men are forever sticking them into places where they don't belong. They are particularly excited about my case because of the challenge in restoring sensation as well as function. The prostate is intact, and they seem confident that they can hook up the complicated plumbing involved in ejaculation. Restoring the ability to urinate is trivially easy, they say.

(The biotechnician in charge of the urogenital phase of the project talked at me for more than an hour, going into unnecessarily grisly detail. It seems that this replacement had been done occasionally even before they had any kind of mechanical substitute by sawing off a short rib and transplanting it, covering it with a skin graft from elsewhere on the body. The recipient thus was blessed with a permanent erection, unfortunately rather strange-looking and short on sensation. My own prosthesis will look very much like the real, shall we say, thing, and new developments in tractor-field mechanics and bionic interfacing should give it realistic response patterns.)

I don't know how to feel about all this. I wish they would leave my blood chemistry alone, so I could have some honest grief or horror. Instead of this placid waiting.

4 SEPTEMBER 2058

Out cold for 13 days and I wake up with eyes. The arm and leg are in place but not powered up yet. I wonder what the eyes look like. (They won't give me a mirror until I have a face.) They feel like wet glass.

Very fancy eyes. I have a box with two dials that I can use to override the default mode; that is, the ability to see only normally. One of them gives me conscious control over pupil dilation, so I can see in almost total darkness or, if for some reason I wanted to, look directly at the sun without discomfort. The other changes the frequency response, so I can see in either the infrared or the ultraviolet. This hospital room looks pretty much the same in ultraviolet, but in infrared, it takes on a whole new aspect. Most of the room's illumination, then, comes from bright bars on the walls, radiant heating. My real arm shows a pulsing tracery of arteries and veins. The other is, of course, not visible except by reflection and is dark blue.

(Later.) Strange I didn't realize I was on the moon. I thought it was a low-gravity ward in Mercy. While I was sleeping, they sent me down to Biotech. Should have figured that out.

5 SEPTEMBER 2058

They turned on the "social" arm and leg and began patterning exercises. I am told to think of a certain movement and do its mirror image with my right arm or leg while attempting to execute it with my left. The trainer helps the cyborg unit along, which generates something like pain, though actually it doesn't resemble any real muscular ache. Maybe it's the way circuits feel when they're overloaded.

By the end of the session, I was able to make a fist without help, though there is hardly enough grip to hold a pencil. I can't raise the leg yet but can make the toes move.

They removed some of the bandages today, from shoulder to hip, and the test-tube skin looks much more real than I had prepared myself for—hairless and somewhat glossy, but the color match is perfect. In infrared it looks different, more uniform in color than the "real" side. I suppose that's because it hasn't aged 40 years.

While putting me through my paces, the technician waxed rhapsodic about how good this arm is going to be—this set of arms, actually. I'm exercising with the "social" one, which looks much more convincing than the ones my co-worker displayed ten years ago (no doubt a matter of money rather than advancing technology). The "working" arm, which I haven't seen yet, will be all metal, capable of being worn on the outside of a space suit. Besides having the two arms, I'll be able to interface with various waldos tailored to specific functions.

Fortunately, I am more ambidextrous than the average person. I broke my right wrist in the second grade and kept rebreaking it through the third, and so learned to write with both hands. All my life, I have been able to print more clearly with the left.

They claim to be cutting down on my medication. If that's the truth, I seem to be adjusting fairly well. Then again, I have nothing in my past experience to use as a basis for comparison. Perhaps this calmness is only a mask for hysteria.

6 SEPTEMBER 2058

Today I was able to tie a simple knot. I can lightly sketch out the letters of the alphabet—a large and childish scrawl but recognizably my own.

I've begun walking after a fashion, supporting myself between parallel bars. (The lack of hand strength is a neural problem, not a muscular one; when rigid, the arm and the leg are as strong as metal crutches.) As I practice, it's amusing to watch the reactions of people who walk into the room—people who aren't paid to mask their horror at being studied by two cold lenses embedded in a swathe of bandages over a shape that is not a head.

Tomorrow they start building my face. I will be essentially unconscious for more than a week. The limb patterning will continue as I sleep, they say.

14 SEPTEMBER 2058

When I was a child, my mother dressed me in costume each Halloween and escorted me around the high-rise, so I could beg for candy. One occasion, I wore the mask of a child star then popular on the cube, a tightly fitting plastic affair that covered the head, squeezing my pudgy features into something more in line with some Platonic ideal of childish beauty.

This face is like that. It is undeniably my face, but the skin is taut and unresponsive. Any attempt at expression produces a grimace.

I have almost normal grip in the hand now, though it is still clumsy. As they hoped, the sensory feedback from the finger tips and the palms seems to be more finely tuned than in my "good" hand. Tracing my new forefinger across my right wrist, I can sense the individual pores, and there is a marked temperature gradient as I pass over tendon or vein. And yet the hand and arm will eventually be capable of superhuman strength.

Touching my new face, I do not feel pores. They have improved on nature in the business of heat exchange.

22 SEPTEMBER 2058

Another week of sleep while they installed the new plumbing. When the anesthetic wore off, I felt a definite *something*—not pain, but neither was it the normal somatic heft of genitalia. Everything was bedded in gauze and bandage, though, and catheterized, so it would feel strange even to a normal person.

(Later.) An aide came in and gingerly snipped away the bandages. He blushed; I don't think fondling was in his job description. When the catheter came out, there was a small sting of pain and relief.

It's not much of a copy. To reconstruct the face, they could consult hundreds of pictures and cubes, but it had never occurred to me that one day it might be useful to have a gallery of pictures of my private parts in various stages of repose. The technicians had approached the problem by bringing me a stack of photos culled from urological texts and pornography and having me sort through them as to closeness of fit.

It was not a task for which I had been well trained, by experience or disposition. Strange as it may seem in this age of unfettered hedonism, I haven't seen another man naked, let alone rampant, since leaving high school, 25 years ago. (I was stationed on Farside for 18 months and never went near a sex bar, preferring an audience of one, even if I had to hire her, as was usually the case.)

So this one is rather longer and thicker than its predecessor— would all men unconsciously exaggerate?—and has only approximately the same aspect when erect. A young man's rakish angle.

Distasteful but necessary to write about the matter of masturbation. At first, it didn't work. With my right hand, it felt like holding another man, which I have never had any desire to do. With the new hand, the process proceeded in the normal way, though I must admit to a voyeuristic aspect. The sensations were extremely acute—ejaculation more forceful than I can remember from youth.

It makes me wonder. In a book I recently read about brain chemistry, the author made a major point of the notion that it was a mistake to completely equate mind with brain. The brain, he said, is in a way only the thickest and most complex segment of the nervous system: It coordinates our consciousness, but the actual mind suffuses through the body in a network of ganglia. In fact, he used sexuality as an example. When a man ruefully observes that his penis has a mind of its own, he is stating part of a larger truth.

But I, in fact, do have actual brains embedded in my new parts: the biochips that process sensory data coming in and action commands going back. Are these brains part of my consciousness the way the rest of my nervous system is? The masturbation experience indicates that they may be in business for themselves.

This is premature speculation, so to speak. We'll see how it feels when I move into a more complex environment, where I'm not so self-absorbed.

23 September 2058

During the night, something evidently clicked. I woke up this morning with full strength in my cyborg limbs. One rail of the bed was twisted out of shape where I must have unconsciously gripped it. I bent it back quite easily.

Some obscure impulse makes me want to keep this talent secret for the time being. The technicians thought I would be able to exert three or four times the normal person's grip; this is obviously much more than that.

But why keep it a secret? I don't know. Let *them* tell *me* why I've done it. After all, this is supposed to be a record of my psychological adjustment or maladjustment.

(Later.) The techs were astonished, ecstatic. I demonstrated a pull of 90 kilograms. I know if I'd actually given it a good yank, I could have pulled the stress machine out of the wall. I'll give them 110 tomorrow and inch my way up to 125.

Obviously, I must be careful with force vectors. If I put too much stress on the normal parts of my body, I could do permanent injury. With my metal fist, I could punch a hole through an air-lock door, but it would probably tear the prosthesis out of its socket. Newton's laws still apply.

Other laws will have to be rewritten.

24 September 2058

I got to work out with three waldos today. A fantastic experience!

The first one was a disembodied hand and arm attached to a stand, the setup they use to train normal people in the use of waldos. The difference is that I don't need a waldo sleeve to imperfectly transmit my wishes to the mechanical double. I can plug into it directly.

I've been using waldos in my work ever since graduate school, but it was never anything like this. Inside the waldo sleeve, you get a clumsy kind of feedback from striated pressor field generators embedded in the plastic. With my setup, the feedback is exactly the kind a normal person feels when he touches an object but much more sensitive. The first time they asked me to pick up an egg, I tossed it up and caught it (no great feat of coordination in lunar gravity, admittedly, but I could have done it as easily in Earth normal).

The next waldo was a large earthmover that Western Mining uses over at Grimaldi Station. That was interesting, not only because of its size but because of the slight communications lag. Grimaldi is only a few dozen kilometers away, but there aren't enough unused data channels between here and there for me to use the land line to communicate with the earthmover hand. I had to relay via Comsat, so there was about a ten-second delay between the thought and the action. It was a fine feeling of power but a little confusing: I would cup my hand and scoop downward and then, a split second too late, would feel the resistance of the regolith—and then casually hold in my palm several *tonnes* of rock and dirt. People were standing around watching; with a flick of my wrist, I could have buried them. Instead, I dutifully dumped it onto the belt to the converter.

But the waldo that most fascinated me was the micro. It had been in use for only a few months; I had heard of it but hadn't had a chance to see it in action. It is a fully articulated hand barely a tenth of a millimeter long. I used it in conjunction with a low-power scanning electron microscope, moving around on the surface of a microcircuit. At that magnification, it looked like a hand on a long stick wandering through the corridors of a building whose walls varied from rough stucco to brushed metal to blistered gray paint, all laced over with thick cables of gold. When necessary, I could bring in another hand, manipulated by my right from inside a waldo sleeve, to help with simple carpenter and machinist tasks that, in the real world, translated into fundamental changes in the quantum-electrodynamic properties of the circuit.

This was the real power: not crushing metal tubes or lifting *tonnes* of rock but pushing electrons around to do my bidding. My first doctorate was in electrical engineering; in a sudden epiphany, I realized that I am the first *actual* electrical engineer in history.

After two hours, they made me stop; said I was showing signs of strain. They put me into a wheelchair, and I did fall asleep on the way back to my room, dreaming dreams of microcosmic and infinite power.

25 September 2058

The metal arm. I expected it to feel fundamentally different from the social one, but of course it doesn't, most of the time. Circuits are circuits. The difference comes under conditions of extreme exertion: The soft hand gives me signals similar to pain if I come close to the level of stress that would harm the fleshlike material. With the metal hand, I can rip off a chunk of steel plate a centimeter thick and feel nothing beyond "muscular" strain. If I had two of them, I could work marvels.

The mechanical leg is not so gifted. It has governors to restrict its strength and range of motion to that of a normal leg, which is reasonable. Even a normal person finds himself brushing the ceiling occasionally in lunar gravity. I could stand up sharply and find myself with a concussion or worse.

I like the metal arm, though. When I'm stronger (hah!), they say, they'll let me go outside and try it with a space suit. Throw something over the horizon.

Starting today, I'm easing back into a semblance of normal life. I'll be staying at Biotech for another six or eight weeks, but I'm patched into my Skyfac office and have started clearing out the backlog of paper-work. Two hours in the morning and two in the afternoon. It's diverting, but I have to admit my heart isn't really in it. Rather be playing with the micro. (Have booked three hours on it tomorrow.)

26 September 2058

They have threaded an optical fiber through the micro's little finger, so I can watch its progress on a screen without being limited to the field of an electron microscope. The picture is fuzzy while the waldo is in motion, but if I hold it still for a few seconds, the computer assist builds up quite a sharp image. I used it to roam all over my right arm and hand, which was fascinating: hairs a tangle of stiff, black stalks, the pores small, damp craters. And everywhere evidence of the skin's slow death: translucent sheaves of desquamated cells.

I've taken to wearing the metal arm rather than the social one. People's stares don't bother me. The metal one will be more useful in my actual work, and I want to get as much practice as possible. There is also an undeniable feeling of power.

27 September 2058

Today I went outside. It was clumsy getting around at first. For the past 11 years, I've used a suit only in zero g, so all of my reflexes are wrong. Still, not much serious can go wrong at a sixth of a g.

It was exhilarating but at the same time frustrating, since I couldn't reveal all of my strength. I did almost overdo it once, starting to tip over a large boulder. Before it tipped, I realized that my left boot had crunched through ten centimeters of regolith in reaction to the amount of force I was applying. So I backed off and discreetly shuffled my foot to fill the telltale hole.

I could, indeed, throw a rock over the horizon. With a sling, I might be able to put a small one into orbit—rent myself out as a lunar launching facility.

(Later.) Most interesting. A pretty nurse who has been on this project since the beginning came into my room after dinner and proposed the obvious experiment. It was wildly successful.

Although my new body starts out with the normal pattern of excitation-plateau-orgasm, the resemblance stops there. I have no refractory period; the process of erection is completely under conscious control. This could make me the most popular man on the moon.

The artificial skin of the penis is as sensitive to tactile differentiation as that of the cyborg fingers: Suddenly, I know more about a woman's internal topography than any man who ever lived— more than any *woman!*

I think tomorrow I'll take a trip to Farside.

28 September 2058

Farside has nine sex bars. I read the guidebook descriptions and then asked a few locals for their recommendations and wound up going to a place cleverly called The Juice Bar.

In fact, the name was not just an expression of coy eroticism. They served nothing but fruit and juices there, most of them fantastically expensive Earth imports. I spent a day's pay on a glass of pear nectar and sought out the most attractive woman in the room.

That in itself was a mistake. I was not physically attractive even before the accident, and the mechanics have faithfully restored my coarse features and slight paunch. I was rebuffed.

So I went to the opposite extreme and looked for the plainest woman. That would be a better test, anyway: Before the accident, I always demanded, and paid for, physical perfection. If I could duplicate the performance of last night with a woman to whom I was not sexually attracted—and do it in public—then my independence from the autonomic nervous system would be proved beyond doubt.

Second mistake. I was never good at small talk, and when I located my paragon of plainness, I began talking about the accident and the singular talent that had resulted from it. She suddenly remembered an appointment elsewhere.

I was not so open with the next woman, also plain. She asked whether there was something wrong with my face, and I told her half of the truth. She was sweetly sympathetic, motherly, which did not endear her to me. It did make her a good subject for the experiment. We left the socializing section of the bar and went back to the so-called love room.

There was an acrid quality to the air that I suppose was compounded of incense and sweat; but, of course, my dry nose was not capable of identifying actual smells. For the first time, I was grateful for that disability; the place probably had the aroma of a well-used locker room. Plus pheromones.

Under the muted lights, red and blue as well as white, more than a dozen couples were engaged more or less actively in various aspects of amorous behavior. A few were frankly staring at others, but most were either absorbed with their own affairs or furtive in their voyeurism. Most of them were on the floor, which was a warm, soft mat, but some were using tables and chairs in fairly ingenious ways. Several of the permutations would no doubt have been impossible or dangerous in Earth's gravity.

We undressed, and she complimented me on my evident spryness. A nearby spectator made a jealous observation. Her own

body was rather flaccid, doughy, and under previous circumstances, I doubt that I would have been able to maintain enthusiasm. There was no problem, however; in fact, I rather enjoyed
it. She required very little foreplay, and I was soon repeating the
odd sensation of hypersensitized exploration—gynecological
spelunking.

She was quite voluble in her pleasure, and although she lasted
less than an hour, we did attract a certain amount of attention.
When she, panting, regretfully declined further exercise, a woman
who had been watching, a rather attractive young blonde, offered
to share her various openings. I obliged her for a while; although
the well was dry, the pump handle was unaffected.

During that performance, I became aware that the pleasure
involved was not a sexual one in any normal sense. Sensual, yes,
in the way that a fine meal is a sensual experience, but with a
remote subtlety that I find difficult to describe. Perhaps there is a
relation to epicurism that is more than metaphorical. Since I can
no longer taste food, a large area of my brain is available for the
evaluation of other experience. It may be that the brain is reorga-
nizing itself in order to take fullest advantage of my new abilities.

By the time the blonde's energy began to flag, several other
women had taken an interest in my satyriasis. I resisted the temptation to find out what this organ's limit was, if, indeed, a limit
existed. My back ached and the right knee was protesting, so I
threw the mental switch and deflated. I left with a minimum of
socializing. (The first woman insisted on buying me something at
the bar. I opted for a banana.)

29 September 2058

Now that I have eyes and both hands, there's no reason to scratch
this diary out with a pen, so I'm entering it into the computer. But
I'm keeping two versions.

I copied everything up to this point and then went back and
edited the versions that I will show to Biotech. It's very polite and
will remain so. For instance, it does not contain the following:

After writing last night's entry, I found myself still full of energy,
and so put into action a plan that has been forming in my mind.

About two in the morning, I went downstairs and broke into

the waldo labs. The entrance is protected by a five-digit combination lock, but, of course, that was no obstacle. My hypersensitive fingers could feel the tumblers rattling into place.

I got the microwaldo set up and then detached my leg. I guided the waldo through the leg's circuitry and easily disabled the governors. The entire operation took less than 20 minutes.

I did have to use a certain amount of care in walking, at first. There was a tendency to rise into the air or to overcompensate by limping. It was under control by the time I got back to my room. So once more, they have proved to be mistaken as to the limits of my abilities.

Testing the strength of the leg with a halfhearted kick, I put a deep dent in the metal wall at the rear of my closet. I'll have to wait until I can be outside, alone, to see what full force can do.

A comparison kick with my flesh leg left no dent but did hurt my great toe.

30 SEPTEMBER 2058

It occurs to me that I feel better about my body than I have in the past 20 years. Who wouldn't? Literally eternal youth in these new limbs and organs; if a part shows signs of wear, it can simply be replaced.

I was angry at the Biotech evaluation board this morning. When I simply inquired as to the practicality of replacing the right arm and leg as well, all but one were horrified. One was amused. I will remember him.

I think the fools are going to order me to leave Nearside in a day or two and go back to Mercy for psychiatric "help." I will leave when I want to, on my own terms.

1 OCTOBER 2058

This is being voice recorded in the Environmental Control Center at Nearside. It is 10:32; they have less than 90 minutes to accede to my demands. Let me backtrack.

After writing last night's entry, I felt a sudden surge of sexual desire. I took the shuttle to Farside and went back to The Juice Bar.

The plain woman from the previous night was waiting, hoping

that I would show up. She was delighted when I suggested that we save money (and whatever residue of modesty we had left) by keeping ourselves to each other back at my room.

I didn't mean to kill her. That was not in my mind at all. But I suppose in my passion, or abandon, I carelessly propped my strong leg against the wall and then thrust with too much strength. At any rate, there was a snap and a tearing sound. She gave a small cry, and the lower half of my body was suddenly awash in blood. I had snapped her spine and evidently at the same time caused considerable internal damage. She must have lost consciousness very quickly, though her heart did not stop beating for nearly a minute.

Disposing of the body was no great problem. In the laundry room, I found a bag large enough to hold her comfortably. Then I went back to the room and put her and the sheet she had besmirched into the bag.

Getting her to the recycler would have been a problem if it had been a normal hour. She looked like nothing so much as a body in a laundry bag. Fortunately, the corridor was deserted.

The lock on the recycler room was child's play. The furnace door was a problem, though: It was easy to unlock, but its diameter was only 25 centimeters.

So I had to disassemble her. To save cleaning up, I did the job inside the laundry bag, which was clumsy and made it difficult to see the fascinating process.

I was so absorbed in watching that I didn't hear the door slide open. But the man who walked in made a slight gurgling sound that I somehow did hear over the cracking of bones. I stepped over to him and killed him with one kick.

I have to admit to a lapse in judgment at that point. I locked the door and went back to the chore at hand. After the woman was completely recycled, I repeated the process with the man—which was much easier. The female's layer of subcutaneous fat made disassembly of the torso a more slippery business.

It really was wasted time (though I did spend part of it thinking out the final touches of the plan I am now engaged upon). I might as well have left both bodies there on the floor. I had kicked the man with great force—enough to throw me to the ground in reaction and badly bruise my right hip—and had split him open from crotch to heart. This made a bad enough mess, even if he hadn't compounded the problem by striking the ceiling. I would never have been able to clean that up, and it's not the sort of thing that would escape notice for long.

At any rate, it was only 20 minutes wasted, and I gained more time than that by disabling the recycler-room lock. I cleaned up, changed clothes, stopped by the waldo lab for a few minutes and then took the slidewalk to the Environmental Control Center.

There was only one young man on duty at the E.C.C. at that hour. I exchanged a few pleasantries with him and then punched him in the heart, softly enough not to make a mess. I put his body where it wouldn't distract me and then attended to the problem of the door.

There's no actual door on the E.C.C., but there is an emergency wall that slides into place if there's a drop in pressure. I typed up a test program simulating an emergency, and the wall obeyed. Then I walked over and twisted a few flanges around. Nobody would be able to get into the center with anything short of a cutting torch.

Sitting was uncomfortable with the bruised hip, but I managed to ease into the console and spend an hour or so studying logic and wiring diagrams. Then I popped off an access plate and moved the microwaldo down the corridors of electronic thought. The intercom began buzzing incessantly, but I didn't let it interfere with my concentration.

Nearside is protected from meteorite strike or (far more likely) structural failure by a series of 128 bulkheads that, like the emergency wall here, can slide into place and isolate any area where there's a pressure drop. It's done automatically, of course, but can also be controlled from here.

What I did, in essence, was to tell each bulkhead that it was under repair and should not close under any circumstance. Then I moved the waldo over to the circuits that controlled the city's eight air locks. With some rather elegant microsurgery, I transferred control of all eight solely to the pressure switch I now hold in my left hand.

It is a negative-pressure button—a dead-man switch taken from a power saw. As long as I hold it down, the inner doors of the air locks will remain locked. If I let go, they will all iris open. The outer doors are already open, as are the ones that connect the air-lock chambers to the suiting-up rooms. No one will be able to make it to a space suit in time. Within 30 seconds, every corridor will be a vacuum. People behind airtight doors may choose between slow asphyxiation and explosive decompression.

My initial plan had been to wire the dead-man switch to my pulse, which would free my good hand and allow me to sleep. That will have to wait. The wiring completed, I turned on the intercom and announced that I would speak to the coordinator and no one else.

When I finally got to talk to him, I told him what I had done and invited him to verify it. That didn't take long. Then I presented my demands:

Surgery to replace the rest of my limbs, of course. The surgery would have to be done while I was conscious (a heartbeat dead-man switch could be subverted by a heart machine) and it would have to be done here, so that I could be assured that nobody had fooled with my circuit changes.

The doctors were called in, and they insisted that such profound surgery couldn't be done under local anesthetic. I knew they were lying, of course—amputation was a fairly routine procedure even before anesthetics were invented. Yes, but I would faint, they said. I told them that I would not, and at any rate, I was willing to take the chance, and no one else had any choice in the matter.

(I have not yet mentioned that the totality of my plan involves replacing all of my internal organs as well as all of the limbs—or at least those organs whose failure could cause untimely death. I will be a true cyborg then, a human brain in an "artificial" body, with the prospect of thousands of years of life. With a few decades—or centuries!—of research, I could even do something about the brain's shortcomings. I would wind up interfaced to EarthNet, with all of human knowledge at my disposal and with my faculties for logic and memory no longer fettered by the slow pace of electrochemical synapse.)

A psychiatrist, talking from Earth, tried to convince me of the error of my ways. He said that the dreadful trauma had "obviously" unhinged me, and the cyborg augmentation, far from effecting a cure, had made my mental derangement worse. He demonstrated, at least to his own satisfaction, that my behavior followed some classical pattern of madness. All this had been taken into consideration, he said, and if I were to give myself up, I would be forgiven my crimes and manumitted into the loving arms of the psychiatric establishment.

I did take time to explain the fundamental errors in his way of thinking. He felt that I had literally lost my identity by losing my face and genitalia and that I was at bottom a "good" person whose essential humanity had been perverted by physical and existential estrangement. Wrong. By his terms, what I actually *am* is an "evil" person whose true nature was revealed to him by the lucky accident that released him from existential propinquity with the common herd.

And evil is the accurate word, not maladjusted or amoral or even criminal. I am as evil by human standards as a human is evil by the standards of an animal raised for food, and the analogy is accurate. I will sacrifice humans not only for my survival but for comfort, curiosity or entertainment. I will allow to live anyone who doesn't bother me and reward generously those who help.

Now they have only 40 minutes. They know I am

(*End of recording.*)

EXCERPT FROM SUMMARY REPORT
1 OCTOBER 2058

I am Dr. Henry Janovski, head of the surgical team that worked on the ill-fated cyborg augmentation of Dr. Wilson Cheetham.

We were fortunate that Dr. Cheetham's insanity did interfere with his normally painstaking, precise nature. If he had spent more time in preparation, I have no doubt that he would have put us in a very difficult fix.

He should have realized that the protecting wall that shut him off from the rest of Nearside was made of steel, an excellent conductor of electricity. If he had insulated himself behind a good dielectric, he could have escaped his fate.

Cheetham's waldo was a marvelous instrument, but basically it was only a pseudo-intelligent servomechanism that obeyed well-defined radio-frequency commands. All we had to do was override the signals that were coming from his own nervous system.

We hooked a powerful amplifier up to the steel wall, making it, in effect, a huge radio transmitter. To generate the signal we wanted amplified, I had a technician put on a waldo sleeve that was holding a box similar to Cheetham's dead-man switch. We wired the hand closed, turned up the power and had the technician strike himself on the chin as hard as he could.

The technician struck himself so hard that he blacked out for a few seconds. Cheetham's resonant action, perhaps 100 times more powerful, drove the bones of his chin up through the top of his skull.

Fortunately, the expensive arm itself was not damaged. It is not evil or insane by itself, of course, as I shall prove.

The experiments will continue, though of course we will be more selective as to subjects. It seems obvious, in retrospect, that we should not use as subjects people who have gone through the kind of trauma that Cheetham suffered. We must use willing volunteers—such as myself.

I am not young, and weakness and an occasional tremor in my hands limit the amount of surgery I can do—much less than my knowledge would allow or my nature desire. My failing left arm I shall have replaced with Cheetham's mechanical marvel, and I will go through training similar to his—but for the good of humanity, not for ill.

What miracles I will perform with the knife!

CHET
WILLIAMSON

SEN YEN BABBO &
THE HEAVENLY HOST

August 1987

A little history here: During the 1980s, *Playboy* was much beleaguered by factions of the increasingly noisy and censorious religious right, which at that time quite untruthfully called itself the Moral Majority. Then, in short order, two of the most pietistic "televangelist" leaders of the right were exposed for sexual misdemeanors and for fraudulent swindling of the faithful. This story is, in part, a satiric reaction to that era and those events. But it stands very well on its own; the juxtaposition of two of the weirder staples of American televised entertainment still holds. Chet Williamson, born in 1948 in Pennsylvania, where he still lives, has written plays, mysteries and a number of well-regarded horror novels, but not much science fiction. This artful near-future take on cybernetics and society indicates that the field would welcome him.

I USED TO TELL my students at the seminary that an evangelical wrestling match was a morality play for our time. Gone were the days of politically ideological wrestling, of grunting Iranian tag teams and fat, sweating pseudo sheiks. Now saints and sinners grappled with each other on a stage of sin and redemption, the struggle between good and evil so clearly delineated that even the most obtuse spectator could comprehend and shout, "Hallelujah!" We could now—thank you, Jesus—see the power, not of a man or even a country, but of the Lord. God was not only good, He was bigger and better than ever.

Unfortunately, He also cursed me with a weakness for libidinous and willing coeds, a weakness that eventually cost me my professorship at the seminary.

It was therefore with a joyful heart that I received a com-call from the Reverend Donald Devout of Denver, a man whose outrageous piety was equaled only by his love of alliteration. "Harry, boy, how *are* you?" His down-home accent was so thick Moses couldn't have parted it, even though he was from Philadelphia, same as me. "Understand you got some problems at the seminary."

It was the first I had heard from Don since we'd been roommates at Good News of the Airwaves Bible College. In the intervening years, he had become the king of evangelical wrestling and had grown reputedly wealthy and definitely famous in the process. "How did you know I'd been fired?" I asked him.

"How did *Daniel* know the dreams of *Nebuchadnezzar? A Vision* came to me in which you dipped into a tender virgin's inner *temple!*"

I was irked. "For heaven's sake, Don, she was twenty-two if she was a—"

"*Blasphemy, too?*" he bellowed so loudly my ear hurt. "But Jesus forgives. So do I. Ever think about the wrestling ministry, Harry? It's a great way to serve the Lord." He was finally speaking without italics. "Your plight has reached my ears just as I have lost one of the Lord's servants. It is a sign."

To make a long sermon short, Don offered me the job of villain manager.

Evangelical wrestling, of course, required villainous instruments of Satan, and villains required managers. The managers were to find appropriately ugly baddies and train and outfit them. Reverend Don, fortunately, paid for the cyberprosthetics.

Cyberprossing was what really made evangelical wrestling succeed. The public never would have stood for it in old-time pro wrestling. The outcry had been bad enough when the old-time wrestlers cut themselves with hidden razor blades. So can you imagine the clamor at seeing hands ripped off, ragged stumps pumping blood (oh, yes, human—Reverend Don also owned a medical center) all over the first few rows? Washed in the blood of the Lamb, indeed.

But evangelical wrestling got away with it. Its popularity was so strong that for a public official to condemn it would be suicidal. Literally. The fans were fans in the worst way—fanatics. And it was a pack of those fanatics who unknowingly made an opening for me.

Sinning Sam Silverstein, who not only managed Pilate the Proud and Horrible Herod but was also a Jew, had been savaged by an angry mob outside the stage door. It seems that Herod and Pilate had unwisely roughed up David and Jonathan in a tag-team match before they had allowed themselves to be battered into submission by David's harp, and the crowd took it out on poor Sam, who was pronounced D.O.A. at Denver General. Bad luck for Sam, good luck for me. Reverend Don gave me a week to find a wrestler. "The uglier and meaner and the bigger enemy of *Christ* the better!" he told me, promising to banklink money for expenses.

I found my man easily enough, a 40ish black brother named Mustafa who was ugly enough and mean enough but depressingly neutral toward Christ. We flew to Denver, where Reverend Don met us. Since our seminary days, he had become a huge, hearty man with a crown of hair like a shellacked air bag. Once in his limo, he wasted no time in telling Mustafa and me what the next few weeks would hold.

"You," he said unto me, "are now Harry the *Heretic,* manager of *Mammon,* and *you,*" he said unto Mustafa, "are *Asphodel,* the Ebony *Demon!*" Then he smiled broadly and generously. "Now, young man, whom the *Lord* hath seen fit to deliver unto me, which hand would you prefer to have replaced—the right or the left?"

Such was my introduction to evangelical wrestling. Mustafa, who required a minimal amount of persuasion and much less money than I would have asked for, chose to have his left hand replaced by a cyberprosthetic one. It was, admittedly, an extraordinary piece of craftsmanship. The technology was so far beyond the myoelectric limbs of the Eighties that it made their owners look like Captain Hook in comparison. Instead of operating through muscle movement, a cyberpros limb is controlled through brain waves whizzing through a micromini implanted beneath the rib cage. Mustafa's new hand, fitted firmly into the slot installed between ulna and radius, did everything a real hand could do, and with extra strength. It was a shame that he would have only the one match in which to show it off publicly.

That Saturday night, we were both extremely nervous as we stood in the ramp waiting to make our entrance. It was nearly eight, and soon Mustafa and I would be on TBS world-wide, seen by tens of millions of people, a significant number of them rabid Bornies howling for Mustafa's blood. Everything was ready. The redpaks and the raw liver had been tucked into the phony wrist, and my man's face had been painted by Reverend Don's make-up artist, though I thought he looked more like a little-theater Mikado than like a demon.

At last I heard Reverend Don introduce me, painting me as one of the great sinners of our age, a man hurled out of the seminary for teaching not only free love and communism but also demonology and photographic techniques in child pornography. The more Reverend Don talked, the more the crowd shrieked out their hatred for me. But his diatribe against me was nothing compared with the number he did on poor Mustafa. There was nothing racially oriented, since Reverend Don had his share of black followers; but when he was finished, there couldn't have been a soul in that arena who believed that Mustafa was anything less than the vilest, most depraved demon of the pit.

For all their hatred, they were well behaved when Mustafa and I entered the arena. They shouted and threw things at us, but nothing heavier than a pair of binoculars. The ring was blazing with light, and high on the eastern wall hung a video screen that displayed a compugenerated Jacob wrestling with the Angel, the same footage that began and ended each show. We climbed through the red-velvet ropes, and then Reverend Don introduced "*Solomon* the Slammer! The Wisest Wrestler beneath the *Heavens!*" Solomon came on, handsome, bearded, golden-robed, surrounded by modestly dressed handmaidens.

The match began, and in a brief time Solomon was slamming the Devil out of poor Mustafa, or Asphodel, as I tried to think of him. The fatal moment at last came to pass, and Solomon grasped the left hand, wrenched and stood up with a cry of godly triumph, holding the hand high above his head, the myriad circuits making the fingers flex and twitch as though still connected to the screaming demon writhing on the floor. Mustafa seemed thoroughly possessed by the spirit of the thing, flailing his arm so that the geyser of blood doused a woman in the front row who had been calling him a "nigger Devil" throughout the match.

Finally, the redpak ran dry and the implanted sensors shut off the pump, the chunks of liver hiding the plastic and metal that formed Mustafa's wrist. His struggle subsided and medicos rushed into the ring with a stretcher, tossed Mustafa onto it and whisked him away before anyone could see that he was still breathing. I followed, shaking my head and making in the air what I thought might be interpreted as arcane signs. I was booed, I was spat upon, but I was not hit. At least not hard.

For his pains, Mustafa received five figures, a ticket back East and the cyberpros hand, a $50,000 consolation prize with which he could win bar bets until the day he died.

As for me, my remuneration was sufficient but not extravagant. Reverend Don kept the big bucks, and I learned as the months went by that charity was one of the areas in which the reverend could have more closely emulated the Master.

The money, you see, is not in the baddies but in the good guys. They're the ones, always angelically handsome (as though goodness had something to do with looks), who get the commercials, the product endorsements, the workout vids, the guest spots on *The 700 Club*. *My* boys got used and abused and tossed back into the anonymity from whence they came, and I spent my days hanging around gyms looking for more canonical fodder. My hopes of managing a hero were nil, because all of them were already managed by—you foretold it—the Reverend of the Ring his divine self. And Don Devout liked it that way.

Weeks went by, and I saw Mary the Virgin trash my gal, the Whore of Babylon; watched David smash my seven-foot-tall Goliath; beheld Moses the Mighty mash my gilded Golden Calf, ripping off his implanted horns and piercing each of his four liquid-hydrogen stomachs with a startling blast of hell-fire. What could a Golden Calf endorse? And a dead one at that? But seeing the calf get sautéed made me think about other livestock, and soon the idea came to me for a hero of my very own.

"Samson," I told Reverend Don after the match that night, while I waited for the angry mob that wanted to kill me to disperse.

He raised an eyebrow that closely resembled a woolly-bear caterpillar. "And a horde of Philistines?" he inquired.

"*One* Philistine. Phil the Philistine."

"Phil the *Fornicating* Philistine!" he amended.

I nodded graciously. "Whatever. But the gimmick is that instead of beating him with the jawbone of an ass, Samson rips off the *Philistine*'s jawbone."

"His . . . jawbone?" Reverend Don's wide and watery eyes glittered, and he stroked his blocky and clean-shaven chin. "His jawbone," he repeated thoughtfully. "I'll have to ask for divine guidance on that one. And find out if cyberpros can rig it up." He shook his head. "*Jawbone*. Sometimes, Harry, in spite of all your sins, I think the *Lord* touches you with *divine* inspiration!"

Maybe so, but the Reverend Don didn't touch me with increased funding after he used my idea. *He* managed Samson, and yours truly found the slob to play Phil the Philistine—an ex-jock jaw-cancer patient who was only too glad to trade a night in the ring for a state-of-the-art job of reconstructive cybernetic surgery. Everyone made out like a bandit except Harry the Heretic.

So the months passed, months of scuffling and hustling, of being the lackey of Reverend Don and the nemesis of good, born-again, wrestling-loving Christians everywhere, months of disguises and subterfuge to avoid being lynched by those same good Bornies. It was a lifestyle that I feared would go on as long as I survived. But that was before Reverend Don found the Hammer of Christ and I found Sen Yen Babbo.

The Hammer, like Samson, was my idea. Reverend Don's imagination had never extended to using a cyberpros limb on a good guy, and when I made the suggestion, hoping against hope that he would let *me* be the one to find and manage the newest servant of Yahweh, his eyes lit up as quickly as my hopes dimmed. I could tell that he thought it was a great idea—an *inspired* idea—and that he would never entrust it to me.

I was right. He didn't. Within three days, he had found the Hammer in the guise of a wrestler at Colorado State. The kid was a senior and a glorious monster, with a face like a horny angel's. He was also a Bornie, all six feet eight inches and 300 pounds of him. Fifty pounds, however, were soon happily sacrificed for a cyberpros right arm, a perfect match for the left, natural one, right down to hair, moles and the tiniest pores. It slotted smoothly into the articular capsule, where it moved effortlessly and without the creaking noises that my own age-weary shoulders make.

At first, the Hammer was simple, trusting and enthusiastic. He didn't seem surprised to learn that the blood, sweat, toil and tears were all an act and didn't care, since the subterfuge was, in his words, "truly justified since it doth magnify the *Lord.*" He spoke in italics, too—the Reverend Don influence. The kid was so nice, in fact, that I was afraid he was going to blow his first match.

The crowd was getting dulled out, as my man, Bad Battlin' Beelzebub, wasn't supposed to give the Hammer the works until after the sixth commercial. Beelzebub was doing all right, roaring and cursing and slamming the Hammer with an occasional forearm to get out of the corners, but the kid didn't seem as if his heart was in it.

I stood at ringside, making sorcerous gestures, yelling to the kid that his mom sacrificed to Baal, trying to get him to show a little zip, all to no avail. But, as we were to learn, the kid needed no urging. He'd been setting us up—us and the whole booing crowd.

Finally it was time. Beelzebub made a move that was amazingly slick for a man of his girth and age and had the kid's right arm wrenched up behind his back, pressing the hand and wrist ever higher, until they touched the kid's neck. Not once did the kid's face display the pain that it would have caused anyone with a *real* right arm.

Now the crowd started to quiet down, so that all 10,000 of them heard the sharp and heart-stopping *crack* that the cyberpros arm made as it split away from the shoulder in a rush of blood and dangling meat.

The crowd gasped. Even *I* gasped. Beelzebub laughed in premature triumph and held the dripping arm above his head with both hands, shouting, "Satanas! Satanas!" which endeared him not at all to the shocked throng, who now started to buzz in a definitely menacing undercurrent, and I wondered if we had gone too far. After all, this had never happened before. Not Elijah nor Solomon nor Daniel nor any of the good guys had ever lost so much as a pinkie, and here we were ripping off an entire *arm*. I felt the blood leave my face as I looked around at all the dream-shattered Bornies apportioning their anger between me and Beelzebub, whose demoniac mirth had begun to be replaced by fear.

And then the Hammer of Christ made his move. Through all of Beelzebub's celebratory posturing, the Hammer had not winced nor cried aloud. He merely stood, his face stony, his shoulder reservoir pumping a steadily diminishing supply of blood onto the ring floor. Now he slowly turned and fixed Beelzebub with an icy glare.

I will never forget that moment—the feel of the flop sweat sticking my sorcerous robe to my flesh, the mixed smells of body odor, popcorn and spilled grape juice, the sound of 10,000 drawn breaths—and, most of all, the look of *deity* on that young, beautiful and human face.

In utter silence, the Hammer of Christ walked the few steps to his adversary and, with one swift move, ripped the cyberpros arm from his hairy hands, raised it over his head like a maul and brought it down on the head of Beelzebub, driving him to the floor of the ring as brutally as Charlton Heston smashed the Golden Calf in *The Ten Commandments*.

The crowd loved it. They yelled and screamed and stomped and cheered and stood up and threw their programs and popcorn boxes and hats and coats and Bibles in the air, then picked up what had come down on their heads and threw it up again. And all the time, the Hammer of Christ kept whomping that cyberpros arm—all 50 pounds of it—down upon the unconscious head and body of my boy Beelzebub, that fat, flabby, dumb 50-year-old widower who had just wanted to make enough money in this one night to move to Florida. It was wrong, all wrong. It had been planned, of course, for the Hammer to take the arm and strike down his opponent—but with a pulled blow. One blow—a fake one—not the deadly storm of them that the Hammer was raining down.

I couldn't do a thing. If the Hammer of Christ didn't lambaste me, the crowd would. I could only watch as the Hammer of Christ, the bastard whose sweet face had fooled all of us there in different ways, beat an ex-pug named Billy Petrossian to death while thousands cheered.

At last he stopped, held up the arm for all to see and pressed it back to his shoulder, guiding it skillfully in a move he had rehearsed for weeks, slotting it so that all those little circuits joined, all the little brain waves zipped and zapped and took that dead, ripped-off arm straight up over his head, where a false and bloody fist clenched in holy, inholistic victory.

The Hammer and Reverend Don found me sitting beside Petrossian's still form when they came into the dressing room ten minutes later. The medicos had left. They were fakes, of course, and death scared them. Reverend Don had a thin smile on his full face, like a little boy who's won a game by cheating but is happy he's won just the same. The Hammer looked ecstatic. "He's dead," I told them. "You killed him."

The Hammer shook his head. "I'm only His instrument. It was the Lord that brought down destruction."

"It was *you* that brought down the arm!"

"I was filled with His spirit."

I couldn't believe it. "It's a *game,* you moron! It's a fake, a show, a fraud! None of it's real; it's not *supposed* to be real!"

Reverend Don smiled, fully now. "We grieve along with you for the loss of our brother here, Harry, but you must remember he died in the service of Christ and is so ensured of a place among the saints."

"A place . . . you mean that's it?" I looked from one face to the other. "That's all there is? Billy Petrossian dies, no sweat? And the Hammer lives to kill another day?"

"The Hammer," Reverend Don intoned, "is the greatest blessing evangelical wrestling has ever seen. He will win more souls to Christ by showing the power of the *Lord* than any servant of Christ in this sorry century."

"But . . . you've got a *dead* man here!"

"Zealousness in defense of the true and good is no crime. The death of this man is a pity, true, and it shall not happen again"— he gave the Hammer a sidelong glance—"but the ministry of the Hammer of Christ must not be stopped by an unfortunate accident."

I grabbed Reverend Don and hustled him into the hallway, away from the Hammer. "Accident? That was no accident—that kid *loved* it. It wasn't necessary, not at all! He's a *killer,* Don!"

"Not with peace but with a *sword,*" Reverend Don reminded me.

I shook my head to try and understand. "You're going to wrestle this kid again? You're going to see he gets off?"

He shrugged. "An accident. One we can avoid in the future. I'll keep him under tighter control, and you find some foes of Christ with tougher skulls."

Reverend Don was serious, and he did what he said. There was an inquiry, but the Hammer was exonerated in full, wrestling being a "high risk" profession. It was not a surprising decision, as Reverend Don's influence reached high. I almost quit, but I didn't.

Instead, I did as Reverend Don had said and searched for hard skulls. I found them at the rate of one a week. It was easier, since they didn't have to undergo cyberprossing. Oh, sure, when they found out they had to wrestle the Hammer of Christ, some of them balked. But Reverend Don kept the Hammer in check, and none of my boys was hurt too badly, except for the one who caught a concussion when he didn't twist his head at the right moment.

Still, I could see that urge in the Hammer, and I feared he would go over that thin edge again. For all his self-professed piety, he was no Christian but a pagan gladiator, and what I had foolishly mistaken for deity in his face had been an angelically pure blood lust.

I came across Sen Yen Babbo in a dirty little gym in Pueblo that looked as if it had tried to be a health spa and failed. The free weights looked well used, while Nautilus machines rusted in the corners. There were no beautiful people there, just a bunch of aging fighters, a few flabby bodybuilders and some young Turks punishing punching bags. I saw no one with the physical oddities that Reverend Don thought made for good villains and was just about to leave when Sen Yen Babbo walked in.

He was the oldest man there, probably in his mid-50s. He was wearing a Gold's Gym T-shirt with so many holes that one saw more flesh than cotton, and that flesh was unpleasant to behold. It was yellow in color, made a muddy ocher by the matted covering of gray-brown body hair that sprouted through the holes in the T-shirt. His bald head looked as though it were made of sponges slapped together with papier-mâché. The nose had been broken times beyond counting, and the ears belonged on a relish tray. He was short and bandy-legged, and his stomach hung several inches over the sagging waistband of his gym shorts. In short, he was a perfect match for the beautiful, godly, diabolical Hammer of Christ.

I walked over to where he'd begun bench pressing a bar with an absurdly large number of iron plates on it. "How you doing?" I asked him. He didn't respond. "That's sure a lot of weight," I observed. He still didn't answer. "My name's Harry," I tried again.

He dropped the bar bell into the supports and looked at me.

"Sen Yen Babbo," he said. I must have looked blank, for he went on immediately, "That's m' *name*."

Sen Yen Babbo turned out to be extremely talkative for a man who didn't talk well. He possessed a host of impediments, all of them acquired from his varied career. Thirty-plus years of prize fighting, professional wrestling and just plain roughhousing with his peers had shattered his jaw, scattered his teeth and cleft his palate until he was left with the barely distinguishable slur of a stroke victim. Still, before long, I was able to make out most of the words and found him astute enough to comprehend the merits of my offer.

"Wan' me ta rassle this *Hammer* guy."

I nodded. "He's not very nice. He'll hit you hard. You have a tough skull?"

He laughed, an unpleasant, gargling sound. "Touch 't," he grounted, lowering his head so that the bald pate faced me like a small boulder. I felt, delicately, and found a slightly yielding top layer and, beneath, a hard, calcified *something*. "Scar tisha," he said proudly. "'F ya can't bus' it open, ya can't hur' me."

"Did anyone ever bust it open?"

"Harh!"

"Well, the Hammer might try."

"Leddim."

Sen Yen Babbo didn't seem averse to losing. He'd lost plenty of times when he was a pro wrestler back in the Eighties. "Think they ledda guy look like me win? Naah, I lose alla time, know howda lose good."

The agreement was made, and I took Sen Yen Babbo to see Reverend Don. The holy man loved Sen Yen Babbo, his face, his body, his manner, everything about him but his name. "Sen Yen Babbo? Nonsense, we'll call him the *Beast*, after the beast in the Book of Revelation."

"Sen Yen Babbo," answered Sen Yen Babbo.

"Pardon?" said Reverend Don.

"Sen Yen Babbo," answered Sen Yen Babbo again.

"I think," I tried to explain, "that he wants to use the name Sen Yen Babbo."

Sen Yen Babbo nodded. "Sen Yen Babbo," he repeated.

"But . . . but it doesn't mean anything; what does it mean?"

"Means *me*," clarified Sen Yen Babbo.

The *VideoGuide* listed the match as the Hammer of Christ *vs.* Sen Yen Babbo.

The night of the match, we went over the procedures one more time. Sen Yen Babbo had practiced with the Hammer all week, and I thought he was ready. Still, there was a lack of precision about him that made me edgy. I wanted him to remember everything that was supposed to happen, because I didn't want him hurt.

"After the third commercial break," I told him again, "is when you go for the right arm. It'll come off easy. I don't know when he'll grab it back from you—he milks that like crazy. But when he does, be ready for the blow and go with it. Don't let him hit you head on, because if he sees he's really hurt you, well, something might snap and he might really bang you up."

Sen Yen Babbo looked at me oddly. "Wha' you so worried about me for, huh?"

"I just don't want anybody to get hurt."

"This Hammer guy, he killed that Petrossian, din' he?" I nodded. "Don' you worry about me. That Petrossian, he had a soft head." When he grinned at me, I was glad he liked me. "You good guy. Don' vorry. Things turn out aw right."

Surprisingly enough, Sen Yen Babbo vas right.

The evening began auspiciously enough. The mob hurled imprecations and a number of popcorn boxes at Sen Yen Babbo and myself as we entered the arena. I was accustomed to it, and it didn't bother him. As he climbed into the ring, a juice bottle bounced off his head, but he gave no indication of its presence. Seeing that made me feel better. He strode immediately to the middle of the ring and twirled about with a body not built for twirling. The long red robe wafted outward like a film of blood, and he roared a guttural challenge to the world at large. Then he spat at the audience.

That was a new one on me and a new one on the audience as well. To be spat upon was bad enough, but to be spat upon by ancient, evil, repulsive Sen Yen Babbo was something else entirely. The first three rows stood en masse and moved toward the ring in a wave. But Sen Yen Babbo swirled around again and roared and stilled the waters as quickly as Jesus ever had. Then he laughed and shouted as clearly as he could, "Bring me the *Christian*."

I was terrified. My previous wrestlers had bullied and blustered but had never spat, and no one had ever called for a *Christian* in that blasphemous tone of voice. It was fast becoming a nasty crowd.

As loudly as they had reviled Sen Yen Babbo, all the more loudly did they cheer the Hammer of Christ as he entered the arena. "Ham-*mer*, Ham-*mer*, Ham-*mer!*" rang the chant as the Scourge of God vaulted over the ropes and landed with a deft bounce. Here was a man who disdained twirling. He simply strode to the center of the ring, smiled a closed-mouth smile and raised his cyberpros right arm, fist clenched, showing the happy people the Hammer of the Hammer.

They cheered and continued to cheer, and I whispered to Sen Yen Babbo, "Third commercial."

He nodded. "Thir' commersh'."

The ring announcements, alternately laudatory and condemnatory, were made by Reverend Don, who looked crisp and clean and holy in a white-silk suit. The Hammer preened, Sen Yen Babbo snarled and the bell rang.

It was a good show. The Hammer leaped and pirouetted and turned, punishing and being punished with grace and style. And Sen Yen Babbo was magnificent in his own right, biting and clawing and gouging with such artistry that had I not known it was all spurious, I would have been easily convinced that real mayhem was occurring. And every chance I got, I whispered *sotto voce* to Sen Yen Babbo, "Third commercial," and he would nod and mumble, "Thir' commersh'."

At last the time had come. Reverend Don had plugged the latest evangelicalwrestling viddiscs for the third time, and we were back to meat slapping meat. Now Sen Yen Babbo broke the Hammer's full nelson, spun, grasped the Hammer of Christ by the wrist and wrenched with all his strength. The arm went taut, snapped and Sen Yen Babbo wrenched again, as though trying to tear that last bit of gristle that tenaciously holds the drumstick to the rest of the Thanksgiving turkey.

The drumstick snapped off in a rush of blood, and Sen Yen Babbo held over his head, like some grisly trophy, the left arm of the Hammer of Christ.

Left arm?

Whoops.

I suppose I had thought everything was all right because the Hammer had not screamed. He had never screamed before, since screaming was not consistent with his miraculous aura. But the reason he didn't scream now was that he had fainted dead away from pain and shock. Reverend Don walked, trembling, to where the Hammer lay, oblivious to the pumping blood that was staining his ice-cream suit. Sen Yen Babbo still stood, the arm above his head, apparently waiting to have it snatched from his hand and get conked on the head with it. All this time, the crowd was deathly still.

At last Sen Yen Babbo turned impatiently and saw Reverend Don bending over the Hammer, saw how pale the Hammer was where he wasn't splashed with red and saw how pale Reverend Don was as well. It was enough to give Sen Yen Babbo pause and make him examine the grisly relic he held. A cursory glance at the strips of muscle and ligament dangling from the shoulder joint told him something was awry, and he then did the only thing that he apparently felt he could do under the circumstances. Clinging desperately to the now-aborted scenario, he attempted to knock himself unconscious with the arm, since it didn't look as though the Hammer of Christ was going to be able to in the near future.

The attempt was unsuccessful. The arm bent limply at the elbow and flopped over Sen Yen Babbo's shoulder. He dropped it and looked at me in dismay.

I could give him no consolation, for I knew that we were doomed. The crowd's stunned silence had ceased, and a low, turbulent roar was slowly growing. In another moment they would be upon us, destroying both the slayer and the manager who had been responsible for the destruction of their hero. Even now they were rising, shoulders hunched forward, eyes burning with the zealous fire of divine retribution. I started to pray.

And the prayer was answered. A voice spoke out that could be heard in each corner of the arena—

"*Six-six-six!*"

At first I thought it was God but quickly realized it was Reverend Don on his mike.

"The mark of the *beast!* Here on his *head!* Hidden in his *hair!* The sign of the *Antichrist!*"

I realized several things at once then. I realized that it was the Hammer's head Reverend Don was referring to and not Sen Yen Babbo's, since Sen Yen Babbo had no hair; and I realized, too, that no wrestler for God, in the six years in which evangelical wrestling flourished, had ever lost a match. And Reverend Don did not intend a wrestler for God to start now. If a wrestler for God lost, then he could be no wrestler for God. Reverend Don was a man who knew how to cut his losses.

"The Hammer of *Christ? No,* my friends—rather the Hammer of the *Antichrist!*" He called to the medicos. "Remove this *pestilence* from our sight!" They rushed into the ring, threw the unconscious and possibly dead Hammer onto the stretcher and dashed out.

"And *here,*" Reverend Don went on, pointing to Sen Yen Babbo, "is God's *instrument!* As the *Lord Jesus* converted *Saul* the *sinner* to *Paul* the *saint,* so he has converted *this* sinner to his *truth!* No longer shall this man be Sen Yen Babbo, but he shall be *Paul* the *Convert!* And as such he shall battle for the *Lord* and smite the heads of the *sinners!*" I almost expected Sen Yen Babbo to decline the name change again, but he seemed to realize the gravity of the situation and accepted the new appellation with good grace.

Then I came to my last realization—that if I did not join in quickly, the train that was bound for glory and riches would leave without me.

"*Hallelujah!*" I cried in letters as italic as I could squeeze from a fear-parched throat, leaping into the ring and embracing first Sen Yen Babbo and a confused Reverend Don, whose microphone I took easily. "I have seen the *light* at *last!* Through my unwitting guidance has this man *Paul* defeated a minion of *Satan!*"

"*M' manager!*" Sen Yen Babbo grunted into the mike.

"Hallelujah! The manager of *Paul* the *Convert!* Born again—as are we *all*—to manage this man against the forces of *evil!* To join hands with *Reverend Don* and rid this good world of the *sin* and the *vermin* that corrupt it!"

I grinned at the man in the strawberry-ice-cream suit, and handed him back his mike. "Right, Don?" I asked him, and he nodded dully as the crowd screamed their delight at the saving of the souls of Sen Yen Babbo and Harry the Heretic.

413

There's not much else to tell. The Hammer lived, which was more than he deserved, and sued Reverend Don when he wouldn't buy him a second cyberpros arm. The Hammer lost, of course. You just don't sue Reverend Don in Colorado. Paul the Convert became, as everyone knows, the most beloved wrestler since Hulk Hogan, and I've managed him ever since, along with the rest of the Apostles, the hottest tag team in the business. They're a good bunch, with a lot less violence and a lot more showmanship, which seems to be the direction in which evangelical wrestling is going.

One more thing. I found out from one of the Apostles that Sen Yen Babbo was a good friend of Billy Petrossian, the pug the Hammer killed in his first match. Maybe, despite the childish ignorance he conveys on *The 700 Club*, Sen Yen Babbo isn't quite as punchy as I gave him credit for being.

The *Lord* works in mysterious ways His blunders to perform.

LUCIUS SHEPARD

FIRE ZONE EMERALD

February 1988

Lucius Shepard's first novel, *Green Eyes,* won him the John D. Campbell Award for Best New Writer. Had the book not appeared in 1984, the year that William Gibson swept the other awards with the celebrated *Neuromancer,* it might have done even better. Born in Lynchburg, Virginia in 1947, and raised in Florida, Shepard's background is in rock and roll; he has published a good deal of poetry which reads as considerably more literary than most rock lyrics. *Life During Wartime,* which takes place in a setting not unlike that of "Fire Zone Emerald," was his second novel, and this was followed by *Kalimantan* (1990) and *The Golden* (1995), an ornate and extraordinary vampire novel. His novella "R & R" won a Nebula and formed the centerpiece of *The Jaguar Hunters* which won the World Fantasy

Award. His second collection, *The Ends of the Earth* picked it up again, while the novella "Barnacle Bill, the Spacer" won a Hugo.

Again and again Shepard's stories return to the Latin American jungle to explore the horrifying, surreal wars of the near future (many were written during the period when Ronald Reagan periodically threatened to engage the U.S. in war with Nicaragua). Drugs, futuristic technology, machismo, battle fatigue, and an extreme war-induced disorientation are common themes in his stories, some of which venture boldly into Latin-American magic realism territory. This one just skirts it.

AINT IT WEIRD, soldier boy?" said the voice in Quinn's ear. "There you are, strollin' along in that little ol' green suit of armor, feelin' all cool and killproof . . . and wham! You're down and hurtin' bad. Gotta admit, though, them suits do a job. Can't recall nobody steppin' onna mine and comin' through it as good as you."

Quinn shook his head to clear the cobwebs. His helmet rattled, which was not good news. He doubted that any of the connections to the computer in his backpack were still intact. But at least he could move his legs, and that was very good news, indeed. The guy talking had a crazed lilt to his voice, and Quinn thought it would be best to take cover. He tried the computer; nothing worked except for map holography. The visor display showed him to be a blinking red dot in the midst of a contoured green glow: 11 miles inside Guatemala from its border with Belize, in the heart of the Peten rain forest, on the eastern edge of Fire Zone Emerald.

"Y' hear me, soldier boy?"

Quinn sat up, wincing as pain shot through his legs. He felt no fear, no panic. Although he had just turned 21, this was his second tour in Guatemala, and he was accustomed to being in tight spots. Besides, there were a lot worse places he might have been stranded. Up until two years before, Emerald had been a staging area for Cuban and guerrilla troops; but following the construction of a string of Allied artillery bases to the west, the enemy had moved their encampments north and—except for recon patrols such as Quinn's—the fire zone had been abandoned.

"No point in playin' possum, man. Me and the boys'll be there in ten, fifteen minutes, and you gonna have to talk to us then."

Ten minutes. Shit! Maybe, Quinn thought, if he talked to the guy, that would slow him down. "Who are you people?" he asked.

"Name's Mathis. Special Forces, formerly attached to the First Infantry." A chuckle. "But you might say we seen the light and opted outa the Service. How 'bout you, man? You gotta name?"

"Quinn. Edward Quinn." He flipped up his visor; heat boiled into the combat suit, overwhelming the cooling system. The suit was scorched and shredded from the knees down; plastic armor glinted in the rips. He looked around for his gun. The cable that had connected it to the computer had been severed, probably by shrapnel from the mine, and the gun was not to be seen. "You run across the rest of my patrol?"

A static-filled silence. "'Fraid I got bad tidin's, Quinn Edward. 'Pears like guerrillas took out your buddies."

Despite the interference, Quinn heard the lie in the voice. He scoped out the terrain, saw that he was sitting in a cathedrallike glade: vaults of leaves pillared by the tapering trunks of ceibas and giant figs. The ground was carpeted with ferns; a thick green shade seemed to well up from the tips of the fronds. Here and there, shafts of golden light penetrated the canopy, and these were so complexly figured with dust motes that they appeared to contain flaws and fracture planes, like artifacts of crystal snapped off in mid-air. On three sides, the glade gave out into dense jungle; but to the east lay a body of murky green water, with a forested island standing about 100 feet out. If he could find his gun, the island might be defensible. Then a few days' rest and he'd be ready for a hike.

"Them boys wasn't no friends of yours," said Mathis. "You hit that mine and they let you lie like meat on the street."

That much Quinn believed. The others had been too wasted on the martial-arts ampules to be trustworthy. Chances were, they simply hadn't wanted the hassle of carrying him.

"They deserved what they got," Mathis went on. "But you, now . . . boy with your luck. Might just be a place for you in the light."

"What's that mean?" Quinn fumbled a dispenser from his hip pouch and ejected two ampules—a pair of silver bullets—into his palm. Two, he figured, should get him walking.

"The light's holy here, man. You sit under them beams shinin' through the canopy, let 'em soak into you, and they'll stir the truth from your mind." Mathis said all this in dead earnest, and Quinn, unable to mask his amusement, said, "Oh, yeah?"

"You remind me of my ol' lieutenant," said Mathis. "Man used to tell me I's crazy, and I'd say to him, 'I ain't ordinary crazy, sir. I'm crazy gone to Jesus.' And I'd 'splain to him what I knew from the light, that we's s'posed to build the kingdom here. Place where a man could live pure. No machines, no pollution." He grunted as if tickled by something. "That's how you be livin' if you can cut it. You gonna learn to hunt with knives, track tapirs by the smell. Hear what weather's comin' by listenin' to the cry of a bird."

"How 'bout the lieutenant?" Quinn asked. "He learn all that?"

"Y' know how it is with lieutenants, man. Sometimes they just don't work out."

Quinn popped an ampule under his nose and inhaled. Waited for the drugs to kick in. The ampules were the Army's way of ensuring that the high incidence of poor battlefield performance during the Vietnam war would not be repeated: Each contained a mist of pseudo endorphins and RNA derivatives that elevated the user's determination and physical potentials to heroic levels for 30 minutes or thereabouts. But Quinn preferred not to rely on them, because of their destructive side effects. Printed on the dispenser was a warning against abuse, one that Mathis—judging by his rap—had ignored. Quinn had heard similar raps from guys whose personalities had been eroded, replaced in part by the generic mystic-warrior personality supplied by the drugs.

"'Course," said Mathis, breaking the silence, "it ain't only the light. It's the queen. She's the one with the light."

"The queen?" Quinn's senses had sharpened. He could see the spidery shapes of monkeys high in the canopy and could hear a hundred new sounds. He spotted the green-plastic stock of his gun protruding from beneath a fern not 20 feet away; he came to his feet, refusing to admit his pain, and went over to it. Both upper and lower barrels were plugged with dirt.

"'Member them Cuban 'speriments where they was linkin' up animals and psychics with computer implants? Usin' 'em for spies?"

"That was just bullshit!" Quinn set off toward the water. He felt disdain for Mathis and recognized that to be a sign of too many ampules.

"It ain't no bullshit. The queen was one of them psychics. She's linked up with this little ol' tiger cat—what the Indians call a *tigrillo*. We ain't never seen her, but we seen the cat. And once we got tuned to her, we could feel her mind workin' on us. But at first, she can slip them thoughts inside your head without you ever knowin'. Twist you round her finger, she can."

"If she's that powerful," said Quinn, smug with the force of his superior logic, "then why's she hidin' from you?"

"She ain't hidin'. We gotta prove ourselves to her. Keep the jungle pure, free of evildoers. Then she'll come to us."

Quinn popped the second ampule. "Evildoers? Like my patrol, huh? That why you wasted my patrol?"

"Whoo-ee!" said Mathis after a pause. "I can't slide nothin' by you, can I, Quinn Edward?"

Quinn's laughter was rich and nutsy: a two-ampule laugh. "Naw," he said, mocking Mathis' corn-pone accent. "Don't reckon you can." He flipped down his visor and waded into the water, barely conscious of the pain in his legs.

"Your buddies wasn't shit for soldiers," said Mathis. "Good thing they come along, though. We was runnin' low on ampules." He made a frustrated noise. "Hey, man. This armor ain't nothin' like the old gear . . . all this computer bullshit. I can't get nothin' crankin' 'cept the radio. Tell me how you work these here guns."

"Just aim and pull." Quinn was waist-deep in water, perhaps a quarter of the way to the island, which from that perspective— with its three towering vine-enlaced trees—looked like the over- grown hulk of a sailing ship anchored in a placid stretch of jade.

"Don't kid a kidder," said Mathis. "I tried that."

"You'll figure it out," Quinn said. "Smart peckerwood like you."

"Man, you gotta attitude problem, don'tcha? But I 'spect the queen'll straighten you out."

"Right! The invisible woman!"

"You'll see her soon enough, man. Ain't gonna be too long 'fore she comes to me."

"To *you?*" Quinn snickered. "That mean you're the king?"

"Maybe." Mathis pitched his voice low and menacing. "Don't go thinkin' I'm just country pie, Quinn Edward. I been up here most of two years, and I got this place down. I can tell when a fly takes a shit! Far as you concerned, I'm lord of the fuckin' jungle."

Quinn bit back a sarcastic response. He should be suckering this guy, determining his strength. Given that Mathis had been on recon prior to deserting, he'd probably started with around 15 men. "You guys taken many casualties?" he asked after slogging another few steps.

"Why you wanna know that? You a man with a plan? Listen up, Quinn Edward. If you figgerin' on takin' us out, 'member them fancy guns didn't help your buddies, and they ain't gonna help you. Even if you could take us out, you'd still have to deal with the queen. Just 'cause she lives out on the island don't mean she ain't keepin' her eye on the shore. You might not believe it, man, but right now, right this second, she's all round you."

"What island?" The trees ahead suddenly seemed haunted-looking.

"Little island out there on the lake. You can see it if you lift your head."

"Can't move my head," said Quinn. "My neck's fucked up."

"Well, you gonna see it soon enough. And once you healed, you take my advice and stay the hell off it. The queen don't look kindly on trespassers."

On reaching the island, Quinn located a firing position from which he could survey the shore: a weedy patch behind a fallen tree trunk hemmed in by bushes. If Mathis was as expert in jungle survival as he claimed, he'd have no trouble discovering where Quinn had gone; and there was no way to tell how strong an influence his imaginary queen exerted, no way to be sure whether the restriction against trespassing had the severity of a taboo or was merely something frowned on. Not wanting to take chances, Quinn spent a frantic few minutes cleaning the lower barrel of his gun, which fired miniature fragmentation grenades.

"Now where'd you get to, Quinn Edward?" said Mathis with mock concern. "Where *did* you get to?"

Quinn scanned the shore. Dark avenues led away between the trees, and as he stared along them, his nerves were keyed by every twitching leaf, every shift of light and shadow. Clouds slid across the sun, muting its glare to a shimmering platinum gray; a palpable vibration underscored the stillness. He tried to think of something pleasant to make the waiting easier, but nothing pleasant occurred to him. He wetted his lips and swallowed. His cooling system set up a whine.

Movement at the margin of the jungle, a shadow resolving into a man wearing olive-drab fatigues and carrying a rifle with a skeleton stock—likely an old M-18. He waded into the lake, and as he closed on the island, Quinn trained his scope on him and saw that he had black shoulder-length hair framing a haggard face; a ragged beard bibbed his chest, and dangling from a thong below the beard was a triangular piece of mirror. Quinn held his fire, waiting for the rest to emerge. But no one else broke cover, and he realized Mathis was testing him, was willing to sacrifice a pawn to check out his weaponry.

"Keep back!" he shouted. But the man kept plodding forward, heaving against the drag of the water. Quinn marveled at the hold Mathis must have over him: He *had* to know he was going to die. Maybe he was too whacked out on ampules to give a shit, or maybe Mathis' queen somehow embodied the promise of a swell afterlife for those who died in battle. Quinn didn't want to kill him, but there was no choice, no point in delaying the inevitable.

He aimed, froze a moment at the sight of the man's fear-widened eyes; then squeezed the trigger.

The hiss of the round blended into the explosion, and the man vanished inside a fireball and geysering water. Monkeys screamed; birds wheeled up from the shore-line trees. A veil of oily smoke drifted across the lake, and within seconds a pair of legs floated to the surface, leaking red. Quinn felt queasy and sick at heart.

"Man, they doin' wonders with ordnance nowadays," said Mathis.

Infuriated, Quinn fired a spread of three rounds into the jungle.

"Not even close, Quinn Edward."

"You're a real regular-Army asshole, aren't you?" said Quinn. "Lettin' some poor fucker draw fire."

"You got me wrong, man! I sent that ol' boy out 'cause I loved him. He been with me almost four years, but his mind was goin', reflexes goin'. You done him a favor, Quinn Edward. Reduced his confusion to zero"—Mathis' tone waxed evangelic—"and let him shine forevermore!"

Quinn had a mental image of Mathis, bearded and haggard, like the guy he'd shot, but taller, rawboned: a gaunt rack of a man with rotting teeth and blown-away pupils. Being able to fit even an imaginary face to his target tuned his rage higher, and he fired again.

"Aw right, man!" Mathis' voice was burred with anger; the cadences of his speech built into a rant. "You want bang-bang, you got it. But you stay out there, the queen'll do the job for me. She don't like nobody creepin' round her in the dark. Makes her crazy. You go on, man! Stay there! She peel you down to meat and sauce, motherfucker!"

His laughter went high into a register that Quinn's speakers distorted, translating it as a hiccuping squeal, and he continued to rave. However, Quinn was no longer listening. His attention was fixed on the dead man's legs, spinning past on the current. A lace of blood eeled from the severed waist. The separate strands seemed to be spelling out characters in some Oriental script; but before Quinn could try to decipher them, they lost coherence and were whirled away by the jade-green medium into which—staring with fierce concentration, giddy with drugs and fatigue—he, too, felt he was dissolving.

At twilight, when streamers of mist unfurled across the water, Quinn stood down from his watch and went to find a secure place in which to pass the night: Considering Mathis' leeriness about his queen's nocturnal temper, he doubted there would be any trouble before morning. He beat his way through the brush and came to an enormous ceiba tree whose trunk split into two main branchings; the split formed a wide crotch that would support him comfortably. He popped an ampule to stave off pain, climbed up and settled himself.

Darkness fell; the mist closed in, blanketing moon and stars. Quinn stared out into pitch-black nothing, too exhausted to think, too buzzed to sleep. Finally, hoping to stimulate thought, he did another ampule. After it had taken effect, he could make out some of the surrounding foliage—vague scrolled shapes, each of which had its own special shine—and he could hear a thousand plops and rustles that blended into a scratchy percussion, its rhythms providing accents for a pulse that seemed to be coming up from the roots of the island. But there were no crunchings in the brush, no footsteps.

No sign of the queen.

What a strange fantasy, he thought, for Mathis to have created. He wondered how Mathis saw her. Blonde, with a ragged
Tarzan-movie skirt? A black woman with a necklace of bones? He
remembered driving down to see his old girlfriend at college and
being struck by a print hung on her dorm-room wall. It had
shown a night jungle, a tiger prowling through fleshy vegetation
and—off to the side—a mysterious-looking woman standing
naked in moon shadow. That would be his image of the queen. It
seemed to him that the woman's eyes had been glowing. . . . But
maybe he was remembering it wrong; maybe it had been the
tiger's eyes. He had liked the print, had peered at the artist's signature and tried to pronounce the name. "Roo-see-aw," he had said,
and his girl had given a haughty sniff and said, "Roo-so. It's Roo-
so." Her attitude had made clear what he had suspected: that he
had lost her. She had experienced a new world, one that had set
its hooks in her; she had outgrown their little North Dakota farming town, and she had outgrown him as well. What the war had
done to him was similar, only the world he had outgrown was a
much wider place: He'd learned that he just wasn't cut out for
peace and quiet anymore.

Frogs chirred, crickets sizzled, and he was reminded of the
hollow near his father's house where he used to go after chores
to be alone, to plan a life of spectacular adventures. Like the
island, it had been a diminutive jungle—secure, yet not insulated from the wild—and recognizing the kinship between the
two places caused him to relax. Soon he nodded out into a
dream, one in which he was 12 years old again, fiddling with the
busted tractor his father had given him to repair. He had never
been able to repair it, but in the dream, he worked a gruesome
miracle. Wherever he touched the metal, blood beaded on the
flaking rust; blood surged rich and dark through the fuel line;
and when he laid his hands on the corroded pistons, steam
seared forth and he saw that the rust had been transformed into
red meat, that his hands had left scorched prints. Then that
meat engine had shuddered to life and lumbered off across the
fields on wheels of black bone, plowing raw gashes in the earth,
sowing seeds that overnight grew into stalks yielding fruit that
exploded on contact with the air.

It was such an odd dream, forged from the materials of his childhood yet embodying an alien sensibility, that he came awake, possessed by the notion that it had been no dream but a sending. For an instant, he thought he saw a lithe shadow at the foot of the tree. The harder he stared at it, though, the less substantial it became, and he decided it must have been a hallucination. But after the shadow had melted away, a wave of languor washed over him, sweeping him down into unconsciousness, manifesting itself so suddenly, so irresistibly, that it seemed no less a sending than the dream.

At first light, Quinn popped an ampule and went to inspect the island, stepping cautiously through the gray mist that still merged jungle and water and sky, pushing through dripping thickets and spider webs diamonded with dew. He was certain Mathis would launch an attack today. Since he had survived a night with the queen, it might be concluded that she favored him, that he now posed a threat to Mathis' union with her—and Mathis wouldn't be able to tolerate that. The best course, Quinn figured, would be to rile Mathis up, to make him react out of anger and to take advantage of the situation.

The island proved to be about 120 feet long, perhaps a third of that across at the widest, and—except for a rocky point at the north end and a clearing some 30 feet south of the ceiba tree—was choked with vegetation. Vines hung in graceful loops like flourishes depended from illuminated letters; ferns clotted the narrow aisles between the bushes; epiphytes bloomed in the crooks of branches, punctuating the grayness with points of crimson and purple. The far side of the island was banked higher than a man could easily reach; but to be safe, Quinn mined the lowest sections with frags. In places where the brush was relatively sparse, he set flares headhigh, connecting them to trip wires that he rigged with vines. Then he walked back and forth among the traps, memorizing their locations.

By the time he had done, the sun had started to burn off the mist, creating pockets of clarity in the gray; and as he headed back to his firing position, it was then he saw the tiger cat crouched in the weeds, lapping at the water. It wasn't much bigger than a house cat, with the delicate build and wedge-shaped head of an Abyssinian, and fine black stripes patterning its tawny fur. Quinn had seen such animals before while on patrol, but the way this one looked, so bright and articulated in contrast to the dull vegetable greens, framed by the eddying mist, it seemed a gateway had been opened onto a more vital world, and he was for the moment too entranced by the sight to consider what it meant. The cat finished its drink, turned to Quinn and studied him; then it snarled, wheeled about and sprang off into the brush.

The instant it vanished, Quinn became troubled by a number of things. How he'd chosen the island as a fortress; how he'd gone straight to the best firing position; how he'd been anticipating Mathis. All this could be chalked up to common sense and good soldiering . . . yet he had been so assured, so definite. The assurance could be an effect of the ampules; but then Mathis had said that the queen could slip thoughts into your head without your knowing—until you became attuned to her, that is. Quinn tasted the flavors of his thoughts, searching for evidence of tampering. He knew he was being ridiculous, but panic flared in him nonetheless and he popped an ampule to pull himself together. OK, he told himself. Let's see what the hell's going on.

For the next half hour, he combed the island, prying into thickets, peering at treetops. He found no trace of the queen, nor did he spot the cat again. But if she could control his mind, she might be guiding him away from her traces. She might be following him, manipulating him like a puppet. He spun around, hoping to catch her unawares. Nothing. Only bushes threaded with mist, trembling in the breeze. He let out a cracked laugh. Christ, he was an idiot! Just because the cat lived on the island didn't mean the queen was real; in fact, the cat might be the core of Mathis' fantasy. It might have inhabited the lake shore, and when Mathis and his men had arrived, it had fled out here to be shut of them . . . or maybe even this thought had been slipped into his head. Quinn was amazed by the subtlety of the delusion, at the elusiveness with which it defied both validation and debunking.

Something crunched in the brush.

Convinced that the noise signaled an actual presence, he swung his gun to cover the bushes. His trigger finger tensed, but after a moment he relaxed. It was the isolation, the general weirdness, that was doing him in, not some bullshit mystery woman. His job was to kill Mathis, and he'd better get to it. And if the queen *were* real, well, then she did favor him and he might have help. He popped an ampule and laughed as it kicked in. Oh, yeah! With modern chemistry and the invisible woman on his side, he'd go through Mathis like a rat through cheese. Like fire through a slum. The drugs—or perhaps it was the pour of a mind more supple than his own—added a lyric coloration to his thoughts, and he saw himself moving with splendid athleticism into an exotic future wherein he killed the king and wed the shadow and ruled in hell forever.

Quinn was low on frags, so he sat down behind the fallen tree trunk and cleaned the upper barrel of his gun: It fired caseless .22-caliber ammunition. Set on automatic, it could chew a man in half; but, wanting to conserve bullets, he set it to fire single shots. When the sun had cleared the tree line, he began calling to Mathis on his radio. There was no response at first, but finally a gassed, irascible voice answered, saying, "Where the fuck you at, Quinn Edward?"

"The island." Quinn injected a wealth of good cheer into his next words. "Hey, you were right about the queen!"

"What you talkin' 'bout?"

"She's beautiful! Most beautiful woman I've ever seen."

"You seen her?" Mathis sounded anxious. "Bullshit!"

Quinn thought about the Rousseau print. "She got dark, satiny skin and black hair down to her ass. And the whites of her eyes, it looks like they're glowin', they're so bright. And her tits, man. They ain't too big, but the way they wobble around"—he let out a lewd cackle—"it makes you wanna get down and frolic with them puppies."

"Bullshit!" Mathis repeated, his voice tight.

"Uh-uh," said Quinn. "It's true. See, the queen's lonely, man. She thought she was gonna have to settle for one of you lovelies, but now she's found somebody who's not so fucked up."

Bullets tore through the bushes on his right.

"Not even close," said Quinn. More fire; splinters flew from the tree trunk. "Tell me, Mathis." He suppressed a giggle. "How long's it been since you had any pussy?" Several guns began to chatter, and he caught sight of a muzzle flash; he pinpointed it with his own fire.

"You son of a bitch!" Mathis screamed.

"Did I get one?" Quinn asked blithely. "What's the matter, man? Wasn't he ripe for the light?"

A hail of fire swept the island. The cap-pistol sounds, the volley of hits on the trunk, the bullets zipping through the leaves, all this enraged Quinn, touched a spark to the violent potential induced by the drugs. But he restrained himself from returning fire, wanting to keep his position hidden. And then, partly because it was another way of ragging Mathis but also because he felt a twinge of alarm, he shouted, "Watch out! You'll hit the queen!"

The firing broke off. "Quinn Edward!" Mathis called.

Quinn kept silent, examining that twinge of alarm, trying to determine if there had been something un-Quinnlike about it.

"Quinn Edward!"

"Yeah, what?"

"It's time," said Mathis, hoarse with anger. "Queen's tellin' me it's time for me to prove myself. I'm comin' at you, man!"

Studying the patterns of blue-green scale flecking the tree trunk, Quinn seemed to see the army of his victims—grim, desanguinated men—and he felt a powerful revulsion at what he had become. But when he answered, his mood swung to the opposite pole. "I'm waitin', asshole!"

"Y' know," said Mathis, suddenly breezy, "I got a feelin' it's gonna come down to you and me, man. 'Cause that's how she wants it. And can't nobody beat me one on one in my own back yard." His breath came as a guttural hiss, and Quinn realized that this sort of breathing was typical of someone who had been overdoing ampules. "I'm gonna overwhelm you, Quinn Edward," Mathis went on. "Gonna be like them ol' Jap movies. Little men with guns actin' all brave and shit till they see somethin' big and hairy comin' at 'em, munchin' treetops and spittin' fire. Then off they run, yellin', 'Tokyo is doomed!'"

For 30 or 40 minutes, Mathis kept up a line of chatter, holding forth on subjects as varied as the Cuban space station and Miami's chances in the A.L. East. He launched into a polemic condemning the new statutes protecting the rights of prostitutes ("Part of the kick's bein' able to bounce 'em round a little, y' know"), then made a case for Antarctica's being the site of the original Garden of Eden and then proposed the theory that every President of the United States had been a member of a secret homosexual society ("Half them First Ladies wasn't nothin' but guys in dresses"). Quinn didn't let himself be drawn into conversation, knowing that Mathis was trying to distract him; but he listened because he was beginning to have a sense of Mathis' character, to understand how he might attack.

Back in Lardcan, Tennessee, or wherever, Mathis had likely been a charismatic figure, glib and expansive, smarter than his friends and willing to lead them from the rear into fights and petty crimes. In some ways, he was a lot like the kid Quinn had been, only Quinn's escapades had been pranks, whereas he believed Mathis had been capable of consequential misdeeds. He could picture him lounging around a gas station, sucking down brews and plotting meanness. The hillbilly con artist out to sucker the Yankee: That would be how he saw himself in relation to Quinn. Sooner or later, he would resort to tricks. That was cool with Quinn; he could handle tricks. But he wasn't going to underestimate Mathis. No way. Mathis had to have a lot on the ball to survive the jungle for two years, to rule a troop of crazed Green Berets. Quinn just hoped Mathis would underestimate him.

The sun swelled into an explosive glare that whitened the sky and made the green of the jungle seem a livid, overripe color. Quinn popped ampules and waited. The inside of his head came to feel heavy with violent urges, as if his thoughts were congealing into a lump of mental *plastique*. Around noon, somebody began to lay down covering fire, spraying bullets back and forth along the bank. Quinn found he could time these sweeps, and after one such had passed him by, he looked out from behind the tree trunk. Four bearded, long-haired men were crossing the lake from different directions, plunging through the water, lifting their knees high. Before ducking back, Quinn shot the two on the left, saw them spun around, their rifles flung away. He timed a second sweep, then picked off the two on the right; he was certain he had killed one, but the other might only have been wounded. The gunfire homed in on him, trimming the bushes overhead. Twigs pinwheeled; cut leaves sailed like paper planes. A centipede had ridden one of the leaves down and was still crawling along its fluted edge. Quinn didn't like its hairy mandibles, its Devil face.

Didn't like the fact that it had survived while men had not. He let it crawl in front of his gun and blew it up in a fountain of dirt and grass.

The firing stopped.

Branches ticking the trunk; water slopping against the bank; drips. Quinn lay motionless, listening. No unnatural noises. But where were those drips coming from? The bullets hadn't splashed up much water. Apprehensions spidered his backbone. He peeked up over the top of the tree trunk . . . and cried out in shock. A man was standing in the water about four feet away, blocking the line of fire from the shore. With the mud freckling his cheeks, strands of bottom weed ribboning his dripping hair, he might have been the wild mad king of the lake—skull face, staring eyes, survival knife dangling loosely in his hand. He blinked at Quinn. Swayed, righted himself, blinked again. His fatigues were plastered to his ribs, and a big bloodstain mapped the hollow of his stomach. The man's cheeks bulged: It looked as if he wanted to speak but was afraid more would come out than just words.

"Jesus . . . shit," he said sluggishly. His eyes half-rolled back; his knees buckled. Then he straightened, glancing around as if waking somewhere unfamiliar. He appeared to notice Quinn, frowned and staggered forward, swinging the knife in a lazy arc.

Quinn got off a round before the man reached him. The bullet seemed to paste a red star under the man's eye, stamping his features with a rapt expression. He fell atop Quinn, atop the gun, which—jammed to automatic—kept firing. Lengths of wet hair hung across Quinn's faceplate, striping his view of branches and sky; the body jolted with the bullets tunneling through.

Two explosions nearby.

Quinn pushed the body away, bellycrawled into the brush and popped an ampule. He heard a *thock* followed by a bubbling scream: Somebody had tripped a flare. He did a count and came up with nine dead—plus the guy laying down covering fire. Mathis, no doubt. It would be nice if that were all of them, but Quinn knew better. Somebody else was out there. He felt him the way a flower feels the sun—autonomic reactions waking, primitive senses coming alert.

He inched deeper into the brush. The drugs burned bright inside him; he had the idea they were forming a manlike shape of glittering particles, an inner man of furious principle. Mats of blight-dappled leaves pressed against his faceplate, then slid away with underwater slowness. It seemed he was burrowing through a mosaic of muted colors and coarse textures into which even the concept of separateness had been subsumed, and so it was that he almost failed to notice the boot: a rotting brown boot with vines for laces, visible behind a spray of leaves about six feet off. The boot shifted, and Quinn saw an olive-drab trouser leg tucked into it.

His gun was wedged beneath him, and he was certain the man would move before he could ease it out. But apparently the man was playing bird dog, his senses straining for a clue to Quinn's whereabouts. Quinn lined the barrel up with the man's calf just above the boot top and checked to make sure it was set on automatic. Then he fired, swinging the barrel back and forth an inch to both sides of his center mark. Blood erupted from the calf, and a hoarse yell was drawn out of Quinn by the terrible hammering of the gun. The man fell, screaming. Quinn tracked the fire across the ground, and the screams were cut short.

The boot was still standing behind the spray of leaves, now sprouting a tattered stump and a shard of bone.

Quinn lowered his head, resting his faceplate in the dirt. It was as if all his rectitude had been spat out through the gun. He lay thoughtless, drained of emotion. Time seemed to collapse around him, burying him beneath a ton of decaying seconds. After a while, a beetle crawled onto the faceplate, walking upside down; it stopped at eye level, tapped its mandibles on the plastic and froze. Staring at its grotesque underparts, Quinn had a glimpse into the nature of his own monstrosity: a tiny armored creature chemically programmed to a life of stalking and biting and, between violences, lapsing into a stunned torpor.

"Quinn Edward?" Mathis whispered.

Quinn lifted his head; the beetle dropped off the faceplate and scurried for cover.

"You got 'em all, didn'tcha?"

Quinn wormed out from under the bush, got to his feet and headed back to the fallen tree trunk.

"Tonight, Quinn Edward. You gonna see my knife flash . . . and then fare thee well." Mathis laughed softly. "It's me she wants, man. She just told me so. Told me I can't lose tonight."

Late afternoon, and Quinn went about disposing of the dead. It wasn't something he would ordinarily have done, yet he felt compelled to be rid of them. He was too weary to puzzle over the compulsion and merely did as it directed, pushing the corpses into the lake. The man who had tripped the flare was lying in some ferns, his face seared down to sinew and laceworks of cartilage; ants were stitching patterns across the blood-sticky bone of the skull. Having to touch the body made Quinn's flesh nettle cold, and bile flooded his throat.

That finished, he sat in the clearing south of the ceiba and popped an ampule. The rays of sunlight slanting through the canopy were as sharply defined as lasers, showing greenish-gold against the backdrop of leaves. Sitting beneath them, he felt guided by no visionary purpose; he was, however, gaining a clearer impression of the queen. He couldn't point to a single thought out of the hundreds that cropped up and say, "That one; that's hers." But as if she were filtering his perceptions, he was coming to know her from everything he experienced. It seemed the island had been steeped in her, its mists and midnights modified by her presence, refined to express her moods; even its overgrown terrain seemed to reflect her nature: shy, secretive, yet full of gentle stirrings. Seductive. He understood now that the process of becoming attuned to her was a process of seduction, one you couldn't resist, because you, too, were being steeped in her. You were forced into a lover's involvement with her, and she was a woman worth loving. Beautiful . . . strong. She'd needed that strength in order to survive, and that was why she couldn't help him against Mathis. The life she offered was free from the terrors of war but demanded vigilance and fortitude. Although she favored him—he was sure of that—his strength would have to be proved. Of course, Mathis had twisted all this into a bizarre religion.

Christ!

Quinn sat up straight. Jesus fucking Christ! He was really losing it—mooning around like some kid fantasizing about a movie star. He'd better get his ass in gear, because Mathis would be coming soon. Tonight. It was interesting how Mathis—knowing his best hope of taking Quinn would be at night—had used his delusion to overcome his fear of the dark, convincing himself that the queen had told him he would win . . . or maybe she *had* told him.

Fuck that, Quinn told himself. He wasn't that far gone.

A gust of wind roused a chorus of whispery vowels from the leaves. Quinn flipped up his visor. It was hot, cloudless, but he could smell rain and the promise of a chill on the wind. He did an ampule. The drugs withdrew the baffles that had been damping the core of his anger. Confidence was a voltage surging through him, keying new increments of strength. He smiled, thinking about the fight to come, and even that smile was an expression of furious strength, a thing of bulked muscle fibers and trembling nerves. He was at the center of strength, in touch with every rustle, his sensitivity fueled by the light-stained brilliance of the leaves. Gazing at the leaves, at their infinite shades of green, he remembered a line of a poem he'd read once: "Green flesh, green hair and eyes of coldest silver . . ." Was that how the queen would be if she were real—transformed into a creature of pure poetry by the unearthly radiance of Fire Zone Emerald? Were they all acting out a mythic drama distilled from the mundane interactions of love and war, performing it in the flawed heart of an immense green jewel whose reality could be glimpsed only by those blind enough to see beyond the chaos of the leaves into its precise facets and fractures? Quinn chuckled at the wasted profundity of his thought and pictured Mathis dead, himself the king of that dead man's illusion, robed in ferns and wearing a leafy crown.

High above, two parrots were flying complicated loops and arcs, avoiding the hanging columns of light as if they were solid.

Just before dusk, a rain squall swept in, lasting only a few minutes but soaking the island. Quinn used it for cover, moving about and rigging more flares. He considered taking a stand on the rocky point at the north end: It commanded a view of both shores, and he might get lucky and spot Mathis as he crossed. But it was risky—Mathis might spot *him*—and he decided his best bet would be to hide, to outwait Mathis. Waiting wasn't Mathis' style. Quinn went back to the ceiba tree and climbed past the crotch to a limb directly beneath an opening in the canopy, shielded by fans of leaves. He switched his gun to its high-explosive setting. Popped an ampule. And waited.

The clouds passed away south, and in the half-light, the bushes below seemed to assume topiary shapes. After 15 minutes, Quinn did another ampule. Violet auras faded in around ferns, pools of shadow quivered and creepers seemed to be slithering like snakes along the branches. A mystic star rose in the west, shining alone above the last pink band of sunset. Quinn stared at it until he thought he understood its sparkling message.

The night that descended was similar to the one in the Rousseau print, with a yellow-globe moon carving geometries of shadow and light from the foliage. A night for tigers, mysterious ladies and dark designs. Barnacled to his branch, Quinn felt that the moonlight was lacquering his combat gear, giving it the semblance of ebony armor with gilt filigree, enforcing upon him the image of a knight about to do battle for his lady. He supposed it was possible that such might actually be the case. It was true that his perception of the queen was growing stronger and more particularized; he even thought he could tell where she was hiding: the rocky point. But he doubted that he could trust the perception—and besides, the battle itself, not its motive, was the significant thing. To reach that peak moment when perfection drew blood, when you muscled confusion aside and—as large as a constellation with the act, as full of stars and blackness and primitive meaning—you were able to look down onto the world and know you had outperformed the ordinary. Nothing, neither an illusory motive nor the illusion of a real motive, could add importance to that.

Shortly after dark, Mathis began to chatter again, regaling Quinn with anecdote and opinion; and by the satisfaction in his voice, Quinn knew he had reached the island. Twenty minutes passed, each of them ebbing away, leaking out of Quinn's store of time like blood dripping from an old wound. Then a burst of white incandescence to the south, throwing vines and bushes into skeletal silhouette . . . and with it a scream. Quinn smiled. The scream had been a dandy imitation of pain, but he wasn't buying it. He eased a flare from his hip pouch. It wouldn't take long for Mathis to give this up.

The white fire died, muffled by the rainsoaked foliage, and finally Mathis said, "You a cautious fella, Quinn Edward."

Quinn popped two ampules.

"I doubt you can keep it up, though," Mathis went on. "I mean, sooner or later you gotta throw caution to the winds."

Quinn barely heard him. He felt he was soaring, that the island was soaring, arrowing through a void whose sole feature it was and approaching the moment for which he had been waiting: a moment of brilliant violence to illuminate the flaws at the heart of the stone, to reveal the shadow play. The first burn of the drugs subsided, and he fixed his eyes on the shadows south of the ceiba tree.

Tension began to creep into Mathis' voice, and Quinn was not surprised when—perhaps five minutes later—he heard the stutter of an M-18: Mathis firing at some movement in the brush. He caught sight of a muzzle flash, lifted his gun. But the next instant, he was struck by an overpowering sense of the queen, one that shocked him with its suddenness.

She was in pain. Wounded by Mathis' fire.

In his mind's eye, Quinn saw a female figure slumped against a boulder, holding her lower leg. The wound wasn't serious, but he could tell she wanted the battle to end before worse could happen.

He was mesmerized by her pervasiveness—it seemed that if he were to flip up his visor, he would breathe her in—and by what appeared to be a new specificity of knowledge about her. Bits of memory were surfacing in his thoughts; though he didn't quite believe it, he could have sworn they were hers: a shanty with a tin roof amid fields of tilled red dirt; someone walking on a beach; a shady place overhung by a branch dripping with orchids, with insects scuttling in and out of the blooms, mining some vein of sweetness. That last memory was associated with the idea that it was a place where she went to daydream, and Quinn felt an intimate resonance with her, with the fact that she—like him—relied on that kind of retreat.

Confused, afraid for her yet half convinced that he had slipped over the edge of sanity, he detonated his flare, aiming it at the opening in the canopy. An umbrella of white light bloomed overhead. He tracked his gun across eerily lit bushes and . . . There! Standing in the clearing to the south, a man wearing combat gear. Before the man could move. Quinn blew him up into marbled smoke and flame. Then, his mind ablaze with victory, he began to shinny down the branch. But as he descended, he realized something was wrong. The man had just stood there, made no attempt to duck or hide. And his gun. It had been like Quinn's own, not an M-18.

He had shot a dummy or a man already dead!

Bullets pounded his back, not penetrating but knocking him out of the tree. Arms flailing, he fell into the bush. Branches tore the gun from his grasp. The armor deadened the impact, but he was dazed, his head throbbing. He clawed free of the bush just as Mathis' helmeted shadow—looking huge in the dying light of the flare—crashed through the brush and drove a rifle stock into his faceplate. The plastic didn't shatter, webbing over with cracks; but by the time Quinn had recovered, Mathis was straddling him, knees pinning his shoulders.

"How 'bout that, motherfucker?" said Mathis, breathing hard.

A knife glinted in his hand, arced downward and thudded into Quinn's neck, deflected by the armor. Quinn heaved, but Mathis forced him back and this time punched at the faceplate with the hilt of the knife. Punched again, and again. Bits of plastic sprayed Quinn's face, and the faceplate was now so thoroughly cracked, it was like looking up through a crust of glittering rime. It wouldn't take many more blows. Desperate, Quinn managed to roll Mathis onto his side, and they grappled silently. His teeth bit down on a sharp plastic chip, and he tasted blood. Still grappling, they struggled to their knees, then to their feet. Their helmets slammed together. The impact came as a hollow click over Quinn's radio, and that click seemed to switch on a part of his mind that was as distant as a flare, calm and observing; he pictured the two of them as black giants with whirling galaxies for hearts and stars articulating their joints, doing battle over the female half of everything. Seeing it that way gave him renewed strength. He wrangled Mathis off balance, and they reeled clumsily through the brush. They fetched up against the trunk of the ceiba tree, and for a few seconds they were frozen like wrestlers muscling for an advantage. Sweat poured down Quinn's face; his arms quivered. Then Mathis tried to butt his faceplate, to finish the job he had begun with the hilt of his knife. Quinn ducked, slipped his hold, planted a shoulder in Mathis' stomach and drove him backward. Mathis twisted as he fell, and Quinn turned him onto his stomach. He wrenched Mathis' knife arm behind his back, pried the knife loose. Probed with the blade, searching for a seam between the plates of neck armor. Then he pressed it just deep enough to prick the skin. Mathis went limp. Silent.

"Where's all the folksy chitchat, man?" said Quinn, excited.

Mathis maintained his silent immobility, and Quinn wondered if he had gone catatonic. Maybe he wouldn't have to kill him. The light from the flare had faded, and the moon-dappled darkness that had filled in reminded Quinn of the patterns of blight on the island leaves: an infection at whose heart they were clamped together like chitinous bugs.

"Bitch!" said Mathis, suddenly straining against Quinn's hold. "You lied, goddamn you!"

"Shut up," said Quinn, annoyed.

"Fuckin' bitch!" Mathis bellowed. "You tricked me!"

"I said to shut up!" Quinn gave him a little jab, but Mathis began to thrash wildly, nearly impaling himself, shouting, "Bitch!"

"Shut the fuck up!" said Quinn, growing angrier but also trying to avoid stabbing Mathis, beginning to feel helpless, to feel that he would have to stab him, that it was all beyond his control.

"I'll kill you, bitch!" screamed Mathis. "I'll . . ."

"Stop it!" Quinn shouted, not sure to whom he was crying out. Inside his chest, a fuming cell of anger was ready to explode.

Mathis writhed and kicked. "I'll cut out your fuckin' . . ."

Poisonous burst of rage. Mandibles snapping shut, Quinn shoved the knife home. Blood guttered in Mathis' throat. One gauntleted hand scrabbled in the dirt, but that was all reflexes.

Quinn sat up, feeling sluggish. There was no glory. It had been a contest essentially decided by a gross stupidity: Mathis' momentary forgetfulness about the armor. But how could he have forgotten? He'd seen what little effect the bullets had. Quinn took off his helmet and sucked in hits of the humid air, watched a slice of moonlight jiggle on Mathis' faceplate. Then a blast of static from his helmet radio, a voice saying, "You copy?"

"Ain't no friendlies in Emerald," said another radio voice. "Musta been beaners sent up that flare. It's a trap."

"Yeah, but I got a reading like infantry gear back there. We should do a sweep over that lake."

Chopper pilots, Quinn realized. But he stared at the helmet with the mute awe of a savage, as if they had been alien voices speaking from a stone. He picked up the helmet, unsure what to say.

Please, no . . .

The words had been audible, and he realized that she had made him hear them in the sighing of the breeze.

Static fizzling. "Get the hell outta here."

The first pilot again. "Do you copy? I repeat, do you copy?"

What, Quinn thought, if this had all been the queen's way of getting rid of Mathis, even down to that last flash of anger; and now, now that he had done the job, wouldn't she get rid of him?

Please stay . . .

Quinn imagined himself back in Dakota, years spent watching cattle die, reading mail-order catalogs, drinking and drinking, comparing the queen to the dowdy farm girl he'd have married, and one night getting a little too morbidly weary of that nothing life and driving out onto the flats and riding the .45-caliber express to nowhere. But at least that was proved, whereas this . . .

Please . . .

A wave of her emotion swept over him, seeding him with her loneliness and longing. He was truly beginning to know her now, to sense the precise configurations of her moods, the stoicism underlying her strength, the . . .

"Fuck it!" said one of the pilots.

The static from Quinn's radio smoothed to a hiss, and the night closed down around him. His feeling of isolation nailed him to the spot. Wind seethed in the massy crown of the ceiba, and he thought he heard again the whispered word *Please.* An icy fluid mounted in his spine. To shore up his confidence, he popped an ampule; and soon the isolation no longer troubled him but, rather, seemed to fit about him like a cloak. This was the path he had been meant to take, the way of courage and character. He got to his feet, unsteady on his injured legs, and eased past Mathis, slipping between two bushes. Ahead of him, the night looked like a floating puzzle of shadow and golden light: No matter how careful he was, he'd never be able to locate all his mines and flares.

But she would guide him.

Or would she? Hadn't she tricked Mathis? Lied to him?

More wind poured through the leaves of the ceiba tree, gusting its word of entreaty; and intimations of pleasure, of sweet green mornings and soft nights, eddied up in the torrent of her thoughts. She surrounded him, undeniable, as real as perfume, as certain as the ground beneath his feet.

For a moment, he was assailed by a new doubt. "God," he said. "Please don't let me be crazy. Not just ordinary crazy."

Please . . .

Then, suffering mutinies of the heart at every step, repelling them with a warrior's conviction, he moved through the darkness at the center of the island toward the rocky point, where—her tiger crouched by her feet, a ripe jungle moon hanging above like the emblem of her mystique—either love or fate might be waiting.

WILLIAM TENN

THE GHOST STANDARD

December 1994

Readers may complain that this anthology is somewhat lacking in alien life forms. It's true. Bug-eyed monsters have taken a back seat to the infinite possibilities awaiting mankind in the future. Here, to redress the situation, is a comic turn complete with both alien and conundrum. William Tenn is the pseudonym of Penn State professor emeritus Philip Klass, born in 1920, who has been publishing witty and satiric short stories since the 1940s, though too rarely in recent years. He has published five collections of stories, and his only novel, *Of Men and Monsters,* appeared in 1963. Tenn was a member of the all-star Playboy Panel: *1984 and Beyond.*

REMEMBER THE ADAGE of the old English legal system: "Let justice be done though the heavens should fall"? Well, *was* justice done in this case?

You have three entities here. An intelligent primate from Sol III—to put it technically, a human. An equally intelligent crustacean from Procyon VII—in other words, a sapient lobstermorph. And a computer of the Malcolm Movis omicron beta design, intelligent enough to plot a course from one stellar system to another and capable of matching most biological minds in games of every sort, from bridge to chess to double zonyak.

Now—add a shipwreck. A leaky old Cascassian freighter comes apart in deep space. I mean quite literally comes apart. Half the engine segment explodes off, the hull develops leaks and begins to collapse, all those who are still alive and manage to make it to lifeboats get away just before the end.

In one such lifeboat you have the human, Juan Kydd, and the lobstermorph, Tuezuzim. And, of course, the Malcolm Movis computer—the resident pilot, navigator and general factotum of the craft.

Kydd and Tuezuzim had known each other for more than two years. Computer programmers of roughly the same level of skill, they had met on the job and had been laid off together. Together they had decided to save money by traveling on the scabrous Cascassian freighter to Sector N-42B5, where there were rumored to be many job opportunities available.

They were in the dining salon, competing in a tough hand of double zonyak, when the disaster occurred. They helped each other scramble into the lifeboat. Activating the computer pilot, they put it into Far Communication Mode to search for rescuers.

443

It informed them that rescue was possible no sooner than 20 days hence, and was quite likely before 30.

Any problems? The lifeboat had air, fuel, more than enough water. But food . . .

It was a Cascassian freighter, remember. The Cascassians, of course, are a silicon-based life-form. For their passengers, the Cascassians had laid in a supply of organic, or carbon-based, food in the galley. But they had not even thought of restocking the lifeboats. So the two non-Cascassians were now imprisoned for some three to four weeks with nothing to eat but the equivalent of sand and gravel.

Or each other, as they realized immediately and simultaneously.

Humans, on their home planet, consider tinier, less-sapient crustaceans such as lobsters and crawfish great delicacies. And back on Procyon VII, as Tuezuzim put it, "We consider it a sign of warm hospitality to be served a small, succulent primate known as spotted morror."

In other words, each of these programmers could eat the other. And survive. There were cooking and refrigerating facilities aboard the lifeboat. With careful management and rationing, meals derived from a full-size computer programmer would last till rescue.

But who was to eat whom? And how was a decision to be reached?

By fighting? Hardly. These were two highly intellectual types, neither of them good physical exemplars of their species.

Kydd was round-shouldered, badly nearsighted and slightly anemic. Tuezuzim was somewhat undersized, half deaf and suffering from one crippled chela. The claw had been twisted at birth and had never matured normally. With these disabilities, both had avoided participation in athletic sports all their lives, especially any sport of a belligerent nature.

Yet the realization that there was nothing else available to eat had already made both voyagers very hungry. What was their almost-friendship compared with the grisly prospect of starvation?

For the record, it was the lobstermorph, Tuezuzim, who suggested a trial by game, with the computer acting as referee and also as executioner of the loser. Again, only for the record and of no importance otherwise, it was the human, Juan Kydd, who suggested that the logical game to decide the issue should be Ghost.

They both liked Ghost and played it whenever they could not play their favorite game—that is, when they lacked zonyak tiles. In the scrambling haste of their emergency exit, they had left both web and tiles in the dining salon. A word game now seemed the sole choice remaining, short of flipping a coin, which—as games-minded programmers—they shrugged off as childishly simplistic. There also was the alternative of trial by physical combat, but that was something that neither found at all attractive.

Since the computer would function as umpire and dispute-settling dictionary as well as executioner, why not make it a three-cornered contest and include the computer as a participant? This would make the game more interesting by adding an unpredictable factor, like a card shuffle. The computer could not lose, of course—they agreed to ignore any letters of Ghost that it picked up.

They kept the ground rules simple: a ten-minute time limit for each letter; no three-letter words; the usual prohibition against proper nouns; and each round would go in the opposite direction from that of the previous round. Thus, both players would have equal challenging opportunities, and neither would be permanently behind the other in the contest.

Also, challenging was to be allowed across the intervening opponent—the computer, not part of the combat.

Having sent off one last distress signal, they addressed themselves to programming the computer for the game (and the instantaneous execution of the loser). Combing through the immense software resources of the computer, they were pleased to discover that its resident dictionaries included *Webster's First* and *Second,* their own joint favorites. They settled on the ancient databases as the supreme arbiters.

The verdict-enforcer took a little more time to organize. Eventually, they decided on what amounted to a pair of electric chairs controlled by the computer. The killing force would be a diverted segment of the lifeboat's Hametz Drive. Each competitor would be fastened to his seat, locked in place by the computer until the game was over. At the crucial moment, when one of them incurred the *t* in Ghost, a single blast of the diverted drive would rip through the loser's brain, and the winner would be released.

"Everything covered?" asked Tuezuzim as they finished their preparations. "A fair contest?"

"Yes, everything's covered," Kydd replied. "All's fair. Let's go."

They went to their respective places: Kydd to a chair, Tuezuzim to the traditional curved bed of the lobstermorph. The computer activated their electronic bonds. They stared at each other and softly said their goodbyes.

We have this last information from the computer. The Malcolm Movis omicron beta is bundled at sale with Altruix 4.0, a fairly complex ethicist program. It was now recording the proceedings, with a view to the expected judicial inquest.

The lobstermorph drew the first *g*. He had challenged Juan Kydd, who had just added an *e* to *t-w-i-s*. Kydd came up with *twisel*, the Anglo-Saxon noun and verb for fork. To Tuezuzim's bitter protests that *twisel* was archaic, the Malcolm Movis pointed out that there had been no prior agreement to exclude archaisms.

Kydd himself was caught a few minutes later. Arrogant over his initial victory, he was helping to construct *laminectomy* ("surgical removal of the posterior arch of a vertebra") by adding *m* after *l-a-m-i-n-e-c-t-o*. True, this would end on the computer's turn, which could incur no penalty letters, but Kydd was willing to settle for a neutral round. Unfortunately, he had momentarily forgotten the basic escape hatch for any seasoned Ghost player—plurals. The Malcolm Movis indicated *i,* and Tuezuzim added the *e* so fast it sounded like an echo. There was absolutely no escape for Kydd from the concluding *s* in *laminectomies.*

And so it went, neck and neck, or, rather, neck and cephalothorax. Tuezuzim pulled ahead for a time and seemed on the verge of victory, as Kydd incurred *g-h-o-s* and then was challenged in a dangerous situation with a questionable word.

"*Dirigibloid?*" Tuezuzim demanded. "You just made that one up. There is no such word. You are simply trying to avoid getting stuck with the *e* of *dirigible.*"

"It certainly is a word," Kydd maintained, perspiring heavily. "As in 'like a dirigible, in the form of or resembling a dirigible.' It can be used, probably has been used, in some piece of technical prose."

"But it's not in *Webster's Second*—and that's the test. Computer, is it in your dictionary?"

"As such, no," the Malcolm Movis replied. "But the word dirigible is derived from the Latin *dirigere,* to direct. It means steerable, as a dirigible balloon. The suffix *-oid* may be added to many words of classical derivation. As in *spheroid* and *colloid* and *asteroid,* for example—"

"Just consider those examples!" Tuezuzim broke in, arguing desperately. "All three have the Greek suffix*-oid* added to words that were originally Greek, not Latin. *Aster* means 'star' in Greek, so with *asteroid* you have 'starlike or in the form of a star.' And *colloid* comes from the Greek *kolla* for 'glue.' Are you trying to tell me that dictionaries on the level of *Webster's First* or *Second* mix Greek with Latin?"

It seemed to the anxiously listening Kydd that the Malcolm Movis computer almost smiled before continuing. "As a matter of fact, in one of those cases, that's exactly what happens. *Webster's Second* describes *spheroid* as deriving from both Greek and Latin. It provides as etymologies, on the one hand, the Greek *sphairoeidēs* (*sphaira,* 'sphere,' plus *eidos,* 'form') and, on the other, the Latin *sphaeroides,* 'ball-like' or 'spherical.' Two different words, both of classical origin. *Dirigibloid* is therefore ruled a valid word."

"I protest that ruling!" Tuezuzim waved his claw angrily. "Data are being most selectively used. I am beginning to detect a prohuman, anti-lobstermorph bias in the computer."

Another faint suggestion of an electromechanical smile. "Once more, a matter of fact," the computer noted silkily. "The Malcolm Movis design team was headed by Dr. Hodgodya Hodgodya, the well-known lobstermorph electronicist. Prohuman, anti-lobstermorph bias is therefore most unlikely to have been built in. *Dirigibloid* is ruled valid; the protest is noted and disallowed. Juan Kydd begins the next round."

Since both opponents were now tagged with *g-h-o-s,* the round coming up would be the rubber, or execution, round. This was most definitely *it.*

Kydd and Tuezuzim looked at each other again. One of them would be dead in a few minutes. Then Kydd looked away and began the round with the letter that had always worked best for him in three-cornered Ghost, the letter *l.*

The computer added *i,* and Tuezuzim, a bit rashly, came up with *m.* He was quite willing for the word to be *limit,* and thus to end on the Malcolm Movis. A null round, and he, Tuezuzim, would be starting the next one.

But Kydd was not interested in a null round this time. He added an *o* to the *l-i-m* and, when the computer supplied a *u,* the developing *limousine* that had to end on Tuezuzim became obvious.

The lobstermorph thought desperately. With a hopeless squeak from deep in his cephalothorax, he said *s.*

It must be recognized here, as the computer testified at the subsequent inquest, that the *s* already completed a word, to wit *limous* ("muddy, slimy"). But the Malcolm Movis pointed out that the individual who should have triumphantly called attention to *limous,* Juan Kydd, was so committed to catching his opponent with *limousine* that he didn't notice.

Limousine moved right along, with an *i* from Kydd and an *n* from the computer. And once again it was up to Tuezuzim.

He waited until his ten-minute time limit had almost expired. Then he came up with a letter. But it wasn't *e.*

It was *o.*

Juan Kydd stared at him. "*L-i-m-o-u-s-i-n-o?*" he said in disbelief, yet already suspecting what the lobstermorph was up to. "I challenge you."

Again Tuezuzim waited a long time. Then, slowly rotating his crippled left chela at Juan Kydd's face, he said, "The word is *limousinoid.*"

"There's no such word! What in hell does it mean?"

"What does it mean? 'Like a limousine, in the form of or resembling a limousine.' It can be used, probably has been used, in some piece of technical prose."

"Referee!" Kydd yelled. "Let's have a ruling. Do you have *limousinoid* in your dictionary?"

"Whether or not it's in the dictionary, Computer," Tuezuzim countered, "it has to be acceptable. If *dirigibloid* can exist, so can *limousinoid.* If *limousinoid* exists, Kydd's challenge is invalid and he gets the *t* of Ghost—and loses. If *limousinoid* doesn't exist, neither does *dirigibloid,* and so Kydd would have lost that earlier round and would therefore now be up to the *t* of Ghost. Either way, he has to lose."

Now it was the Malcolm Movis that took its time. Five full minutes it considered. As it testified later, it need not have done so; its conclusion was reached in microseconds. "But," it noted in its testimony at the inquest, "an interesting principle was involved here that required the use of this unnecessary time. Justice, it is said, not only must be done, but must *seem* to be done. Only the appearance of lengthy, careful consideration would make justice *seem* to be done in this case."

Five minutes—and then, at last, the Malcolm Movis gave its verdict.

"There is no valid equation here between *dirigibloid* and *limousinoid*. Since *dirigible* is a word derived from the so-called classic languages, it may add the Greek suffix *-oid*. *Limousine,* on the other hand, derives from French, a Romance language. It comes from Limousin, an old province of France. The suffix *-oid* cannot therefore be used properly with it—Romance French and classical Greek may not be mixed."

The Malcolm Movis paused now for three or four musical beats before going on. Juan Kydd and Tuezuzim stared at it, the human's mouth moving silently, the crustacean's antennae beginning to vibrate in frantic disagreement.

"Tuezuzim has incurred *t,* the last letter of Ghost," the computer announced. "He has lost."

"I protest!" Tuezuzim screamed. "Bias! Bias! If no *limousinoid,* then no *dirigibl—*"

"Protest disallowed." And the blast of the Hametz Drive tore through the lobstermorph. "Your meals, Mr. Kydd," the computer said courteously.

The inquest, on Karpis VIII of Sector N-42B5, was a swift affair. The backup tapes of the Malcolm Movis were examined; Juan Kydd was merely asked if he had anything to add (he did not).

But the verdict surprised almost everyone, especially Kydd. He was ordered held for trial. The charge? Aggravated cannibalism in deep space.

Of course, our present definition of interspecies cannibalism derives from this case:

The act of cannibalism is not to be construed as limited to the eating of members of one's own species. In modern terms of widespread travel through deep space, it may be said to occur whenever one highly intelligent individual kills and consumes another highly intelligent individual. Intelligence has always been extremely difficult to define precisely, but it will be here and henceforth understood to involve the capacity to understand and play the terrestrial game of Ghost. It is not to be understood as solely limited to this capacity, but if an individual, of whatever biological construction, possesses such capacity, the killing, consuming and assimilating of that individual shall be perceived as an act of cannibalism and is to be punished in terms of whatever statutes relate to cannibalism in that time and that place.

—*The Galaxy v. Kydd, Karpis VIII, C17603.*

Now, Karpis VIII was pretty much a rough-and-ready frontier planet. It was still a rather wide-open place with a fairly tolerant attitude toward most violent crime. As a result, Juan Kydd was assessed a moderate fine, which he was able to pay after two months of working at his new job in computer programming.

The Malcolm Movis computer did not fare nearly as well.

First, it was held as a crucial party to the crime and an accessory before the fact. It was treated as a responsible and intelligent individual, since it had unquestionably demonstrated the capacity to understand and play the terrestrial game of Ghost. Its plea of nonbiological construction (and therefore noninvolvement in legal proceedings pertaining to living creatures) was disallowed on the ground that the silicon-based Cascassians who had built the ship and lifeboat were now also subject to this definition of cannibalism. If silicon-chemistry intelligence could be considered biological, the court ruled, so inevitably must silicon-electronics.

Furthermore, and perhaps most damaging, the computer was held to have lied in a critical situation—or, at least, to have withheld information by not telling the whole truth. When Tuezuzim had accused it of anti-lobstermorph bias, it had pointed to the fact that the Malcolm Movis omicron beta had been designed by a lobstermorph and that anti-lobstermorph bias was therefore highly unlikely. The *whole* truth, however, was that the designer, Dr.

Hodgodya, was living in self-imposed exile at the time because he hated his entire species and, in fact, had expressed this hatred in numerous satirical essays and one long narrative poem. In other words, anti-lobstermorph bias *had* been built in and the computer knew it.

To this the computer protested that it was, after all, only a computer. As such, it had to answer questions as simply and directly as possible. It was the questioner's job to formulate and ask the right questions.

"Not in this case," the court held. "The Malcolm Movis omicron beta was not functioning as a simple question-and-answer machine but as a judge and umpire. Its obligations included total honesty and full information. The possibility of anti-lobstermorph bias had to be openly considered and admitted."

The Malcolm Movis did not give up. "But you had two top-notch programmers in Kydd and Tuezuzim. Could it not be taken for granted that they would already know a good deal about the design history of a computer in such general use? Surely for such knowledgeable individuals not every *i* has to be dotted, not every *t* has to be crossed."

"Software people!" the court responded. "What do they know about fancy hardware?"

The computer was eventually found guilty of being an accessory to the crime of cannibalism and was ordered to pay a fine. Though this was a much smaller fine than the one incurred by Juan Kydd, the Malcolm Movis, unlike Kydd, had no financial resources and no way of acquiring any.

That made for a touchy situation. On a freewheeling planet such as Karpis VIII, judges and statutes might wink a bit at killers and even cannibals. But never at out-and-out deadbeats. The court ruled that if the computer could not pay its fine, it still could not evade appropriate punishment. "Let justice be done!"

The court ordered that the Malcolm Movis omicron beta be wired in perpetuity into the checkout counter of a local supermarket. The computer requested that instead it be disassembled forthwith and its parts scattered. The request was denied.

So.

You decide. Was justice done?

TERRY BISSON

AN OFFICE ROMANCE

February 1997

From Kentucky, Terry Bisson, born in 1942, eventually arrived in Brooklyn, New York, though a complex labyrinth involving tobacco farming, automobile repair, a hippie commune, advertising copy-writing, and a stint in publishing. His first novel, *Wyrldmaker,* appeared in 1981, followed by *Talking Man.* By the 1990s, his attitude toward science fiction had become decidedly tongue-in-cheek: *Voyage to the Red Planet* puts a film crew on an umbrella-shaped spaceship named the *Mary Poppins,* while his latest book is *Pirates of the Universe.* Bisson wrote no short stories till the 1990s, but he imme-diately demonstrated a knack for them—his beginner's effort, the funny and surreal "Bears Discover Fire," became the first and only story ever to sweep every genre award, the Hugo, the Nebula, and several others. Bisson's sly take on the much ballyhooed cyberpunk revolution, droll, charming, and thoroughly contemporary, points to one direction science fiction may be heading in the future.

THE FIRST TIME Ken678 saw
Mary97, he was in Municipal Real Estate, queued for a pickup for
Closings. She stood two spaces in front of him: blue skirt, orange
tie, slightly convex white blouse, like every other female icon. He
didn't know she was a Mary; he couldn't see which face she had.
But she held her Folder in both hands, as old-timers often did, and
when the queue scrolled forward he saw her fingernails.

They were red.

Just then the queue flickered and scrolled again, and she was
gone. Ken was intrigued, but he promptly forgot about her. It was
a busy time of year, and he was running like crazy from Call to
Task. Later that week he saw her again, paused at an open Window
in the Corridor between Copy and Send. He slowed as he passed
her, by turning his Folder sideways—a trick he had learned. There
were those red fingernails again. It was curious.

Fingernails were not on the Option Menu.

Red was not on the Color Menu, either.

Ken used the weekend to visit his mother at the Home. It was her
birthday or anniversary or something like that. Ken hated weekends. He had grown used to his Ken face and felt uncomfortable
without it. He hated his old name, which his mother insisted on
calling him. He hated how grim and terrifying things were outside. To avoid panic he closed his eyes and hummed—out here, he
could do both—trying to simulate the peaceful hum of the Office.

But there is no substitute for the real thing, and Ken didn't
relax until the week restarted and he was back inside. He loved the
soft electron buzz of the search engines, the busy streaming icons,
the dull butter shine of the Corridors, the shimmering Windows

with their relaxing scenes of the environment. He loved his life and he loved his work.

That was the week he met Mary—or rather, she met him.

Ken678 had just retrieved a Folder of documents from Search and was taking it to Print. He could see by the blur of icons ahead that there was going to be a long queue at the Bus leaving Commercial, so he paused in the Corridor; waitstates were encouraged in high traffic zones.

He opened a Window by resting his Folder on the sill. There was no air, of course, but there was a nice view. The scene was the same in every Window in Microserf Office 6.9: cobblestones and quiet cafés and chestnut trees in bloom. April in Paris.

Ken heard a voice.

<Beautiful, isn't it?>

<What?> he said, confused. Two icons couldn't open the same Window, and yet there she was beside him. Red fingernails and all.

<April in Paris,> she said.

<I know. But how—>

<A little trick I learned.> She pointed to her Folder, stacked on top of his, flush right.

<—did you do that?> he finished because it was in his buffer. She had the Mary face, which, it so happened, was his favorite. And the red fingernails.

<When they are flush right the Window reads us as one icon,> she said.

<Probably reads only the right edge,> Ken said. <Neat.>

<The name's Mary,> she said. <Mary97.>

<Ken678.>

<You slowed when you passed me last week, Ken. Neat trick, too. I figure that made you almost worth an intro. Most of the workaholics here in City Hall are pretty unsociable.>

Ken showed her his Folder trick even though she seemed to know it already.

<How long have you been at City?> he asked.

<Too long.>

<How come I have never seen you before?>

<Maybe you saw me but didn't notice me,> she said. She held up a hand with red fingernails. <I didn't always have these.>

<Where'd you get them?>

<It's a secret.>

<They're pretty neat,> Ken said.

<Is that pretty or neat?>

<Both.>

<Are you flirting with me?> she asked, smiling that Mary smile.

Ken tried to think of an answer, but he was too slow. Her Folder was blinking, a waitstate interrupt, and she was gone.

A few cycles later in the week he saw her again, paused at an open Window in the Corridor between Copy and Verify. He slid his Folder over hers, flush right, and he was standing beside her, looking out into April in Paris.

<You learn fast,> she said.

<I have a good teacher,> he said. Then he said what he had been rehearsing over and over: <And what if I was?>

<Was what?>

<Flirting.>

<That would be OK,> she said, smiling the Mary smile.

Ken678 wished for the first time that the Ken face had a smile. His Folder was flickering, but he didn't want to leave yet. <How long have you been at City?> he asked again.

<Forever,> she said. She was exaggerating, of course, but in a sense it was true. She told Ken she had been at City Hall when Microserf Office 6.9 was installed. <Before Office, records were stored in a basement, in metal drawers, and accessed by hand. I helped put it all on disk. Data entry, it was called.>

<Entry?>

<This was before the neural interface. We sat *outside* and reached in through a Keyboard and looked in through a sort of window that they called a Monitor. There was nobody *in* Office. Just pictures of files and stuff. There was no April in Paris, of course. That was added later to prevent claustrophobia.>

Ken678 calculated in his head. How old did that make Mary— 55? 60? It didn't matter. All icons are young, and all females are beautiful.

Ken had never had a friend before, in or out of the Office. Much less a girlfriend. He found himself hurrying his Calls and Tasks so he could cruise the Corridors looking for Mary97. He could usually find her at an open Window, gazing at the cobblestones and the little cafés, the blooming chestnut trees. Mary loved April in Paris. <It's so romantic there,> she said. <Can't you just imagine yourself walking down the boulevard?>

<I guess,> Ken said. But in fact he couldn't. He didn't like to imagine things. He preferred real life, or at least Microserf Office 6.9. He loved standing at the Window beside her, listening to her soft Mary voice, answering in his deep Ken voice.

<How did you get here?> she asked. Ken told her he had been hired as a temp, transporting scanned-in midcentury documents up the long stairway from Archives to Active.

<My name wasn't Ken then, of course,> he said. <All the temp icons wore gray, male and female alike. We were neural-interfaced through helmets instead of earrings. None of the regular Office workers spoke to us, or even noticed us. We worked 14-, 15-cycle days.>

<And you loved it,> Mary said.

<I loved it,> Ken admitted. <I found what I was looking for. I loved being inside.> And he told her how wonderful and strange it had felt, at first, to be an icon; to see himself as he walked around, as if he were both inside and outside his own body.

<Of course, it seems normal now,> he said.

<It is,> Mary said. And she smiled that Mary smile.

Several weeks passed before Ken got up the courage to make what he thought of as "his move."

They were at the Window where he had first spoken with her, in the Corridor between Copy and Verify. Her hand was resting on the sill, red fingernails shimmering, and he put his hand exactly over it. Even though he couldn't actually feel it, it felt good.

He was afraid she would move her hand, but instead she smiled that Mary smile and said, <I didn't think you were ever going to do that.>

<I've been wanting to since I first saw you,> he said.

She moved her fingers under his. It almost tingled. <Want to see what makes them red?>

<You mean your secret?>

<It'll be our secret. You know the Browser between Deeds and Taxes? Meet me there in three cycles.>

The Browser was a circular connector with no Windows. Ken met Mary at Select All and followed her toward Insert, where the doors got smaller and closer together.

<Ever hear of an Easter Egg?> she asked.

<Sure,> Ken said. <A programmer's surprise that is hidden in the software. An unauthorized subroutine that's not in the manual. Sometimes humorous or even obscene. Easter Eggs are routinely—>

<You're just repeating what you learned in Orientation,> Mary said.

<—found and cleared from commercial software by background Debuggers and Optimizers.> Ken finished because it was already in his buffer.

<But that's OK,> she said. <Here we are.>

Mary97 led him into a small Windowless room. There was nothing in it but a tiny, heart-shaped table.

<This room was erased but never overwritten,> Mary said. <The Optimizer must have missed it. That's why the Easter Egg is still here. I discovered it by accident.>

On the table were three playing cards. Two were facedown and one was faceup: the ten of diamonds.

<Ready?> Without waiting for Ken's answer, Mary turned the ten of diamonds facedown. Her fingernails were no longer red.

<Now you try it,> she said.

Ken backed away.

<Don't get nervous. This card does not do anything; it just changes the Option. Go ahead!>

Reluctantly, Ken turned up the ten of diamonds.

Mary's fingernails were red again. Nothing happened to his own.

<That first card works just for girls,> Mary said.

<Neat,> Ken said, relaxing a little.

<There's plenty more,> Mary said. <Ready?>

<I guess.>

Mary turned up the second card. It was the queen of hearts. As soon as she turned it up, Ken heard a *clippety-clop,* and a Window opened in the Windowless room.

In the Window it was April in Paris.

Ken saw a gray horse coming straight down the center of the boulevard. It wore no harness, but its tail and mane were bobbed. Its enormous red penis was almost dragging the cobblestones.

<See the horse?> Mary97 said. She was standing beside Ken at the Window. Her convex white blouse and orange tie both were gone. She was wearing a red lace brassiere. The sheer cups were full. The narrow straps were taut. The tops of her plump breasts were round and bright as moons.

Ken678 couldn't move or speak. It was terrifying and wonderful at the same time. Mary's hands were behind her back, unfastening her brassiere. There! But just as the cups started to fall away from her breasts, a whistle blew.

The horse had stopped in the middle of the boulevard. A gendarme was running toward it, waving a stick.

The Window closed. Mary97 was standing at the table, wearing her convex white blouse and orange tie again. Only the ten of diamonds was faceup.

<You turned the card down too soon,> Ken said. He had wanted to see her nipples.

<The queen turns herself down,> Mary said. <An Easter Egg is a closed algorithm. Runs itself once it gets started. Did you like it? And don't say you guess.>

She smiled that Mary smile and Ken tried to think of what to say. But both their Folders were blinking, waitstate interrupts, and she was gone.

Ken found her a couple cycles later at their usual meeting place, at the open Window in the Corridor between Copy and Verify.

<Like it?> he said. <I loved it.>

<Are you flirting with me?> Mary97 asked.

<What if I am?> he said, and the familiar words were almost as good as a smile.

<Then come with me.>

Ken678 followed Mary97 to the Browser twice more that week. Each time was the same; each time was perfect. As soon as Mary turned over the queen of hearts, Ken heard a *clippetyclop.* A Window opened in the Windowless room and there was the horse again, coming down the boulevard, its enormous penis almost dragging the cobblestones. Mary97's ripe, round, perfect breasts were spilling over the top of her red lace brassiere as she said, <See the horse?> and reached behind her back, unfastening—

Unfastening her bra! And just as the cups started to fall away, just as Ken678 was about to see her nipples, a gendarme's whistle blew and Mary97 was wearing the white blouse again and the orange tie. The Window was closed, the queen of hearts facedown.

<The only problem with Easter Eggs,> Mary said, <is that they are always the same. Whoever designed this one obviously had a case of arrested development.>

<I like always the same,> Ken replied.

As he left for the weekend, Ken678 scanned the crowd of office regulars filing down the long steps of City Hall. Which woman was Mary97? There was, of course, no way of knowing. They were all ages, all nationalities, but they all looked the same with their blank stares, neural-interface gold earrings, and mesh marks from their net gloves.

The weekend seemed to last forever. As soon as the week restarted, Ken raced through his Calls and Tasks, then cruised the Corridors until he found Mary at "their" spot, the open Window between Copy and Verify.

<Isn't it romantic?> she said, looking out into April in Paris.

<I guess,> said Ken impatiently. He was thinking of her hands behind her back, unfastening.

<What could be more romantic?> she asked, and he could tell she was teasing.

<A red brassiere,> he said.

<Then come with me,> she said.

They met in the Browser three times that week. Three times Ken678 heard the horse, three times he watched the red lace brassiere falling away, falling away. That week was the closest to happiness he would ever come.

<Do you ever wonder what's under the third card?> Mary97 asked. They were standing at the Window between Copy and Verify. A

new week had barely restarted. In April in Paris the chestnuts were in bloom above the cobblestones. The cafés were empty. A few stick figures in the distance were getting in and out of carriages.

<I guess,> Ken678 said, though it wasn't true. He didn't like to wonder.

<Me too,> said Mary.

When they met a few cycles later in the Windowless room off the Browser, Mary put her red-fingernailed hand on the third card and said, <There's one way to find out.>

Ken didn't answer. He felt a sudden chill.

<We both have to do it,> she said. <You turn up the queen and I'll turn up the third card. Ready?>

<I guess,> Ken said, though it was a lie.

The third card was the ace of spades. As soon as it was turned up, Ken knew something was wrong.

Something felt different.

It was the cobblestones under his feet.

It was April in Paris and Ken678 was walking down the boulevard. Mary97 was beside him. She was wearing a lowcut, sleeveless peasant blouse and a long, full skirt.

Ken was terrified. Where was the Window? Where was the Windowless room? <Where are we?> he asked.

<We are *in* April in Paris,> Mary said. <*In*side the environment! Isn't it exciting?>

Ken tried to stop walking, but he couldn't. <I think we're stuck,> he said. He tried to close his eyes to avoid panic, but he couldn't.

Mary just smiled the Mary smile and they walked along the boulevard, under the blooming chestnut trees. They passed a café, they turned a corner; they passed another café, turned another corner. It was always the same. The same trees, the same cafés, the same cobblestones. The carriages and stick figures in the distance never got any closer.

<Isn't it romantic?> Mary said. <And don't say you guess.>

She looked different somehow. Maybe it was the outfit. Her peasant blouse was cut very low. Ken tried to look down it but couldn't.

They passed another café. This time Mary97 turned in, and Ken was sitting across from her at a small sidewalk table.

<Voilà!> she said. <This Easter Egg is more interactive. You just have to look for new ways to do things.> She was still smiling that Mary smile. The table was heart-shaped, like the table in the Windowless room. Ken leaned across it but still couldn't see down her blouse.

<Isn't it romantic!> Mary said. <Why don't you let me order?>

<It's time to head back,> Ken said. <I'll bet our Folders—>

<Don't be silly,> Mary said, opening the menu.

<—are blinking like crazy,> he finished because it was already in his buffer.

A waiter appeared. He wore a white shirt and black pants. Ken tried to look at his face, but he didn't exactly have one. There were only three items on the menu:

WALK

ROOM

HOME

Mary pointed at ROOM, and before she had closed the menu they were in a wedge-shaped attic room with French doors, sitting on the edge of a bed. Now Ken could see down Mary97's blouse. In fact he could see his two hands reach out and pull it down, uncovering her two plump, perfect breasts. Her nipples were as big and as brown as cookies. Through the French doors Ken could see the Eiffel Tower and the boulevard.

<Mary,> he said as she helped him pull up her skirt. Smiling that Mary smile, she lay back with her blouse and skirt both bunched around her waist. Ken heard a familiar *clippety-clop* from the boulevard below as Mary spread her plump, perfect thighs wide.

<April in Paris,> she said. Her red-tipped fingers pulled her little French underpants to one side and

He kissed her sweet mouth. <Mary!> he said.

Her red-tipped fingers pulled her little French underpants to one side and

He kissed her sweet red mouth. <Mary!> he said.

Her red-tipped fingers pulled her little French underpants to one side and

He kissed her sweet red cookie mouth. <Mary!> he said.

A gendarme's whistle blew and they were back at the sidewalk café. The menu was closed on the heart-shaped table. <Did you like that?> Mary asked. <And don't say you guess.>

<Like it? I loved it,> Ken said. <But shouldn't we head back?>

<Back?> Mary shrugged. Ken didn't know she could shrug. She was holding a glass of green liquid.

Ken opened the menu and the faceless waiter appeared.

There were three items on the menu. Before Mary could point, Ken pointed at HOME, and the table and the waiter were gone. He and Mary97 were in the Windowless room, and the cards were facedown except for the ten of diamonds.

<Why do you want to spoil everything?> Mary said.

<I don't—> Ken started, but he never got to finish. His Folder was blinking, waitstate interrupt, and he was gone.

<It *was* romantic,> Ken678 insisted a few cycles later when he joined Mary97 in their usual spot, at the Window in the Corridor between Copy and Verify. <And I did love it.>

<Then why were you so nervous?>

<Was I nervous?>

She smiled that Mary smile.

<Because I just get nervous,> Ken said. <Because April in Paris is not really part of Microserf Office 6.9.>

<Sure it is. It's the environment.>

<It's just Wallpaper. We're not supposed to be *in* there.>

<It's an Easter Egg,> Mary97 said. <We're not supposed to be having an office romance, either.>

<An office romance,> Ken said. <Is that what we're having?>

<Come with me and I'll show you,> Mary said, and he did. And she did.

And he did and she did and they did. He met her three times that week and three times the next week, every spare moment, it seemed. The cobblestones and the cafés still made Ken678 nervous, but he loved the wedge-shaped attic room. He loved Mary's nipples as big and as brown as cookies; loved her blouse and skirt bunched around her waist as she lay on her back with her plump, perfect thighs spread wide; loved the *clippety-clop* and her red-tipped fingers and her little French underpants pulled to one side; loved her.

It was, after all, a love affair.

The problem was, Mary97 never wanted to go back to Microserf Office 6.9. After the wedge-shaped room she wanted to walk on the boulevard under the blooming chestnut trees, or sit in a café watching the stick figures get in and out of carriages in the distance.

<Isn't it romantic?> she would say, swirling the green liquid in her glass.

<Time to head back,> Ken would say. <I'll bet our Folders are blinking like crazy.>

<You always say that,> Mary would always say.

Ken678 had always hated weekends because he missed the warm electron buzz of Microserf Office 6.9, but now he missed it during the week as well. If he wanted to be with Mary97 (and he did, he did!) it meant April in Paris. Ken missed "their" Window in the Corridor between Copy and Verify. He missed the busy streaming icons and the Folders bulging with files and blinking with Calls and Tasks. He missed the red brassiere.

<What happens,> Ken asked late one week <if we turn over just the queen?>

He was turning over just the queen.

<Nothing,> Mary answered. <Nothing but the red brassiere.>

She was already turning over the ace.

<We need to talk,> Ken678 said finally. It was April in Paris, as usual. He was walking with Mary97 along the boulevard, under the blooming chestnut trees.

<What about?> she asked. She turned a corner, then another.

<Things,> he said.

<Isn't it romantic?> she said as she turned into a café.

<I guess,> he said. <But—>

<I hate it when you say that,> Mary said.

<—I miss the Office,> Ken finished because it was already in his buffer.

Mary97 shrugged. <To each his own.> She swirled the green liquid in her glass. It was thick as syrup; it clung to the sides of the glass. Ken had the feeling she was looking through him instead of at him. He tried to see down her peasant blouse but couldn't.

<I thought you wanted to talk,> Mary said.

<I did. We did,> Ken said. He reached for the menu.

Mary pulled it away. <I'm not in the mood.>

<We should be getting back, then,> Ken said. <I'll bet our Folders are blinking like crazy.>

Mary shrugged. <Go ahead,> she said.

<What?>

<You miss the Office. I don't. I'm going to stay here.>

<Here?> Ken tried to look around. He could look in only one direction, toward the boulevard.

<Why not?> Mary said. <Who's going to miss me there?> She took another drink of the green liquid and opened the menu. Ken was confused. Had she been drinking it all along?

And why were there four items on the menu?

<Me,> Ken suggested.

But the waiter had already appeared; he, at least, was still the same.

<Go ahead, go for it,> Mary said, and Ken pointed at HOME. Mary was pointing at the new item on the menu: STAY.

That weekend was the longest of Ken678's life. As soon as the week restarted, he hurried to the Corridor between Copy and Verify, hoping against hope. But there was no Window open and, of course, no Mary97.

He looked for her between Calls and Tasks, checking every queue, every Corridor. Finally, toward the middle of the week, he went to the Windowless room off the Browser by himself, for the first time.

Mary97's Folder was gone. The cards on the tiny, heart-shaped table were facedown, except the ten of diamonds.

He turned up the queen of hearts, but nothing happened. He wasn't surprised.

He turned up the ace of spades and felt the cobblestones under his feet. It was April in Paris. The chestnuts were in bloom, but Ken678 felt no joy. Only a sort of thick sorrow.

He turned into the first café and there she was, sitting at the heart-shaped table.

<Look who's here,> she said.

<Your Folder is gone,> Ken said. <It was in the room when I got

back, blinking like crazy. But that was before the weekend. Now it's gone.>

Mary shrugged. <I'm not going back there anyway.>

<What happened to us?> Ken asked.

<Nothing happened to us,> Mary said. <Something happened to me. Remember when you found what you were looking for? Well, I found what I was looking for. I like it here.>

Mary pushed the glass of green liquid toward him. <You could like it here, too,> she said.

Ken didn't answer. He was afraid if he did he would start to cry, even though Kens can't cry.

<But it's OK,> Mary97 said. She even smiled her Mary smile. She took another sip and opened the menu. The waiter appeared, and she pointed to ROOM, and Ken knew somehow that this was to be the last time.

In the wedge-shaped attic room, he could see down Mary's blouse perfectly. Then his hands were cupping her plump, perfect breasts for the last time. Through the French doors he could see the Eiffel Tower and the boulevard. <Mary!> he said, and she lay back with her blouse and skirt both bunched around her waist, and he knew somehow it was the last time. He heard a familiar *clippety-clop* from the boulevard as she spread her perfect thighs and said <April in Paris!> Her red-tipped fingers pulled her little French underpants to one side and Ken knew somehow it was the last time.

He kissed her sweet red cookie mouth. <Mary!> he said. She pulled her little French underpants to one side and he knew somehow it was the last time.

<Mary!> he said.

It was the last time.

A gendarme's whistle blew and they were back at the sidewalk café. The menu was closed on the heart-shaped table. <Are you flirting with me?> Mary asked.

What a sad joke she is making, Ken678 thought. He tried to smile even though Kens can't smile.

<You're supposed to answer, What if I am?> Mary said. She took another drink of the green liquid. She swirled it jauntily. No matter how much she drank there was always plenty left.

<Time to head back,> Ken said. <My Folder will be blinking like crazy.>

<I understand. It's OK. Come and see me sometime,> she said. <And don't say, I guess.>

Ken678 nodded even though Kens can't nod. It was more like a stiff bow. Mary97 opened the menu. The waiter came and Ken pointed to HOME.

Ken678 spent the next two weeks working like crazy. He was all over Microserf Office 6.9. As soon as his Folder blinked he was off, on Call, triple Tasking, burning up the Corridors. He avoided the Corridor between Copy and Verify, though, just as he avoided the Browser. He almost paused at an open Window once. But he didn't want to look at April in Paris. It was too lonely without Mary.

Four weeks passed before Ken678 went back to the Windowless room in the Browser. He dreaded seeing the cards on the heart-shaped table. But the cards were gone. Even the table was gone. Ken saw the scuff marks along the wall, and he realized that the Optimizer had been through. The room had been erased again and was being overwritten.

When he left the room he was no longer lonely. He was accompanied by a great sorrow.

The next week he went by the room again and found it filled with empty Folders. Perhaps one of them was Mary97's. Now that the Easter Egg was gone, Ken678 no longer felt guilty about not going to see Mary97. He was free to love Microserf Office 6.9 again, free to enjoy the soft electron buzz, the busy streaming icons and the long, silent queues. But at least once a week he stops by the Corridor between Copy and Verify and opens the Window. You might find him there even now, looking out into April in Paris. The chestnuts are in bloom, the cobblestones shine, the carriages are letting off stick figures in the distance. The cafés are almost empty. A lone figure sits at a tiny table, a figure that might be her.

They say you never get over your first love. Then Mary97 must have been my first love, Ken678 likes to think. He has no interest in getting over her. He loves to remember her red fingernails, her soft Mary voice and her Mary smile, her nipples as big and as brown as cookies, her little French underpants pulled to one side—her.

The figure in the café must be Mary97. Ken678 hopes so. He hopes she is OK in April in Paris. He hopes she is as happy as she once made, is still making, him. He hopes she is as wonderfully sad.

But look: His Folder is blinking like crazy, a waitstate interrupt, and it's time to go.